BALLISTIC

ALSO BY MARKO KLOOS

FRONTLINES

THE PALLADIUM WARS

BALLISTIC

THE · PALLADIUM · WARS

MARKO KLOOS

Published by 47North, Seattle

www.apub.com

Amazon, the Amazon logo, and 47North are trademarks of Amazon.com, Inc., or its affiliates.

ISBN-13: 9781542090056 (hardcover)
ISBN-10: 1542090059 (hardcover)

ISBN-13: 9781542090070 (paperback)
ISBN-10: 1542090075 (paperback)

Cover design by Shasti O'Leary Soudant

Printed in the United States of America

First edition

For Lyra, the artist. I love you as much as you don't love hugs.

When it is peace, then we may view again
With new-won eyes each other's truer form
And wonder. Grown more loving-kind and warm
We'll grasp firm hands and laugh at the old pain,
When it is peace. But until peace, the storm,
The darkness and the thunder and the rain.

—Charles Hamilton Sorley

CHAPTER 1

ADEN

Zephyr streaked through the void faster than Aden had ever traveled before. *Faster than most people have ever traveled before,* he corrected himself as he watched the holographic plot on the top bulkhead. They were hurtling down the dotted trajectory of the current shortest-time traffic lane from Rhodia to Pallas, the small mountain planet that made the most distant orbit around the system's sun. The acceleration readout next to *Zephyr*'s icon showed the improbable number of fifteen g. Most civilian ships maxed out at seven or eight, and even warships rarely managed more than ten. At some point, gravmag generators demanded an infinite amount of energy, and then the laws of physics kicked in and imposed a hard speed limit.

"T-minus eight for turnaround burn," Maya, the pilot, announced from her workstation up on the command deck. She was fully in her element, both hands on the flight controls, comfortably reclining in her gravity couch. Aden had been on *Zephyr* for three months, and this was the first time they were pushing the engine hard enough against the gravmag generator's limit to feel the weight of uncompensated acceleration.

Zephyr was roughly the same size as *Cloud Dancer*, the ill-fated ship that had carried Aden off Rhodia three months ago, but that was where the similarities ended. *Cloud Dancer* had been old and worn, with the marks of many years of interplanetary travel. *Zephyr* looked far more polished. Everything on board worked the way it had been designed, and nothing was worn out or broken. It was easily the most modern ship Aden had ever seen, although his sample size was admittedly small and consisted mostly of well-used Gretian Navy ships. His berthing compartment was just as small as the one on *Cloud Dancer*, but it was much more comfortable, with well-thought-out storage cubbies and a retractable toilet-and-sink combo. It was claustrophobic compared to the officer-sized residence unit in the Rhodian prison arcology, but Aden had gotten used to the smaller space. In a way, it was cozier than his old residence unit, which had always felt empty and impersonal because he never had enough belongings to fill it up and make it his own.

"What's the status of our slow friends?" Captain Decker asked.

Next to Aden, Henry Siboniso, the ship's first officer, used the controls suspended in front of his gravity couch to increase the scale of the holographic plot projection until it showed most of the space between *Zephyr* and Pallas. He highlighted a ship icon labeled OMV Lady Mina and clicked his tongue.

"They're not even at turnaround yet," Henry said. "Going down the track at a steady ten point two. Unless they find an extra notch or two on their throttle, we'll beat them by almost an hour."

Decker chuckled softly. "Well, the bet was their idea. Not that we stand to win much after we fill up again at Pallas."

"We could back off a g or two," Maya suggested. "Save some reactor fuel. We'll still beat them. It's first past the inner marker, not first one to dock."

"Crew poll," Decker said. "It's everyone's money, after all. Sound off. Who wants to save a few thousand on the fuel bill? We'll stand to make profit on the bet if we don't blow the whole wager out of the drive cone."

"Not me. I'll kick in a few hundred if I have to," Maya said without taking her eyes off the control screen in front of her. She looked like she was having way too good of a time to even consider her own proposal.

"If you're going to show off, might as well show off big," Henry said.

"I don't care for this extended high-g shit, but I can suffer it for a little while longer, I guess," Tristan Dorn said from his gravity couch behind Aden. He was the ship's medic and the oldest member of the crew, a tall and lanky Oceanian in his fifties with a craggy face and short white hair. Aden found it liberating that almost everyone on *Zephyr* was his own age or older, and far more experienced. Only Maya, the pilot, and Tess, the engineer, were not in their forties yet. It was the first time since his early days in the Blackguards that he was the most junior and least experienced member of a team, but there was a certain freedom in taking orders instead of giving them, in learning instead of having to be responsible for someone else's development.

As their new linguist, he'd been hired to do all the talking and listening whenever the crew needed someone who was completely fluent in Rhodian or Gretian. Universal-translator AI was incredibly useful for everyday interactions between people from different cultures, but even with quantum-state computing, it couldn't catch nuance, dialect, or inflection as well as a multilingual human could. And *Zephyr* sometimes moved in circles where people didn't want to be easily understood by outsiders.

"What about you, Aden?" Captain Decker asked. "You want to keep the throttle open, or have a little more money in your ledger when we dock?"

"I get a vote, too?"

"Of course you do. You're a member of the crew. Profits get split eight ways. The more fuel we burn, the smaller the payout once we get to Pallas. Might be nothing left over when *Lady Mina* pays up."

"What's the advantage of staying on the throttle if we're going to win either way?" Aden asked.

"It's good advertising," Decker said. She pointed at the situational display projected above them. "Every ship in the neighborhood has us on their plots right now. And the telemetry data from our transponder is public record."

"Everyone with a comtab can get on the Mnemosyne and see that this ship can do fifteen g sustained," Henry added. "Reminds people where to look if they need to hire a fast courier."

"Then let's keep the throttle open," Aden said. "That bet was bonus money anyway, right? Might as well invest it on advertising."

Decker's brief smile told Aden that she approved of his vote. He had gone out of his way to be agreeable as a new member of the crew, and he'd mostly gone with whatever he perceived to be the majority consensus. Fortunately, the other crew members were easy enough to get along with. Aden was glad he no longer had to mediate disputes or deal with the social dynamics of an entire company of troops that had been mostly in their teens and twenties when the war ended, and who had never known anything but top-down discipline.

"Tess?" Decker asked the last person on the maneuvering deck who hadn't voiced an opinion yet.

"Keep going. And we have a bit more zip in reserve, if you want to open it up a little more," Tess said from her gravity couch. She was scrolling through data readouts on her chair's control tab, and there wasn't a bit of strain in her voice from the added gravity of acceleration.

"We're going plenty fast for a good show. No need to go all out and tip our hand," Decker said. "Save the reserve for when we need it. All right, six votes for, none against. Steady as she goes, Maya."

"That's affirmative. T-minus six to turnaround," Maya said. "*Lady Mina* is still on inbound burn, still chugging at nine point two g."

"They can kiss that pot goodbye already," Henry said with satisfaction in his voice. Except for him and Maya, the crew was Oceanian, so that was the language they usually spoke on the ship, and Henry's Palladian-accented Oceanian sounded strangely musical to Aden, who wasn't used to hearing that inflection. Henry Siboniso had a deep voice, and his low register combined with the Palladian habit of softening consonants made him sound almost mournful.

"I think we gave ourselves a fair handicap. And they accepted the terms. I can't help it if we're still the fastest kids in the neighborhood," Decker said.

Aden had expected the turnaround burn transition to be unpleasant, but Maya handled the ship as if they were transporting a thousand crates of fresh eggs in the cargo hold. The gravity couches were on floor-mounted gimbals. The computer pivoted them to minimize acceleration forces as Maya flipped the ship end over end to commence the deceleration burn. Aden couldn't tell if it was her manual skill on the throttle or merely sophisticated piloting software, but the acceleration faded out and returned so gradually that his couch didn't have any work to do. There were a few moments of near weightlessness that made his stomach rise a little, and then the acceleration readout was climbing once more until Aden felt the weight of uncorrected gravity settling on his chest again.

"Turnaround complete. Estimated time to the inner marker is one hour, fifteen minutes, thirty-seven seconds," Maya announced to the maneuvering deck.

"You want to get something from Rhodia to Pallas any faster, you have to strap it to a missile," Tess said next to Aden. Every member of the crew wore overalls, but Tess was the only one who had hers slipped down to her waist, with the sleeves tied like a belt. Tess's internal thermostat seemed to run about five degrees higher than everyone else's.

Much of the time, she wore just a sleeveless black compression shirt underneath her overalls that showed off the skin art on her well-toned arms, beautiful pictures of wolves and foxes done in color-changing ink. He hadn't been around people with tattoos very much because body art was not allowed in the Gretian military, and it surprised him to realize that he found it attractive, at least on Tess. It matched her personality somehow.

"What if the gravmag array fails while we're pulling this much acceleration?" Aden asked, and he regretted it right away when he found that he didn't really want to hear the answer. Tess supplied it anyway.

"You'll die of a cerebral hemorrhage in about ten seconds," she said in a tone that sounded almost cheerful. "I'll die in fifteen. Maya can probably hang on for twenty. Fifteen gravities will knock us all out before Maya can back off the burn. But don't worry. Those arrays are super reliable."

"Don't let her freak you out. The fail-safe circuit runs on palladium pathways. It will cut the thrust in about ten nanoseconds," Maya contributed from above. "We'll all just have a bitch of a hangover. Maybe a nosebleed or two."

"Good to know," Aden said. "Has that ever happened before?"

"Not yet. But we hardly ever push fifteen plus. Everything running at near max, it cranks up the chance of system failure." Tess put her head back against the headrest of the gravity couch and closed her eyes.

"Outer marker coming up in sixteen minutes," Maya said. "Our exhaust plume is something else. They can probably spot us on infrared all the way from Acheron."

"Aden, contact Pallas Center and knock on the door," Captain Decker said.

"Yes, ma'am."

Aden brought up the comms screen on his control pad, grateful for something to do. His previous communications experience had been limited to the military protocol in basic training, and he hadn't touched a comms console in half a decade before he joined the *Zephyr* crew, but modern comms gear interfaces were almost as easy to figure out as comtabs. Henry had trained him on the comms station for two weeks until the first officer had been satisfied that Aden had learned the ins and outs of the gear. He selected the approach channel for Pallas Station and sent a handshake sequence, then went through the voice protocol.

"Pallas Center, OMV-2022 at sixteen to the outer marker, requesting approach vector for Pallas One dock."

"OMV-2022, proceed direct middle marker via route Delta."

"Proceed direct middle marker via route Delta, OMV-2022," Aden read back. The voice comms were mostly a courteous formality because the data link between the ship and the control center showed the same information on the navigation console before the voice exchange was even finished, but old rituals died hard even in the age of instant system-wide data traffic.

"We're in the queue for Pallas One," Aden reported to the command deck.

"Thank you. Now get *Lady Mina* on comms so we can gloat a little."

"Yes, ma'am. Private or general?"

"Use tight-beam, our ears only. Nobody else needs to know about our little wager."

"Affirmative." Aden opened a tight-beam connection to the other ship. Instead of broadcasting their conversation on the general channel or using voice-to-data over the Mnemosyne, *Zephyr*'s comms computer directed a laser emitter at *Lady Mina*'s hull so they could talk via direct private connection. There were ways to eavesdrop on a tight-beam link, but it was much harder to do than intercepting the data stream on the Mnemosyne or simply running an encrypted radio broadcast through a decryption algorithm. It took the computer a few seconds to align the emitter and take aim at *Lady Mina*, which was still accelerating toward their turnaround burn marker somewhere on the track ahead of *Zephyr*.

"*Lady Mina*, this is *Zephyr*. I have the captain on the link for you."

"Go ahead, *Zephyr*."

"We're doing our deceleration burn right now," Captain Decker said. "I think at this point it's pretty safe to say we'll be docking before you do."

"Don't take this the wrong way, but I'm still holding out hope. If your containment field shits the bed, you'll overshoot and miss your approach by half a day at your speed."

"That's not likely to happen," Decker replied.

"Not likely. Not impossible either. We'll transfer the pot when we see your docking link popping up on the 'Syne. And gods. I knew you were faster, but I had no idea how much."

"Yeah, she can work up a fair sprint," Decker replied. "We'll see you all at Trader Khan's in a few. And remember to pay up the minute we dock. *Zephyr* out."

"Trader Khan's," Tristan said, in a tone that sounded like reverence and dread in equal measure. "Haven't been there in, what, six months?"

He looked at Aden and grinned.

"You've never been to Trader Khan's."

"Never been to Pallas," Aden confirmed.

"They serve some fierce chow. Hottest food this side of Acheron. Last time I had their spicy goat tarkari, I was feeling the burn for two days, if you know what I mean."

"They make you pick a hotness grade when you order," Tess added. "Scale of one to ten. Only pick a number above five if you are used to Acheroni or Palladian food. And only go all the way up to ten if you don't mind chemical burns on your esophagus."

"If nothing falls off the ship in the next hour and a half, we even stand to make a bit of money on the bet," Decker said from above.

The command deck had only two gravity couches on it, one for the pilot and one for the captain, so Decker and Maya were always three meters above everyone else when the ship was at maneuvering stations.

Aden still wasn't fully used to the difference in orientation between a building on flat ground in normal g and a starship under acceleration. The top of the ship was the front while they were in motion, but when the drive and the gravmag rotor were off, there was no front or back, up or down. Aden was used to living his life in the horizontal plane, but on spaceships, everything was oriented vertically, small decks stacked on top of each other like the floors in a tall and narrow high-rise building.

"How are we doing with thermal management?" Decker asked.

Tess consulted her screen.

"Heat sinks are good. Not quite up to eighty percent of passive thermal limits yet. We have some breathing room."

"Good to know. All hands, prep for arrival and hard dock. I want something strong and cold in front of me without delay. Let's make sure we're all buttoned up so the dockmaster doesn't have cause to give us any shit."

———

The crew spent the remaining hour running through system checklists and bantering. Aden did the required approach check-ins when they passed the outer, then the middle marker. They received their final approach direction once they were at the inner marker, and he shunted the data over to Maya's station and confirmed it verbally at the same time.

"Cleared for final and hard dock at Alpha Five-Three, OMV-2022," he read back to Pallas One's docking control.

"Inbound for Alpha Five-Three," Maya confirmed. "ETA eleven minutes."

Zephyr finished her counterburn the moment they passed the inner marker. They had scrubbed all the speed they'd worked up at great fuel expense over the last few hours, and now the ship was coasting on the residual velocity, just a few meters per second below the mandated speed limit beyond the inner marker. Maya turned the ship bow forward with the maneuvering thrusters again, then turned the controls over to the computer.

"Two hours, twenty-nine minutes, thirty-eight seconds from the RP3 beacon to the inner marker," she said.

Both Henry and Decker whistled softly.

Next to Aden, Tess merely let out a satisfied little chuckle.

"That's almost a half hour off the old record," Decker said from above. "Be a good while before anyone beats that run, I think."

Aden switched the display in front of him to show an outside view of the ship. He knew what Pallas looked like from pictures and Mnemosyne feeds, but it was something different to see the planet from only a few thousand kilometers away, even if it was through yet another camera lens. Pallas was small, the second smallest of Gaia's planets after Hades, but it looked the most intimidating from space. Maybe that was just his subconscious at work, his knowledge that Gretia had suffered most of its wartime casualties down there on the mountainsides and in the tunnels, but the planet looked unwelcoming—harsh and austere.

"Never been here, huh?" Tristan said when he saw what Aden was viewing.

"Never," Aden repeated. "Have you been down to the surface?"

"Yes, a few times. Had some leisure time, wanted to see what it was like. And try something other than whatever they serve the tourists up on the stations."

Tristan pointed at the expanse of the planet that filled up most of the camera's field of view. It was daylight on the hemisphere below Pallas Three, and Aden could see the mountains down there even from orbit. The sunlight glistened on the ice-covered peaks and the waters of the narrow seas between the mountain chains, higher mountains and deeper seas than anywhere else in the system.

"All the cities are on the equator," Tristan said. "On terraces halfway up the mountains. Only place where it's warm enough. The stations are right above, on tethers. Freight climber takes five days to get from the ground to the station. You could see the cable if we came in at a lower approach angle. Acheroni graphene."

"Five days," Aden said. "You must have wanted to see the place badly."

"Oh, they make it worth the trip. Great restaurants in the passenger climbers. And let me tell you, the views are worth it. Gods, and the liquor. Watching a sunset from a bar that's a thousand kilometers above the mountaintops while sipping a hundred-year-old Rhodian whisky, that'll almost make you believe in the gods. If the gravity wasn't such a bitch, I'd retire down there."

"Tristan's been everywhere." Tess stretched in her gravity couch and yawned. "He ranks the planets strictly by food and drink. I think he's planning to do a travel guide someday."

"Nobody wants to watch me get drunk on five different planets."

"Six planets," Aden corrected.

"You couldn't get me to drink with Gretians if you gave me a thousand ags and a free week in the finest pleasure house on Acheron," Tristan said.

Aden felt his cheeks flush, and he was glad that everyone was strapped into their couches and mostly looking at the screens projected in front of the bulkhead instead of sitting around the table on the galley deck, where everyone would have noticed. Nobody on the crew had questioned his fictional background, and the only person who knew—Captain Decker—had kept the information to herself, leaving it up to him to determine when to come clean. Aden didn't know when that would be, but he knew it wasn't now, not yet. In the last three months, he had gotten comfortable with the rest of the crew, and he felt they had started to accept him as more than just a temporary addition. But revealing to a mostly Oceanian crew that he had mirror-imaged his actual lineage and citizenship, that he was a Gretian with an Oceanian mother instead of the other way around, would probably cause them to leave him at the next space station. Tristan's casually hostile remark about Gretians just confirmed Aden's instinct again. If they found out he had been a Blackguard as well, Aden thought there was a nontrivial chance Henry would just walk him down to the airlock deck and flush him out into space on the spot.

Right now, Aden silently thanked his mother every day for insisting that he learn both Gretian and Oceanian from the time he was old enough to start talking, and for spending months on her home planet with him every year despite his father's dislike for her extended family visits. Plenty of people in his linguistics classes at the Gretian military academy had learned flawless Oceanian, but to his ears, none of them had really sounded like natives because they didn't have a local accent. They didn't sound like they were *from* anywhere. He sounded like an Oceanian from the city of Chryseis because his mother was one, and she had spoken with him in Oceanian almost exclusively whenever his father wasn't around. The ability to switch his brain between languages had been as automatic as breathing to him.

His mother had left the family when his sister Solveig was just a little girl, too young to keep building on those neural pathways on her own without a constant conversation partner and model. He had continued to keep in touch with Solveig in the Mnemosyne since he'd reestablished contact with her after his release from prison, and when he had switched to Oceanian with her a few times just to see how much of their mother's influence had stuck, Solveig had been fluent, but her upbringing had tainted her Oceanian with a prominent Gretian accent.

In the last few months, he had started to think of himself as Oceanian, convinced that it was almost the truth anyway, that his citizenship had been the result of a coin flip that could have landed on the other side just as easily. Maybe he was Aden Ragnar, and maybe he had been Aden Jansen all along. Whoever he was now, he wasn't a Gretian Blackguard major named Aden Robertson anymore, and if he could have erased the seventeen years he had lived under that name, he would have done so without a second thought.

CHAPTER 2

DUNSTAN

"Someone's in a big hurry," Lieutenant Bosworth said. "Look at this, sir. He's practically leaving contrails in space."

Lieutenant Commander Dunstan Park, master of RNS *Minotaur*, swiveled around in his seat to look at the plot table, where his second-in-command was slowly turning the projection with his hands to isolate a slice of the stellar map. *Minotaur* was loitering in space off the current shipping lane from Rhodia to Pallas, gathering and collating data from the Mnemosyne and her own sensors to keep track of everything around her, sitting like a spider in the center of an electronic web.

"Let's see that," Dunstan said. "Anything off about him?"

"Negative, sir. It's an Oceanian courier. Flight plan checks out. They're just going fast enough to travel back in time."

Bosworth isolated a segment of the plot and magnified it. It showed a portion of the main traffic lane as a dotted line. Half a dozen different ships were strung along the line like pearls on a bracelet, each with their ID tag and vital data next to their color-coded icon. The one Bosworth had pointed out was going down the lane so fast that it looked like an antiship missile homing in on a target.

"They are really moving. What's the acceleration?"

Bosworth checked the number and let out a low whistle.

"Fifteen g, sir."

"Good gods. Must be an express delivery. Check the type and registry. I didn't think there was a merchant out there that could pull that sort of acceleration."

On the other side of the plot table, Lieutenant Mayler opened a data window above his console and consulted the database. When he found the information, he flicked the relevant pages over to Bosworth's plot display, where they attached themselves to the fast-moving icon.

"OMV-2022 *Zephyr*," Mayler said. "Database says she's a speed yacht. Tanaka Spaceworks model two thirty-nine."

"Want me to ping them for a status check?" Bosworth asked.

"No, let them do their thing," Dunstan replied. "They're not breaking any regulations. But do save that drive profile for future reference. I'm not sure we have anything in the fleet that can chase something this fast."

"They can outrun us, but they can't outrun a Mnemosyne signal. Speed is fine, but system-wide arrest powers are final."

"Quite right, Bosworth. But still." Dunstan looked at the speed readout of OMV *Zephyr* again with some envy. Minotaur could do ten g, and maybe break eleven with all the systems running at 100 percent. An extra four g on top of that would make her almost invulnerable against anything launched at her from more than a hundred kilometers away. The ship's defensive AI gained a few million calculations with each second they could put between themselves and an incoming threat, and an extra g or two could make the difference between life or death in a close fight.

"Look at that power output, on a five-hundred-ton hull. That's a ridiculously large drive for a hull that size," Mayler contributed. "Speed yacht, she's made of composites, most likely. No armor, no weapons."

"Speed is a kind of armor, too, Lieutenant. You don't need titanium plating if you're not around to take the hit," Dunstan replied. "All right, sports time is over. Let's get the big picture again. We're the only RN ship in the area today. It won't do if we miss a pirate because we're busy watching a speed run."

Lieutenant Bosworth closed the data readouts and restored the plot display to its default magnification state, which showed most of the space between Rhodia and Pallas and all the active traffic going back and forth on the transit route. Even though the two planets were almost in opposition this month, and the lowest-energy transfer path between them was at its shortest in four decades, it was still a lot of space to patrol for the handful of light cruisers and frigates the navy had assigned to police duties. Information traveled between ships and planets in an instant, but ships did not. Even for a fast warship like *Minotaur*, it took hours or days to reach a merchant who was shouting for assistance, and the pirates that were plaguing the transit lanes didn't give the courtesy of advance notice before attacking. Most of the time, the navy ships arrived too late to do anything but write reports or pluck escape pods out of space.

Dunstan leaned back in his chair and took a sip of his coffee. He looked around in the Action Information Center and watched the command crew return to their tasks. Bosworth and Mayler were the most senior members of his command staff, and they were both ten years his junior. Most of the fresh AIC crew, like Midshipman Boyer, were younger than the ship. *Minotaur* had been a bit long in the tooth even before the big war had started, and while the networked systems and the weapons had been upgraded to keep with the times over the years, the hull was showing its age more and more with every deployment. But with the resurgence in piracy since last year, the Rhodian Navy was chronically short on deep-space patrol units now, and fleet command had postponed the planned decommissioning of *Minotaur* in favor of one more refit and overhaul.

"Prepare to end silent running," Dunstan ordered. "All hands, get ready for gravity. Helm, spin us around and do a wake check. And then bring the drive up and float us over to the transit lane."

"Wake check, aye," Midshipman Boyer said from the helm station. "Commencing turn."

The plot spun slowly as Boyer turned the ship with the maneuvering thrusters until the nose and the main sensor array pointed at the area of space behind *Minotaur*. Dunstan watched the holographic display as they completed their turn, but no surprise contacts popped up in the neighborhood. They had caught one pirate by doing a routine wake check three months ago, and ever since then, Dunstan had a tingly feeling in the pit of his stomach every time they repeated the maneuver.

"Wake check is negative, sir," Lieutenant Mayler said.

"All right. Boyer, bring her back around and light the drive. One gravity, nice and leisurely."

"Turn around and burn for one g, aye," Midshipman Boyer acknowledged.

A dozen decks below the AIC, *Minotaur*'s plasma drive came to life with a low thrumming sound. Dunstan felt his own weight again as the acceleration pushed him back into his gravity couch, a welcome sensation after a few hours of weightlessness. He unbuckled his harness and got out of the couch, then stretched his legs and back slowly with a low, satisfied groan.

Over by the plot table, a flashing red message popped up above the situational display.

"Incoming priority transmission, sir," Lieutenant Bosworth called out.

"I see it." Dunstan walked over to the plot table and plucked the message off the display, then expanded it to see the content. When he was finished reading it, he let out a breath he didn't remember holding.

"It's a crash buoy signal," he told the AIC crew. "It's from RNS *Danae*. Just the automated broadcast, nothing else."

He flicked the message over to Lieutenant Bosworth's station.

"Bosworth, check where *Danae* is supposed to be right now, and see if you can get a hold of them on comms."

"Aye, sir," Bosworth replied. He brought up a screen and started populating it with data. Dunstan looked at the plot, which showed every ship in a ten-million-kilometer sphere around *Minotaur*. The situational display had no hint of trouble—no other warships, no unidentified contacts, just dozens of civilian freighters and transports plodding from planet to planet on the lowest-energy transfer routes and going about their business.

"Maybe it's a malfunction," he thought out loud. "*Danae* popped one of her crash buoys by accident."

"Their last position update was two hours ago," Bosworth said. "They were just short of Oceana space and getting ready for turnaround."

"What about comms?"

"No luck, sir. Their node is offline. They're either running silent, or their comms gear is malfunctioning."

"All the way down to the tertiary circuits? Doubtful."

Dunstan looked at the display and tried to ignore the unsettling feeling that had lodged in his middle suddenly.

"Whatever happened to them, we have to go and render assistance. Bring the gravmag system online. Helm, lay in a course for the location of that buoy and prepare for a full burn. Everyone will be suited up and in their couches in five minutes. And let fleet know that we've picked up a crash beacon from *Danae* and intend to investigate."

"Aye, sir," Boyer and Bosworth acknowledged at the same time.

And let's hope it's just a spectacular tech glitch, Dunstan thought as he walked over to the suit locker on the far bulkhead of the AIC to put on his vacsuit. There were other explanations for a fleet unit dropping off the network and releasing a crash buoy, but he didn't want to contemplate those. *Danae* was a light cruiser, twenty years newer and twice as big and powerful as *Minotaur*. Light cruisers were designed to hunt and kill pirates, even well-armed ones, and they didn't fall prey to ambushes, especially not ones so sudden that the crew wouldn't be able to get a detailed distress call out. But when Dunstan looked at the flashing red text of the crash buoy broadcast, that unsettling feeling in his middle intensified.

"And see who else is in the neighborhood," he said. "Check with the Oceanians, too. I'd feel better with some backup behind us. Even if it's just one of their little patrol corvettes."

——

Even at nine gravities, it took *Minotaur* four and a half hours to intercept the source of the automated crash buoy signal, and with every passing hour, Dunstan's feeling of unease grew. Halfway through the intercept trajectory, *Minotaur* had to flip around and counterburn, which turned the main sensor array away from their direction of travel. On the plot, the crash buoy sent out its signal with the mindless regularity of a computer brain, one broadcast every thirty seconds.

Thirty minutes out, Dunstan connected the oxygen feed of his suit to the couch and reclined into the high-g position.

"XO, sound action stations. Tactical, energize the point defense and set it to standby mode. Send out the recon drones for an active sensor sweep. No point staying quiet. If someone's waiting for us, they've seen us coming already."

The sharp, grating klaxon sound of the action stations alarm rang out in the AIC. Every member of the crew was now buckling into a gravity couch and plugging in life-support lines. Even an armored warship was a fragile object in the hostile environment of space, and in the history of zero-g warfare, no ship had ever been in a shooting engagement without taking at least some damage. The couches kept bodies from crashing into things while the defensive AI maneuvered the ship, and the supply umbilicals kept them breathing if the hull got pierced by shrapnel or rail-gun projectiles. But Dunstan knew that he wasn't the only human with an instinctive aversion to being strapped to a stationary couch in the face of danger. It went against the fight-or-flight instinct, and no amount of training or experience would ever make him fully comfortable with going into a dangerous situation immobilized on his back.

"Point defense is energized and on standby," Lieutenant Mayler said. "Drones away."

On the tactical display, two dozen red triangles swarmed out from the center of the orb and rushed outward at a hundred meters per second in a wedge-shaped formation. The recon drones extended the eyes and ears of *Minotaur* and allowed her crew to see the area of space that was obscured by the visual and radiation noise of their drive plume.

"Drones going to active mode in three . . . two . . . one. Drones are on line and active, sir."

In the space ahead, all around the spot where the computer had placed the marker for the emergency beacon, sensor echoes started popping into existence, first dozens and then hundreds. Dunstan's dread increased even before the AI had analyzed the data and labeled the new contacts in the color that stood for INERT/BALLISTIC. The debris field was a hundred kilometers across and still expanding.

"Give me an optical feed," he said, even though he already knew what he would see.

Mayler brought up another overlay and expanded it. The AI stitched the feed from the drones together into a cohesive image that reminded Dunstan of the internment yard carnage they had witnessed firsthand three months ago.

The debris field was a hundred kilometers across and still expanding. Whatever had happened to the light cruiser *Danae* had been sudden and catastrophic. Some of the bits and pieces careening through the darkness were recognizable as shards of laminate armor, still wearing the titanium-gray paint layer that was standard on RN warships, but much of the rest looked like the result of a high-velocity collision between a small space station and an asteroid. When the optical sensors picked up the first unmistakable floating bodies, Dunstan let out a low sigh. He had seen lots of dead sailors during the war—some of them in one piece and looking like they were merely sleeping, some torn to bits so thoroughly that only the shredded remains of pressure suits clinging to them identified them as body parts, some just reduced to dissipating clouds of viscera and body fluids. But most of his crew had not been in active service in the war, and this would be their first exposure to the realities of death in space combat. It was an unforgiving environment even when nobody was shooting at you.

"Bosworth, contact fleet command and let them know we've reached the crash buoy location, and that we have spotted a large debris field. Transmit our telemetry data and tell them to send whatever recovery teams are in the area. And we'll be on station awhile, so ask for some extra guns out here. Whoever did this may still be in the neighborhood."

"Aye, sir," Bosworth replied.

"Any word from the Oceanians yet?"

"They have a corvette on the way, but it's still six hours out."

"So it'll be all us for a while. Run out the drones for max coverage. I want early warning if someone's trying to sneak up on us."

"Aye, sir." Bosworth was tight-lipped and slightly pale, and the temperature in the AIC seemed to have dropped several degrees in the last few minutes.

"What do you think happened here, sir?" Boyer asked.

"I have no idea yet, Boyer. If they ran into that stolen fuzzhead cruiser, they would have gotten off a contact report. And I can't imagine there's a pirate out there with enough firepower to just blot one of our light cruisers out of space like that. Not if the crew was alert and awake."

"*Danae*'s Point Defense System is better than ours," Mayler said. "And they have twice the missile tubes we do. *Had*," he corrected himself with an unhappy shake of his head.

Dunstan looked at the optical feed composite from the drones again. At this distance, the resolution of the imagery was still too low to make out fine details, but some of the floating objects looked like bodies in vacsuits. If the ship had blown apart so suddenly that the command crew never had the time to send a warning or distress signal, the chances were slim that anyone had made it to the escape pods. But *Minotaur* would be looking anyway, because that's what *Danae*'s crew would do for them if the roles were reversed.

"Thirteen minutes to turnaround, sir," Boyer said.

"Very well. As soon as we turn, go active on all sensors and take us toward that crash beacon. Let's hope some of them made it out alive."

CHAPTER 3
IDINA

The patrol gyrofoil hung in the summer sky above Sandvik, its rotors churning the hot air. Idina looked at the temperature readout on the flight control screens. It was a sticky thirty degrees Celsius outside, and the cabin's environmental controls kept the inside at a much more agreeable twenty-one degrees.

"I'm not sure I could ever get completely used to the weather on this planet," Idina said.

"Is it too hot for you, Sergeant?" Captain Dahl asked. "I can turn the climate down a few degrees."

Idina's Gretian police partner was watching the screen projection in front of her, which showed a magnified high-resolution image of the city streets a thousand meters below the gyrofoil. The surveillance hardware on these prewar police flyers wasn't as good as military gear, but even from this altitude, Dahl could still zoom in on an individual closely enough to read the text on their comtab screen if she wanted.

"It's not the heat," Idina replied. "I don't mind the heat. It's the seasons."

"I keep forgetting they do not have those on the other planets. What is the weather like on Pallas?"

"Cold. Windy. Ten, twelve degrees on a warm day. But it doesn't matter much inside the mountains. It's always eighteen degrees underground. This place?" Idina gestured at the view of the Gretian capital outside the gyrofoil's large observation windows that had tinted themselves almost fully to keep out the sun. "I'm on my third tour here on Gretia, and it still feels unnatural. One month you need heaters in your armor, the next month you need coolant packs."

"And in the spring and autumn, sometimes you need both on the same day," Dahl said, smiling, without taking her eyes off the display.

After the May bombing in Principal Square, the weekly protest marches had abated gradually as the Alliance and the Gretian police had cracked down on mass demonstrations, and the heat of the summer had all but suffocated the rest. But for the first time since the beginning of summer, there was a sizable crowd gathered below, one that had nothing to do with political discontent. It was the first day of the socaball season, and the gathering was happening at Sandvik's stadium.

For all their political differences, every planet in the system shared the socaball passion. Gretia had exported the sport when they had started to colonize the rest of the system, and it was the one cultural constant, the single unaltered piece of their common heritage everyone had willingly retained, all centered on a ball and a square field measuring one hundred meters on each side. It was equal parts strategy and athletics, brains and muscles, fast-paced and exciting. Idina had played it as a child, but she didn't usually watch matches except during the interplanetary contest that took place every three years. The last one had been held ten years ago. None had happened during the war—stylized battle on the socaball field had been superseded by real warfare—and everyone had been too busy picking up the pieces to concern themselves with restarting the contest when the war ended. But the Gretians had received permission to reestablish their planetary league two years after the war, and the games had provided a diversion from the hardships of the postwar years that had been welcomed by occupiers and occupied alike.

"That is dedication. Standing in the heat like that just to see a ninety-minute match. They could all be at home and watching everything in perfect comfort," Idina said.

Down below, the crowds funneled through the newly installed security measures the occupation authorities now required for large public events. As people arrived on the plaza in front of the stadium, they had to walk through sensor fields that could detect weapons and explosives. The sensors were unobtrusive and didn't look like obvious policing or military hardware. They were large see-through panels that appeared to be safety barriers or weather shielding to the uninitiated. Everyone who wanted to get into the stadium had to walk into a twenty-meter tunnel made up of panel segments. The AI connected to the panel sensors could scan a person from head to toe in a few milliseconds, and it could sniff out anything that could be made to go boom, even the components to binary explosives before they were mixed together. Anyone walking through the passage with a weapon would be intercepted by the police officers on the far end of the sensor pathway. If the system detected a bomb, it could erect a set of blast walls from its base and seal off the tunnel in just a few seconds. For a culture so conditioned toward structure and hierarchy, the Gretians had a surprising fetish for privacy rights in the public sphere, but few had objected to the new surveillance measures after the May bombings.

"I do not follow the sport, but all of my colleagues do," Dahl said. "I am given to understand that the experience is quite different when one is actually present in the stadium."

"I'll have to take their word for it. There just isn't much that will make me overcome my dislike for getting stuck in crowds."

"Then I'm afraid you may have chosen the wrong profession," Dahl replied with the faint smile Idina knew well by now. She had gotten used to her partner's expressions and the translator bud's annoyingly stilted interpretation of Dahl's Gretian, and after three months on patrol with the woman, Idina understood a fair number of Gretian words. Police and military work involved a lot of repetitive phrases. Cruising around with a Gretian police officer was almost an ideal way to pick up the language, at least certain aspects of it. On her patrols in the city over the last few months, she had become particularly proficient in the recognition of invective and obscenities.

At least they're peaceful, Idina thought. *And I'm not down there in riot gear getting piss-filled bags thrown at me. Let them bake in the sun and watch their silly ball game.*

The console chirped a subdued alert and projected another screen into the space between Idina and Dahl. The Gretian police captain brought it over to her side of the cabin and inspected the data.

"One of the sensor fields just alerted," she read. "Number eleven, by the east entrance."

Idina focused the gyrofoil's surveillance array onto the spot Dahl had indicated and magnified the view. A steady stream of spectators was moving through the sensor field, but nothing looked out of the ordinary. The police officers at the end of the security gate had clearly received the same alert because they were squaring off toward the oncoming pedestrians with unmistakably attentive body language.

"What is going on, post eleven?" Dahl sent on the tactical channel. In the security gate, the civilians had noticed that something wasn't right, but then the officers at the end of the tunnel stepped aside to clear the way and kept waving the crowd along.

"False positive, Captain," someone from the post guard replied. *"Secondary scan shows nothing. Nobody in the sensor field is armed."*

"That wasn't a false positive," Dahl said to Idina. "Those look different."

She expanded the data field in front of her and rotated it a little so Idina could see the contents of the projection.

"That's a near-field return from an asset chip," she said. "One from a duty weapon. One that wasn't there before. Military or police. But it's not one of ours. The central database doesn't recognize the code."

Idina looked at it and ran it through her military data link. It came back with a result just a moment later, and she sat up as straight in her seat as her safety harness would let her.

"It's Palladian," she said. "It's a sidearm. Pallas Brigade military issue. Where did the sensor get that return?"

"The chip in the gun sent an automatic proximity ID when it picked up the interrogation by the sensor. Twenty meters from the eastern edge of the security lock."

"See if you can get a visual on that spot from the moment the chip went active," Idina said. She was proficient with the gyrofoil's systems after a few months of flying around in it, but it still took her conscious mental effort to navigate the controls for the surveillance suite's multitude of data streams. Dahl had been patrolling in this vehicle type for a decade, and she could do any task four times as fast. Whenever speed was of the essence, Idina was happy to let the Gretian take charge.

"All units, be advised that someone armed with a military-grade sidearm just tried to enter security lock eleven. They're still out there, so be alert," Idina sent to the Joint Security Patrol troops embedded with the Gretian police. They were down to one JSP to every four Gretian officers—not because the JSP had reduced their numbers, but because the Gretian police had grown bigger and more competent with every passing month. But the JSP troopers were still in charge of their counterparts when it looked like the riot shields or the guns were about to come out. Her troopers sent their acknowledgments wordlessly through the data link.

"Got him," Dahl said with satisfaction in her voice. "Male, one hundred seventy centimeters, light-colored short hair, light-blue bodysuit, white vest." She froze the sensor image on-screen and pushed a duplicate to Idina. "He walked toward the checkpoint and stopped short when he noticed the sensor locks. Turned around and walked back east."

"He knew security would see the gun if he walked through the scanner. He may not know we already got a ping on him from the asset chip in the gun," Idina replied. She sent the image to all her JSP troopers over the platoon's data link. The JSP soldiers and their Gretian patrol partners had shared voice channels, but the police and military data networks still didn't talk to each other. Even after five years of nominal peace and improving cooperation, the Alliance still wasn't willing to let a recent enemy interface with its sensitive data infrastructure.

"If he is on foot, he is no more than a hundred meters away," Dahl said. She brought up two more display projections. The gyrofoil kept doing its slow autopilot loops high above the stadium square, but the sensor package was mounted in an underbelly pod that could monitor all directions at once.

"I see him," she announced a few moments later. "Light-blue thermal suit, walking on Eleventh and crossing the intersection with Twentieth."

On the visual feed, their quarry was easy to spot. His light-blue bodysuit didn't particularly stand out among the Gretian fashion choices of the crowd, but he was one of the few people moving against the current flow of foot traffic, away from the stadium instead of toward it. Dahl put a sensor marker on him for the AI to track. Then she disengaged the autopilot and brought the gyrofoil around in a lazy turn toward the west, away from the stadium and Eleventh Street.

"Don't you want to follow him? The optics won't be able to track him once we lose line of sight."

Dahl shook her head.

"If we fly in his direction, he may notice. Then he will know we are following him. There are too many indoor galleries and passages in this area. If he goes into one of those, we will not find him again."

Idina checked the dispersal of her JSP troopers on the tactical map. All of them were on the square, working the security checkpoints with the Gretian police officers, with hundreds of people between them and the end of Eleventh Street, where the suspect had gone. Even if she sent a team in pursuit, it would take them a while to make their way through the crowd.

"Any of yours close enough to do an intercept?"

Dahl checked her own map and shook her head.

"Everyone is tied up. The closest patrol not on stadium duty is replying to a disturbance at the entertainment center on Fifth and Fourteenth. We are the closest unit. I am already bringing us around to fly ahead of him, out of sight."

"You know, for patrol supervisors, we spend an awful lot of time on the ground," Idina said, and Dahl's mouth twitched her little smile again.

"That just means we are doing our jobs right. Prepare for a quick drop."

Idina's harness tightened automatically as Dahl put the gyrofoil into a steep descent and increased speed. Dahl kept them on a westerly course until they had dropped enough altitude to break line of sight with the suspect, who was still walking down Eleventh Street in no hurry. When they were almost at the level of the highest buildings in the area, Dahl nudged the gyrofoil into a left-hand turn that brought them parallel with Eleventh.

"All units, we have the suspect in sight and are moving to apprehend," Idina told her JSP officers. "Stay vigilant in case there are more."

For a city of Sandvik's size, even the JSP and the beefed-up Gretian police were not enough to keep eyes on everything, so the JSP had a few dozen high-endurance surveillance drones on call. They did not patrol the city from above on a regular basis because the Gretians objected to their presence without cause, but today there were six of them on station, three thousand meters above the city and all but invisible to the naked eye. Idina tapped into the network and assigned the closest one to shift its patrol pattern and focus its attention on her and Dahl. If something went sideways during the arrest, the drone would be their guardian spirit.

"All right, we have the eyes in the sky on us. Where are we putting down?"

Dahl pointed at a spot on the navigation display.

"There, in that little square past the intersection with Forty-Fourth. He will not see us landing, and we can turn the corner and come down Eleventh right when he is just a grid away. If he runs when he sees us, we will be close enough to follow."

"Let's do it," Idina said and surreptitiously flexed her right hand. She was a soldier, not a police officer, and most of the time she found police work boring and frustratingly restrictive. But chasing down live quarry was one of the few exciting activities of this assignment. The adrenaline rush from the threat of impending conflict made her feel awake and alive. It was the challenge of the chase more than the tussle at the end that gave her enjoyment. Too few of the belligerent Gretians she had fought during an arrest had any direct experience with Palladians, and they always overestimated their own abilities against a short, stocky woman who was used to living under 20 percent higher gravity than they did. Fighting them was never a challenge, but she always enjoyed seeing the look of astonished surprise on the face of some young Gretian hothead after getting put on his ass by a woman who was two heads shorter.

———

Dahl put the gyrofoil down on the square, drawing a few curious looks from passersby. There was a fountain nearby that sprayed changing water patterns into the air, something that would have been a scandalous waste of water on every other world in the system. The mist from the sprayers permeated the air above the square. Idina climbed out of the gyrofoil and enjoyed the sensation of cool humidity on her face.

"Here we go," Dahl said. She had left her helmet on, something she rarely did on patrol because she felt it depersonalized her and encouraged conflict escalation. In the beginning, Idina had entertained the idea of patrolling without a helmet, but the bombing a few months prior had dissipated the notion completely. To her, planning to put on a helmet only when trouble required it was like flying in a gyrofoil without a safety harness and planning to buckle up just before a crash. Dahl wore her green police bodysuit as always, but now it was reinforced with ballistic armor on her chest, back, and shoulders.

Idina was in full light scout armor, tinted dark blue and emblazoned with "JSP" and MILITARY POLICE. It wasn't the most comfortable setup in the summer heat even with the built-in cooling system, but it would keep out bullets and shrapnel, and Idina had learned long ago that it was impossible to predict when those would start flying.

"I don't like it when guns are in play," Dahl said, echoing the sentiment of Idina's thoughts. "It never ends well. Somebody ruins a life one way or the other. Theirs or someone else's."

They crossed the intersection and turned onto Eleventh Street. Overhead, the drone kept watch, silently and invisibly, transmitting a visual stream to Idina's helmet display. The street was not as busy as she would have liked, not enough people for her and Dahl to disappear among. But it didn't matter. The suspect in the blue bodysuit and the white thermal vest was walking toward them, looking at a comtab screen projection as he rushed down Eleventh. He was close enough for Idina to make out his face: a young man, short and slender, with a fashionable asymmetrical haircut that was colored stark white and wearing a wraparound sun visor. He could have been any of the kids they usually chased off the front steps of the Sandvik vactrain station on a weekend night. Idina maintained her casual pace, trying to pretend that she wasn't walking with a purpose. If they got close enough to rush him, they could secure him before he could draw his stolen gun and make things complicated for everyone. Eleventh Street wasn't very crowded, but there were still plenty of people around, and Idina didn't like the idea of having to fire her weapon here. Even with the aim assist of her suit, rounds could miss their target, or overpenetrate it and strike someone who didn't need to get shot. Out in the field as an infantry trooper, she'd rarely had to think about things like collateral damage or restrain her firepower for fear of hitting the wrong target. The AI in her armor wouldn't let her fire on a friendly accidentally, and all the people on her side had their own armor, which would deflect stray rounds and ricochets.

And that's why soldiers don't make good police officers, she thought.

"Eighty meters," Dahl said, with her head turned pointedly to the side as if she were merely looking at the food stand they were passing instead of tracking their target. "Do you see anyone who might be walking with him as rear guard?"

Idina studied the live overhead footage from the drone again. It was strange to see Dahl and herself from this perspective, like unsuspecting targets in the crosshairs of a missile strike.

"I don't think so. Can't rule it out, though."

"When we make contact, I will secure him quickly and you will stand guard," Dahl said.

"You got it," Idina replied. Her brain didn't like to concede the possibility that anyone on this street could be working in tandem with their suspect. In this setting, the other side didn't wear uniforms or armor, so anyone could be on the suspect's team, and she wouldn't know it until they started drawing fire. For a moment, she considered telling Dahl to back off and call in the JSP's quick-reaction team. But that would be an overwhelming and very public show of force, overkill for what was most likely just a single armed and unaware suspect, and they were too far along in the original plan already.

"Fifty meters," Dahl said. The suspect's attention was still absorbed by the contents of his comtab screen. He was striding along briskly but without unusual haste. His step had the slight swagger common to young men in every culture. The thermal vest he was wearing to mitigate the summer heat showed no sign of the gun he was likely hiding underneath, no telltale bulge, no muzzle poking out from beneath the lower hem.

The suspect looked up. The pace of his stride faltered. Idina could practically hear the gears in his brain grinding to a halt as he spotted the two police officers only a few dozen steps away from him. In the next second, he would either continue walking and try to be inconspicuous, or he would let his brain's flight-or-fight response make the call for him.

"*Shit,*" Idina said.

His brain chose *flight*. He whirled around and ran back up Eleventh Street, arms and legs pumping.

She took off after him, not having to wonder whether Dahl would follow. She had never been a fast runner, and the light armor she was wearing weighed her down a little, but Gretia's lower gravity turned Palladians into high-performance athletes. Pedestrians jumped aside with exclamations of irritation and surprise as she dashed down the street after the running kid in the light-blue bodysuit. He looked over his shoulder and redoubled his efforts. When she was just a few meters away from him, he nimbly hooked to the left and ran toward the entrance of a nearby indoor gallery. She was faster, but he was smaller and had less mass to swing around, and she couldn't match his turn at the same speed and overshot her mark. By the time she had changed direction, he was twenty meters in front of her again. Dahl had been slightly behind Idina and was able to adjust her own trajectory more quickly. She reached the kid and grabbed him by the back of his thermal vest. In one impressively quick motion, he rolled his shoulders and slipped out of the vest, then ran into the gallery, a wide passageway lined with shops.

Dahl stumbled and almost fell to her knees. She caught herself and took off after the kid again, still holding his vest. Idina overtook her, once again at a full run. Between the two of them, the kid had no chance to make it out of there. Another look over his shoulder seemed to make him realize it as well. He took another sharp turn, this one to the right. Idina could almost smell the fear trailing in his wake, a panicked prey animal fleeing from two predators and realizing it had run into a dead end. She saw the pistol now, tucked into a pocket high up on the waist of his bodysuit.

"Gun, gun, gun," she called out to make sure that Dahl was aware of the confirmed threat, even though she was certain the other woman had seen it as well.

He ran into a shop that sold custom-printed clothing, knocking over a display near the entrance and sending sample bodysuits flying through the air. Dahl yelled something in Gretian that Idina's translator didn't understand. The kid slipped and crashed into an order terminal, toppling it over as he fell. The store attendant, too surprised to react to the sudden intrusion, started to voice a protest, but backed away from the entrance when he saw Dahl and Idina barging into the store behind their quarry.

When the kid rose from the pile of clothing samples that had fallen on top of him, he had the pistol in one hand. He wasn't aiming it at anyone in particular yet as he was struggling back to his feet, but Idina's adrenaline spiked at the sight of the weapon's muzzle swinging in her general direction. She unlocked her own weapon and drew it from its holster. Next to her, Dahl's gun was already out and aimed at the kid. The Gretian police sidearms still used visual aiming assists in the form of a green laser chevron. The tip of the chevron was square in the middle of the kid's chest. Even though Dahl's suit didn't have automatic aiming servos and she had just run a sprint, the green laser mark didn't waver very much.

"Drop the weapon *now*," Dahl commanded in a loud voice that wasn't quite a shout.

The kid didn't drop the pistol, but he didn't raise his arm any further. His wraparound sun visor had fallen off his head when he had crashed into the sales terminal. His eyes were wide and fearful.

"If you move that gun toward us another centimeter, we will shoot you," Dahl told him. "We are in armor. You are not. If you try your luck, we will both have a very bad day. But yours will be worse than mine."

The kid appeared shaken. For a moment, the gun in his hand dipped a little, and it looked like he wasn't willing to try his luck.

"Tell him the gun probably won't work anyway," Idina said. "It's coded to its owner's biometric profile."

His expression of wide-eyed fear mixed with anger. Before Dahl could provide the translation, the kid spat in Idina's direction.

"Fuck off, occupier," he said. "You do not belong here. You cannot give me orders. You do not have the right."

"She did not give you an order," Dahl said. "I did. And I do have the right."

For a few heartbeats, they were at an impasse. The kid was angry, but not enough to let that emotion override his survival instincts. He was still holding the gun though, and Idina could tell that his ego wouldn't just let him obey Dahl's commands without a gesture of defiance. He needed a nudge to get him away from the precipice. To her relief, Dahl read the situation the same way.

"You do not want it to end like this," Dahl told him, in a gentler tone. "Dying here, now, for no reason. You will not leave a mark. You want to matter, do you not?"

From the way the kid's posture changed and his gaze flicked from Dahl's face to the floor and then back, Idina could tell that she had picked the right angle. He let out a long, shaky breath and slowly put the pistol on the ground. As soon as his hand had left the grip of the weapon, Dahl was in front of him and kicked it away.

Idina stood back while the Gretian police captain put restraints on the kid. She let out a long breath of her own and opened her helmet's visor. She always hated the feeling of light-headed nausea from a rapidly receding adrenaline high. But she knew that she would have hated seeing this kid on the ground with bloody holes in his chest even more, seeing the light go out of his eyes forever and knowing that she'd had a hand in it. She walked over to where Dahl had kicked the weapon and picked it up to inspect it. It was an older model, superseded by a more modern handgun over a decade ago, but the brigade usually phased their gear out gradually, and some troopers just liked to hang on to what they knew well. She ejected the magazine block. It was still unused, twenty factory-loaded caseless rounds stacked in a staggered column, white propellant blocks topped with red explosive-tipped rounds. Her scout armor would have stopped them, but only just, and she wouldn't have wanted to bet on her helmet's face shield standing up to more than one.

With the magazine feed empty, she cycled the weapon manually, aimed it at the floor, and pulled the trigger. The weapon's haptic grip panel vibrated against her palm, the signal for a successful dry firing. Someone had hacked the biometric lock on this pistol, and if the kid had pulled the trigger with the ammunition block still inserted, it would have fired. She checked the cadence selector on the side of the gun. It was set to salvo mode. One pull of the trigger would have let loose three rounds at once, each powerful enough to punch through light armor or blow a hole the size of a fist into an unprotected body.

You stupid, reckless child, she thought. *What were you going to do with this in the middle of a crowded stadium?*

When they were outside on the street again, the restrained kid walking between them under Dahl's control, Idina had to make an effort to keep her knees from shaking. She took a few slow breaths and allowed herself a long sip from her armor's water cartridge. Back at the gyrofoil, the kid blinked up into the hot sun, then closed his eyes while they waited for Dahl to open the passenger hatch, as if he were feeling the sensation of warmth on his face for the first time.

"Tell him he's lucky. He almost didn't get to see the sun again," Idina said to Dahl.

"Oh, I think he knows that already," Dahl replied.

CHAPTER 4

SOLVEIG

When she was on her morning runs, Solveig felt like she was the only person alive on Gretia.

The exercise trail was a seven-point-five-kilometer loop that started and ended at the gymnasium behind the house. Falk Ragnar thought that running in a straight line was boring, so the trail meandered like a river, looping and curving around natural obstacles instead of cutting through them. Solveig had run the trail thousands of times, and she knew every little twist and bend. The first kilometer and a half snaked through the fruit tree orchards before making a long downhill turn toward a brook. When she was still running for best time, she'd use the downslope to pick up speed and let the gravity assist shave twenty or thirty seconds off the total, but she couldn't run against herself constantly and expect to improve her time each day.

Instead, Solveig had set herself a new challenge, one that would be achievable every single day if she remained focused on the task. Now she ran for accuracy, not speed. Every morning, she set out to run the trail to the same time down to the second, aiming to step back onto the wooden deck between the gymnasium and the pool exactly thirty minutes after starting her loop. With precision as the new benchmark measure, it made no sense to speed up on the downslope because it messed up her rhythm and timing, so she paced herself, enjoying the lessened effort and taking in the smells and sounds instead. It was summer; the early-morning air was cool and fragrant with the smells of dew-covered grass, and tiny pollination drones were silently flitting from tree to tree and flower to flower all over the orchard. All of this tranquil beauty was carefully managed and groomed, of course, but out here it was easy enough for Solveig to let herself be fooled by the illusion of unspoiled nature. She knew that even though nobody else was in sight, there were security drones high in the sky above the estate, monitoring her run. If she showed any signs of distress, she wouldn't even have to use the flexible comtab bracelet she was wearing around her wrist. Marten or one of the other corporate security agents would be overhead in a gyrofoil in less than a minute. The estate was ringed with multiple layers of sensors. Whether by land or air, nothing bigger than a pollination drone could make it onto the Ragnar homestead unseen and unchallenged. But all of those guardians did their work out of sight and earshot, so for half an hour every morning, Solveig pretended they did not exist.

Six minutes, thirty seconds. Bottom out at the brook and start up the hill again.

She passed the little bend where the path came closest to the softly murmuring waters of the brook that marked the edge of the orchard. Her left foot hit the side of the trail in that spot right at the six-minute, thirty-second mark, and Solveig nodded with satisfaction. From here, it was a brief stretch uphill, eighty-six meters of incline followed by a thirty-meter stretch of even ground. Then the path took another left turn and led across the brook on a small wooden bridge. Beyond, the forest began, purposefully untidy rows of graybark oaks that had been planted here decades before she was born. Now the trees were ten, fifteen meters tall, and the path that snaked along between them was entirely in the shade. Solveig took deep breaths through her nose, soaking in the smell of dark soil and tree sap, and listened to the soft rustling of the leaves in the morning breeze as she ran.

Eleven minutes, forty-five seconds. Pass the edge of the forest and turn toward the lake.

She was right at the mark when the chime of an incoming comms link yanked her out of her meditative state and back into the real world, shattering the illusion of solitude. Solveig let out an angry huff, touched the bracelet on her wrist without looking down, and flicked a finger to accept the link. Half a meter in front of her, a screen projected itself and kept exact pace as she continued running down the forest path.

"Go ahead," she said, trying to hold back the irritation from her voice.

"Miss Solveig, I apologize for the interruption." The face on the screen belonged to Bernard, the majordomo of the Ragnar estate.

"Let me guess. *Papa.*"

Bernard inclined his head. "He wishes to see you at the gymnasium right away when you return to the house. And again, I am sorry for disturbing your morning run."

"It's all right, Bernard. Tell Papa I will be sure to stop by."

Bernard nodded again, and Solveig swiped the screen projection in front of her out of existence to terminate the link. There was no reason for her father to have Bernard yank on her leash when she would have been back at the house in twenty minutes anyway, but he rarely missed an opportunity to remind everyone exactly whose schedule and desires still had priority here at the family estate.

I wonder if he'd do the same to Aden, she thought. *Whistle him back from his morning run early just because he can.*

If the war hadn't happened, her older brother would be the heir to the business. He'd be getting ready to head out to the office right now instead of hiding somewhere in the system under a pseudonym. She had talked to him a few times over the Mnemosyne since he had resurfaced three months ago, but they always had to keep their contact brief because of corporate security. For some reason, Aden didn't want their father to know that he was talking to her. Respecting that wish made Solveig a coconspirator because Falk would not accept any excuse if he found out that she hadn't told him.

Solveig thought about getting back into her flow state, but between having to check the time on her wristband and her irritation at the interruption, it had dissipated like morning fog in the sunshine, and she wasn't about to worsen her mood by trying and failing to conjure it again. She passed the edge of the forest and took her turn toward the lake, then slackened her run to a slow trot. If Papa got to ruin her run this morning, she'd take her time getting back to the house and enjoy the quiet for a little while longer. He could make her bend her agenda to his, but he couldn't make her hurry.

———

Her father was doing a sword kata in the middle of the gym floor when she walked in. Solveig watched from the entrance as he went through the motions slowly and deliberately. The sword he was using was his favorite, a slender and elegant two-hander with a slightly curved blade and a sloped cross guard. He moved it into a low guard position, parried upward, then turned the blade and executed the counterattack: downward stroke from left to right, then right to left, then straight down the centerline. In her mind, she reviewed the parries she would have needed to block each attack, the mirror image of her father's kata, opposite-direction blocks while moving backward to make him extend his reach. Falk Ragnar finished his kata, then returned his sword to its sheath with a quick and precise movement. Her father was still fit, lean, and muscular, even at seventy, thanks to the healthiest lifestyle and the best genetic regeneration treatments money could buy.

"Did you have a good run?"

"I did," she said, unwilling to admit that he'd messed up the most relaxing part of her day.

"Good. I like that you are keeping that routine. So much has changed since you went off to university. I'm glad to see that some things haven't."

"You've kept to your routines, too," Solveig said. "I've seen you do that kata a thousand times. I bet I could set a timer to it."

"That's how you measure real skill, Solveig. Reliable repeatability, not peak performance."

Falk nodded over at the equipment rack on the back wall of the gymnasium.

"Come on. Put on some armor, pick a sword. When's the last time you sparred? Let's see if you remember which end of the blade to use."

"Papa, I just ran the path. I'm sweaty and I need a shower. And I need to be at the landing pad at seven thirty."

"You're the boss at Ragnar. Or rather, you will be. You can take ten minutes to humor me. The pilot on duty will wait for you, I promise."

Solveig didn't feel like sparring, but she knew that her father wouldn't take a refusal for an answer without kindling discord. She walked over to the equipment rack and put on the adaptive armor they used for sparring with live blades. It was made of several layers of slash- and stab-proof synthetic spidersilk, cushioned by a layer of kinetic gel to absorb impacts. Falk Ragnar did not use blunt practice blades, even if it meant that sparring partners had to wear armor that cost as much as a decent gyrofoil.

While her armor was adjusting itself to her body shape, she looked at the blades on the rack. Her father had rotated out some of the weapons as his whims and preferences had changed over the years, but some of the swords she had used years ago were still there. He was using his favored curved two-handed blade, which was excellent at slashing and only so-so at thrusting. She finished her inventory and picked the weapon that was best suited for countering his sword. She couldn't match him for strength, but she knew she was faster and more agile, and she made a smaller target. The sword she pulled from the rack was a simple one-hander with a narrow, lightweight blade and a basket-shaped hand guard. She tested the balance and slashed the air with it. The tip of the blade made a sharp whistling sound. She repeated the motion a few more times, hoping to cement in her father's subconscious that she intended to match his style of sweeping strikes, where his heavier blade with its curved geometry would have an advantage.

When they both had their armor in place and the face shields of their helmets lowered, they took up opposing positions in the middle of the gymnasium floor. Falk nodded at her, and Solveig returned the gesture.

"Sensei, begin scoring," he told the gymnasium's AI. "First to three strikes, lethal strike ends the fight."

"First to three strikes wins, lethal strike wins instantly," the AI confirmed. *"You may begin."*

Falk launched into his first attack as soon as the buzzer sounded. He struck from the low guard position, the same left-right, right-left combination he had used at the end of his kata. Solveig parried both in quick succession, her blade so fast that it was merely a blur in the air between them, and the sound of steel clashing on steel rang through the gymnasium. He finished with the centerline strike, and she sidestepped it, then lashed out with her sword and lanced the tip of her blade along the side of Falk's right arm. Without the armor, she would have sliced him open from wrist to elbow, but the armor merely marked the hit visually. An angry-looking pulsating red line appeared in the spot where the tip of her sword had touched the white fabric of the armor.

"Point," the AI said. *"Nonlethal strike. Miss Solveig leads, one to nothing."*

They returned to their guard positions. Falk changed his grip and shifted into a high guard, the sword curving down in front of him, shielding his other arm.

"I almost forgot how quick you are," he said. Solveig thought she could detect admiration in his voice.

"I'm just glad I used the right end," she replied.

She feigned a swipe at the arm she had just struck, and he pulled back and deflected like she knew he would. She let him tap her blade downward, then used the momentum for a straight thrust at his chest. He spun away, but only barely, the tip of her sword missing his armor by the barest fraction of a millimeter. The shifting of his hands on the hilt of his sword alerted her to his next strike, a horizontal sweep at shoulder height. She ducked underneath the slicing blade, then rolled backward and came back up in a guard position. He pressed the attack, this time less predictably than his preferred kata combination, and his blade tagged her on the thigh on the finishing downstroke.

"Point. Nonlethal strike. The score is one to one."

"Now we'd both be bleeding all over the floor," Falk said with a satisfied smile. Solveig looked at the spot where his blade would have cut deeply into her thigh. The armor's AI dutifully marked the potential wound in bright red that started pulsating like a heartbeat. In a real fight, she'd be hobbled now, but if her hit on his arm had been real, he'd have no use of his main sword arm. The fight would be a stalemate, with his offense and her mobility both neutralized, neither being able to strike the other decisively. They would have wounded each other grievously with no outcome, no clear victory to claim for their sacrifice, both worse off than before.

Solveig knew that she'd be able to wear him down now, that the fire of his competitive spirit was only truly coming alive with the first point he had scored. He would get confident, and that would make him overly rash and hasty. But she also knew that if she beat him by points, he'd insist on a rematch until she conceded one, and if she beat him with a lethal strike, he'd be in a dark mood for the rest of the week. So when he crossed steel with her again on the next exchange, she invited a diagonal strike by lowering her stance into an imperfect guard just a little. He took the opening and let her goad him into committing to the strike. When it came, she tried to block it with her own blade, knowing that she wouldn't be able to arrest his momentum. His blade crashed into hers, driving it against the side of her neck and shoulder, and he used his energy advantage to slide his sword down the edge of her blade until it made contact with her neck. The buzzer sounded.

"Lethal strike. The fight ends. Master Ragnar wins."

They both looked at each other, panting with the exertion of their exchange, even though the whole fight had taken less than a minute. Then Falk flashed his toothy grin and sheathed his sword.

"Not bad at all, for someone who's out of practice. I would have bet money that you wouldn't score at all. Come on, let's get cleaned up and meet in the kitchen for breakfast. I have something to ask of you."

———

Falk was sitting at the kitchen table already when she got there twenty minutes later. He was wearing an all-black outfit, a flattering buttonless tunic with a high collar and sleeves that ended just below the elbows. There was a news stream playing on a screen projection, and when he saw her walking through the entry archway, he waved at the screen to turn off the sound.

"I'm trying some of your tea," he said and lifted his mug to show her. "Hope you don't mind."

"Not at all," Solveig said. "It's a Palladian blend. Most people I know think it's too strong."

"I didn't even know they could grow tea on that craggy rock of theirs. Come, have a seat. Did you put in your breakfast order already? Greta got some fresh shallows crabs from Oceana. The soft-shelled kind. Great in eggs."

Solveig walked over to the beverage station and filled a mug of her own with tea. The soundless news stream was showing a crowd in front of the old High Council building in Sandvik, half a kilometer from the square where Ragnar Tower stood. The deadly bombing on Principal Square three months ago had been all the excuse the Alliance needed to crack down on the protests that had been growing more heated and violent. Now the mere sight of an impact weapon was enough to draw the swift response of a JSP patrol, and if it looked like an assembly was about to slide out of control, there was a full JSP platoon on the scene in minutes.

The breakfast she had requested from the kitchen staff was waiting for her in the service station. She took the plated arrangement of poached eggs and corn mash to the table and sat down, then spread butter on the mash and cut the eggs with her fork to pierce the yolks. They were just on the right side of runny this morning.

"So what do you want to ask me?"

"I have a suggestion for you. Unofficially, of course. I'm not supposed to have a hand in how you run the business." Falk took a sip from his mug and watched over the rim as she took the first bite of her breakfast.

"A suggestion," Solveig repeated. Her father wasn't in the habit of making those. When he conveyed his opinion, he usually expected agreement or compliance.

"We—*you*—have to renegotiate terms with Hanzo soon. The terms we got from them three years ago are about to expire, and I think you're in a good position to get more favorable ones. Now that the dust from the war has settled a bit."

"The graphene contracts," Solveig said, and Falk nodded.

"Hanzo would have given us better terms back then, but their main customer is Oceana. And you know the level of the grudge those people are holding against us. They made sure the Acheroni would charge us the highest net they could squeeze out of us. And we had no choice but to take it."

We invaded Oceana, Solveig thought. *We occupied it for four years. Of course they're holding a grudge. We are, aren't we? We're still protesting our occupation after five years.*

"And you think we're in a better position now," she said instead.

"Of course we are. I mean, we're not back to normal yet. Probably won't be for another three years. But we're back up to fifty percent of prewar. They need more Alon; we need more graphene. It's no longer a one-sided deal. Now we have more Alon to use for leverage. If they refuse to revisit the shit terms they gave us, they get shit terms from us in return. With a grin, of course, because they're all about *etiquette.*"

He smiled without humor and took another sip from his mug.

"And that's where you come in, Solveig."

"You want *me* to negotiate with Hanzo?"

"I'm not telling you to do anything. I'm not allowed, remember? I am just giving you some parental advice."

"Papa, I've been a vice president for three months. I'm hardly the most qualified person for that job. I've never negotiated foreign contracts."

"You have a magister in interplanetary business," Falk said. "But you also have something nobody else at the company has right now. The family name that's on the side of the building."

She felt her face flush.

"I want to get assignments on my own merit, Papa. Not because I am a Ragnar. I already get enough side-eye at work because I get to have an executive office at twenty-three."

Falk shook his head lightly and flashed a smile again.

"For this assignment, the fact that you're a Ragnar makes you the most qualified negotiator."

"And how is that?"

"It's their etiquette thing. You don't know their culture yet."

"I took four years of Acheroni in school. My instructor was from Acheron. I know a *little* about the place."

"They have really peculiar ideas about *respect*. Especially as it relates to family and business. We could send Magnus or one of the other VPs, of course. But you're the heir. You have the name. In their culture, you outrank everyone else in the company. Sending you would be a major show of respect in their eyes. The terms are almost secondary, really. You'd get better ones than Magnus because his negotiating skills won't count as much as your lineage."

"So you want *me* to be the company lead for the Hanzo talk."

"I want you to go to *Acheron*, Solveig. Meet with them face-to-face. These people will really respect the gesture if a Ragnar makes the trip in person. It will put us on much better footing with them than a Mnemosyne conference. You can't drink on a deal with a hologram."

The low-level dread Solveig had been feeling at taking on the responsibility was suddenly tempered by the excitement she felt at the prospect of a trip to Acheron. She had never been there—the war had started when she was just fourteen and at boarding school—and the idea of being let off her leash to see a different planet again for the first time in a decade was almost irresistible. Still, she kept her carefully neutral expression and pretended that she was unsure about the whole thing.

"I'd still want to take one of the VPs along. Maybe Alvar or Gisbert."

"Of course." Falk nodded. "You'll be going with a full delegation, plus security. But you'll be in charge. Which means that you'll get the credit for the result if Hanzo makes concessions. And they will."

And I'll get the blame if they don't, Solveig thought.

"Well," she said, and took another bite of her breakfast. "I *am* a Ragnar. And that name on my door says 'vice president' next to it. Might as well get acclimated to the water in the big pool."

Falk smiled, this time with genuine pleasure at her invocation of her name and status. She knew that losing the firm was the most grievous wound he had ever suffered, even more so than losing his son or his wife, and putting a balm on that wound would always let her score easy points with him.

Thinking about her brother, Aden, made her excitement flare up again. She'd be off the planet for a little while, and it would be easier to get around Papa's informant network when she was a few million kilometers away from Gretia. Corporate security had tracked Aden on Gretia, but they had lost him again as soon as they had found him, and as far as Solveig knew, neither Papa nor the company's intelligence division had discovered his new identity or his current whereabouts. All they knew was that he had left Oceana three months ago.

Maybe I can meet up with him, she thought. *Finally see him in person again.* They had exchanged brief messages, but he had only told her that he had a new job on a ship, and that he was traveling the system. He was always reluctant to share his exact location because he knew that Ragnar's corporate intelligence was still looking for him after he had barely escaped them in Adrasteia three months ago. They couldn't arrest him, but they could blow open his fake ID and take him home to Papa, and that was as good as a prison sentence.

"All right," she said. "I'll go to Acheron. And I'll come back with better terms for the graphene contract."

"I have no doubt." Falk grinned broadly. "Thank you for taking my advice."

"And do you think I can schedule a bit of time for fun stuff? I want to do some sightseeing while I'm there. I hear it's a pretty exciting place."

"Of course you can. Once the business is done, your time is yours. And now that you're swimming in the big pool, you'll get to learn another family business rule."

"And what's that?"

"What happens off-world stays off-world," he said with a conspiratorial wink.

She responded with what she hoped was a shy smile and ate another spoonful of her corn mash and eggs.

Oh, you can very much count on that, Papa.

CHAPTER 5

ADEN

Pallas One was immense, a floating city in space that looked nothing like any other orbital station Aden had ever seen. It had hundreds of docking berths, some empty, most occupied by ships of all sizes: freighters, passenger shuttles, yachts, and courier ships like *Zephyr*, and the command modules of the great ore haulers that supplied the other planets with the uranium and palladium that fueled the economies in the Gaia system. Planets without the palladium necessary for large-scale gravmag compensators had to build spin stations if they wanted to operate under gravity, but Pallas could have gravity on anything they wanted in space without having to make it spin, no matter the shape or size.

From the vantage point of *Zephyr*'s bow sensors, Aden could finally see the cable that tethered the station to a mountainside terrace on the equator of Pallas. A cargo climber left the station as he watched, exterior lights blinking on every corner of the octagonal freight containers attached to the climber's core. It descended on the cable at a brisk rate of speed, and Aden followed its path until it dropped from view below the edge of the screen projection. Below, the planet loomed, huge and gray and covered in clouds. Even the atmosphere had the color of frozen rock from up here. This place had been the reason for the war, trillions of tons of easily mineable ore and all the known palladium in the system, the grand prize for which Gretia had contested against everyone else. They had held a chunk of it for a year at ludicrous human cost, then lost it all again, and the war along with it. He wondered how many Gretian soldiers were still entombed down there in collapsed tunnels or crushed at the bottom of miles-deep mountain gorges, all dead for less than nothing. Dropping onto that planet into battle from orbit must have felt like jumping into a hell that was beyond even the reach of the gods. It twisted his stomach just to imagine it.

What were they thinking? Aden mused. *That anyone could defeat the people who chose to live on that? It doesn't want us on it. It doesn't want anyone on it. It looks like it would shrug off all life like a minor case of fleas if it had a mind to do it.*

"It's a sight, isn't it?" Tristan said next to him, pulling Aden out of his dark thoughts. He nodded slowly in response with what he hoped was a sufficiently awestruck expression.

They coasted into position for the docking maneuver, propelled only by occasional quick bursts from the ship's thrusters. The helm was under the control of the station's AI now, but Maya still had her hands near her own flight controls, ready to override Pallas One if anything started to look wrong. Aden had yet to meet a single pilot who fully trusted any AI with their ship.

"Get ready for one g, people. Engaging clamps in three . . . two . . . one," Maya announced. The hull shuddered lightly with the contact of the clamps locking onto the hard points on *Zephyr*'s hull.

They had been weightless since Maya cut the main drive a little while ago when the deceleration burn was finished, but as *Zephyr* engaged the docking clamps and entered Pallas One's powerful gravmag field, Aden could feel gravity returning gradually, turning the deck flooring into *down* again.

"In position for hard dock at Alpha Five Three. And here comes the docking collar." Maya watched the process on the visual feed from the ship's starboard hull, where a flexible passageway extended from the side of the station and connected with the outer airlock ring of *Zephyr*.

"Service lines are connected. Collar is pressurizing. *Annnnnnnd . . .* we have atmo. Green lights on the starboard airlock. Hard dock confirmed. You can all get up and stretch your legs until we get security clearance to come across."

"About time," Tess said next to Aden. She raised her gravity couch into the seated configuration and unbuckled her harness with one well-practiced move. "Because I really, really have to get rid of some internal ballast."

"After you, then," Aden said.

———

Down in the airlock deck, Captain Decker activated the screen projection of her wrist comtab. Aden watched as she cycled through a few data fields.

"*Lady Mina* just paid up," she declared. "They'll whine about this for a while."

"Let them demand a rematch," Maya said.

Aden had no idea what Maya had done before joining *Zephyr*, but judging by the experience level of the rest of the crew, he guessed it was an interesting story if she managed to get the pilot job at her age. She was twenty-seven, the youngest member of the crew by half a decade. She was also the shortest, with the slight build of an Acheroni, and she wore her dark hair shaved close to her skull. In his three months on the ship, he hadn't had many conversations with her, and he had only stopped wanting to take it personally when he had noticed that she didn't chat much with the rest of the crew either.

"They're not going to do us that favor," Decker replied. "The 'Syne data says they only barely broke ten g, and I bet they were giving it all they had."

She flicked her finger across the projected screen in front of her comtab to shuffle some data around and turned her wrist to make the projection disappear again.

"I subtracted the refueling cost for what we burned on that sprint and split up what's left between all of us. Let's go drink it away, because it's not enough to do much else with it."

"No, this is good." Henry had retrieved a jacket from one of the lockers in the airlock deck and was putting it on over his flight suit with care. "We get to replace the fuel and get a little drunk, no more. It was a perfect amount for a wager. Not enough to cause hard feelings."

Aden noticed that Henry hadn't bothered to take off the kukri he usually wore in a locking sheath on his left side. None of the stations Aden had ever set foot into allowed weapons, but he figured that the ship's first officer knew the regulations, and that he had a reason for what he was doing.

The last one to arrive at the airlock deck was Tess, who climbed up the ladderway from the engineering deck. She had put on the top of her flight suit properly again, though it looked like it was a fresh suit from the locker in her berthing compartment.

"Reactor is on standby. Temps are back down to normal. I want to inspect the heat sinks visually from the outside before we head out again—make sure nothing fell off. Took a while longer to bleed off the residual than I would have liked."

"Your baby," Decker said. "But be absolutely sure if we need to dip into the maintenance budget right before the three-year overhaul."

It felt odd to walk through a docking collar instead of floating through it. Pallas One's gravmag rotors generated one g everywhere on the station, right out to all the ships that had physical contact with it. Rumor had it that the Palladians were on the verge of introducing gravity-based atmospheric containment fields, and the next generation of space stations wouldn't need docking clamps and collars anymore. Technology had marched on again at a brisk pace after the stasis imposed by the war, when every economy in the system had been churning out weapons and war material to shovel into the furnace of conflict.

At the end of the Alpha docking section, they had to pass through a security checkpoint before they could enter the main part of the station. Aden watched as Tristan stepped through the scanner array, then Decker, then Maya. When it was Henry's turn, the flooring underneath his feet lit up in red, but the Palladian security officer merely saluted and let him pass despite the curved thirty-centimeter blade hanging from Henry's belt in a magnetic sheath.

"Veteran perk," Tess explained when Aden looked at her with a raised eyebrow.

"How so?"

"Pallas Brigade. You know the thing with their knives, right?"

"Sort of. I know it's a traditional thing."

"They get a kukri when they make it through training. The sheath is coded to the owner. The kukri won't come out for anyone else. You see someone with a kukri and a sheath like that, he's brigade or used to be. And they are exempt from weapons laws. On Pallas anyway."

Aden took his turn through the scanner. The floor under his feet remained green. He waited on the other side for Tess to take her turn.

"Well," Aden said when she had rejoined him. "The knife thing is a little strict. I mean, I get that a gun can poke a hole into a pressure hull. But how much damage can you do to station infrastructure with a knife?"

Tess chuckled.

"Those kukris have monomolecular blades. The sheath keeps them that way. I've seen Henry stick that thing right through the primary locking clamp on an escape pod hatch. They are trusting their veterans an awful lot, letting them keep those things everywhere they go."

Tristan had been walking a few steps ahead of them. Now he slowed his step a little so they could catch up.

"The knife ban isn't for people like Henry," he said. "It's for morons like us. Spacers from somewhere else. So we don't stab each other at the bar after we get fucked up on Pallas liquor."

Aden smiled, not sure whether to take it as a joke or as a legitimate fact.

"So Palladian food is a ten on the spicy scale, and everyone else is a two or a three except for Acheron," he recalled, and Tristan nodded.

"Where does their alcohol rank?" Aden asked.

"What's your number two or three on that scale?"

"I don't know. Maybe a Rhodian malt. Or a seaweed infusion from Adrasteia. The midgrade stuff, not the garbage that comes in a plastic bladder."

"In that case, the shit up here is a fifteen," Tristan said. "And you're buying the first round, by the way."

"Why, because I'm the new crew member?"

Tristan laughed, pleased to be able to deliver the punch line.

"No, because you may not be conscious enough after the first round to buy another."

CHAPTER 6
DUNSTAN

RNS *Danae* was a light cruiser of the D class. At her commissioning, only seven years ago, she had been 150 meters long from the tip of her bow array to the end of her drive cone, and she had weighed over five thousand tons in standard gravity. The torn and mangled hull remnant that was drifting in space in front of *Minotaur* was barely bigger than a patrol corvette. *Minotaur*'s AIC was dead silent as they circled *Danae*'s wreckage at a safe distance, letting the AI map out every square millimeter of what was left of the other ship.

"That's the bow section," Mayler finally said. He brought up a schematic of a D-class cruiser and superimposed it on the visual feed. "Maneuvering deck, AIC, airlock, and pod deck. Everything below the pod deck is gone."

"That was no gun cruiser," Dunstan said.

"I don't think so, sir. There aren't any impact holes in what's left of the hull. Whatever hit them, it wasn't a rail-gun salvo."

"Like something grabbed the ship in the middle and just ripped it apart." Bosworth zoomed in on the visual to take a closer look at the twisted and ragged edges of the shattered hull plating.

"More like it blew up from the inside," Dunstan said. "Look how that armor plating is bowed out, and how the hull has buckled—here and here." He indicated the spots on the screen.

"Maybe it wasn't an attack after all. Maybe they had a technical malfunction. Hypervelocity debris going through their missile magazine, something like that."

"We're still looking at a hundred dead crew. I doubt they'd appreciate the distinction," Dunstan replied. "Anything at all on the emergency channel?"

"No, sir. We've been sounding off on all frequencies since we came out of the burn and flipped. The only thing broadcasting is the crash buoy. No life pods, no suit transmitters, nothing."

"The front section is still more or less in one piece. They should have gotten at least a few pods off, even if all the power circuits went dead at the same time. What in Hades happened here?"

Nobody in the AIC ventured a guess at an answer.

"Helm, get us behind what's left of their command section and match the rotation of the wreckage," Dunstan ordered. "Keep your distance. Make it five hundred meters."

"Aye, sir," Midshipman Boyer replied. "Coming about and matching rotation."

Boyer used the maneuvering thrusters of the ship to line up *Minotaur* with the remains of *Danae*, then initiated a longitudinal spin that matched the movement of the cruiser's mangled bow section exactly. Dunstan noted with satisfaction that she accomplished the feat manually, without letting the ship's AI take over the final adjustments.

"Rotation is in sync, sir. We are holding station five hundred meters astern and turning at one point three meters per second."

"Very well, Boyer."

Looking up into the violated hull of *Danae* felt like staring into the open chest cavity of a corpse. Severed fiber links and supply lines snaked out of dented and cracked bulkheads. *Minotaur* only had one central ladderway along the ship's spine, but the D-class cruisers like *Danae* were large enough to have two. They went from the maneuvering deck at the top of the ship all the way to the reactor room at the bottom, and seeing both of them open to space made it look to Dunstan like the trachea and esophagus visible in the neck of a severed head.

"XO, tell the marines to get a boarding party suited up. I want them to go over there and see if they can make it up the open ladderways to the command deck. But no risky business. Anything they can't open manually or with the plasma cutters, leave it for the recovery team once they get here. If the data core is still intact, the fleet techs will figure it out. Right now, we are looking for survivors. Understood?"

"Aye, sir," Bosworth replied and punched up the comms link on his console. "Marine country, this is the XO. Sergeant Bosca, you are going for a little stroll. Get your team geared up for EVA and meet me on the airlock deck in fifteen minutes."

———

The AIC crew watched as the boarding team from *Minotaur*'s marine detachment launched from the airlock a short while later. The marines fired short bursts from the thrusters of their EVA suits and coasted over to the remains of RNS *Danae* in irregular intervals, spaced apart widely so that one explosion or rail-gun salvo couldn't blot the entire team out of space at once. The armor suits for boarding actions were coated in a layer of flat black carbon composite that made their wearers very tiny sensor targets, and even to the optics from *Minotaur*'s sensors, the marines were almost invisible against the nothingness of deep space as they covered the distance to the wreck in radio silence. When they were almost at what was now the stern of the wreck, each marine turned and fired thrusters toward their target to slow down again. Dunstan had some experience with EVA suits, and trying to stop at a particular point in space was a hard thing to accomplish, but these marines trained for boarding actions constantly, and he watched with some pride as the team turned and burned, then got into position on the outside of the torn hull with pinpoint accuracy. One by one, they disappeared inside the wreckage.

"*Minotaur*, this is Bosca. We are at the aft end of the central ladderway pair. One is blocked about ten meters in. The other seems mostly clear."

The telemetry from the marines' EVA suits came online and showed eight different helmet view perspectives, which Lieutenant Bosworth arranged in an arc over the main tactical display.

"Send up the bots and see what it looks like up top," Dunstan ordered. "Remember—no unnecessary risks. Anything looks like it's about to blow, you pull your team out."

"Understood, sir."

Bosca's perspective shifted as the marine sergeant looked up the dark ladderwell, then tapped a control on his lower left arm. Half a dozen little personal recon drones, each the size of a thumb, ejected from recesses in Bosca's armor and swarmed up into the ladderwell to scout the wreckage above the team.

"This girl really got her back snapped in half," Bosca said and looked around for the benefit of the AIC crew. "Everything below frame forty is gone, and the rest isn't looking so good. I don't think there's an airtight deck left above us. There are shrapnel holes all over these bulkheads."

Dunstan and Bosworth exchanged a look.

"That was a war shot," Bosworth said. "Hit it right in the sweet spot, dead center next to the missile silo."

Dunstan looked at the array of visual feeds from the marine helmets again. The evidence was undeniable: scorch marks and jagged holes in bulkheads that only had one likely source. He had only ever seen battle damage like this during the war, when ships took hits from armor-piercing antiship missiles that got through the point defenses.

"I hate to agree with you, Lieutenant. Because that means there's someone out there who's deliberately gunning for navy ships. Someone who can get close enough to a modern light cruiser to get a missile through her point defenses and blow her in half before her crew can even send an alert."

"Something stealthy," Bosworth offered. "Like the ghost we were chasing around the internment yard right before the fuzzhead fleet blew all to hell. But they launched on us, remember? The point defense got both missiles. And our systems aren't half as good as what's on a D-class cruiser."

Dunstan shrugged.

"Best guess? We knew they were sneaking around out there. We had active drones out to pin them down. They launched from over sixty klicks out as soon as we got a solid sensor return. Maybe they knew they couldn't get any closer without us burning through their stealth. This crew here had no idea anyone was in the neighborhood."

"The point defense only takes two seconds to fully energize once it detects incoming," Lieutenant Mayler said from his station. "Even if the crew didn't set it to active status manually. Another second at most for the AI to fire the emitters."

"Two seconds," Dunstan repeated. "They were less than five klicks away when they launched. Maybe less than three."

"Nobody is that stealthy," Bosworth said.

"It appears that *someone* is, Lieutenant. Because if they launched close enough to beat the point defense AI on a D class, it means they were just about close enough to read the registry number off the hull."

"*Minotaur*, Bosca." The voice of the marine sergeant cut into their discussion.

"Go ahead, Sergeant," Dunstan said.

"The drones made it up the ladderwell to the pod deck hatch. It's sealed, but there's no atmo showing on the other side of that bulkhead. I'm going up to cut the interlock open."

"Affirmative. But go easy with it."

"*Reckless* isn't on the menu for me right now, sir. Stand by."

———

They watched Bosca float up into the ladderwell until he reached the sealed hatch of the pod deck, ten meters up from where the ship had been blown in half. The pressure indicators next to the hatch showed a red triangle, indicating there was no air on the other side. The indicators were mechanical and needed no power, but even if they were somehow faulty, Dunstan knew that Bosca would not be able to open the steel hatch up into a pressurized deck because the pressure would keep it in its seal even with the interlocks cut away. Bosca turned on the plasma cutter in his EVA armor and went to work, slicing through the bulkhead plating slowly and expertly. When he was finished, he turned the plasma cutter off and took a deep breath that sounded just a tiny bit ragged.

"Here goes," he said. "Boarding team, stand by for a quick exit if you hear a really loud noise."

He pushed up against the hatch with the palm of his armored hand. Dunstan heard the power-assist servos let out a little whine as Bosca increased the force of his push gradually. The hatch broke away soundlessly and slowly floated upward into the airless deck above him.

"Pod deck confirmed depressurized," he reported. "First element, move up to my position. Second element, stay put at the bottom of Ladderway Beta. Let's see if anyone's left in here."

———

In the beams of the team's helmet lights, two bodies were floating in the pod deck, surrounded by drifting spheres of liquid and pieces of debris. Both dead crew members were in regular shipboard jumpsuits, not EVA gear. One wore the rank of a lieutenant, the other was a midshipman, which meant they had come down from the command deck to get into the escape pods when the ship blew apart. It was only one deck down, but whatever happened had taken place too fast for them to make the pods before the rest of the ship got depressurized.

"They weren't suited up," Bosca muttered. "Shit way to die."

He turned his head to pan the sensors and his helmet light around the pod deck. This was the place where the crew from the top half of the ship would have gone to get into the escape pods. The circular access hatches of the pod chutes ringed the deck, four to each side of the octagonal inner hull. Thirty-two pods holding six people each, enough to evacuate the entire crew even if the other pod deck, seven decks down and below the secondary crew quarters, was somehow inaccessible or out of commission. Bosca and his team moved around the deck and checked pod hatches. It seemed to take an agonizingly long time to Dunstan.

"Six launched," Sergeant Bosca finally reported. "Or they got blown out of the hull in the explosion. The rest are still here, but they're all empty."

"Gods-damn it," Dunstan muttered. Even if those six pods had been full to the last seat, *Danae* had lost at least two-thirds of her crew instantly.

"I'm not picking up any pod transponders at all, sir," Lieutenant Mayler said from the tactical station. "Neither are the drones."

Dunstan shook his head slowly.

"Sergeant Bosca, check the command deck for survivors, then go through the rest of the hull as far as you can access it safely. Then gather your team and return to the ship."

"Aye, sir," Bosca replied in a clipped voice. The marine sergeant was the most experienced person on the ship aside from Dunstan. He'd seen the war from start to finish in the front lines of battle. Dunstan knew that he and Bosca had come to the same conclusion. But six of the pods had launched, and if there was even the faintest chance that someone had survived, they would scour the area until they found the pod or exceeded the maximum time of the crew's likely survival because that was what *Danae*'s crew would have done for them.

"XO, send an update to command. Boyer, lay in a patrol course, standard expanding ladder search pattern. Mayler, run the drones out as far as they will reach and still give us telemetry. We're doing a maximum power sensor sweep as we go. Warm up the point defense as soon as the marines get back to the airlock. I don't want us to get caught with our overalls down like *Danae*. Let's find our people if they're out there."

"Yes, sir," the AIC crew replied, even the ones he hadn't addressed directly. Dunstan leaned back in his chair, and the sudden weight on his chest felt like they had already lit the drive and pushed it to the grav-mag compensator's limit. They would look for the pods from *Danae*, but he was certain they wouldn't find any. The new breed of pirate that had cropped up in the last year had taken to destroying escape pods to eliminate witnesses. He doubted that whoever had the means and the motive to destroy a cruiser with all hands would show its pods more mercy. He knew that *Danae* was dead, and so was her crew. Whatever ship had ambushed her was still out there, and if they could do this to a light cruiser, there were few ships in the fleet that were safe. And that did not include old workhorse frigates that had been a bit long in the tooth a decade ago already.

"And XO? Increase pod drills," he added. "One per watch cycle."

Nobody in the AIC voiced dissent.

CHAPTER 7

IDINA

The Gretian police headquarters looked exactly like the impersonal technocratic monument to efficiency Idina had expected it to be when she was first assigned to the JSP. It was all glass and polished stainless steel, white walls and floors. Even the workstations were white, all the furniture seemingly from the same manufacturing line. There wasn't a mismatched chair in the building.

"Maybe I shouldn't come into the room with you," Idina said to Dahl, who was striding down the hallway with her. They were both in their regular bodysuits now—dark-blue JSP color for Idina, green-and-silver Gretian police for Dahl—and it felt good to spend the rest of the day out of armor. The atmosphere in this place had changed over the last few years. At first, the Gretian officers had resented the supervision of the JSP troopers. Then they had settled into a long détente of grudging cooperation. But since the indiscriminate bombing three months ago that had claimed the lives of Gretians and Alliance troops alike, Idina noticed no more frowns or scowls when she walked these hallways. Now she even got acknowledging nods and occasional smiles from the Gretians.

"Why would you not?" Dahl asked.

"I'm a foreign occupier. He'll just get all worked up again."

"And that is exactly why you should be in the room," Dahl said. "It will make him angry. And emotion sometimes overrides the part of our brains that acts as a safety catch for our mouths. You know how young men are."

An incoming message made Idina's comtab chirp, and she flicked a projection into her field of view to check the contents.

"JSP tracked the inventory chip and the serial number of the gun," she said to Dahl.

"Does it give us any clue how he got his hands on it?"

Idina read the brief database entry attached to the message, then swiped the projection away to close it.

"It was issued to a brigade corporal who died in battle. On Pallas, at the start of the Gretian invasion."

"Huh," Dahl said. "Pallas. So how did it get all the way to Gretia and into the hands of a local juvenile, after all this time?"

Idina thought about it, and there was only one likely conclusion that fit the data. If the brigade had recovered the weapon with the body of its owner, they would have reissued it to someone else, or taken it out of the inventory if it had been damaged beyond repair. Either way, there would be a database entry attached to the asset tag to document the transfer. But its service history ended with that of its last sanctioned user.

"Some Gretian Blackguard took it home," she said to Dahl. "As a war trophy. Or to sell it on the black market."

"That would be in violation of military regulations," Dahl said.

"And Gretian soldiers would never violate regulations, right?"

Dahl shrugged with a little smile.

"Young men and emotions."

———

The young man sitting on the other side of the interrogation room was wearing a detention suit. It was rather less fashionable than the blue-and-white outfit he'd worn when they had arrested him the day before, but his body language was every bit as cocky and defiant as it had been during his transport and processing. He sat as spread legged as the built-in movement limiters of his suit would allow, arms crossed in front of his chest, and he looked at Dahl and Idina with contempt when they entered the room.

"Good day," Dahl said to him. He returned the greeting with a scowl. Idina thought about saying the same greeting in her halting Gretian to rile him up and get the interrogation started on the lively side, then decided against it. Dahl was the expert here, and she'd let the other woman determine the steps of the dance.

They sat down at the other side of the Alon barrier that split the room in two and separated detainees and questioners. Dahl had explained to Idina that the barrier wasn't really necessary because the detention suits would immobilize the suspects if they became violent, but that it was in place to rule out even the possibility of physical contact.

"I have to inform you that this room is monitored by four different AI systems. One for the state prosecutor, one for your defense, one for public record, and one for the police. Whatever you say will be entered into all of them."

The kid shrugged.

"It does not matter. This is all a sham anyway. You are not even in charge here. They are." He nodded at Idina, then glared at Dahl again. "You should be ashamed, doing their dirty work for them. Arresting your own people. Taking orders from the occupiers. No serfdom," he added. Idina knew the slogan well enough by now that she didn't have to rely on the AI translator to figure it out.

"That is a catchy phrase," Dahl said. "I have heard it often lately. But let me assure you that I am in charge here. I was in charge here before you were born. And I will still be in charge here long after the Palladians and the Rhodians have gone home again. I do my work in the same way, with or without them. Their presence makes no difference to me."

"That is a load of *excrement*," the kid said. Idina was positive that the AI's translation of the word in her ear was overly formal because she knew that expletive in the original by now as well.

Dahl nodded. Her expression was almost sad, a mother having to deal with a misbehaving favorite child whose punishment she dreaded.

She took an ID pass out of her pocket and held it up to read from it.

"Haimo Keller. Twenty years old. You work at the spaceport, as a traffic-controller apprentice."

He looked at her without a change in expression, as if even acknowledging what she already knew about him would constitute recognition of her authority.

"What were you going to do with a loaded military weapon in a sports arena?" she asked.

"I was not going to do anything. I have the gun for protection. When I saw the scanners, I turned and walked away. What is wrong with going armed? Their kind walk around with weapons all the time. And this is our planet, not theirs."

Dahl sighed.

"Let me explain to you the depth of the pool of *excrement* in which you are currently trying to hold your head above the surface, Haimo Keller," Dahl said. "Based on the evidence, the court has already convicted you of the crime of possessing and carrying a restricted weapon without authorization. The conviction means your security clearance at the spaceport has been revoked automatically. I am sorry to inform you that your apprenticeship will be terminated."

Haimo tried to maintain his self-control, but Idina could see that Dahl's words were rapidly deflating his composure. He looked around the room, then back at Dahl.

"I get my certificate next week," he said in disbelief. "My three-year certificate. I worked for it. I earned it. I passed all the exams. And the final test."

Dahl shook her head.

"I am sorry, but that will not be happening, Haimo. A weapons offense makes you ineligible for that profession."

"There must be *something* I can do." He glanced at Idina, then back at Dahl. "I was just carrying that gun. I did not shoot anyone. I did not even enter the stadium. Why would you come to ask me questions if I am already convicted? Are you not supposed to offer me something so I will cooperate? What is the *point*?"

He almost shouted the last word. Now there was fear in his eyes again—not the wide-eyed panic from yesterday when they had aimed their guns at him, but something just as raw. Dahl had yanked the floor out from underneath his feet, and now he was in a tumble that he had not expected.

"The point is this," Dahl said. "Your conviction already means a mandatory detention term. That is something you will not be able to avoid. You made that choice when you tried to carry an unauthorized weapon of war into a public gathering."

Idina almost felt sorry for the kid, who was visibly recoiling at Dahl's calm and certain declaration. He'd had a night in detention to work up a tough and defiant exterior for what was to come, his turn at standing up to the oppressor, and she had torn it down in just a few moments without even raising her voice.

"But your level of cooperation will determine where you serve that term," Dahl continued.

She nodded at Idina.

"This Palladian soldier here has so far declined to have you charged with pointing a weapon at her. The weapon you were carrying was taken from one of her comrades. She would like to find out where you got it, and how. Right now, you are only looking at one to three years of rehabilitative detention in the Sandvik Center of Justice."

Haimo looked at Idina. She was pleased to see that he made a conscious effort to keep his expression as far away from hostility as he could manage.

"But if this soldier here is not happy with your degree of contrition, she will have that charge added after all. And then it becomes an Alliance matter. The judge may decide that the severity of the offense merits a term on Landfall."

From the desperation that flashed up in his expression, Idina could tell that Haimo was familiar with Landfall Island. It was a penal facility off the coast of the mostly uninhabitable northern continent of Gretia. It had no walls or electric security fields because it didn't need them to keep people in. There was a thousand-kilometer exclusion zone around it, and anyone who escaped would have to try to make it home across a frigid, mountainous wasteland with no life of any kind on it.

"Think about it," Dahl continued. "One to three years at Sandvik. Family visits. You can even earn curated Mnemosyne access. Or three to five years on Landfall. That is a long time to spend on a frozen rock in the middle of nowhere."

Haimo covered his face with his hands and blew a long, ragged breath into his palms. He slowly rubbed his eyes. When his hands came down again, all of his defiance had leaked out of him, and he seemed ten centimeters shorter than before.

"I will tell you about the gun," he said.

"You are making a wise decision, Haimo," Dahl said gently.

He nodded at her and sat up straight.

"But before you start, let me just tell you that I have been doing this for a very long time," she said in the same soft and caring tone. "When you say things like 'occupiers,' or 'no serfdom,' I know I am not hearing you. I am hearing the person who put those phrases into your head. When you tell me the details about the gun, make sure I only hear you. Because I will know the difference."

Haimo looked at the floor between his feet and nodded again.

"I bought it from someone I met, someone from work," he said. "One of the technicians from the maintenance line."

"What is his name?" Dahl asked.

"Vigi. His name is Vigi Fuldas. He is into all this military stuff. Collects it at his place. He has a workshop where he tinkers with it. The gun was not supposed to be able to fire, but he reprogrammed it so it could. I gave him a thousand ags for it."

"How did you get to know Vigi? You were training to be a flight controller. You do not have any business at the maintenance line."

"At one of the rallies," Haimo said. "The Loyalists. We found out later that we both worked at the same place. If you go see him, please do not tell him I told you about the gun," he said.

"That is not going to be up to me alone, Haimo. Now tell me everything you know about Vigi, please. Leave out no detail, even if it does not seem important to you."

———

"You made that look easy," Idina said when they had finished the interrogation and Haimo had returned to his detainment suite. "The kid is lucky he got you for an interrogator. The Pallas way would have been to bang his head against that Alon screen until information started falling out of his mouth."

"It was easy," Dahl said. "And I find that a little worrying."

"You don't think he was telling the truth?"

They were walking through the main atrium of the police head-quarters. Almost every officer who passed Dahl gave her a respectful nod or spoke a greeting. In the middle of the atrium, a reflection pool showed a perfect image of the ceiling above, the surface of the water smooth as a mirror.

"I do not think he was lying to us," Dahl replied. "But he was not telling us the facts from the right angle. He told us what he knew, but in the way he guessed we wanted to hear it."

Idina knew that both the Gretian police and the Alliance intelligence service were already seeking out everything there was to know about both Haimo and his work friend Vigi Fuldas. If the story had holes, they would shine a light through them soon enough, and Haimo wasn't going anywhere for a while. But Dahl's sliver of worry had now transferred to Idina as well. Everything in the interrogation room had gone right as far as she could gauge, but Dahl had done this sort of thing a thousand times, and if she thought something was a little off, Idina had no cause to disagree.

They paused next to the pool and looked at their own reflections, which were almost perfect negatives of each other: Dahl's white hair and light skin to Idina's black hair and dark skin.

"Do you ever tire of it?" Dahl asked.

"Tire of what?"

"Being here. In a place that is not your home. Spending your days and your energy keeping the peace among strangers. Enduring the *seasons*."

Idina considered the question.

"I get tired," she said. "It's strange, when I think about it. How much harder it is to keep your finger off the trigger than to pull it. I've been training to pull triggers all my life."

"The Pallas way," Dahl said, and Idina smiled.

"It would have worked on Haimo, beating the information out of him. And it would have been faster," Dahl said. "This way is harder. But I am not sure I would want to be a police officer in a place where being a police officer is easy."

The reflecting pool performed its function almost too well, like most things designed by Gretians. Idina could see all the lines in her face that hadn't been there just a year ago, the furrows on her forehead and the deep wrinkles at the corners of her eyes. She stuck a finger into her reflection and made the water ripple a little, but it returned to perfect stillness just a few moments later.

"You could have shot him, back in that shop," Dahl said. "He had a weapon in his hand, a loaded weapon. He was not obeying our commands. We still would have gotten a gun off the streets. We would have been in the right, legally. But we wouldn't know about the technician who sold it to him. The one who has the tools and the knowledge to bypass the biometric lock on a military sidearm."

"If you weren't going to take the shot, I wasn't going to either," Idina said. "You're better at not pulling triggers than I am."

Dahl smiled at her statement.

"You are not so terrible at it yourself. That young fool gets to live out the rest of his life. In exchange for a year in the detention facility. Someday he will look back at this and realize just how low a price that was."

Idina checked the time. She had dismissed her platoon three hours ago already, and the next JSP platoon on the roster was now out on patrol in the city with their Gretian counterparts, a new pair of patrol supervisors in the air above them. Technically, she had sat in on that interrogation on her free time.

"I need to head back to the base and check in with Lieutenant Liu before he sends the quick-reaction unit after me," she said. "I'll see you at 0800 for patrol."

"Take some rest," Dahl said. "Today was not a bad day."

"No, it wasn't," Idina said. "Not a bad day at all."

When she walked across the atrium to the elevators, her legs started to ache, as if she had given them permission to show their fatigue by thinking about the end of her shift. A passing Gretian police sergeant glanced at the kukri on her left side with curiosity, then gave her a friendly nod. On her right side, the pistol counterbalanced the blade. The familiar weight of her gear usually comforted her, but tonight it felt like she was back in Pallas gravity. Maybe she *was* starting to tire of it all.

———

Back at JSP Base Sandvik, the company building was lit up in purple and gold, the colors of Pallas. The buildings of the JSP companies all had white exteriors, and the Hadeans had started a fad last month by projecting stripes of orange light on the front of their building at night to make the structure look like the flag of Hades. All the other companies had followed suit in short order: Acheroni yellow, Oceanian blue, Rhodian red. The Palladian CO had held out longest, but it seemed that even Major Malik wasn't immune to peer pressure. She suspected that he had most likely started to play along just to preserve the uniformity of the battalion square's appearance, even if the new trend was a little gaudy.

Lieutenant Liu's office was empty, and the door was locked. Idina shuffled off to her own office to log the day and sign off for the night.

"Color Sergeant Chaudhary," Major Malik said when she walked past his door. She stopped and turned on her heel.

"Sorry, sir. I thought everyone had left for the evening. Lieutenant Liu's office is closed."

"Everyone but me and Second Platoon, it seems. Come in, please."

"*Sir.*"

She stepped into the company commander's office. He was a hands-off sort of leader and trusted his lieutenants and senior sergeants to run their platoons without constant micromanaging. With her ever-changing patrol shift rotation, she hadn't talked to him directly in a month or more.

"I'm late off patrol because we had to do an interrogation at the Gretian HQ. The stadium suspect with the weapon," she said.

"Yes, I saw that in the logs. Good work. You don't spend much time in the air, do you?"

"No, sir. Much easier to get good intel on the ground."

"I've checked the roster history. You've put in a lot of extra time since Principal Square. More than any other platoon sergeant."

"I'm not much for sitting around the base and polishing my kukri, sir."

"That makes two of us," he said. "But that's mostly what I seem to be doing with my time these days. Have a seat, Colors."

Idina did as she was told and watched as the major turned around and looked out of his window at the battalion square and its newly multicolored assembly of buildings.

"I predict that light show will last until the next Palladian rotates in as battalion commander," he said. "How have you been feeling lately?"

The question took her off guard.

"Fine, sir," she said, trying to gauge his intent. Was she in for a dressing-down?

"Lieutenant Liu has shared some concerns about you. He forwarded me your medical data from the last few weeks." He opened a screen and showed her a data page.

"There is nothing wrong with me, sir."

"Your vital statistics say otherwise, Sergeant. Your muscle mass loss is right at the limit, and your lung capacity is down by almost a double-digit percentage. You've been off Pallas for too long."

"I have two months left in this tour, sir," she said.

"You've done your last two tours back-to-back," Major Malik said. "Two consecutive tours off-world is the hard limit. But this looks to me like you've hit your limit a little early. Maybe it's the pace you've been keeping up since Principal Square. Maybe it's your age. Infantry duty is hard on the body. But if you don't return to Pallas soon, you'll be medically unfit for duty in a few months. At your age and time in service, it would be hard to catch up. You'd have to spend too much time rebuilding muscle and getting your bone density back up for brigade medical to clear you for infantry duty again. They may just decide that you've done your share and transfer you to an admin unit."

The thought horrified her.

"Sir. I have no intention of spending my time until retirement as a recruiter. Or curating the brigade museum. I'm an infantry sergeant."

"Then you will gladly follow the order I am about to give you. The next replenishment group from Pallas arrives at the end of this week. When they return home, you will be going with them. Corporal Noor from Blue Section is about to get his sergeant stripes. I will have Lieutenant Liu bump him up to platoon NCO for the remainder of Fifth Platoon's deployment."

Idina tried not to show her shock.

"Sir, I can't go home now. There's still work to be done."

"There's *always* work to be done," Major Malik said. "We will be here for years to come, Sergeant. We have plenty of people to do it. No need for you to grind yourself down to the bone for this place personally."

"I don't want to leave my platoon early, sir," she protested, but she knew that it was a futile argument, that the major had made his decision.

"It's just two months early, Colors. Noor can handle the platoon. You brought your squad leaders up well."

He wiped the projection in front of him away with a flick of his wrist and nodded toward the door.

"You *will* be on that flight home in a week, Color Sergeant Chaudhary. That is an order. I suggest you go on light duty until your departure. Go home and recuperate. And if you decide that you still haven't had enough of this planet, you can put in a request for another

JSP assignment. But not until you've spent at least a year in normal Pallas gravity. Dismissed, Sergeant."

Idina got out of her chair and saluted. The legs that had felt achy and tired earlier now just felt numb, like temporary prosthetics. She turned on her left heel and stiffly walked toward the door.

"I have to say I am a little surprised, Colors," Major Malik said when she was at the threshold. "After all that has happened to you, I figured you would be glad to get out of this place a little early."

She paused at the door, her mind as numb as her legs felt right now.

"Things got a little . . . *complicated*, sir," she said.

CHAPTER 8

SOLVEIG

"Miss Solveig?"

Solveig looked up from the data pad she was holding between her hands and turned off the Acheroni language refresher she had been studying for the last half hour. Her assistant Anja stood at the door just outside the threshold, one hand resting on the translucent frame she had just lightly rapped with her knuckles to announce her presence.

"Yes, Anja?"

"Edric from security would like to know how late you will be needing the gyrofoil home. He wanted me to remind you that there are new flight restrictions in place now."

Solveig looked over to the window, where the sun had mostly settled behind the skyline of Sandvik. She hadn't noticed the time because the streets were always lit at the same level—as the sun went down, the illumination of the roadways and buildings increased gradually. Down on street level, the sun never really set. She used to enjoy that about city life, but after a few months of spending her nights back in the countryside, it seemed unnatural.

"I'm afraid I haven't kept track of my time very well today," she said. Anja smiled, but Solveig could tell that her assistant was trying to gauge whether she was being blamed somehow. Solveig wondered if Anja had been here when her father sat in the big chair, then decided that she was probably too young, but she had clearly been around long enough for the corporate culture to imprint on her.

His spirit is still all over this place, she thought. *Everyone's always jumpy and worried.*

Solveig checked the time. "What's the new regulation again?"

"No air traffic over Principal Square after 2100 hours," Anja replied. "If you wish to stay beyond that time, Edric will have to ferry you to the spaceport in a ground pod for a transit flight home."

"Ugh." Solveig made a face. "That's on the other end of the city. Too much trouble for a twenty-minute flight home. Tell Edric not to waste his time just because I can't stick to my own schedule. I'll be on the rooftop pad at 2030."

"Very well, Miss Solveig. I will let him know."

Anja withdrew politely and walked down the hallway out of sight. Solveig was the only person on the executive floor who liked to work with her door open. Everyone else kept theirs closed, and many of the department directors and vice presidents turned on their offices' glass tinting for privacy. Falk Ragnar would have forbidden the practice outside of confidential meetings. It pleased Solveig that at least this little bit of slack had made its way into the attitudes on the top floor, even if it had taken half a decade.

She put down her data pad and looked at the screen projections above her desk. There was never an end to the flow of data in a company like Ragnar Industries, not even the postwar incarnation that was still operating at half throttle. Ragnar was the hub of hundreds of supply spokes. Every day, many millions of ags' worth of raw materials and finished goods changed hands, entered inventories and left them again, each transaction creating a digital footprint. As much as the Alliance had squeezed the company as a critical wartime supplier, everyone still needed Alon, and only Ragnar and its subcontractors could produce it.

But the size of the network required to keep the flow of goods going was so immense that no single person could possibly have their hands on every lever simultaneously, know every layer and sublayer of the structure. And yet her father had done it for decades. Sometimes she wondered whether he had intentionally set things up to be complex enough that only he would always know exactly which lever to pull to get a specific result. For three months now, Solveig had tried to dig into all the digital strata that made up Ragnar Industries, and she had barely scratched the surface.

She checked the time again. It was almost 1900 hours, so she had ninety minutes to finish the tasks she had set for herself today. The screens surrounding her kept scrolling information she had requested, data fields overlaid on data fields. Anja's interruption had pulled her out of the flow of her Acheroni language lesson, and Solveig decided that she didn't have a mind for data analysis anymore. The lesson had been on food—ordering in a restaurant—and it had put her in the mood for something spicy. She waved all the screens above her desk surface out of existence with a single gesture and got out of her chair to stretch.

"Vigdis, I'm stepping out for a bit. Run the dine-in protocol until 2130 hours, please."

"Understood. The dine-in protocol is in effect. Have a good evening," the AI replied. Solveig had made a few tweaks to the way her personal AI reported her presence in the office to the network whenever she wanted to go out for a bite to eat without a security entourage. If Marten or any of his underlings checked her location in the system, it would still show her in her office, with a privacy flag enabled so they'd know not to disturb her in person. If they came close to the office anyway, the AI would have her seem to wander off to the canteen or one of the exercise facilities downstairs. Her access pass to the building was now temporarily assigned to a fictitious ID so she could leave and return without getting an earful from Marten about security protocol. It wasn't bulletproof—all that had to happen to blow her little sleight of hand

was for Marten to give closer scrutiny to the surveillance data or cross paths with her in one of the entrance lobbies of the building—but she figured the fallout would be tolerable. After all, she was just going out for Acheroni food, not plotting with the competition or trying to steal the company's cash reserves.

———

The summer evening was warm and humid. Solveig walked away from Ragnar Tower on streets that were still busy with activity—people heading home from work late or heading out to enjoy their diversions.

There was a street nearby where the eateries were closed during the day but open all night, catering to the leisure crowd and the busy people looking for an easy dinner on the way home. There was no theme or system to the agglomeration of food stalls and tiny sit-in places here—Gretian comfort snacks, Oceanian seafood, Acheroni stew shops, all peacefully coexisting shoulder to shoulder on the same strip of real estate. Solveig's favorite place on this street was an Acheroni joint so narrow that it could only fit a single row of tiny tables inside next to the counter, and on busy nights she had to wait a good while for her turn to order, but she had never been disappointed with the food. She knew that Magnus would have a fit if he saw her in the middle of the evening crowds without a bodyguard. But nobody cared. Nobody knew that her name was on the side of the nearby office tower that stood tallest among all the ones around Principal Square. There was a freedom to her occasional clandestine dinner excursions that made her feel a little like she was at university again, when the weight of responsibility and expectations hadn't yet settled on her shoulders. There had been no security detail back then. She had just been one of the students, and her father seemed to have deemed her too valuable to venture out into public only when she was of legal age, with a degree that finally qualified her to start at Ragnar and step into the role he had intended for her.

Solveig ordered her food, then stood in line to wait for its preparation. It was a busy evening, and all the little tables inside were taken. She kept an eye on them as she moved along the line to the pickup station. Sometimes the timing was in her favor, and another guest got ready to vacate their table just as she was ready to claim it.

The person sitting at the last table in the back had a familiar face. It took her a moment to recognize him because she had only seen it once, three months ago. It was the young police detective who had questioned her on the day before the Principal Square bombing. She had never heard from him again. The police probably had other things to do after the worst terrorist attack in the planet's history. Just as she started to turn her head away so he wouldn't recognize her, their eyes locked, and he gave her a friendly nod.

So much for anonymity, she thought.

When she had received her food container, the layout of the place required her to make a turn at the very back and walk past all the guest tables on the way out. Nobody was going through the telltale motions of preparing to leave yet.

"Miss Ragnar," the detective said when he saw her scanning the line of tables as she walked by. "You can sit here if you want. No offense taken if you don't."

He gestured at the empty seat across the table from him. She knew that on Acheron, where space was always at a premium, it was perfectly acceptable and necessary to share a table with a stranger. But Gretian customs were very different. Offering someone a seat at one's table was a gesture of high courtesy. Solveig didn't want to be rude. Besides, eating her food while sitting down was better than eating it on the walk back to the office. She placed her food container on the table and sat down across from the detective.

"Thank you. Berg, isn't it? Criminal Detective Berg."

"You have a good memory," he said. "We met quite a while ago. You must have been busy since then."

He was as good-looking as she remembered, unruly brown hair curling down the back of his neck and touching his collar. He wore a purple compression shirt that went well with his green eyes. The form-fitting top accentuated the fact that he was in very good shape. Just as she had done three months ago, she briefly wondered if the police had sent him to question her specifically because he was young and handsome. For a moment, the low-grade paranoia programmed into her since childhood made her suspect that he was here on purpose again, that this was a setup to get more information out of her in an informal setting, but then she dismissed the thought as illogical. He had been here first, and he'd had no way of knowing she would step out for dinner tonight at this exact time and choose this place out of a hundred other options on this street.

He nodded at her food container.

"I hadn't marked you for someone who likes spicy food," he said. "What grade is that?"

"Five," she said. "I'm still working my way up the scale. Yours?"

"Eight. Sometimes nine if I feel daring." He smiled at the little wince she gave him. "I have to eat out because the smell annoys the other detectives when I bring Acheroni food back to the office. They all have solid, traditional Gretian palates."

"Starches, dairy, and meat proteins," Solveig said. "Salt and sugar and maybe a little pepper."

"And gods forbid you use too much of that. They think soy sauce is spicy," he said.

She couldn't suppress a little laugh, and he smiled, obviously pleased to have gotten that reaction out of her.

"It must be busy for you, too, if you're still out here at this hour," she said.

"Tempers get shorter in the summer. People are outside more. And we just had the first socaball match of the season this afternoon. Thank the gods that Sandvik won. Whenever they lose, we get really busy."

Solveig ate her meal deliberately, mindful of the potential for sauce splattering her clean blue suit. She wanted to be annoyed at the fact that she cared about not making a mess in front of Detective Berg. It meant acknowledging to herself that she found him attractive. But it was an unexpected and almost pleasant annoyance.

"What about you? Working late tonight?" he asked.

"I want to tell you I am so busy that I don't have time for leisure. That I only go home to sleep. The sort of thing you're supposed to say as a corporate executive."

She looked around as if to make sure nobody was listening in, then lowered her voice a little to pretend she was sharing a secret.

"The truth is that the food in our executive kitchen is boring. So I sneak out for dinner sometimes."

"You're a vice president at Ragnar," Berg said. "I'm sure they could make you whatever you told them."

"That's not a good use of executive power," Solveig replied. "It's not my personal kitchen. It's the company kitchen. Besides, it's a good excuse to get some fresh air."

He nodded and took a few bites of his own food. She watched him pick up the glistening black noodles of his dish with the sticks, then expertly wind them into a ball before putting them into his mouth.

"Do you live in the city?" he asked.

Solveig shook her head.

"No, I'm staying at the family place. At least until I get a feel for this routine. I just started three months ago. I'm still trying to find the right rate of swing for this pendulum."

"That's a good way to put it," he said. "I'm not sure I could move into the same place with my parents again. I was glad to be away. It's nice to see them every few months, but we all do better when we have our own space. I barely spend time at home anyway. And when I do, it's at the strangest hours. It would drive them crazy after a while."

"Where do you live?"

"I have a place in the outer ring, near the spaceport. Sometimes I stay late, or I don't want to deal with the tube travel, and then I just rent a sleeping pod in the city for the night."

Solveig suddenly felt keenly aware of the gap in life circumstances that existed between her and almost everyone else who was close to her age. She had a company gyrofoil standing by to ferry her back home to sleep, to a huge family estate with a security detachment, dozens of rooms, and a fully staffed kitchen with its own vegetable gardens and fishponds. He had to take a long tube ride home because he couldn't afford a place inside the main city ring, and when he stayed out in the city overnight, it was by necessity and not choice. Things that were adventures or acts of rebellion for her were just regular life for normal people.

"The investigation was a dead end, by the way," he said around a mouthful of noodles.

"The investigation," Solveig repeated.

"The one I helped conduct at Ragnar when I questioned you. Three months ago. The glove from Lagertha Land Systems. It was a dead end. In case you're wondering if I'm just trying to get information out of you."

"Oh. I figured you would have been by to ask more questions if it wasn't resolved."

"It was like you said. Lagertha closed down after the war, and the military records can't tell us who received that glove."

"So we are both just civilians right now," she said.

"Off the clock and off the record," he confirmed. "No legal or ethical pitfalls."

They continued their meal. She kept sneaking glances at him when his attention was on his noodles to wind them up for another bite. Detective Berg's brown hair was lightly curled, and it looked a little too unruly for a police officer. She suspected he got a lot of comments about it at work. It could be that he was duplicitous, that he was trying to use her as an easy wedge to get more intelligence about Ragnar Industries. But she was very good at smelling out intent. It had been a necessary survival skill for most of her life. And from the way he was glancing at her whenever he thought she was paying attention to her own food or the surroundings, she suspected she had his intent figured out with a fair degree of accuracy.

Besides, sometimes it was fun to throw caution to the wind.

"Off the record," she said. "You have a personal comtab with you?"

He looked surprised, but then he nodded and pulled the device out of a pocket. He held it up to show her, the questioning expression still on his face. She took her own comtab out and tapped it against his.

"That's my private node, not the business one. For the next time you are off the clock and in the mood for some spicy food. And you feel like having company. No legal or ethical pitfalls."

Berg looked at the node information flashing across his screen. She had formulated the offer in casual terms. If he wasn't interested, or if he was with someone else, it would be easy for him to be politely noncommittal without rejecting her outright.

He smiled and tucked his comtab away again.

"I will take you up on that."

———

She barely avoided being late for her ride home. When she stepped through the rooftop access door, it was 2128 hours. Tonight, ninety minutes had passed much more quickly than usual.

On the rooftop landing pad, Edric was waiting for her next to the gyrofoil that would bring her home. Solveig stopped at the edge of the pad for a moment and turned to look at the city. The sun had set, leaving only a faint streak of purple and red at the horizon. Down in the streets, thousands of AI-controlled pods formed never-ending rivers of blinking lights that crisscrossed each other and converged in the distance. The evening air carried the smells of the city, ozone and warm steel and sunbaked photovoltaic glass.

"Good evening, Miss Solveig," Edric said when she walked over to the gyrofoil's open door. "You look like you had a good day."

"How so, Edric?" she asked.

"You look pleased."

Edric climbed into the cabin behind her and closed the door. A few moments later, the pilot started the rotors and lifted off into the night sky. Solveig checked her reflection in the window next to her seat. There was a little smile stuck in the corners of her mouth after all, she saw, one that wasn't usually there after a long day at Ragnar.

———

When she walked the path from the landing pad to the main house half an hour later, the music from the house was so loud that she could already hear it halfway across the central terrace. The noise increased exponentially when the front door sensed her approach and opened. An orchestral soundtrack, heavy with percussion and dramatic. Solveig sighed. She knew how her father's day had been going, and where she would find him tonight.

"Computer, turn it down seventy percent," she shouted at the housekeeping AI. The thundering drums lowered their volume to a more tolerable level. She made her way straight to the bar next to the main sitting room. If he wanted company—and on nights like this, he usually did—there was no avoiding him. If she went to bed without stopping to see him, he'd just have her summoned anyway.

Falk Ragnar sat at the bar, on one of his old-fashioned stools that were covered in ancient leather. A screen projection was floating in front of a wall, taking up the entire side of the room. It was playing three news streams side by side, with the sound turned off.

"You are going to make yourself deaf, Papa," she said when she walked in. "Listening to music at that volume."

"Cochlear replacements are cheap," he said. "Takes half an hour. I've had it done twice already."

He patted the bar stool next to his.

"Daughter of mine. Come on, have a drink with me before you go to bed. You worked late. You've earned one."

She could tell by the light slur in his speech that the drink in front of him wasn't his first tonight, or the second. There was a bottle by his right hand. She recognized the label—Rhodian single malt that was older than she was, a thousand-ag bottle of liquor. As much as her father detested the Rhodians, his hatred did not let him deny himself the pleasure of their finest and most expensive distillates.

"Sure," she said, knowing that he wouldn't take no for an answer. "But just a little."

He took another glass from the overhead rack and put it down on the counter, then poured a finger's height of liquor into it. Even drunk, he had supreme physical control. He'd sway just like anyone else, but she had never seen him stumble or fall while intoxicated, not even when he'd had an entire bottle by himself, and he never threw up. Solveig sat down on the stool and touched glasses with him. It wasn't her sort of drink, but she could understand why people enjoyed it. There was an almost infinite complexity to the flavor. She held the sip of liquor on her tongue for a moment and breathed in through her nose before swallowing, just like he had taught her, and he nodded his approval.

"He should have been like you," he said. "Aden."

She took another sip of the liquor to avoid a reply. There was no good way to bring up Aden with her father, and she was surprised he had broached that subject on his own. Maybe he wasn't even on his third drink anymore.

"You went and walked the path. You got top grades. And then you took the chair. The one he was supposed to claim. And instead, he runs off and becomes a *soldier*." He emphasized the word like it was the name of a distasteful medical condition.

"Have you heard anything?" Solveig asked.

Falk shook his head.

"He disappeared again. But corporate intel did some digging. He joined up the year he left. Went into military intelligence. Linguistics. Sat out the war on Oceana, if the records have it right. He spent five years in a POW camp on Rhodia. Five years, and not a word to us. Not even a Mnemosyne message. While we were thinking he was dead. Why would he do that, Solveig?"

He slugged the rest of the liquor in his glass and gently set it down next to the bottle.

"Have I been a bad father?" he asked without looking at her. "Am I a terrible person?"

"Absolutely not," she said. "You've always made sure I've had everything I needed. I wouldn't be who I am without you, Papa."

It was another learned skill that came with growing up a Ragnar— the ability to sense what an audience wanted to hear, and then delivering it in just the right way to confirm their biases or the validity of their fears. It worked on almost everyone, and when her father was drunk enough, it even worked on him.

"Why would he throw all of this away and waste his life like that? He could have been running half the planet. Not translating enemy field manuals for the fucking Blackguards. They have *software* that can do that job. Why would he turn his back on all of this? On you and me?"

There was no right answer to that question, none that her father would accept, so she didn't even make the attempt.

"I was *six* the year he left," she said. "I barely even remember him. I can't tell you why he would. I don't know who he is. Or who he *was*."

"Fair enough." Falk looked at the bottle as if considering whether to pour another. He picked up his glass and lightly clinked the bottom of it against the neck of the bottle, then set it down again.

"What *really* happened back then?" she asked. "Between the two of you?"

Her father stared off into the space behind the bar. His jaw muscles flexed slowly. For a few moments, she thought he might be drunk and introspective enough to make a hole in the wall he had been keeping up in front of that part of the family history for seventeen years and allow her a peek through the crack. Then he shook his head.

"Just silly stuff, now. I've told you it was about a girl. Boys that age, it's always about love. They think they're the first ones to discover it. Trust me, it wasn't anything worth seventeen years of silence."

He looked at her with glassy eyes and smiled. It was a different smile from his usual toothy display of dominance. There was genuine sadness in it. But she could tell that this was as much authentic, unfiltered emotion as that bottle of liquor could get out of him tonight, and that she had asked the question half a glass too soon.

"I really shouldn't keep you up, Solveig. You've had a long day. Go get some rest."

Solveig knew when she was being dismissed. She leaned in and kissed him on the cheek.

"All right, Papa. Have a good night. I'll see you at breakfast."

She climbed off the bar stool and walked past the screen projections that were still silently shouting out three different newscasts at once, data streams overlaid with data streams, a torrent of structured chaos.

I wonder if it looks like that in his head all the time, she thought.

CHAPTER 9

ADEN

The dish in front of him, retained in the little cast-iron pan the server had put on the table with a gestured warning against touching the handle, sizzled with the residual heat from cooking. The smell wasn't unappetizing, but the strong scent of spices almost singed the hairs in his nostrils, and Aden knew that he'd most likely get chemical burns on his tongue from eating whatever was in that shallow pan.

"If this makes the hangover worse, I am absolutely blaming you," he told Tristan, who sat across from him, arms folded, elbows on the table surface, an amused expression on his face.

"It will make you forget about the hangover," Tristan said. "It can cure anything. Up to and possibly including the pain from a stab wound."

"What is it called again?"

Aden poked the dish with a fork. He could identify the eggs on top, but the ingredients underneath were a mystery. Everything had been blended together into a layer of baked mush that had shades of red, orange, and green.

"I can't pronounce the Palladian word, but I can tell you what everyone else calls it. Spacers' Sunrise."

"Spacers' Sunrise," Aden repeated.

"Break up the eggs with your fork and stir them in with the mix. You want to break the yolks and make them run into the mush," Tristan said.

A panoramic window ran the length of the wall on the guest-table side of the eatery. It was really a large holographic screen layer, but they had set it into a frame that looked like a bulkhead viewport and then put a thin layer of Alon on top to make the mimicry complete. The screen showed an outside view of the station, Pallas looming underneath, spaceships arriving and departing in a steady stream. Aden wondered if it was a live view or recorded footage played on an endless loop, but he gave up trying to look for repetitive patterns after a minute. It was something that would please space tourists, but he had to admit it was nicer to look at than a naked bulkhead.

He touched the Alon layer covering the screen and rested his palm on it for a moment. It was cool to the touch and as smooth as polished steel. Every piece of Alon in the system came from his family's factories, Ragnar Industries' most important product. He had known all its lucrative properties by the time he was six. Transparent ceramic, 90 percent as hard as diamond, highly resistant to bullets and shrapnel, impervious to corrosion. Only a diamond or another piece of Alon could make a scratch in it. Every spaceship ever built had viewports somewhere, and every viewport was a slab of Alon that had made Ragnar a healthy profit on its way along the chain of manufacture, distribution, and sale. This screen cover was a tiny part of the tether that had tied him to a different destiny once, the tether he had unintentionally transferred to his sister Solveig's ankle when he left home. Aden withdrew his palm from the Alon layer and picked up his fork again.

"I still feel like hammered shit," he told Tristan. "I'm not sure I'm up for culinary experiments."

"Just try it," Tristan said. His craggy face had permanent smile lines etched into it. He was tall and lean, with unruly white hair that always looked like he had just taken off a helmet.

Aden tried to determine whether he was being set up for a practical joke—make the new guy puke his guts out after a bender, ha ha—or if Tristan was really just sharing some of his extensive knowledge of the system's culinary cultures without bad intent. It was probably the latter, he decided. Tristan was too good-natured to play mean pranks. And even if it was an initiation ritual of sorts, Aden figured it was best to be a good sport and play along. He gamely filled up a fork, making sure to get equal amounts of egg and mush, and took his first bite.

The spiciness was a fair bit beyond his usual tolerance level. It made his tongue burn, then the roof of his mouth, then his throat. He felt his nose starting to run almost instantly. But it wasn't just all nuclear heat. The egg yolks blended with the ingredients in the base dish into a flavor that was surprisingly complex even in its ferocious intensity.

Tristan watched with a glint in his eyes as Aden swallowed the first bite, then another. After his third bite, he had to put the fork down and tear off a piece of the table liner to wipe his nose, then another to dab the tears from his eyes.

"Well," Aden said in a strangled-sounding voice. "You're right about one thing. I'm not even feeling the hangover anymore."

Tristan laughed. "It stops hurting halfway through the pan. And by the time you're done, you'll find yourself thinking you might want another."

Captain Decker and Henry appeared at the door of the eatery, and Tristan gave them a lazy wave to get their attention. They walked over to Aden and Tristan's table and sat down on the free chairs. Henry looked at Aden's dish and said a Palladian word, approval in his voice. Aden assumed it was the native name of the dish.

"Really, Tristan?" Decker said. "His first time on Pallas One, and you're taking him to have that for breakfast."

"He's doing fine," Tristan said. "Better than I thought he would."

"I can't have our new linguist taking up residence in the head on the galley deck for the next two days. Or on IV fluids in the medical bay."

"Where are the others?" Tristan asked.

"Tess has been doing an exterior hull check on the heat sink array on *Zephyr* since 0600. Maya is off doing Maya things, like she does."

"Tess is doing EVA after drinking with us last night?" Aden couldn't even fathom getting into an EVA suit right now. They were not designed to handle sudden gastric emergencies.

"She knows her limits," Decker said and watched pointedly as he wiped his nose again. "Apparently you don't know yours quite yet."

"How do you like it?" Henry asked Aden.

"I think it's pretty good. I'll let you know for sure once the numbness on my tongue wears off."

Henry chuckled. Decker just shook her head, but Aden could see the little smile turning up the corners of her mouth almost imperceptibly. Aden knew that she was the crew member closest to him in age—he was forty-two; she was forty-three. But she was at the top of the hierarchy aboard *Zephyr*, and he was all the way at the bottom, junior to even Maya, who was just about young enough to be his daughter. It had been a strange dynamic at first, but he found it liberating in a way. In the prison arcology, he had been responsible for managing the conduct and daily tasks of over a hundred people for half a decade. Here, he only had to do what he was told. He was only responsible for his own actions, his accomplishments and failures. There was a certain freedom to it. Maybe it was the only freedom that really mattered.

"We have a new contract," Decker announced. "As soon as Tess is done with her business, we are out of here. So do your last-minute shopping now if you need to stock up on anything."

"Off the contract board?" Tristan asked, and Decker shook her head.

"Half the stuff on the board is for runs to Hades. Most of the rest wasn't worth our fuel or time. This one's back-channel."

"What's wrong with Hades runs?" Aden asked.

"We don't have the rating for Hades approaches," Henry replied. "It's so close to the sun, you need heavy shielding. Too much heat and radiation."

"They build special freighters just for that run," Decker added. "Hades beats up ships. Everything has to be shielded. Triple-redundant systems, special pilot certification, and it all adds to the tab. Not worth it for a hull our size."

"So what's the job?" Tristan asked.

"Courier run. We're heading out to pick up some cargo and deliver it."

"Speed or discretion?"

"We'll go over it on the ship," Decker said. "Take your time with breakfast. But don't be late, or we'll have to wait half a day for another slot. Everyone needs to be back on the ship and buckled in by 1100. If we miss our slot, whoever made us late gets to eat the additional departure fee."

———

Aden didn't know anything about Pallas One, but Tristan seemed more than happy to act as tour guide for him. They went to the standard-gravity mercantile concourse, where a few dozen shops offered their wares to tourists and commercial freighter crews.

"The shops with the music playing and the guys in the bright Pallas garb out front, you don't want to go into those," Tristan advised. "Those are tourist traps. For the transit crowd that doesn't have the time to go down to the surface. Authentic Pallas crafts and clothing, for a hefty premium."

"Authentic, huh?" Aden eyed one of the shops Tristan had indicated.

"Some sucker is going to drop three hundred ags on a genuine hand-forged ceremonial kukri that was probably stamped out of a sheet of recycled scrap metal in a trinket factory on Hades. And when the happy customer carries his purchase out of the shop to take it home and hang it on the wall of his living unit, that shopkeeper is going to replace it with an identical one from a storage bin in the back."

"What about that honorable Palladian warrior spirit?" Aden asked.

"You want to see some warrior spirit, go buy something from that guy in the bright-blue tunic and then ask to return it for a refund."

———

They went to a shop in a side corridor of the concourse Aden never would have ventured into on his own. From what he could tell, the other customers in the place were all freighter crews, cargo hands from the freight-dock level, or maintenance crews in grease-stained overalls. He felt out of place in his nearly new flight suit. Nobody here sold or bought counterfeit kukris or Palladian garb. Instead, the shop offered a wildly diverse mix of goods: comtabs, tool sets, energy cells in all sizes and formats, a variety of food items, and hundreds of other diversions or necessities for a working life in space.

"You've done some time," Tristan observed when Aden had collected his purchases from the dispenser chute at the exit.

"What do you mean?" Aden's hand briefly froze on the pack of freeze-dried crackers he was about to stuff into his sling pack.

"You've been in a detention center. And not just for a week or two."

"What makes you say that?"

"You shop like a prisoner," Tristan said and nodded at the small pile of purchases in front of Aden. "Like you're in a detention commissary. Personal hygiene products. So you don't have to use the issue stuff and smell like everyone else. Packaged comfort foods. Stuff that doesn't need equipment to warm up or rehydrate. Little private pleasures you can keep in your locker until you can use them up."

"Sounds like you know a thing or two about that," Aden replied, trying to figure out Tristan's intent.

"A lot of us do. Spacers are a rough lot. We bounce around between six worlds. Six different sets of rules, customs, regulations. It's not hard to piss off authority."

"I've done some time," Aden admitted.

"For what?"

"Being in the wrong place at the wrong time. With the wrong people."

Tristan's purchases slid out of the dispenser chute into the pickup tray, and he began collecting them without hurry.

"Ah, yes. The number-one cause of incarceration."

The items in Tristan's little pile of supplies looked mostly unfamiliar to Aden.

"What is the veteran spacer buying for the ride, then?" he asked.

"Spices. Freeze-dried herbs. Pepper sauce. So I can keep turning those prepackaged galley meals on the ship into something edible. Other than that, I've got all the stuff I need."

Tristan picked up his bag and slung it over his shoulder.

"Never own more things than you can carry off the ship in one hand. It just makes life complicated. Weighs you down."

Aden smiled. He had already followed that philosophy for the last five years, albeit not by choice.

"I think I have that covered right now," he said.

When they left the shop, he glanced back at the variety on the shelves. Once, in a previous life, he'd had enough money at his disposal to buy the place empty in a single transaction. If the shop owner told him right now he could pick a thousand ags in merchandise for free, he wouldn't know what to choose beyond the items he had already purchased. He couldn't even remember what the old Aden had liked, what he would have bought for a thousand ags in this place. It was like trying to remember details from last night's fleeting dream. The ID pass in his pocket was a lie, but it marked a break in his life that was real. There was very little left of Aden Robertson, and he didn't know Aden Ragnar well enough anymore to judge just how much of him had remained. Three lives, three names, and he was less sure of who he really was than he had ever been.

———

They were all early for the departure. Maya was the last to make it through the docking collar and onto the ship. Aden knew by now that she was always the first to leave and the last to come back, no matter where they had docked in the last three months.

Whenever Captain Decker wanted to call an all-hands meeting, they gathered around the table in the galley because it was the only space on the ship where everyone could sit down together and face each other. Aden didn't know how long he would have to be a member of the crew for him to stop feeling like he was sitting down at dinner as the houseguest of another family, but three months hadn't been enough time yet.

"Someone is paying us double rate for a cargo haul," Decker said when everyone had settled in. "Ship-to-ship pickup somewhere off the beaten path. Discreet delivery to another ship. The client would really like to avoid official entanglements."

"So we're running incognito for this one," Maya clarified.

"We haven't had to do that in a while. It's a good way to stay in practice."

"How much cargo?" Tess asked.

"One container, two hundred and eighty kilos gross," Decker said.

"Lot of money to be shelling out for hauling a quarter ton." Tristan sat back in his chair and folded his arms across his chest. "That must be some fine contraband. Where do they need it? Past the customs blockade at Gretia?"

Decker shook her head.

"Nothing that difficult. The rendezvous point is some random spot in Rhodian space. Should be easy enough to avoid the Rhody navy. They're busy with their antipiracy patrols on the regular transfer routes. The whole affair is a four-day run. We go out, pick up the cargo, bring it to the drop-off point, and collect our fee times two. And then we head to Acheron for the three-year overhaul."

She looked around the table.

"Everyone on board with this?"

Maya and Henry nodded.

"I just keep her running. You point her to whatever makes the money show up on my ledger," Tess said.

"Double rate for four days of running dirty. And we get to Acheron a week ahead of schedule," Tristan summed up. "I'm fine with it."

Decker looked at Aden, and every other pair of eyes at the table followed.

"What about you, Aden?" she asked.

"Do we want to know what we're delivering?" he replied.

"That's part of why they're willing to pay us double rate," Decker said. "They're purchasing a 'don't ask, don't tell' policy. That's generally implied in the no-haggle up-front bonus."

"So it's probably illegal."

"Oh, it's *definitely* illegal," Tristan said.

"And if the Rhodian Navy catches us?"

"Then we will be in some deep shit," Maya said. "The idea is to not get caught. This ship is a black hole in space when we're rigged for dirty running. And even if the Rhodies somehow detect us, we can outrun anything they have."

"It's a risk," Tess said. "But the fun ones usually are."

Flying dirty in Rhodian space meant a risk to end up with the ship impounded and the crew in detention. It wasn't the illegal nature of the job that bothered him, it was the fact that it would break Rhodian law. If they got caught, he'd go back to one of their prison arcologies just for being a Blackguard on parole, even if the others got off lightly. But those were not fears he could voice in front of everyone at the table. The rest of the crew thought it was worth the risk. None of them seemed concerned. He figured they had the experience to gauge the chance of failure and weigh it against the benefits more accurately than he could.

"I'll go along with it," Aden said.

"We're unanimous, then." Tess rapped the table with her knuckles. "I'll send them the acceptance and collect their deposit."

"Did this have to be unanimous?" Aden asked.

"Of course," Tristan replied for the captain. "Any decision that can get us all in shackles or dead, everyone needs to be on board with it or it's a no go."

"Does that change your answer?" Decker asked.

Aden considered it for a moment. They had given him the power to pull the plug on a lucrative contract on his vote alone, let his one voice override all of theirs, because they believed they didn't have the right to make that decision for him.

"No, it doesn't," he said.

I just hope we all *know what we are doing,* he thought as they got up from the table to take their places on the maneuvering deck.

CHAPTER 10

IDINA

A warm rain was falling out of the night sky above Joint Base Sandvik. Out on the landing pad, Idina and Dahl walked through puddles on the way to their patrol gyrofoil. The summer thunderstorm had made the temperature drop by a few degrees, but it was still warm enough for Idina to keep the cooling system running under her light armor, if only to reduce the humidity she felt on her skin. The summer storms here were mild, with breezy air and short, gentle bursts of rain. At home on Pallas, storms could rage for days, and flying a gyrofoil in the middle of one was as safe a suicide method as jumping off a city terrace into the kilometers-deep chasm below.

"I'm sorry to report that this week will be my last one on patrol with you," she said to Dahl. The older woman gave her a surprised look.

"Have you grown tired of this place after all?"

"It's not that. My commanding officer is ordering me back home two months early. Medical leave," she said, spitting out the last two words with distaste. "We have to go back home on a regular basis. Our bone density and muscle mass deteriorate too much in your low gravity."

"I see." Dahl looked disappointed, an emotion Idina rarely saw on her face. "That is unfortunate. I think we work well together. And I have grown rather accustomed to our chats."

"As have I," Idina said. The Idina from six months ago would have been aghast at the idea of regret over having to leave Gretia or ending a duty assignment that caused her to cooperate with a Gretian every day. But the emotion was there, and it was pointless to deny its existence.

"I would have thought a military as well equipped as yours would have a high-g facility for rehabilitation. To save the flight home every few months," Dahl said.

"That takes gravmag generators," Idina said. "Too expensive to justify for just a company that rotates out half its personnel every six months anyway. You know how stingy bureaucracies can be."

"Oh, yes," Dahl said. "By the time we get new equipment, it is usually five to ten years out of date already."

They went up to their assigned gyrofoil and did their walk-around check wordlessly. Dahl brought up the checklist on a comtab projection and worked through it just like she did before every flight. The Gretian police captain never let routine lull her into complacency, not even after decades on the job. It was one of the stereotypical Gretian qualities that Idina had to grudgingly admire. Dahl would have made an excellent platoon sergeant, no matter how often she insisted that she wasn't cut out to be a soldier.

They took off into the rainy night sky at exactly 2200 hours as always. Idina spent the five-minute flight to the platoon's assigned patrol sector checking in with her JSP troopers and reviewing their intended deployment locations. Sandvik was a big city, and their joint platoon only had forty pairs of patrol officers between them. Every night, the AI set patrol spots and assignments, based on the current security situation and previously observed call patterns, to maximize the coverage they could provide with just eighty officers per sector.

"I really do wish I could finish this deployment with you," Idina said after she had made all her usual comms check-ins. "I don't like leaving jobs undone. And you'll have to get used to a new Palladian in that passenger seat."

Dahl shrugged.

"I will be fine. I have had to get used to many different partners over the years. At least it will only be two months if we end up disliking each other."

"Sergeant Noor was supposed to be riding with you today already. I'm supposed to be on light duty. I just haven't managed to redo the patrol assignments yet. I may not get around to it before I leave."

"I see," Dahl said with a wry smile. "I will make sure you do not strain yourself excessively."

"Maybe we can actually wrap a few things up this week. What's the word on the arms-dealer mechanic the kid from yesterday mentioned? Has someone been out to see him yet?"

"Vigi Fuldas," Dahl said.

"That's the name."

"We have put in a request for a detention order. But the Hall of Justice is not working off its backlog very quickly. They expect to have an order ready by the end of the week."

"The guy is converting illegal military weapons for the black market, and the Hall of Justice thinks that's not an urgent enough matter," Idina summarized. "That's not very efficient."

"They issue the detention orders," Dahl said. "We have to wait for one before we can search his place. That is the way the system works. If I start searching homes without judicial consent, the system is no longer in place. Without the system, I am not a police officer anymore. Just someone with a weapon and a meaningless word written on my armor. And then Vigi Fuldas can claim the right to search my place, too, as long as he brings a bigger gun."

Idina felt a pang of irritation at Dahl's calm and matter-of-fact chastening. Every day, the woman confirmed some of her prejudices about Gretians and then completely dispelled them again.

They flew in silence for a few minutes. The gyrofoil's autopilot corrected for the wind gusts so efficiently that it might as well have been a still and cloudless summer night out there for all the difference it made to the smoothness of the ride. Dahl started their patrol pattern a thousand meters above the bustling streets as always.

"What does the term 'loophole' mean to you, Sergeant Chaudhary?" Dahl asked.

Idina thought about the question.

"A loophole is a way to do something that is against the spirit of the rules without violating them openly," she answered.

Dahl nodded.

"That is not a bad definition. In my experience, a loophole is a thing that is allowed when the person who calls it a 'loophole' would rather see it forbidden but does not have the ability to make it so."

"Interesting perspective," Idina said.

"On an unrelated subject, I have found out something interesting about Vigi Fuldas," Dahl continued. "He lives outside of our patrol sector, which puts his residence out of our area of responsibility. But he travels to work on the Artery. And he changes Artery trains at Philharmony Station, which *is* in our patrol sector."

Idina looked at Dahl with a raised eyebrow, but the other woman maintained the unreadable expression she had probably mastered decades ago.

"That's an interesting fact," she replied.

"I thought so, too."

Idina brought up a map of Sandvik and isolated Philharmony Station, then laughed when she magnified the view.

"That's barely in our sector. The border line goes right through that station," she said. "Half of it is in the Oceanian sector."

"That is true," Dahl conceded. "But our half is the one with the main entrance. And all the transfer platforms."

Idina laughed again.

"That is one tiny loophole. We have jurisdiction there. But it won't do us any good unless we just happen to be there when he changes trains, and we spot him. And somehow get to him before he jumps on the next Artery train or leaves by the eastern entrance."

"If we knew his work schedule, we wouldn't have to happen to be there."

Idina finally figured out Dahl's intent. She shook her head with a grin.

"That's a sort of rule-bending ingenuity I hadn't expected from you."

"I am glad I still manage to confound your expectations sometimes," Dahl said.

"Do we know his work schedule?"

Dahl nodded.

"He works from 1600 hours to 0000 hours this week. The Artery ride from the spaceport to Philharmony Station takes thirty-one minutes."

Idina checked the time. It was 2210. They would be on station until 0600 hours tomorrow morning. If they encountered Vigi Fuldas in their sector during their shift, they could detain and question him without waiting for a judicial order.

"I know you are ordered to be on light duty," Dahl said. "And you have the final authority here on military security matters. But I am the patrol supervisor for the Gretian police in this sector tonight. And I think that the platform at Philharmony Station has not had a foot patrol checking on things in a good while. At around 0030 hours tonight, I may decide that all patrols are either tied up or too far away, and that I want to take a good look around. Personally. And you would have to accompany me. Regardless of your commander's wishes."

"Well," Idina said. "If you did *that*, I really wouldn't have a choice. Those are the rules."

Dahl shrugged, and Idina could see the hint of a smile in the corners of her mouth.

Prejudices dispelled once again, Idina thought.

The Artery transit stations in the center of the city were built underground, but only barely. Idina and Dahl walked down the soft and gradual incline that led from the surface of the Philharmony plaza to the main station entrance below. The station had an entrance atrium, and the ceiling of it was also the surface of the plaza above, made from a layered grid of energy-collecting panels that were set to be completely translucent at night. As they walked through the entrance and into the atrium, Idina looked up at the see-through ceiling, where the rain was collecting in puddles that refracted the lights from the nearby buildings and advertising projections.

Even after midnight, the atrium was still bustling with activity. Late-night commuters were making their way through a crowd that seemed to be mostly young Gretians out for nighttime entertainment, socializing inside the covered court while the summer thunderstorm was passing over the city. Half a dozen food vendors were selling snacks and drinks from mobile stations set up at regular intervals. Idina followed Dahl as she walked through the atrium and past the vendors. Someone in a small group of young men standing nearby saw her coming and jokingly offered up his friend for arrest. Dahl declined the offer, and they laughed as she walked by.

"I did not do it, take this one instead," Dahl said to Idina over the helmet comms. "They all think they are the first ones to think of that joke."

The Artery was a network of magnetic suspension trains that crisscrossed the city and connected major points of interest. It was one of the Gretian engineering achievements Idina could admire without reservation because it didn't have a military application. The trains were sleek and white, and they moved over their smooth magnetic pathways in almost complete silence. The only way to tell that one was about to come out of the pathway's tunnel was the slight change in air pressure right before it emerged. The platform beyond the atrium was divided by color markings, one side green and the other blue. As they walked out onto the green half of the platform, a train glided out of the tube on the blue side and slowed to a gentle stop. Everywhere else in the Gaia system, the screen projections for timetables and directions in transit centers were at least bilingual—the local language plus Rhodian, the de facto common language since the end of the war—but the Gretian signage remained defiantly Gretian only.

"It is now 0032 hours," Dahl said. "The green-line train from the spaceport is due at 0040. Let us hope he did not miss it. There will not be another until 0110."

They paced the platform while they waited, drawing occasional looks from passing commuters. Idina's translator picked up snippets of conversation here and there, background noises of everyday life, mundane and routine. It had taken her a while to shake off her constant fear of another ambush, but she'd always have the professional paranoia of an infantry soldier. This wasn't quite the hostile territory it used to be, but it was still unfriendly ground. She knew that the minute she let herself forget that fact, fate would remind her of it in unpleasant ways. Police duty required that she let people get closer to her than she'd ever allow a civilian from a former enemy planet in an infantry setting, and it was mentally tiring—watching hands in pockets, scanning waistlines for bumps and bulges that could be concealed weapons, looking for objects that were out of place. Human brains had a practical bandwidth for information, and it wasn't difficult to probe the limits of it by having to be alert for threats in a place full of people, where an attack could come from anyone and anywhere.

The minutes ticked by slowly, unmoved by Idina's desire to hurry the minute marker along on its path toward the hour mark on her helmet display's chronometer.

"Thirty seconds," Dahl finally said. "He will be on the next train on the green side. Or we will have to make an excuse to spend another thirty minutes down here."

The train came out of its pathway tube and stopped silently. Idina noted that the doors opened at precisely 0040 and zero seconds.

"Look casual," Dahl advised.

"I'm wearing light armor that has the word POLICE stenciled on it in reflective letters," Idina pointed out. "It's not the best outfit for staying unnoticed."

"That is the joke," Dahl said.

"Gretian humor. I didn't think it existed."

"We get to make one joke per week. There are ration cards."

This got an actual laugh from Idina, and Dahl smiled with satisfaction without taking her eyes off the crowd alighting from the train doors. To give her hands something to do, Idina checked her equipment by touch as they waited: kukri, stun stick, restraints, riot shield handle, sidearm.

"There he is," Dahl said and turned her head to the right. "Green bodysuit, brown vest, orange sling pack."

Idina followed her gaze and saw the suspect, who was walking off the train while looking at the screen projection of his comtab. Vigi Fuldas had the physique of someone who regularly lifted heavy things for a living. There were stains on his green bodysuit, and his white-and-red hard-shell work boots were scuffed and dirty. She tried to will him to pay attention to his screen just a few moments longer, but as Dahl set herself in motion, he extinguished the screen and glanced in their direction. His face froze in the familiar expression of the unpleasantly surprised, a blend of shock and momentary paralysis. Then he turned toward the atrium and ran.

They dashed after him. He sprinted off the platform and into the wide passageway that connected the transit tubes to the atrium. Once again Idina was amazed at the speed Dahl was able to work up at short notice even with ten kilos of equipment weighing down her duty belt.

He almost made the atrium, but then he looked over his shoulder, and seeing Dahl almost within grabbing range made him flinch and stumble. He bumped into a fellow commuter, and his momentum carried him sideways into a store's merchandise rack. Snack packages and electronic trinkets scattered all over the floor of the passage. Dahl and Idina swooped in from two sides, and Vigi Fuldas backpedaled with wide and panicked eyes. He looked from them to the atrium and the distant exit doors.

"Help," he shouted. *"Someone help!"*

The racket had already drawn the attention of the nearby crowd, and Vigi's cries seemed to signal that there might be good entertainment to be had. As Dahl hauled him to his feet and prepared to put the restraints on him, he looked over his shoulder at the slowly gathering crowd and repeated his loud pleas.

"If you do not shut up, I will stun you unconscious and have my colleague carry you out of here on her shoulder," Dahl said, irritation in her voice.

He jerked away from Dahl, and she lost her grip. When she lunged to grab him again, he kicked out with his hard-shell boots and connected with the armor pad on her thigh. She gave him a shove with both hands, which sent him stumbling backward but didn't quite bring him down.

"Have it your way," Dahl said and pulled her stun stick from her belt.

She swung it at him, but he dodged the first swing. For a man of his build, he was surprisingly nimble. When she took another swing, he had his orange sling pack in his hands and parried her blow with it. All around them, a crowd of mostly young men had closed in to watch the event. They had the attention of almost everyone in earshot now, and with every passing second, it would get more difficult to walk out of this place without incident. Idina decided to cut the proceedings short. She dashed toward Fuldas, shrugged off the blow from the pack he was swinging her way, and bodychecked him. He was over a head taller and muscular for a Gretian, but the collision finally knocked him on his ass and sent him skidding across the passage floor for a meter or two. When she hauled him to his feet and turned him toward Dahl so she could put the restraints on him, Fuldas shouted for help again. Some people in the crowd that all but surrounded them by now responded with whistling and jeers.

When Idina's hands were free again, she turned to look for the path out. When she saw the hostile faces surrounding her, she realized that her move had been a mistake. Their own police officer roughing up Vigi was not a noteworthy event, but seeing a foreign occupation soldier mixing it up with him had riled up some of the spectators. Crowd dynamics were volatile. The smallest spark of aggression could erupt into a conflagration very quickly, and groups of young men were the most flammable kindling of all.

"All available units, I need backup for crowd control now," she sent on her platoon channel. "Home in on our location and put the Quick Reaction Force on alert."

A kid with a scruffy red chin beard squared off in front of Dahl and Fuldas.

"Why are you so mean?" he said. "Why are you so *mean*?"

It seemed like a mild and slightly ridiculous accusation to Idina, but she knew that the translator tended to err on the side of excessive formality. He kept saying the phrase, getting closer to Dahl with each repetition, until he was standing just beyond arm's length. Behind him, the crowd jeered again, which seemed to encourage him. The space between them and the rest of the crowd grew smaller with every moment.

"Back off and be on your way," Dahl said in her command voice. She brought up her stun stick to keep the kid from getting nose to nose with her while she only had one hand free. Fuldas used the opportunity to unbalance her slightly by yanking his body weight away from her. The kid with the chin tuft reached out and grabbed Dahl by the wrist, then tried to take the stun stick out of her hand.

With that move, the mob decided that the show had turned from a spectator to a participation event. Several young men crowded around them, encouraged by Dahl's momentary lack of a stern response. Dahl recovered her hold on the stick and brought it down on the side of her attacker's head, putting an end to his ongoing lamentation of their meanness. But Idina knew that the scale had already tipped. She took the riot shield handle from her belt and activated it. Before the cruciform frame could fully deploy, someone crashed into her, pushed by another member of the crowd, and the shield handle fell from her hand and clattered to the ground. She shoved the kid back toward the crowd, but they were too close and too numerous. Next to her, two more young men had pushed Dahl backward and against the window of a nearby shop while others were pulling Fuldas away from her.

Idina pushed her way toward Dahl and put one of them in a headlock from behind, then yanked him away. She felt people reaching for her arms, her helmet, the remaining equipment on her belt. Someone tried to yank her sidearm from its holster. Idina lashed out with her elbow and was rewarded with a cry of pain, and the hand left her pistol's grip again. She felt the blow of a kick against her back armor and stumbled forward against Dahl, who had freed herself with the help of her stun stick. Then it was just blows and kicks, too many for her to deflect with her hands and arms. For a moment, she had the impulse to draw her sidearm, but even if she could get it clear from its holster, she knew they'd wrestle it away from her before she could get off more than a random round or two. In the sudden rush of bodies against and around her, she lost track of Dahl and Fuldas.

"Officers under duress," she shouted into her comms. In just a minute or two, the first backup units would arrive, but a minute seemed like a very long time right now.

Someone tried to take her down by wrapping his arms around her legs. She shrugged him off with a knee thrust and a kick. If she ended up on the ground, she knew they would swarm her and kick her to pieces, armor or not. She took a wide stance, knees bent to lower her center of gravity, and punched back at every arm or leg that was coming her way. All she saw in the faces around her was anger and hatred. The crowd had found a convenient adapter to channel their testosterone and their resentment, and she knew they wouldn't stop now until someone died, and maybe not even then.

I'm like a robot in this armor, she thought. *They're just kicking a robot to bits. I'm not a person to them.*

She reached up, unlocked her helmet, and pulled it off her head, then swung it around and cracked it right across the nearest face. Then she shouted out her fear and anger. It was the height of idiocy to take the helmet off in a melee. But everyone needed to see that she was *someone,* not *something.* If they beat her to death, they'd at least have a face to haunt them in their dreams, not just an anonymous helmet visor.

The crowd retreated a little in collective surprise. It was just enough space for her to reach down and draw her kukri from its sheath in a wide sweeping motion. The blade made a ringing sound as it cleared the sheath and carved through the air molecules in front of her. Instantly, the crowd recoiled away from her as if she had just sprouted meter-long steel thorns all over her body.

So you have heard of these, Idina thought with grim satisfaction. She swung the blade in a flashy and aggressive flourish. Nobody tried to take the kukri from her hands. If they had, she would have started lopping off hands and arms and heads, and then there would be much more blood on the floor than just her own at the end.

Now there was fear in some of the eyes and faces around her. She kept moving the kukri in slow and deliberate flourishes. It was a strange thing, but people often seemed to fear edged weapons more than firearms. Maybe it was because getting shot was an abstract concept very few of them had ever experienced. But she knew that almost everyone in the crowd had gotten cut before, knew the bright pain when a sharp blade sliced open skin and tissue.

"When this cuts you, you don't even bleed. Not at first," she growled at them in Palladian she knew they wouldn't understand. But the strange and aggressive-sounding words seemed to add to the tempering effect of the kukri she was swinging, and she followed them up with a grin.

There was another commotion to her right, behind the crowd in the atrium. Idina didn't have her tactical screen in front of her right eye because her helmet was on the ground three meters away from her, but she knew that the other patrol teams had started to arrive. A ripple of nervous energy seemed to go through the crowd. With the threat of dismemberment in front of them and the certainty of detainment coming up from behind, the fire went out of their eyes, and they started to disperse. Within a few moments, most were rushing toward the east entrance, away from the police officers and JSP troopers Idina knew were now advancing through the atrium. She made no attempt to stop any of them. Her and Dahl's helmet sensors had registered all the faces, and the AI back at the police headquarters would be able to match them to their owners' ID passes in just a few seconds.

Dahl stood a few meters away, breathing hard. She had never lowered her helmet visor during the encounter. In the space between them, four of the attacking crowd were splayed out on the floor of the passage, knocked out by Dahl's stun stick or Idina's helmet blow.

Vigi Fuldas was gone.

Idina gritted her teeth and suppressed a particularly profane curse involving all the gods and their various genitalia. Her heart was still hammering in her chest. She sheathed her kukri and walked over to her helmet, then picked it up and placed it back on her head. As soon as she did, comms traffic assaulted her ears.

"Well," Dahl said, pushing the words out in quick bursts between her fast breaths. "That did not go quite as planned."

CHAPTER 11

SOLVEIG

Seeing Acheron with her own eyes for the first time felt like she was fulfilling an old promise.

At university, most of her classmates had chosen Rhodian or Oceanian for their foreign-language requirements because those were the easiest to learn for Gretians. Solveig had chosen Acheroni, which was more difficult by several orders of magnitude. It took four times as long for a native Gretian to get proficient in Acheroni than any of the other system languages except Palladian. But Acheron was where Ragnar had its most important business partners, and she had always found the culture fascinating. So she had slogged through four years of grueling classes, learning a new writing system and wrapping her vocal cords around new ways to make sounds while most of her friends were breezing through their tourist Rhodian. But the payoff was waiting for her just ten thousand kilometers off the corporate yacht's bow right now. Acheron's atmosphere was all swirls of yellow and orange, constantly in furious movement. The surface was somewhere below that thick layer of corrosive clouds, too hot and with far too much atmospheric pressure for human settlement. Acheron's life was all in the middle layer of its atmosphere, fifty kilometers above the surface, where the cities rode the invisible currents in normal pressure and perpetual twenty-degree weather.

"You said this is your first visit to a different planet?" Gisbert asked. Her corporate chaperone was the vice president of operations, a tall man with a generic sort of handsomeness that went well with his generic personality. He was one of the old guard her father had hired and molded, people smart enough to be adequate and not adventurous enough to swim against the current.

Solveig nodded, finding herself unable to tear her attention away from the large viewscreen on the forward bulkhead of the executive compartment. There was an almost hypnotic quality to the swirl patterns in the atmosphere. The planet stood out against the darkness of space like a semiprecious gemstone on a black velvet cushion.

"I was *fourteen* when the war started," she said. "And by the time I went off to university, we'd lost. First Papa said I was too young for trips, then it was too dangerous, then I was too busy with school."

"Sometimes I forget how young you are, Miss Ragnar. You carry yourself like you've been at this for a decade."

Solveig gave him the smile he'd expect for the compliment.

So he'll be using his face time with the Old Man's daughter and heir for some career building, she thought.

"It's too bad that it has to be this one for your first," Gisbert said. "It's not a pretty planet. I mean, there really isn't anything to see. You can't even spot the surface. It's all just noxious clouds. But I guess they're all lacking compared to home."

"Well, then someone needs to explain the war to me again," Solveig replied. "If none of the other planets measure up to what we had already, I mean."

She could tell that he was trying to figure out how to take her comment, and whether she really wanted an answer. He went the safe and easy route and smiled noncommittally, the way people smiled when they'd been told a joke they didn't get. Solveig picked up her water bulb and took a long sip to have an excuse to look at the screen again, so Gisbert wouldn't think she was trying to engage in deep conversation on the subject.

Just noxious clouds, she thought. *What insight.* Those noxious clouds were the source of Acheron's main export, the reason for its wealth and shipbuilding prowess. Graphene, extracted from atmospheric carbon, let the Acheroni build lightweight and resilient spaceships, corrosion-proof habitat modules for Oceana's floating cities, and a thousand other things that had become indispensable to the system economy. The Acheroni corporations mined sulfur and metals from the surface of their planet, but their real riches came from the atmosphere in which their cities were suspended.

Solveig's assistant Anja came up the spiral staircase that connected all the decks and walked to the seating area. She was wearing her hair in the usual tight braid, and her face was always composed and business neutral whenever she was around any of the vice presidents, but Solveig thought she saw just a fleeting shade of dislike on it when Anja looked over at Gisbert before stopping next to Solveig's seat.

"We will be docking in twenty minutes, Miss Solveig," Anja said. "The flight crew wanted me to remind you that Acheron Six is a spin station, so moving around will feel a little weird once you are off the ship. But we are docking on the outer ring, so it shouldn't be too disorienting."

"I'm sure I'll be able to manage, Anja. Tell the flight crew I thank them for the advice and their skill. It has been a very smooth ride."

"Yes, Miss Solveig. We will not be on the station for long. The Hanzo people are already waiting to take us down to Coriolis City."

Anja walked off again in her purposeful gait and ascended the staircase to the flight deck to deliver the compliment from the VIP. Solveig turned her attention to the viewscreen one more time.

"Well, at least it's only five days, right?" Gisbert said.

She nodded and took another sip from her water bulb.

Too bad it's only five days, she thought. *A million people on Coriolis City, and almost nobody knows the Ragnar name. I want to spend a month down there.*

———

Hanzo Industries had a team waiting to escort the Ragnar delegation all the way from the airlock. The head of the escort team was a fashionably dressed young man with high cheekbones that looked sharp enough to cut paper. He introduced himself as Kee in fluent Gretian, and he showed pleasant surprise when Solveig returned the greeting with the proper phrases in Acheroni.

"Please forgive my mistakes," she continued in the same language once she had reeled off the formal greeting, just so he wouldn't think she had merely memorized the basics. *"I am still learning."*

Kee's smile widened. "You honor us with the mere effort. Your pronunciation is very good. And nobody would be so impolite as to correct your mistakes."

"Your Gretian is much better than my Acheroni," Solveig said and returned the smile. "Where did you learn it?"

"It was my choice in business school. I've taken instruction ever since. Thank you for your very kind assessment."

If there was an ID pass check and a security screening here at the station, Solveig never saw it as they were whisked through the passageways to their atmospheric connection. Their little delegation was just six strong—Solveig, Gisbert, their two personal assistants, and two protection specialists from Marten's corporate security division. Marten had put himself on the roster as her personal bodyguard, and only a considerable amount of gentle pleading and careful arguing had convinced him that there was no point in tying up the head of corporate security with an off-world assignment for a week and a half, and that one of his underlings could do the job just as well. Acheron was the most neutral of the planets when it came to attitudes toward Gretia. They hadn't been invaded, and they'd had no major ground force to commit to the vicious land battles on Pallas. They'd contributed ships to the Alliance fleet and marines to the occupation forces on Gretia, but most Acheroni had been untouched by the war. If anything, the staggering hull loss rates had meant increased business for their fleet yards.

The atmospheric shuttle was sleek and narrow, and the interior was a study in elegant simplicity that would have pleased her father's sense of aesthetics—white and silver, ceramics and polished steel, cleanliness and efficiency. As profoundly divergent as their cultures were in many respects, there was a surprising amount of overlap. Solveig supposed that Acheron's population density made efficiency and adherence to rules a critical necessity. On Acheron, taking up more space for yourself and your things than absolutely necessary was a major social infraction. The constant need for moderation had resulted in a minimalism by necessity that Solveig found appealing.

"Would you like to view the outside on the descent, or should we leave the screen off?" Kee asked when they were all strapped in. "Some like to see the clouds, but the winds are very fast here. It can be unsettling to have a visual reference on the final approach."

"I'd like to see it," Solveig said quickly before Gisbert could open his mouth and ask for the blind descent option. "It's my first time here. I want to see everything."

"Very well," Kee said. He waved a screen into existence in front of him and tapped a few controls. The entire top half of the shuttle cabin seemingly turned translucent. Solveig had to suppress a gasp at the effectiveness of the illusion. It looked like someone had cut the roof off and replaced it with a giant seamless Alon cupola. Next to her, Gisbert's complexion turned slightly green, but she knew he wouldn't dare to contradict her request.

As the shuttle undocked and began its descent into the atmosphere, she leaned back to take it all in. Overhead, the station ring receded swiftly. Gisbert let out a tiny groan and closed his eyes.

The ride into the upper layers of the atmosphere was a spectacular light show. The superheated plasma streaming past the optical sensors made it look like they were inside a comet. It obscured her view of the planet and only left a sliver of star-dotted space at the very top of the cabin ceiling for a few minutes. Then the cocoon of fire around them started to recede. A few minutes later, the shuttle leveled out its descent, and the view was clear again. The atmosphere looked like a roiling river of red and yellow and ochre shades, stretching out as far as she could see. It was amazing to think that people could not just survive places like this, but thrive and expand and shape their societies, maximizing the benefits of their new environments while minimizing the drawbacks.

On the forward bulkhead, a new projection appeared, this one showing an informational display of their flight path to Coriolis City. Kee sat in front of her, facing the back of the cabin, and he smiled as he watched her gaze in awe at all the color and movement outside.

"Beautiful," Solveig said. "I've never seen anything like it."

"The clouds are sulfuric acid," he said, pronouncing the words carefully. "The atmosphere is mostly carbon dioxide." His Acheroni accent was light, but it came out stronger with the scientific terms.

"How did it feel to have blue skies and breathable air on Gretia?" she asked.

"To be honest, it was unsettling. The sky looks all wrong. And not seeing a dome overhead was frightening at first. But it is nice once you get used to it. I liked the winds a lot."

"The winds?"

Kee nodded and smiled in reminiscence.

"Our cities have domes. There is no wind. The temperature is always the same. You can't feel the wind on Acheron. It's not possible to go outside the dome without a suit and helmet. I liked the winds on Gretia. Like the air is stroking my face with kindness."

"I like that analogy," she said. "I guess you never really think about something you experience every day."

"It's a little different for us." He gestured at the swirling clouds outside. "This is our world every day. But we always have to think about everything. The air inside the dome. The clouds outside. One is good to breathe, the other is not."

Someone spoke into his earpiece, and he put a finger on it and sat up.

"We are starting our landing approach," he said.

"Can we see the front sensor feed, too?" Solveig asked.

"Certainly." He swiveled his chair around and made a screen with his thumb and forefinger. A few taps later, the forward bulkhead disappeared, and Solveig let out a soft gasp.

"Coriolis City," Kee said. "It looks like we are close already, but we are almost a hundred kilometers away. It's deceiving to the eye because the city is so big."

In front of them, a skyline was floating above the clouds. She had viewed images of the Acheroni sky cities on the Mnemosyne, but seeing one with her own eyes was something else entirely. Even from this distance, it looked enormous. The dome reflected the patterns in the surrounding cloud cover. The gas-filled double torus that kept everything afloat in the atmospheric current roped around the base of the dome like a well-fed snake snuggling its next meal. Solveig saw tendrils extending from the edges of the city's base, some trailing off into the clouds below, some reaching higher toward the sun.

"What are those?" she said and pointed at them in turn.

"The ones that go below are collectors," Kee said. "Sulfuric acid from the clouds, for turning into water. The ones that go up are collectors, too, but for solar energy."

As they got closer, Solveig's sense of scale improved, but it didn't help to get her mind around the immensity of the city. She couldn't even gauge the size of the base or the height of the dome. Even the tallest buildings of that skyline didn't reach farther up than a quarter of the distance to the peak of the dome above. It was almost the size of Sandvik, but it was floating in the atmosphere, not spread out on solid ground.

"A million people," she said in wonder.

"Our biggest city," Kee said. "There will never be another one this big. All the others are smaller, and all the future ones will be, too. Coriolis City is ten kilometers across. But we found that the ideal size is seven kilometers, five hundred thousand people. Some of the newer ones are only five kilometers. Much easier to keep in equilibrium, only two hundred fifty thousand people. A million is a little too much."

Solveig watched the projection on the forward bulkhead all the way through the approach. The base of the city took up more of her field of view with every passing kilometer. The speed readout on the screen showed they were traveling at three hundred fifty kilometers per hour, but the city was floating on the same atmospheric rapids at the same speed, so the rate of closure was almost leisurely. She had expected the ride to be bumpy, but the shuttle hardly moved in the current. She had taken gyrofoil rides on Gretia that had been more unpleasant. It did not feel like they were traveling through the fastest-moving atmosphere in the system. She concluded that the shuttles had exceptionally capable AI to compensate for the movement of the currents, supremely gifted pilots, or a combination of both.

They came in low over the lip of the city base. The spaceport was in a wide, trough-shaped depression on the surface of the base. The torus of the city extended downward in her field of view, an immense silvery-white ring of flexible composite, inflated with ludicrous amounts of helium and hydrogen. Solveig knew the basics of the physics—in this dense atmosphere, even the breathable air under the dome was a lifting gas—but the book knowledge didn't make the sight of a floating city any more believable. It was as if the Acheroni had tricked gravity somehow.

The shuttle touched down on its designated landing pad. A minute later, a large airlock door opened in the station wall in front of them, and the entire pad moved into the lock. Behind the ship, the door closed again to keep out the atmosphere. Then Solveig's view blurred as several dispenser frames passed over the shuttle in rapid succession and doused it in foamy liquid.

"Decontamination," Kee explained. "To neutralize the sulfuric acid on the hull. Not as friendly as air."

An attendant appeared and offered refreshments while they were waiting for the decon process to finish. Solveig accepted some water and a small bowl of almonds.

"It must be annoying to have to wait this out every time you land," she said. "Just when you're ready to get off the shuttle."

Kee smiled.

"Not at all. I want to think it's like taking a shower when I get home from work. It cleans the outside world off. And it gets me in the mood to relax."

Finally, the sensors seemed to be satisfied that the shuttle was clean. The inner airlock door opened, and the shuttle moved into the spaceport's arrival ring. The attendants helped them out of the safety harnesses. It felt good to be able to stand up again. When the main door of the shuttle opened to let them deplane, the Acheroni attendants deferred to Solveig, gesturing for her to go first and nodding their heads respectfully. She thanked them in Acheroni, which got her more smiles. Then she walked across into the docking collar.

Here we go, she thought. *My first steps on a different world.*

The welcoming committee waiting for them in the arrivals lounge was several times larger than the little Ragnar delegation. Hanzo Industries seemed to be determined to make sure that Solveig didn't feel slighted by a lack of people to greet her. As far as she knew, there hadn't been a Ragnar family member on Acheron since the war began, and the attention she was receiving made it look like they feared it would be another ten years until the next one stopped by. She accepted a bouquet of beautiful Acheroni orchids and exchanged greetings and nods with a line of Hanzo representatives that seemed to renew itself constantly. Gisbert and the rest of the Ragnar delegation had their translator buds in their ears, but Solveig was determined to get a return on all those years of Acheroni, and she exchanged greetings in the local language, knowing that Kee was nearby to iron out any bumps in the discourse. Her efforts were far better received than she knew the quality of her Acheroni warranted, but it gave her a sense of accomplishment nonetheless.

Finally, the welcome parade came to a close. Solveig handed her orchid bouquet to Anja and let Kee and one of the senior Hanzo people take her into their middle for the walk out to what she presumed was their transportation into the city.

The spaceport had a main atrium, but calling it by that noun seemed hopelessly inadequate as a descriptor. Solveig let slip her second amazed gasp of the day. The side of the spaceport facing into the city was a massive viewport without any visible seams, at least two hundred meters from one side to the other and fifty meters tall. It gave an unobstructed view of the bustle beyond. Coriolis City was like the busiest part of Sandvik, but cloned and then stacked on top of itself three or four times, countless rows of tall, gleaming buildings competing for air and sunlight, crisscrossed by streets that looked like canyons carved through mountains. Gyrofoils were flitting down those canyons on many different flight levels in streams that seemed to diverge and converge hundreds of times from her vantage point at ground level. There were advertising projections everywhere on building walls and above storefronts, flashing and pulsing and cycling through slogans. Through the massive viewport, it was a sudden and overwhelming visual onslaught, Acheron introducing itself to visitors with a handful of fireworks to the face. Solveig had lived in and near Sandvik, biggest city of the biggest and oldest planet in the system, for most of her life. But seeing just this slice of Acheron's largest city through the viewport of the station made her feel like a backwater colonist. There was no doubt in her mind that the Acheroni had designed this in-your-face presentation with the purpose to impress and awe, and she had to concede that it excelled at that.

"What do you think?" Kee asked her. Both the Hanzo men by her side were scanning her face, waiting for a reaction.

"It's the best thing I've ever seen," she said, momentarily robbed of her entire Acheroni vocabulary.

———

Hanzo had a fleet of surface transport pods waiting. They were all four seaters, and Cuthbert, Solveig's corporate security agent, insisted on riding with her and Anja. Kee took the fourth seat, eager to show off his home city some more.

Coriolis City was everything she had expected it to be, and at the same time it was nothing like her expectations. According to Kee, the social topography of Acheron cities was the opposite of that of any other large city she knew. The street level was the most desirable layer, not the top floors, and the outside of the city was more desirable than the center. The transport pod had a clear roof, and Solveig could see countless skyways connecting buildings in every direction.

"Our fresh air comes from below, not above," Kee explained when she asked him the reasons for the difference. "Our outer ring is closer to the dome. Better views, closer to the periphery parks. And if you live at street level, you don't have to waste time with vertical travel."

Their column rode along kilometer after kilometer of sensory overload. Solveig saw hundreds of shops, businesses, amusement complexes, and residence towers, interspersed with parks and plazas and unfamiliar buildings whose mystery was only enhanced by the fact that she couldn't read much of the signage. Acheroni writing was the hardest part of learning the language, and it was difficult to decipher syllable sequences when they were spelled out on holographic projections she passed at fifty kilometers per hour. It was all so wildly foreign and unusual that it made her heart leap in her chest with every unfamiliar sighting.

I'm finally here, she thought. *I finally get to see another planet. And Papa is a hundred million kilometers away right now.*

Then she looked over at Cuthbert. The security officer caught her glance and smiled curtly, then returned his attention to the street outside of his window again. Solveig suppressed a sigh. As long as she had him tagging along, she knew that Papa would only be as far away from her as the comtab in Cuthbert's suit pocket, thanks to the instant data traffic of the Mnemosyne.

The unintended drawbacks of quantum entanglement, she thought.

Her private comtab hummed its brief incoming message alert. She pulled it out of her pocket and looked at the contents of the message in the palm of her hand, unwilling to open a screen projection that Cuthbert would be able to read in mirror image.

Do you have dinner plans yet?

She smiled and looked out of the window. From what she could tell, every third or fourth shop out there was a noodle joint.

I do, but you'll find it tricky to join me. I'm on Acheron on business. Tonight it's whatever the locals are having. Wish me luck with the spice scale gamble.

She sent the reply off into the Mnemosyne to Detective Berg. His response came just a few seconds later.

Jealous.

She tucked the comtab away again and smiled at the thought of the tousled-haired detective scratching his head and writing his one-word response in the middle of the culinary row in Sandvik. Right now, not even the presence of Papa's electronic leash in Cuthbert's pocket would temper her enjoyment of something she had been looking forward to since the first week of university. And if Cuthbert wanted to report in detail on the walk to the nearest noodle shop she had planned for the evening, he was welcome to waste his time, and Papa's, too.

CHAPTER 12

ADEN

"*What* a piece of junk," Tess said in an awestruck voice. The expression on her face was a blend of disgust and admiration. "If that shit bucket can pull more than three g without shaking itself apart, I'll eat a square meter of their deck lining."

The image on the forward bulkhead projection was a high-resolution visual of the ship they were supposed to meet for cargo transfer. Aden knew next to nothing about spaceships, but even he could tell that the ship a hundred kilometers off their starboard bow was beyond its best space-going years. It was a freighter of some sort, considerably larger than *Zephyr*, but it didn't look sleek and new like their little speed yacht. It looked like it had been assembled out of spare parts from half a dozen ships, and none of those parts looked like they were originally designed to fit together in this fashion.

"It's no wonder they need to hire someone for a stealth run," Maya said. "That would be the worst smuggling ship ever. The Rhodies could get a sensor return from a million klicks away."

"Look at that," Tess pointed. "Someone welded on external tanks to extend the range. They just ran twenty meters of fuel line externally so it would connect to the original feed without having to cut into bulkheads. If you try to dock that contraption at Oceana, the station controller will have a coronary event. I'm not sure we should even be this close to them."

"Well, at least we know they're not pirates," Captain Decker said. "Not in that."

"During the war, the Rhodies and the fuzzheads would fuck each other up with Q-ships sometimes," Tristan cautioned from his gravity couch next to Aden's. "They'd arm the shit out of a freighter and weld a bunch of junk to it to make it look like some run-down cargo tug, fake a transponder ID. Patrol corvette pulls alongside for inspection, blam. Full broadside."

"That's no Q-ship," Maya scoffed. "There's a bunch of shit welded to it, all right. But it's no decoy. That's genuine junkyard engineering."

She cycled through a database of hull profiles with her free hand.

"Even the AI can't quite figure it out. But it looks like it came out of an Oceanian shipyard. A long, long time ago. Maybe one of the Delphine-class protein haulers. They built about a hundred subvariants of those."

"Aden, contact the OMV *Rickety Garbage* over there. Tell them we're here, and that we are about to come alongside for cargo transfer," Decker said. "Low-power tight-beam."

"Yes, ma'am," Aden replied. He brought up the screen for the ship-to-ship comms.

"*Very* low power," Maya added. "You don't want to set that hull on fire with a few watts too many."

———

The *Rickety Garbage* went by the name of *Iron Pig*, which even Maya had to admit was a pretty good moniker for a junkyard special. They came alongside twenty minutes later, flying a more cautious approach than usual. Up close, the patchwork nature of the other ship was even more apparent. Aden hadn't known that there was such a thing as an ugly weld seam, but it was included on the long list of engineering sins Tess spotted and called out on their approach.

"I just hope they still have a standard docking ring underneath all that," she concluded. "I'm not transferring a quarter ton of cargo via zip line at one g."

"Speed and course matched at one-g acceleration," Maya announced from above. "Ready to commence in-flight docking."

Tess stopped her engineering critique and concentrated on the screen in front of her. She went through the docking sequence with practiced speed. They were all back in vacsuits now, which was standard attire for any operations that carried the risk of hull damage. In this case, the likelihood seemed a fair bit greater than normal as far as Aden could tell, which made his suit a comfort instead of a nuisance. Whenever he started to let himself forget that a spaceship was just a fragile cylinder of air traveling through a vacuum that was hostile to life in a million ways, something usually came up that reminded him of that fact in unpleasant ways. He watched Tess and the contents of her screen as she extended *Zephyr*'s docking collar to mate up with the attachment ring around *Iron Pig*'s airlock.

"Green light," she said when the collar had connected and locked into place. "Pressurizing now. Docking collar has atmo. We are good to go, boys and girls."

"*Iron Pig*, we show a hard lock on the collar," Aden sent to the other ship. "Ready to commence transfer operations."

"*Zephyr, we confirm a hard lock as well,*" the other side replied. Whoever was on *Iron Pig*'s comms spoke Rhodian with a nondescript inflection. Most crews ran voice traffic in their native language and let the comms AI on the receiving end translate their speech as needed, but Aden liked to listen to the original voice whenever he could. It was a good way to keep his own ear attuned to the different accents and dialects.

"Is the neighborhood clear?" Decker asked.

"Nothing but us and this death trap here for at least a million klicks," Maya replied.

"All right. Let's get on with this so we can be on our way. I don't want to fly alongside that thing any longer than we must. Henry and Tess, go down to the airlock deck and receive the cargo. Aden, go with them and lend a hand if they need it. We'll keep an eye on things from up here."

Aden unbuckled his harness and got out of his gravity couch. When Henry climbed down from the command platform, he saw that the first officer wore his kukri on his left side, attached to the utility loops on the outside of the vacsuit.

"Maya, do a weapons scan when their people are in the collar," Decker said. "Anyone carries any hardware, you put a hard seal on the airlock, and we'll see where it goes from there."

"You got it."

It hadn't really occurred to Aden before that *Zephyr*, with all its speed and stealth, might be vulnerable to pirates just like any other civilian merchant. But they hadn't done an in-flight transfer with anyone since he got on board, and it was logical that this was a calculated security risk. They could outrun any ship or hide from it, but allowing a physical connection between airlocks out here in the middle of nowhere instead of the safety of a space station constituted one half of a forced boarding process already, and it was the difficult half.

He climbed down the ladder to the airlock deck. Henry and Tess followed him, and he cleared the space underneath the ladder as soon as his feet were on the deck. When they were all through the maneuvering-deck hatch, Aden watched the hatch cover swing into place and seal off the opening.

Henry walked over to the main airlock and opened the inner hatch. The outer hatch had a small Alon porthole in it. He stepped in front of it and peeked through.

"Let's see what they have for us," he said.

Tess accessed the control pad next to the inner hatch and projected a screen that showed the outside of the ship just beyond the airlock. The hull of *Iron Pig* loomed like a dirty steel wall just ten meters away. The other ship had been painted once, but whatever was left of the original coat was so worn and bleached by sunlight that Aden couldn't even guess at the colors.

The other ship's airlock hatch opened slowly, retracting backward and into the hull in two halves that were separated diagonally. Three people were in the airlock on the other side, a freight container on a transfer float between them. They made their way out into the pressurized docking collar, pushing the float along in front.

"Weapons check negative," Maya said over their helmet comms. "That doesn't mean they don't have sharp sticks or something."

"I'm not too worried about sharp sticks," Henry said. He pulled the hardware release handle on the control panel and twisted it to disarm the locking mechanism. The outer airlock hatch unlocked and slid sideways into its recess in the hull.

The three *Iron Pig* crew members who walked into *Zephyr*'s airlock deck a few moments later looked like they belonged on a different ship. Their pressure suits were all new, or close to it. It took Aden a moment to figure out why their appearance stood out to him beyond their newness. Most freighter crews had company-branded suits with name tags, patches, and various personal touches. These were plain and uniform, with no identifying markers.

Henry raised the visor on his helmet in a customary gesture of welcome. Face shields of pressure-suit helmets were coated with an opaque radiation layer that obscured the face of the wearer, so it was good manners to raise them before talking in a pressurized environment. Aden and Tess followed suit. After a moment, the visitors raised theirs as well. One of them looked around and nodded his approval.

"That's a nice ship," he said in Rhodian. "Hanzo built?"

"Tanaka," Henry replied, and the other man nodded again.

"Ah. Custom shop. Not many of those around. Never seen this model before."

"Is that all of it?" Henry asked. "That one container."

"Yes, that's all of it. You got a spot in mind? It's 278.55 kilos."

Henry pointed at one of the cargo markers on the deck flooring.

"Over there on the green one will do."

The visitors moved their float over to the green marker Henry had indicated and lowered the container onto it. Tess walked over to inspect the cargo from all angles. When she was satisfied that it was just a standard quarter-height shipping container that was properly locked and sealed, she activated the hold-downs, and four clamps extended from recesses in the deck flooring to secure the container on each corner.

"It's not tripping the explosives scan," Maya told them from the command deck. Henry nodded. Just because it wasn't a bomb didn't mean the contents weren't dangerous, but at least they wouldn't get blown to pieces by a clever salvager who was after the palladium in the rotor assembly of their gravmag compensator. Aden tried to guess the nature of the cargo. *Weapons? Drugs? A deadly virus prototype? A fugitive in cryo?* It could be two hundred-plus kilos of anything. The only certainty he had was that it was illegal, otherwise the owners wouldn't need to hire an expensive courier to smuggle it into Rhodian space. When he had agreed to take the contract with the rest of the crew, the idea of a smuggling run had seemed vaguely exciting and adventurous. Now that the goods were bolted down on *Zephyr*'s deck, it felt unsettling.

"Everything looks good," Tess said.

"If that's all you have for us, then we'll be on our way," Henry told the *Iron Pig* crew members. "Thank you for your business. We'll deliver on time. We always do."

"We aren't worried," their leader said. Aden noticed that he was the only one of them who had spoken. "Safe and profitable travels."

Their visitors filed out of the airlock again, pushing their empty float. The one with the float had to go first because of the bulk of the device. His two colleagues lingered in the airlock as they waited their turn to step into the collar. Just before they stepped out, one of them said something in a low voice to his companion, who chuckled.

Something about the exchange triggered vague recognition in Aden's brain. He hadn't understood what the *Iron Pig* spacer had said to his leader—he was standing at the foot of the ladderway, and they'd had their exchange in the airlock, ten meters away and facing away from him—but it had sounded familiar somehow, as if it had involved some mostly forgotten vocabulary from a language course twenty years ago.

Henry closed the airlock hatch behind the departing spacers. He stepped back into the main deck and sealed the inner hatch as well.

"Cargo secured and airlock buttoned up," he said over the ship-board comms to Decker and Maya.

"Understood," Decker replied. "Come on up and strap in so we can get out of here. Maya is getting twitchy with that safety hazard right off our port side."

Overhead, the maneuvering-deck hatch unlocked and opened. Aden started the brief climb to the deck above. Before he passed through the hatch opening, he glanced at the cargo container that was now securely clamped to the deck below. It was a regulation-sized yellow polymer Class I container, identical to dozens they had transported before. But something about this whole exchange made Aden feel uneasy about that plastic box, and he couldn't figure out why.

It's your first smuggling run, he reminded himself when he strapped himself into his gravity couch again. *It would be shocking if it didn't make you uneasy.*

Henry and Tess didn't seem worried. Tess took her place on the gravity couch to Aden's left. Henry's was on the other side of the deck, facing Aden and Tess. Tristan sat on Aden's right side. There were two more couches on the maneuvering deck, but they were empty because

Zephyr had space on board for two extra bodies. Each of the ship's two crew berth decks had one berthing compartment that stood empty, intended for temporary passengers. Tess and Henry strapped in without hurry and reclined their couches into maneuvering position to prepare for acceleration.

"Docking collar retracted and secured," Maya said. "We are clear and free to maneuver. Burning for one and a half g. Farewell and safe journey, *Iron Pig*."

"And best of luck with the *safe* part," Tess said in a low voice.

———

They spent the next eight hours doglegging a course in preparation for their stealth run into Rhodian space. The biggest giveaway of a ship outside the regular transfer lanes was always the drive signature, followed by the heat output. Every time Maya burned after a course change to hurl *Zephyr* down a new trajectory, Tess altered the power curve of the drive. Finally, Maya and Decker were happy with the amount of navigational subterfuge and did a final course correction and acceleration burn that would take them into the general neighborhood of their drop-off coordinates. When they crossed over into Rhodian space a little while later, they were coasting ballistic, with the main drive shut down and the heat sinks retracted. It was the interplanetary equivalent of leaving one's ID pass at home before walking the streets at night while wearing a mask. Anyone who spotted them would have no illusions about their intentions. But *Zephyr* was small and fast, difficult to see and harder still to chase down, and designed to be good at sneaking.

Coasting in stealth mode sounded exciting, but it was a major pain in the ass, Aden found. With their main drive off, they had momentum but no acceleration. Without acceleration, they had no gravity. The rest of the crew handled zero g like the experienced professionals they were. But Aden wasn't a spacer, and he found that easy everyday tasks turned into difficult physics puzzles in zero g. He had to use the toilet with vacuum attachments to avoid floating around in the head with a big bubble of his own urine, and every time he sat or lay down anywhere, he had to strap in to stay in place.

"You know, they used to have tourist flights for zero g," Tristan said when Aden muttered a curse after banging his shin on the edge of the mess deck table while trying to stick a graceful landing.

"They did?" Aden gave Tristan a skeptical look and strapped the seat's lap belt around his waist.

"Back when spaceflight was new again, right before the colonization wave. People would pay good money to go up into orbit around Gretia and experience an hour or two of floating around."

"That idea sounds dumb enough to be plausible," Aden said.

"I'm not even kidding. People shelling out tens of thousands for a little bit of constant free fall. And now you have to have money to avoid zero g. Cheaper to get passage on a freighter without a gravmag array."

"I guess everyone figured out that being weightless is only fun for those first two hours. Until they have to eat and drink. Or empty their bladders."

"Gravmag changed everything," Tristan said. "Cut the transit times between the planets by fifty, seventy, ninety percent. Before, they all had to chug along at one g almost all the time. And then, boom. Want to make a three-day run at seven g? Crank up that fusion drive. Talk about supercharging system commerce."

Tristan held out a squeeze bottle.

"Here, give this a try."

Aden eyed the bottle for a moment before taking it from Tristan.

"Is that going to have me bouncing off the walls in here?"

"No, it's pepper sauce. I mixed it before we went to stealth. Used some of the stuff I bought on Pallas One. Don't worry. It's a lot tamer than Spacers' Sunrise."

Aden took the cap off the spout and squeezed a very small quantity of the sauce into his mouth. In zero g, even eating and drinking felt unnatural. Without the assist from gravity, food and liquids didn't stay on the tongue or go down the esophagus easily.

"It's good," he said. "Really good. Bit of a kick, but just a small one." Something about the taste reminded him of the vegetable fields at his family's estate, the way they smelled in the autumn sun when the produce was ripe. "Tastes like liquid sunshine."

"That's what I'll call it," Tristan said with a smile. "Liquid Sunshine. I think it'll go well with the soy base in the galley meals."

"That better not be alcohol," Tess said from the doorway as she floated through it. "You know we're not supposed to drink on stealth runs."

"It's hot sauce," Aden said. "Tristan mixed it. To improve the freeze-dried dinners."

"Some of those are beyond salvation, I fear." Tess reached the table and grabbed the zero-g handle that was protruding from the surface on one end. She flipped herself around and took a seat, far more gracefully than Aden had managed.

"That awful oversalted veggie layer thing in particular," she continued. "The number-eleven meal. I could swear it's fifty percent sodium. I don't think anyone likes that one. I don't know why we keep buying it."

"It's a package deal from the distributor. Major price break if you buy unbroken variety boxes," Tristan said.

Tess was wearing the sleeves of her flight suit tied around her waist again. Her orange undershirt had a faded Tanaka Spaceworks logo on it. Aden had noticed that most spacers either wore their hair short, or long enough to be tied back in a zero-g environment. Tess had gone the second route. Her black hair was mostly gathered in a tail, but a few unruly strands had come loose. She blew one out of her face, and it drifted away from her eyes in slow motion. The Aden from ten years ago wouldn't have thought of her as his type. Now he didn't even know if he still had a type, but he found himself attracted to her low-key competence. Tess was quietly good at many things. She knew the ship inside and out, and she was the best nuts-and-bolts engineer he had ever worked with, both in her understanding of systems and her hands-on skills with wrench and welder. She played a string instrument Aden didn't recognize—their berthing compartments were adjacent, and sometimes he could hear the soft plucking of the strings through the partitioning wall from her side when she practiced. And she did drawings in physical media, on old-fashioned sheets of paper, using charcoal sticks and colored pencils that had to be sharpened and replaced frequently.

She'd done charcoal portraits of the whole crew. They were part of a group of intricate drawings that decorated the bulkheads down in the engineering workshop. Light and shadow, shape and texture, all brought into existence just by the pressure and tilt of a piece of sharpened charcoal. Aden had always considered engineering and art two different branches of the skill tree far away from each other, but Tess seemed to excel at both in equal measure. He was neither artsy nor technically inclined, and watching her quiet and confident mastery at both work and play sometimes made him feel inadequate and uninteresting. Mostly, however, she made him want to get to know her better.

"Twelve more hours of this, then the handover, then eighteen to get back to the busy neighborhood," Tristan said. "That's four or five meals out of the box. Chances are good you'll draw a number eleven at some point."

Aden let go of Tristan's bottle of Liquid Sunshine and gave it a nudge toward Tess. It tumbled through the air above the table, slowly flipping end over end.

"If you do, this might help," he said. She caught the bottle and squirted out a dab, which coalesced into a little red sphere in the zero-g environment. Tess snatched it up with her mouth.

"That's really good," she proclaimed, and Tristan smiled with satisfaction.

"Five box meal surprises in a row," she said. "I know they're paying double fee for hauling that cargo. But some hardships can't be compensated fairly."

"What do you think we're hauling?" Tristan asked.

Tess shrugged. "Maya says it's not explosives or ammunition. If they're paying double to hire a stealth ship, it's contraband, no question. The drop-off is somewhere in space, so we're just a leg in the delivery, and not the final one."

"Something that's going to end up on Rhodia. What's their main prohibitionist fetish?"

"Synthetic stims," Aden replied. "But everyone has those banned. Black-market cybernetics. Military weapons. Anything with combat AI in it."

"You worried we're smuggling some sort of assassin robot?" Tess said.

"I just know I'm worried," he admitted. "It won't matter what kind of contraband it is if we get caught, right? So I'm not sure I want to know about it."

He recalled the exchange he had witnessed on the airlock deck ten hours earlier.

"It was just something one of them said to the other. When they were leaving the ship. Just a quick exchange, three or four words. I couldn't quite make out what they were saying. But it rubbed me the wrong way, you know? Gave me a bad feeling."

"You didn't hear them? Or you didn't understand what they were saying?" Tess asked.

"I was three or four meters too far to hear them well enough. They were facing away from me and talking to each other."

"If it's bothering you that much, you can just check the sensor records from the airlock," she said. "If they were still in the airlock, the audio feed probably picked them up just fine."

He felt a little stupid. Of course the ship would have sensors monitoring the only access lock, the one through which everyone had to go if they wanted to enter or leave.

"How do I do that?"

"Come on." Tess unbuckled her lap belt and pushed herself away from the table. "I'll show you."

———

They floated down to the airlock deck. Tess drifted over to the control panel of the airlock and brought up a screen. The cargo container sat where they had secured it hours earlier, still just a silent piece of heavy-duty polymer.

"All right, here's the data from when they walked in. Come here and scrub this to the point where you think they said something to each other."

Aden floated next to her and started to drift away again slowly. He looked for a handhold but didn't see one in reach. Tess reached up and pulled him next to her.

He took over the screen and advanced the visuals to the point where the *Iron Pig* crew had completed their delivery and started to make their way back. The one with the empty float went first. Then the other two stepped into the airlock. He froze it just before the left one turned his head, increased the audio volume, and tapped the Continue field. It was a high-resolution image, and the audio was crystal clear, as if someone had spoken loudly into his ear.

This time he heard the words sharply. At first, he again failed to understand them, but then it was like a rusty cog in his brain had loosened and was starting to turn in sync with the machinery once more. He rushed to repeat the segment. The words didn't change. A twisting sensation had materialized in his stomach that had nothing to do with the zero-g environment.

"We have to show this to the captain," he said.

———

"Let me get this perfectly straight," Decker said ten minutes later. The crew was assembled in front of the viewscreen on the airlock deck, and Aden had replayed the sensor recording for them half a dozen times. Now that he knew what the spacer had said to his comrade, the words became clearer and more obvious with every viewing.

"You're saying the transport is a setup because of the slang you heard coming out of this man's mouth," Decker said and pointed at the frozen image of the *Iron Pig* spacer on the screen.

"Not just a setup," he said. "They think we won't be there anymore once everything's concluded."

"Because he said we had a nice ship."

"That's not quite what he said. Well, it is, but not in that way. It's how he used that phrase."

"Run it by the people who aren't linguists," Henry said. "What the fuck kind of language was he using? Didn't sound like anything to me. The AI didn't recognize it either."

"That's the point," Aden said. "It's a cryptolect."

"A cryptolect," Decker repeated.

"Yeah. A cant. What you speak when you don't want to be over-heard. You know how the dockhands and the mechanics at the stations have their own slang? Sort of like that. Only it's like a whole different language altogether."

"And you know that slang," Henry said. "Without a doubt."

Aden nodded.

"So what the fuck is it?"

"It's from Gretia. It's a cant the bad boys use among themselves. The crime syndicates."

"But it's not Gretian," Decker said. Aden shook his head.

"They carried it over from some Old Earth language. I mean, they still speak Gretian to each other. They just pepper it with this cant. Use different verbs and nouns. Make such a hash of it that even the AI can't figure it out past the basics."

"And you would know this how exactly? Studied it in language school?"

Aden shook his head. "I told you my mother was Gretian. I spent a lot of time there when I was a child. Three months every summer."

"And you worked your way into the local criminal underworld at age twelve," Henry said. "That's how you recognize their vocabulary."

Aden looked around, anxiety squeezing his chest and constricting his lungs. Everyone looked back at him with various degrees of incredulity. Only Maya had a neutral expression on her face as she listened to his continued attempts at an explanation.

"Some of it worked its way into slang over the decades," he said. "The kids in Sandvik use a bunch of loanwords from it. It's what you speak when you want to sound tough. Because the real tough guys speak it."

He played back the sensor record again.

"Three words. The first means 'not good.' The other two mean 'nice ship.' But the way he used the first one, it's more like 'too bad.' You use that word in that context, you mean a regrettable event. He was saying, 'What a shame, that's a nice ship.' And it was casual. Dismissive. Like it was unavoidable."

The airlock deck was silent for a moment. Decker studied the frozen faces of the *Iron Pig* spacers on the viewscreen with a frown.

"I believe him," Maya said. "I mean, I believe that he believes in what he's saying. Look at him. He's scared."

Tess coasted over to the cargo box and placed a hand on the lid.

"What are we hauling here?" she said softly.

"All right," Decker said. "Let's hear opinions. Aden says that there's evidence these people aren't going to honor their end of the contract. Likely in a bad way."

She nodded over at the cargo container.

"If we break contract, we'll piss off the customer. We'll lose the fee and the money for all the fuel we've burned so far. And we'll take a hit to our reputation. They'll give us bad marks on the exchange."

"We don't break contract and Aden's right, we all end up dead maybe," Tess said.

There was another silence, this one longer than the first. Aden had never wanted more in his life to be wrong. If they blew off the contract because of him, it would harm their livelihoods, maybe even cost them the ship.

"I don't think we have enough evidence to make that call yet," Maya said. "But I know that I would really like to see what's in that container. Because I don't want to get killed over it. And I think that the contents may help with our decision."

"Breaking customer confidentiality," Henry cautioned. "That's almost as bad as skipping out on a contract and just stealing the cargo."

"I vote to open it and have a look, take it from there," Tristan said.

"Same here," Tess said.

"I'd love to be proven wrong," Aden said. "I want us to open that and find a thousand counterfeit comtabs or something."

"All right," Decker said. "Tess, how do you feel about that security lock on the container? Think you can hack it?"

"Officially? That's a high-grade lock, best encryption money can buy. Takes years to hack, if you can do it at all."

"And unofficially?"

"*Unofficially*, let me float down to engineering and get my data deck," Tess said. "I'll have that thing open in five minutes."

———

Tess hadn't oversold her abilities. Four minutes and forty seconds after she had connected her data link, the latches of the container receded with an authoritative click that made everyone on the deck jump a little.

"Let's see what you are," she said. She unplugged her data link from the lock and tucked away her deck before it could float off and get damaged. Then she popped the locking latches on the container lid and carefully opened it to peek inside.

"Huh," she said.

She swung the lid open all the way so they could all see the contents. There was a second container nestled into the first one, set into an elaborate latticework of spacers and buffers. This container was flat black, and it had handling warnings in bright-yellow writing all around it.

"That's a Category Six hard-shielded cargo box," Tess said. "No wonder the scanners didn't pick up shit. That's for critical freight. Valuable critical freight. Like a memory core with half a billion ags on it."

"Or two hundred kilos of palladium," Henry said.

"Still want to open it?" Tess asked. "This might make an entire planet fall on our heads, people."

"Do it," Decker said.

Tess opened the lock on the second container as well. This one took more time, and when she was finished, the locking bolts retracted into the casing with a barely audible little snap. She grasped the lid with both hands and lifted it up. It came away cleanly, displaying a layer of impact foam. In the middle of it, a meter-long matte gray cylinder with the diameter of a dinner plate was snugly embedded in a precise cutout. It had markings on it, but Aden couldn't read them from his angle.

"Mother*fucker*," Tess said. Her tone was almost casual, but if they hadn't been in zero g, Aden could tell that she would have had to sit down hard. Next to him, Henry muttered what he assumed was the Palladian version of the same curse.

"Is that palladium?" Aden asked.

"That," Tess said after a moment of silence, "is a Mark Sixteen tactical nuclear warhead."

CHAPTER 13

DUNSTAN

Dunstan huffed through the last three of his twenty pull-ups. Each one took more effort, and only the knowledge that the twentieth was the last one made him summon the willpower to get his chin over the bar. *Minotaur* was on the way home at one standard g of acceleration, but on the pull-ups, he could have sworn that a cheeky engineer increased the burn by 10 percent every time his commander started a set, just to vex the Old Man. It was a more comforting theory than having to face that, at forty-six years old, he couldn't bang out twenty pull-ups with the same ease as he could when he was a cadet.

He dropped from the bar and reached for his towel to wipe the sweat from his face. Next to him, the intercom panel chirped.

"Bosworth here. Sorry to disturb you on your off watch, sir, but do you have a few minutes to come up to the AIC? It's kind of urgent, I think."

Dunstan finished wiping his face before replying.

"Of course, Lieutenant. But I have to tell you that your timing is lousy. A minute earlier, and I would have had an excuse to skip the pull-ups. I'll be there in a moment."

———

"I'm eighty percent sure this is a prank or a trick of some sort," Lieutenant Bosworth said when Dunstan stepped into the AIC, still in his sweaty exercise clothes.

"It's not a good time and place for pranks. What do you have?"

"We just got pinged by an Oceanian courier boat. They say they're on a delivery run. And they just discovered that their contract cargo is a nuke."

Dunstan stopped in his tracks and blinked.

"I'm sorry, Lieutenant. Could you run that by me again? Because I thought you said they have a *nuke*."

"I did, sir. And it appears they do. Their engineer sent imagery. It looks like a Mark Sixteen. Or a very convincing mock-up of one."

He brought up the image and showed the screen to Dunstan.

"Variable-yield tactical nuclear warhead, ten to five hundred kilotons. The engineer says her scanners show a plutonium fission core. The radiation profile is consistent with the warhead type."

"That's just wonderful," Dunstan said. "Where are they now?"

"They requested a rendezvous to turn over the warhead to the authorities. We just gave them permission to approach on an intercept vector. But I ordered them to stay at least a hundred klicks from us or anyone else. Time to rendezvous is two hours, thirty-one minutes."

"I suppose I have time to shower," Dunstan said.

"Yes, sir."

Dunstan looked at the plot, where *Minotaur* sat in the center of a bubble of mostly empty space. They had three days left to go on their low burn to Rhodia, where a long-overdue shore leave and overhaul was waiting for them.

Three more days, and it would have been someone else's interesting problem, Dunstan thought.

"I hope you are correct, Bosworth. About the odds for an elaborate prank. Because if it isn't one, we're about to make system-wide news."

Thirty minutes before the intercept, *Minotaur* was at action stations. Dunstan had never heard of a pirate blowing up a navy ship with a suicide nuke. But this year had seen new firsts for a lot of unusual things, and he didn't want *Minotaur* to gain immortality as a fresh textbook example at the academy. There was no exact protocol for dealing with nuclear warheads on civilian ships because there weren't supposed to be any nukes on civilian ships. Not even the few armed private security contractors in the system were authorized to carry atomic warheads.

"Tell them to come about and fly a parallel course no closer than a hundred klicks off our port side," Dunstan said. "That ship is not coming closer until we have that warhead and the crew secured."

"Aye, sir," Lieutenant Mayler said.

"They're coming in nice and clean, by the book," Bosworth commented. He was looking at the plot, where a single ship icon was closing the distance with *Minotaur* slowly. "Transponder on, position lights blinking, steady course at one g."

"Once they get into position, give them a few sweeps with the targeting system. Not a hard lock yet. But let them know we have guns pointing in their general direction. I don't think they'll try anything dumb, but you never know."

"We've seen them before," Bosworth said. "That ID. OMV-2022 *Zephyr*. It's that quick little ship we watched off Pallas a few days ago."

"The one that pulled fifteen g," Dunstan said. "What does the database say?"

"Everything matches, sir. Transponder ID, drive signature, hull profile. Tanaka Spaceworks model two thirty-nine, registered as OMV *Zephyr* in the database three years ago. They seem to be who they say they are."

"That's something," Dunstan replied. It made it more likely they were telling the truth, but it didn't tell him a thing about how they could have ended up with a nuclear warhead in their cargo compartment by accident. There was no way to get a nuke through a space station's cargo transfer facilities without triggering twenty different kinds of alarms.

"Does the database say anything about authorized armaments on that ship?"

"Negative, sir. She's not certified for offensive weapons." Bosworth whistled softly through his teeth as he scrolled through the list of *Zephyr*'s sanctioned modifications. "She does have a killer point-defense array, though. Megawatt-class emitters, fully integrated defensive AI. That's some pretty expensive kit for a fast courier."

"Especially one that can sustain fifteen g. At a hundred K, we may even have trouble getting a missile through."

"There's no *may* about it, sir," Mayler said from the tactical station. "If they decide to go to full burn and set their point defense active, we'll never score a hit. Not at that distance."

"Well, there's no way we are letting them closer until that nuke is secured, and Bosca and his marines have gone through their ship from top to bottom. We'll just have to play this out for now and assume they aren't lying."

"Just imagine," Midshipman Boyer said. "Checking that cargo and finding out you're carrying half a megaton of boom in your hold. I bet there wasn't a clean flight suit left on that deck."

———

The boarding was a calculated risk—Dunstan figured that if the other ship wanted to blow itself up, its crew wouldn't be happy with a mere squad of Rhodian marines to take with them. But he still felt a familiar anxiety as he watched the boarding skiff leave its docking recess on *Minotaur* and make its way over to OMV *Zephyr*, which was obediently holding a parallel course just a little over a hundred kilometers away. Boarding actions were always inherently dangerous, and the presence of an unsecured nuclear warhead added an unsettling variable.

The skiff approached *Zephyr*, then changed course to come alongside. With the little skiff next to the courier ship, Dunstan saw that *Zephyr* was barely three times longer. It was a sleek ship, or as sleek as the designer could bend the blueprint around the general cylindrical shape required for a modern spaceship. Most civilian ships had their exterior sensor arrays and auxiliary gear on top of the pressure hull with no concern for stealth, but he could tell that some thought had gone into making this little courier less observable to eyes or sensors. Whatever protruded from the hull was set into streamlined fairings, and the hull plating itself had been coated with a nonreflective layer. On stern and bow, he saw the telltale emitter cupolas of point-defense energy mounts.

"What does the database have on that class?" he asked. "Tanaka model two thirty-nine."

"It's barely a class," Mayler replied. "Custom run of four. Built as speed and pleasure yachts. They named them after the four winds. This one was launched first, but it wasn't officially registered until two years later."

"Whatever that thing was when they launched it, I know I am not looking at a speed yacht. What do you want to bet they spent the first two years on a custom retrofit right out of the shipyard?"

"I've seen lots of yachts with electronic countermeasure suites," Bosworth said. "But I've never seen one with an ECM suite and a Point Defense System. That's expensive tech."

"And an expensive restricted-technology permit on top of it all." Dunstan watched the optical feed, where the skiff was extending its docking collar toward *Zephyr*'s airlock. "While we have them nearby, let's get every little bit of data we can. Feed it to the AI for some sims to compare to our past encounters. See if we may have run into them before without knowing about it."

"You think they were the sensor echo from the internment yard, sir?" Mayler asked.

On the screen, the sensors of the skiff gave them a high-resolution view of *Zephyr*'s hull. The spotlights from the little boarding craft seemed to get soaked up and dimmed by the exterior coating that covered most of the other ship.

"It's small, it's stealthy with intent, and we know it's very fast. You put those three properties together in a civilian ship, and I start to get nervous. But unless Bosca finds an internal launch tube tucked away somewhere in the hull, I'd say it's unlikely."

"*Minotaur*, Bosca," the marine sergeant sent from the skiff. "We have a hard dock. Commencing boarding ops."

"Fast but thorough, Sergeant," Dunstan said. "Secure the nuke, detain the crew, search the ship for contraband. Specifically unauthorized weapons and munitions."

"Affirmative," Bosca replied.

The first boarding team crossed the docking collar and entered *Zephyr*'s airlock. Ten seconds later, the second team followed. If something was going to happen, it would be now, when the boarding party was in the most vulnerable stage of the process. Two minutes of comms silence passed. There was no gunfire, and the tethered combination of boarding skiff and courier ship did not disappear in a blinding nuclear fireball. Dunstan allowed himself to relax just a little.

"*Minotaur*, Bosca. Nuke is secured, six crew detained without incident. I'm sending them over in the skiff with second team while first team and I search the ship."

"Very good, Bosca. What's the ordnance tech's word on the warhead?"

"He says it's the fission core. It doesn't have a fuse assembly, so it's safe to bring over to *Minotaur*."

"Understood. We are standing by to receive the skiff with the crew. Take your time with the search. I think these people will be with us for a little while."

"You want to have the master-at-arms put them in the brig for now, sir?" Bosworth asked.

Dunstan thought about it, then shook his head.

"I don't want to treat them like prisoners just yet. They contacted us. They asked to surrender that warhead. Let's give them the benefit of the doubt for now and assume they've been telling the truth. But I do want to talk to them separately when they're on board. Have the marines move them to the officers' mess once they get here."

"Aye, sir. I'll let the master-at-arms know."

———

The Oceanian captain was a woman with blue eyes and blonde hair, which she wore in a tight braid. She had a no-nonsense air about her, but Dunstan could tell that she was off balance right now, separated from her ship and with her immediate fate in the hands of the Rhodian Navy. The marine who had escorted her into the compartment stepped outside and took up position out of sight next to the open door.

"Please," Dunstan said. "Have a seat."

She sat down in front of his workstation, hands resting on her thighs. He could tell that she was trying to figure out the level of shit she had gotten herself into. Dunstan didn't need to ask her name, or anything else about her. While the *Zephyr* crew had still been in transit on the skiff, he had pulled all their ID files off the database. Her name was Ronja Decker, she was forty-three years old, and she'd had a commercial command license for twelve years after serving as second and first officer on a variety of freighters and ore haulers.

"Welcome to *Minotaur*, Captain Decker," he said. "I'm Lieutenant Commander Park, the CO of this ship."

"Thank you, Commander. I'm sorry to have to drop such a mess into your lap. But we were in Rhodian space when we discovered the nature of our cargo, and I ordered my comms officer to contact the nearest Rhodian warship immediately. That happened to be you."

"Chance has it in for me," Dunstan said. She flashed a sympathetic smile.

"Quite a ship you have there," he said. "It started out life as a Tanaka type two thirty-nine. I like what you've done with it. That's a lot of expensive custom work. You must be doing well."

"*Zephyr* is owned by a small consortium," Decker said. "They thought the niche potential justified the investment. So far, we've been able to keep them happy."

"Well, I'm afraid you won't be making a profit on this run. The Rhodian Navy is confiscating the warhead you've been hauling. But you knew that would happen when you contacted us."

Decker nodded.

"Sometimes you end up eating a week of operating costs. We will manage."

"Not that I don't applaud your adherence to interplanetary law in this instance, but I can't imagine you were at all keen on letting us have such a close look at your ship. I must wonder why you turned that cargo over instead of just returning it. Or dumping it in deep space somewhere."

"Because that's not a load of inert iron ore or a pallet of stims we're talking about," she said. "It's a thermonuclear warhead. I don't deal in those. And I don't want to be involved with anyone who does."

"We've both been behind the stick for too long to play pretend, Captain. Your boat isn't a standard courier. In fact, if I had to go to a shipyard and say, 'Take this yacht and turn it into something that's perfect for smuggling,' I think it would look a lot like that. So forgive me some degree of skepticism. That's one of the risks you take when you accept contracts that involve unregulated ship-to-ship cargo transfers in the middle of nowhere."

Captain Decker smiled wryly.

"We take above-the-table business most of the time. High-value express delivery. Sometimes passengers. And sometimes we do discreet cargo hauls if the rate is good enough. But we don't do weapons or munitions. Nobody's getting hurt by a few crates of tax-free comtabs."

"Like you said, that cargo you brought with you isn't that. Looks like you need to improve your screening process. Something a little more reliable than the honor system."

"My chief engineer and my pilot both scanned that container when it came on board. It came up clean. They used a Category Six security capsule for that warhead. I've never even seen one of those outside of a classified government environment."

"So you got duped," Dunstan said. "Happens to the most diligent sometimes. And you did the right thing. But that's still a thermonuclear warhead. A weapon of mass destruction. Subject to strict interplanetary control treaties."

He leaned back and folded his arms across his chest.

"I can't just bring that nuke back to Rhodia and hand it over without comment. Fleet command is going to go ballistic over this. Just the knowledge that there are unaccounted nukes floating around on the black market is going to set a whole lot of people on edge. You will have to turn over every bit of data from your ship, because intelligence will want to take your records apart forensically."

"We will hand over whatever they want," Decker said.

"You need to pick your customers with more care, Captain Decker," Dunstan said. "I imagine your consortium would be very unhappy if you lost your operating license. Or your ship. I'm the Rhodian Navy out here right now. If I decide to impound it, nobody is going to stop me."

He was pleased to see a little bit of genuine distress poking through the cracks in Captain Decker's cool composure. If he impounded *Zephyr*, her career would be over, and her crew would have a hard time getting hired on other ships.

"I know your kind," he said. "Independent commercial skippers in fast little ships. You start taking shady contracts in between the legal work. Start thinking you're hot shit because you got some contraband past a slow-ass customs boat or two. The real world isn't like that, Captain. Sooner or later someone pulls one over on you. And then you end up on some third-rate orbital transfer station loading containers all day for a living, and you wonder how it all went sideways. If you're lucky."

"You can impound my ship," Decker said after a moment of consideration. "That's your right. The consortium would file suit and get her back. Probably. But they'd give her to someone else; you're right about that."

She shook her head and sighed.

"I got a little careless, and I messed up. I just figured we would get some good will for coming to you on our own accord. For making sure there isn't a nuclear warhead out there going back to sender. Or floating around in space for some salvager to find."

The shrug that followed was resigned and defiant in equal measure.

"I've loaded containers for a living before. It wasn't such a bad life."

———

Zephyr's crew was an interesting bunch. The first officer was a veteran of the Pallas Brigade, and Dunstan knew in the first thirty seconds of their talk that nothing he could say would scare that man, someone who had fought Gretian Blackguards hand to hand in the tunnels of his home world. Bosca had reported that the only moment of friction during the boarding had happened when he had asked the Palladian to turn over his kukri. Pallas and Rhodia were staunch allies, and the brigade was as respected on Rhodia as it was at home, but nobody under Dunstan's command could extend that respect to letting a detainee keep a monomolecular blade in his possession. Luckily, *Zephyr*'s first officer had seen the logic of the argument and grudgingly surrendered his kukri to the Rhodian marines before things could get unpleasant.

The pilot was a young Acheroni woman with a buzz cut and an attitude. She only gave short and sullen answers, and she didn't even try to hide her dislike for Dunstan's authority. The medic was a tall and white-haired Oceanian who was friendly and almost gregarious, as if he had no worries about their situation at all. The mechanic was Oceanian as well. She was the only one who was nervous, the only member of the crew whose behavior fit the severity of their predicament, but Dunstan got the impression that she was mostly worried about her ship, not her personal fate. All of them had some mud splatters in their personal histories, but Dunstan knew what a crew of incorrigible hard cases looked like, and this was not one of those. The only other crew member was the ship's comms officer and linguist, and he was the one whose background gave Dunstan concern.

———

"Aden Jansen," Dunstan read off the projection from his terminal. "You're the language expert."

"I am," the comms officer said in flawless Rhodian. His hair was slightly shaggy looking, and he had a short reddish beard that was just three days too old to be called stubble. From the way he had walked in, Dunstan could tell some military bearing.

"All the other crew members agree that you probably saved their lives," Dunstan said. "When you figured out what your customers were talking about before they left your ship."

Jansen smiled, but it was a curt smile, as if he was uncomfortable with receiving the credit. There was a nervousness radiating from him that wasn't just worry about the possibility of being held in Rhodian Navy detention for a few weeks.

"So, good job on that," Dunstan continued. "They all owe you a drink once the dust settles. I think you were right to warn them, and I think they were right to listen to you."

"Thank you," Jansen said. "But why do I have the feeling that you don't just want to congratulate me and send me on my way?"

"First I have to figure out what I am dealing with here. Or who I am dealing with."

Dunstan brought up a data screen.

"You see, when we submitted everyone's ID passes to the system for a check, they all came back green. Except for yours. That one came back yellow. That means 'pending.'"

He rotated the data field in the air between them so Jansen could see it as well.

"Now, there are good reasons why a background check might come back pending instead of an instant clearance. It could be that the link with the Oceanian database is a little shaky from all the way out here. But your three Oceanian crewmates all came back green instantly, so I don't think that's the issue."

Dunstan put a hand on his chin and tapped the side of his nose with his index finger.

"A more common reason is that the data on the pass doesn't quite match the database entries all the way, and that the system needs to do a more thorough algorithm check to give a certain reply."

"I've used my ID pass to scan in all over the system," Jansen said. "Never had an issue."

"Those entry scans are running off a common database. The background check we ran goes through the respective planetary databases. Takes longer, but it's more thorough."

Jansen looked at him impassively, but Dunstan could tell that this was not a welcome development. There was a flicker in the linguist's gaze that hadn't been there just a few moments ago.

"When I get a yellow on an ID pass, I usually put in a system request for an extended ID check. That can take an hour, sometimes two. But I have no place else to be for a while."

Dunstan extinguished the screen between them.

"I think that you really don't want me to send that extended ID check request. I think that you paid someone a fair chunk of ledger for that pass, which is why you are getting through scan-ins everywhere. But I also think that it's not your real ID. Or maybe it is, but you had the data tweaked a little. Maybe had something erased or added."

Now there was definitely a whiff of panic in the linguist's expression, and Dunstan took it as encouragement to press on while he had the man off balance.

"We can play this in two ways. I can put in the request, and we can wait for the return. If we go that way, we'll be sitting here for a while. Or you can fess up and tell me why your ID pass is coming up yellow. Same result, but one will make me considerably less cranky."

Jansen closed his eyes and exhaled slowly.

"It doesn't have to be a big deal," Dunstan encouraged. "I may not even give a shit. I have a nuclear warhead to deal with today. I don't care about a fake job clearance right now. Or whatever it is that's making you all jumpy."

Jansen opened his eyes again and suddenly seemed deflated somehow. It was like looking at a different person.

"I paid twenty-five K for it," he said in a resigned voice. "It's real, but the person on it isn't."

Dunstan nodded, pleased to have his instincts validated.

"So who is the *real* you? And remember, I may not care. I just like to know who I'm talking to. Especially when there's a surprise nuke involved."

"I'm Gretian. My name is Aden Ragnar. My service name was Aden Robertson. I was a prisoner of war on Rhodia until this May. I ended up on Oceana and bought a real-fake ID because I didn't want to return to Gretia."

"This May," Dunstan repeated. "Five years. So you're a Blackguard."

"I *was* a Blackguard," Jansen said. "Linguist, not infantry. Military intelligence. I was a major."

"Company commander," Dunstan said, and Jansen nodded.

"Signals Intelligence Company 300. We were stationed on Oceana all the way through the war."

"Well, isn't that something." Dunstan looked at the man sitting across the workstation from him. He tried to imagine Jansen-Ragnar-Robertson in a Blackguard uniform, but his brain couldn't quite make that stretch right now.

It's the beard, he decided. *Beards don't look right on Gretian soldiers.*

He studied Jansen's face, looking for a glimmer of that haughty Gretian air of superiority he had seen in the expression of every fucking Blackguard he had ever encountered. They had been the shock troops of the Gretian army, the most dedicated and obedient of the lot. But there was nothing like that in this one. He just looked defeated, resigned, tired.

Dunstan's first instinct was to call in the marine stationed in the passageway outside and have Jansen hauled off to the brig. He found that he had already started to open his mouth to do just that. Then he closed it again and took a deep breath.

All his crewmates said they found the nuke because of him, Dunstan thought. *He must have known his ID would fall apart. We've had him as a prisoner for five years. And he warned them anyway. Because this is all he has left.*

He wondered how he would feel in Jansen's stead, at the mercy of a Gretian officer after losing the war to them, after spending half a decade in their custody.

We're the same rank, Dunstan thought. *Same job. Same age, give or take a few years. He once had a company. I still have a ship. If just a few battles had gone their way instead of ours, I'd be the one in that chair right now.*

"The captain knows, but the others don't," Jansen said. "When you put me in the brig, just tell them I'm a wanted criminal. Make up whatever crime you want. Don't tell them I'm Gretian."

Somehow, that statement triggered a spark of pity in Dunstan. Maybe it was a combination of everything—Jansen's scraggly beard, his flawless Rhodian, his concern for the crew that had accepted him—but it left Dunstan with no angle to vent his anger. There was nothing left to beat down. Jansen was so desperate to deny his old identity that he would rather have his new friends think he was a thief or murderer than discover he was Gretian. Dunstan knew he could never forgive Gretia for starting a war that killed dozens of his friends. He wouldn't forgive the Blackguards for being in the vanguard of conquest. But right now, he knew that he would find no satisfaction in locking this man up, not after his act of caring for the safety of his fellow crew, even knowing that it would probably expose him.

What the hells, Dunstan thought. *He got a nuke out of circulation. That's a net good. Not enough to let him off the hook for his past. But enough to let him off for today.*

"We're in Rhodian space," he said. "Your Oceana ID pass is Oceana's issue. I won't make it mine today. There's more important stuff sitting in my cargo hold right now."

Jansen looked up in wide-eyed surprise. Dunstan could almost see the shock that went through him from head to toe. If hope had a scent, the compartment would suddenly be redolent with it.

"Go rejoin your crew. Keep your secret for another day," Dunstan said.

"Thank you, Commander," Jansen replied.

Dunstan nodded.

"It will come up yellow again somewhere. That ID pass of yours. Keep that in mind. And you may want to come clean with your crew before it does."

———

The AIC was the nerve center of the ship, always staffed and busy, but it could be the loneliest place on board as far as Dunstan was concerned. They had to send off a report to fleet command, but that would trigger a response containing orders, and those would take away whatever elbow room he still had to make his own calls. It had been three hours since they'd boarded *Zephyr*, and Bosca and his team had finished searching the ship. There was no hidden missile tube, no concealed rail-gun mount. They had a few sidearms in the arms locker, properly secured, and all were registered and authorized. Other than that, the only weapon-like item on board was the set of kitchen knives the cook had tucked away in a storage roll in his berthing compartment.

Mayler approached him while he was looking at the plot, lost in thought.

"Sir, we got data on that warhead. The AI found a match for the radiation profile."

Dunstan looked up. "We know where it came from?"

"We do. It's one of the Mark Sixteens from RNS *Nike*."

"I thought *Nike* was lost with all hands at the First Battle of Oceana."

"That's what the database says. But it said the same thing about RNS *Daphne*."

"And we ran into *Daphne* just three months ago," Dunstan conceded. "There were a lot of ships wrecked in that battle. We lost that one big. No way for us to salvage. The fuzzheads had all the time they needed."

"Makes you wonder how many more they got," Mayler said. "*Nike* had four nuclear launch tubes."

"That's something I'd rather not think about right now, Lieutenant. Or I'll need more than a drink to help me sleep tonight."

They looked at the tactical display, empty except for the solitary icon representing OMV *Zephyr*, which was patiently hanging in space a hundred klicks away, waiting for its crew to return.

"Have you decided what to do with the merchant crew, sir?" Mayler asked.

Dunstan rubbed his forehead with a soft groan.

"I haven't quite figured that out yet, Lieutenant. But I am about to go down to the officers' mess to talk to them, so I guess I should make up my mind before I get there."

———

The *Zephyr* crew were sitting around two of the tables in the mess when Dunstan and Sergeant Bosca walked in. They all got out of their seats at the same time and stood to face Dunstan.

"Apologies for the wait," he said. "I had a few things to sort out. Nukes tend to make the simple things complex."

They looked at him with unconcealed anticipation. It seemed that the long stretch of uncertainty had even served to temper the attitude of the pilot a little because she had dropped the hostile glares.

"You've acted mostly by the book. I mean, after the part where you took on unregulated cargo. I've decided that it isn't in the interests of the Rhodian Navy to add another complication to everyone's day. And if we detain and prosecute you, it will just deter others from making a similar call of conscience. You are free to return to your ship and be on your way."

Dunstan held up his hand to interrupt their audible expressions of relief.

"*But.* You will transmit all your data connected with the incident before you leave. And I can't guarantee that the fleet won't call on your testimony or even demand access to your ship. The Rhodian Navy will keep an eye on you for a while. I would suggest you become more selective regarding the contracts you accept."

"Thank you, Commander," Captain Decker said. She held out her hand, and he shook it. They all filed out of the room behind Bosca. The last one to step across the threshold was the Palladian first officer.

"Master Siboniso," Dunstan said.

The first officer stopped at the door and turned his head. *"Sir."*

"One last word to the wise," Dunstan said. "You just turned over a nuke to the authorities. The kind of people who deal in nukes are the kind of people who won't just accept a refund and an apology. Consider keeping a very low profile for a little while."

Siboniso inclined his head in acknowledgment and stepped across the threshold to follow his shipmates.

You may yet wish we had detained you after all, Dunstan thought.

CHAPTER 14

IDINA

To the west, the skyline of Sandvik was glowing with the fading remnants of a dark-red sunset. From the company square at the JSP base, it looked like the city was on fire.

Is it a red sunset or a red sunrise that's supposed to be a bad omen? Idina wondered as she walked across the square and toward the liaison building. The summer storms of the last few days had lifted, and the air was pleasantly cool tonight. The breeze had dried out the puddles the downpours had left in their wake. It was easily the nicest day she had experienced on this planet since she got here for her third tour of occupation duty, but it irritated her a little, as if the planet had been holding back its good weather on purpose until just before her departure. The emotion was irrational, of course—planets were spheres of rock and water, with no consciousness or capacity for intent. But having to fend off two dozen angry Gretian youths with her kukri just the night before had soured her attitude a bit, and she let her brain indulge in the act of bias confirmation.

Gods, even my grudges have diminished in this gravity. Maybe it is time to go back to Pallas.

The liaison building was busier than usual tonight. In addition to Idina's Fifth Platoon and their usual Gretian police counterparts, a squad of the JSP's Quick Reaction Force had arrived for the pre-shift briefing, adding a dozen troopers to tonight's headcount. Idina had feared that Dahl would be absent tonight for some reason—rattled by the event last night or grounded by her superior—but the tall Gretian police captain was at the front of the room as always, helmet under her arm, hair in her customary tight braid. All things considered, everyone involved in the tussle had gotten off lightly. Idina and Dahl had collected a few bruises, and one of the belligerent youths had gotten his nose broken when Idina had smacked her helmet into his face. But nobody had died, and none had found out how terribly easily a Pallas Brigade kukri could amputate limbs.

Idina walked to the front of the room, right down the multicolored paint stripe that had segregated the JSP troopers and their Gretian patrol partners for the first few years of the occupation. The colored stripe had been crisp and glossy on Idina's first JSP assignment. Now it was dull and faded, scuffed and worn down by the many boot soles that had crossed the demarcation, and nobody had seen a point in refreshing the paint.

The room was awash in the din of low conversation. The QRF troopers stood out in the crowd in their tactical outfits, which were flat black and considerably more aggressive looking than the standard blue JSP patrol suits with their police markings. The leader of the QRF squad was a hard-faced Rhodian lieutenant whose biceps strained the short sleeves of his ballistic undershirt. He was standing next to Dahl, talking to her in a low voice. Dahl looked up when she saw Idina striding up to them.

"Good evening, Sergeant," she said.

"Good evening, Captain. *Lieutenant*," she added with a nod in the Rhodian's direction. The JSP had switched to police protocol when they were around their Gretian counterparts, which meant no salutes and no calling a room to attention when a superior walked in. It had taken weeks for her to stop feeling like she was committing insubordination.

"Good evening, Color Sergeant. Looks like you have some excitement scheduled tonight," the lieutenant said.

"Let's hope it won't be exciting at all," Idina replied. "I want to get this fellow off the street and into custody without anyone getting wind of it. We had plenty of excitement on our first try."

She looked at Dahl and inclined her head toward the assembled troopers.

"Your room, Captain."

Dahl nodded and turned to face the crowd.

"Attention, please," she said. The din of conversation in the room stopped, and within a few seconds, all eyes were on the Gretian captain.

"Tonight, we are going to effect a high-risk arrest," Dahl said. "The suspect is one Vigi Fuldas. You all have the relevant data on your briefing log. He eluded our first attempt to arrest him last night at Philharmony Station. The suspect is a known arms trafficker who has already resisted arrest aggressively. That is why we have requested the assistance of the Quick Reaction Force."

Dahl created a screen and flicked it over her shoulder, where it expanded to fill most of the back wall. It showed a three-dimensional map of a location in Sandvik. An image of Vigi Fuldas along with his vital data hovered in the upper-left quadrant of the map.

"As the suspect was already under judicial watch prior to the attempted arrest, we were able to track his movements since last night, despite his considerable efforts to elude surveillance. He has not returned to his residence. We lost track of him for a few hours, but this afternoon, a facial recognition unit in the Artery network caught sight of him in western Sandvik near his place of employment. He has checked into a capsule hotel near the Sandvik Spaceport using a forged identity pass. It is likely that he is preparing to leave the planet to evade further apprehension measures."

Dahl isolated a section of the map and magnified it. It showed an intersection surrounded by a variety of commercial buildings.

"The suspect has rented a capsule in the Worlds Travel Lodge at 12 West and 2 North. Tonight at 0300, we will leave a minimal number of patrol units on their usual stations. The rest will establish a perimeter around the 12W and 2N intersection for a block in either direction. There is an Artery transit station just half a block north on 2N, so pay attention to that escape vector. Apprehension will be done by the QRF, which will enter the facility from the rooftop emergency access and secure the floor, then proceed to the capsule, where the suspect will hopefully be in the deepest phase of his REM sleep. The JSP patrols will maintain the block of the intersection and the quarantine of the building until the QRF unit leader reports a successful apprehension. Once the suspect is in QRF custody, they will evacuate the area with him via gyrofoil, and the patrol units will lift the block and return to their assigned sectors. If all goes as planned and expected, the operation will conclude at 0315. Does anyone have questions?"

Idina watched as Dahl answered the few clarification requests that followed her prompt. After months of joint briefings and patrols, even the Alliance troops deferred to the Gretian police captain, talking with the same level of respect and courtesy they would use if Dahl wore a Pallas Brigade uniform instead. The JSP concept of joint responsibility and integration had been a full success, even if it had taken years to work out the friction and smooth out the burrs. But this was the only unqualified success of the occupation, achieved by the cooperation of a group of people used to discipline and teamwork. Idina wasn't sure the model could ever be transplanted into a civilian setting, not with everyone trying to pull the rope in different directions.

"If we don't have to fire a shot or use our stun sticks tonight, it'll be a good op," Idina added when there were no more questions from the troopers. "But don't get complacent just because the streets are quiet. Things can turn to shit in a hot second."

———

"Maybe I'm getting too old for this business," Idina said when she was back in the gyrofoil with Dahl and on the way to their patrol sector. The sun had set completely now, leaving only the faintest streak of purple lingering above the horizon.

"You are not too old," Dahl said. "You are in better shape than any of our new officers fresh from police school."

"I will be thirty-seven this year," Idina replied. "Seventeen years of service. That's ancient for an infantry soldier. If I don't take retirement in three years, they will shunt me off into a support slot until I get bored enough."

"And why not retire? You have done more than your share for the Alliance, I think."

"I have done this since I was twenty. I don't really know how to do anything else."

"You will only be forty. That leaves more than half a lifetime to learn something else."

"Infantry skills don't translate well into the civilian world. There isn't much call there for killing people or breaking their stuff," Idina said.

"You would make a fair police officer," Dahl suggested.

"Not my calling. I don't have the temperament. When those people overwhelmed us last night, I was ready to chop off some hands and feet."

"And you would have been in the right," Dahl said. "I was a moment away from deploying my sidearm. And I do not have that impulse very often. Maybe I am getting too old for this business as well."

"What a team we make," Idina said with a smile and looked out over the city. Her eyes had gotten used to the wide-open spaces on Gretia, the way her gaze could drift over the landscape all the way to the far horizon when the weather was clear. Maybe it was the knowledge that her time here was about to end, but for the first time, the thought of leaving this place for good made her feel strangely melancholic. She'd done three deployments to Gretia, and she was at the end of her infantry career. There was little chance they'd approve her for a fourth off-world tour, not after having to cut this one short because of medical issues. After this week, she would never see this sight again.

At least I had a full career, she thought. Half the squad she had lost in the ambush three months ago had consisted of privates on their first off-world deployments, kids with less than two years in the brigade. Self-pity wasn't the Pallas way, and she had no right to sadness at the thought of going home when so many others couldn't.

"I have three years until retirement as well," Dahl said. "I will be fifty-two in two months. The age limit for patrol officers is fifty-five. If I want to stay on any longer, I have to move up into the administrative branch."

"Shoving you off into a support slot," Idina said with a smile.

"Until I get bored enough," Dahl said. "It appears we are in the same pair of shoes, as they say."

Idina chuckled.

"I don't think the translator got that idiom quite right."

———

Thirty minutes before the scheduled arrest, a dozen patrol gyrofoils left their regular sectors and started converging in the night sky above western Sandvik.

Dahl had set their craft's autopilot to fly a three-kilometer racetrack orbit with the Worlds Travel Lodge building at its center. The sensor array in the gyrofoil's chin turret was locked onto the middle of the intersection in front of the building, and Idina watched the image on her surveillance screen shift its perspective slightly as their aspect to the target kept changing gradually. At half past two, there was only sporadic surface pod traffic. This part of Sandvik was dotted with commercial and industrial facilities catering to the nearby spaceport and its customers, and there was little to draw late-night crowds that could be in the way or interfere with an arrest. According to Dahl, it was the perfect location for a high-risk arrest.

"Guest count of the hotel is thirteen," Dahl read off the surveillance report. "Including our friend. There are only three other people on the floor with him."

"When's the last time they got eyeballs on him?"

"The second shift spotted him entering the building at 2023. The concierge scanner has his counterfeit ID pass checking in for floor access at 2025. We have had the building under continuous surveillance since then."

"Did they get a good look at his face?"

Dahl isolated an image from the surveillance feed and magnified it. Fuldas hadn't even tried to change his appearance in any way. He was still wearing the same hairstyle and beard. Only the clothes on his body were different from what he had worn the night before, and he had exchanged the small pack he had carried for a larger travel bag.

"Yeah, that's our guy, all right," Idina said. "I'm looking forward to having a little talk with him back at the office."

"The departure registry shows that he booked passage to Acheron on a consumer goods freighter. It departs in two days. But his shuttle transfer to the orbital station is scheduled for tomorrow at 1100 hours already."

"I guess he figured it was safer to get off the planet as soon as he could. Wonder what he wants on Acheron."

"We will be able to ask him in a little while," Dahl said. "Unless he does something foolish when the QRF try to detain him."

"They'll try nonlethals first. But if he pulls out a gun, it's not going to be pretty. They won't take chances."

They did a few more laps of the aerial racetrack in silence. Somewhere on the fourth floor of the hotel a thousand meters below them, Vigi Fuldas was holed up in a capsule bed the size of a roomy coffin, unaware of the nearly company-sized force that was homing in on his location.

A status message popped up on the tactical display, followed by a new unit icon. The QRF's combat gyrofoil had lifted off from Joint Base Sandvik ten minutes to the east.

"All units, the QRF bird is inbound at this time," she sent to her platoon. "Go time in nine minutes, forty-five seconds."

The platoon's teams sent their acknowledgments, a cascade of green check marks scrolling down the left side of her helmet display. A dozen two-officer teams stood ready to swoop in and secure every intersection in a two-block radius around the hotel in a few seconds. Even if Fuldas was still awake and happened to be near a window, he would have just a few moments of warning before the QRF team was on his floor and at the door of his capsule. And this time, there wouldn't be a crowd around to interfere with the arrest.

She focused on the sensor image of the intersection again. The streets were still and empty. The only movement came from an advertising projection above the entrance of the business next door to the hotel, looping through a text scroll that promised BULK FREIGHT TO HADES/ACHERON: GUARANTEED BEST RATES AT SANDPORT. This would be Fuldas's last sight in freedom before they hauled him off to the police headquarters in restraints.

"Five minutes out," the QRF lieutenant sent. *"On-scene JSP supervisor, give me a go/no-go for deployment."*

Idina checked the screen one last time. A solitary transport pod rolled through the intersection and continued past the hotel without slowing down. The advertisement continued to flog its cheap bulk-freight rates to the empty neighborhood. There was no movement on the rooftops, nobody crouching in the shadows. She took a deep breath and let it out slowly.

"QRF Actual, you are *go* for deployment," she replied.

"Copy go for deployment. ETA four minutes, thirty seconds."

"All units, QRF is cleared to deploy. Take up staging positions at two hundred meters and watch your surroundings on the descent. We have a lot of birds in this airspace right now."

The combat gyrofoil came in low and fast from the west. It was a smaller platoon-sized transport, not the enormous eight-engined beast that could deliver an entire company in a single lift, but it still dwarfed the little four-passenger patrol units. Idina and Dahl watched from their high vantage point as the QRF gyrofoil descended onto the intersection, engines tilted backward to scrub forward momentum. Twenty meters above the hotel rooftop, the machine came to a stationary hover. The shrouded rotors of the engine nacelles made a low humming sound that reverberated back from the concrete and steel surfaces of the surrounding buildings. On the intersection, the downwash from the engines blew around dust and debris. A dozen rappelling lines dropped down from the belly hatch of the ship, and the QRF troopers began their quick descent.

"All units, take up blocking positions," Idina sent. "Everybody on the ground *now, now, now.*"

The much-smaller patrol gyrofoils swarmed down from their staging altitude and landed on their assigned intersections almost at the same second. As soon as they were on the ground, their pilots turned on the emergency lighting and deployed warning screen projections that blocked the intersections in all four directions.

On the hotel rooftop, the QRF troopers had disengaged from their lines. The combat gyrofoil gunned its engines and started a steep ascent, then swung around and took up a covering position a hundred meters away. The troopers lined up at the rooftop access door and swiftly filed through it. Ten seconds after the combat gyrofoil had pulled into its deployment hover, all the QRF members were inside the staircase and on the way to the suspect's floor.

Not bad for a bunch of Rhodians, Idina thought.

"He's barely going to have time to scratch his ass before they haul him out of that capsule," she said to Dahl, who was watching intently as the action unfolded on the surveillance screen.

For a few long moments, there was silence again. The rooftop access door stood open, casting a long shadow in the searchlight from the nearby combat gyrofoil. On the tactical overlay, the outlines of the QRF squad descended to the fourth floor and lined up for entry. The lead trooper unlocked the door with the law enforcement override, and they rushed through, weapons at the ready. Idina felt like holding her breath when the QRF troopers filed into the capsule suite beyond. If Fuldas was awake and in a mind to put up resistance, they would hear gunfire any second. She imagined him cowering at the back of his sleeping capsule, clutching a stolen Palladian pistol loaded with dual-purpose explosive ammunition, the same shit he had sold the idiot kid they had arrested the other day. The QRF troopers all wore medium assault armor, but none of the other nighttime guests in that building did, and dual-purpose explosive rounds could travel through the interior walls of the place like a kukri could punch through a slice of stale bread.

Ten more seconds passed in silence.

"Subject is in custody," the QRF team leader sent. "We are on the way out."

Idina exhaled sharply. "Copy that, QRF Actual. The perimeter is secured. No activity other than our people."

"Affirmative. We are leaving through the front entrance in thirty seconds."

"Yellow Two, clear your intersection for the QRF bird," Idina sent to the patrol unit closest to the building. "Let's wrap this up and get out of here."

"Looks like our friend will not be making his flight tomorrow," Dahl said.

"Yeah, it's a shame. What's the world coming to when a man can't even sell stolen military weapons to young hotheads in peace?"

Down below, one of the patrol gyrofoils left its blocking position on the intersection to make space for the QRF combat gyrofoil hovering nearby. When the smaller unit was out of the way, the QRF bird moved in and set down in the middle of the intersection. The patrol units were deliberately nonmartial in appearance, but the combat gyrofoil was obviously and unapologetically a military craft, all aggressive angles and flat black paint. Once things got dangerous enough for the QRF to come into play, the intimidation factor of an armored war machine reinforced the message that the time for a nonconfrontational approach had passed.

"All that running and hiding. And in the end, he only got another day of freedom. Now he is going to go to Landfall for a few years," Dahl said.

"Should have thought of that before he ran and left us to the crowd," Idina grumbled. "I hope he freezes his ass off up there while he contemplates the error of his ways."

She magnified the view on the surveillance screen to show the front of the hotel. The tactical overlay showed the gaggle of QRF troopers and their prisoner emerging from the staircase in the interior of the building and moving through the foyer to the entrance doors. Two troopers had Fuldas between them, and the rest were in tactical formation in front and behind, securing their egress in every direction. But there was nobody to oppose the arrest tonight. The foyer was empty, and the next pedestrian on Idina's display was five blocks away. As the group approached the door, Idina zoomed in on Fuldas's face. He looked bleary-eyed and satisfyingly scared. The QRF had dragged him out of the sleeping capsule and hauled him off without letting him put on clothes, and he was wearing only his undershirt and shorts, padding across the marble floor of the foyer barefooted.

The front door opened, and Idina's screen washed out into gray noise. For a heartbeat, she thought something had passed in front of the sensor. Then the gyrofoil rocked violently, as if a giant fist had struck it a glancing blow from below. Idina's helmet smacked into the side of the seat's headrest. The bone-shaking thunderclap of a high-order explosion followed just a moment later. On the gyrofoil's system displays, yellow and red warning lights started flashing for attention, accompanied by the discordant trilling of alarms. For a few seconds, the craft spun wildly, the horizon in front of the windshield replaced by city streets and buildings that flashed by entirely too close for comfort. Idina fumbled for the emergency eject lever at the front of her seat.

"Do not touch that," Dahl commanded from the left. "Not until I say."

The Gretian police captain had her hands on the controls now. A few heartbeats later, the gyrofoil righted itself, and the horizon reappeared. Idina looked out of the side window and saw a rooftop close enough that she could have jumped out onto it without even twisting an ankle. Dahl swung the gyrofoil around to the right and deftly avoided an antenna array jutting out of the corner of the rooftop. They climbed away again, the rotors of the craft whining in an unusually belabored pitch. The alarms were still shrilling an unnerving concert in a variety of pitches and volumes.

"We have one engine out and another about to fail," Dahl announced. Her voice was cool and matter-of-fact, but Idina could see the tension and intense focus in the older woman's face.

"Well, put us down before it does," Idina said. Her head was still swimming with the impact against the headrest and the sudden onslaught of chaotic noise and motion.

"That is the idea," Dahl said. "What happened just now?"

Idina brought up her surveillance feed again, but the screen only showed an error message: FEED OFFLINE. Every sensor in the gyrofoil's chin pod flashed a yellow or red status. She cursed and closed the screen once more, then looked outside to get her bearings. A cloud of smoke and dust was rising into the night sky to their left, covering a three-block area and diffusing the lights from the nearby buildings. Idina could hear debris bouncing off the top of the gyrofoil like scattered hail.

"Bomb, bomb, bomb," she sent to the platoon. "All units, report your status. Check in, everyone."

One by one, the patrol units returned their status messages through the data network: green, green, yellow, green, yellow.

No red, she thought. *Don't come up red.*

When all the teams had reported in, she breathed a sigh of relief. No red status messages. Several injuries, but no dead. Whatever trap had just sprung, it had mostly spared her troopers. But her people hadn't been the only ones on the scene. The QRF squad had been inside the building. She tapped over to their channel with dread.

"QRF Actual, Yellow One Niner," Idina sent. "Report your status."

The channel remained silent.

"QRF Actual, come in," she tried again. "Any QRF team members, check in."

For a few long moments, there was nothing but static on the comms. Then one of her troopers chimed in on the all-platoon channel. He sounded as dazed and shaken as she felt.

"One Niner, this is Yellow Two. They're gone, Colors. The building's gone. And the one next to it. Went up right in front of us. Nothing but a pile of rubble left."

"Gods-damn it." Idina gritted her teeth and banged her helmet against the headrest of her seat. She took a deep breath to collect herself and tapped over to the JSP emergency channel.

"Alliance units, this is Yellow One Niner in charge of Sector Five. We have a major high-order explosives incident at location grid Delta

One Three. Our QRF squad is down. There are civilian casualties. Requesting assistance from all available alert forces in the AO. I repeat, send all available alert forces in the AO."

Next to her, Dahl sent her own emergency message to the Gretian police network, speaking calmly but forcefully while piloting the stricken gyrofoil to a landing spot on an intersection below. Idina looked around with renewed concern. If the explosion was part of an ambush, her lightly armed troops would be easy pickings, especially if the attackers were equipped like the people who had killed her squad three months ago. Her light scout armor suddenly felt woefully inadequate.

"All units, watch your surroundings and stay alert. This may just be the opening bell. And stay clear of the site until we have backup with explosives sniffers behind us. The bastards may have planted secondaries to catch first responders. I repeat, do not approach the site," she told her troops on the platoon channel.

"Colors, there are QRF people in there," one of her squad leaders replied. She checked the broadcast ID.

"Corporal Bandhari, you *will* follow protocol. Stay the hells away unless you see someone crawling out of the rubble right in front of you. That's a fucking order. *Acknowledge.*"

It took a moment for Bandhari to respond, and when he did, she could practically hear his teeth grind.

"Affirmative, Color Sergeant."

Go ahead and hate me for that, Idina thought. *At least you'll be alive to hate.*

Dahl steered the gyrofoil around a building corner and descended onto the intersection beyond. When they were just a few meters above the ground, the craft lurched again and dropped forward and to the right. Dahl tried to correct the veer, but they were too low, and the remaining engines of the gyrofoil didn't have the power left to pull them out of the drop. They hit the ground at an angle with a resounding crash. Idina lost sight of the world outside as the automated crash system filled the cabin with flame-retardant kinetic foam. She felt the craft skid across the road surface and spin to a grinding stop.

"Are you all right?" Dahl asked. Her voice sounded muffled through the layer of hardened foam that now separated them.

"As far as I can tell," Idina replied. "You?"

"The same. Pull the red lever above your door. We need to get out of here."

Idina looked for the lever, which was partially covered in dried foam. She grabbed it and yanked it down, and the door on her side of the gyrofoil fell out of its frame, accompanied by the dull cracks of emergency charges. She released her seat harness and hoisted herself out of the craft while Dahl did the same on the other side. They had come to rest with the right side of the gyrofoil's nose against a building. Idina took cover between the vehicle and the nearest wall and drew her sidearm from its holster. The tactical screen projection on her helmet visor kept resetting itself, so she shut off her data monocle and opened her helmet. The warm night air smelled like dust and artillery propellant.

They did it again, she thought. *Binary explosives. They were waiting for us all along. The whole thing was a setup from the start.*

Dahl came around the back of the gyrofoil, gun in hand. She looked a little dazed behind the clear shield of her helmet visor. Idina pulled her behind cover and scanned the street beyond the gyrofoil for threats. If the enemy—whoever they were—had camouflaged riflemen or rail guns in position, the light armor on the craft would be little protection. Any moment, Idina expected to hear the threat detector in her armor alerting her to the spike in EM radiation generated by a charging rail gun, hidden on a rooftop or behind a distant storefront, ready to tear her platoon to pieces.

The street remained quiet and empty. The only movement in her field of vision was the holographic advertising on a storefront in the distance.

"My tactical screen is out," she said on the platoon channel. "Squad leaders, give me a status report."

"We are securing the perimeter around the site," Corporal Bandhari replied. "None of us were closer than half a block. The QRF transmitters are all offline, Colors."

"Anyone got eyes on the building?"

"I'm on the northeast corner," Corporal Shakya sent. "The whole thing collapsed when the ground floor went. Blue section is taking off right now for overhead cover."

"Blue section, do you read?"

"Loud and clear, Colors," Corporal Noor replied. "We have you on tactical. You're a block and a half to the northeast."

"Noor, you're in charge for now from up there. Our ride is down and my tactical link is out. Captain Dahl and I are going to make our way to the site on foot. Keep overwatch and have purple and yellow sections redeploy for perimeter security."

"Understood, Colors," Noor said. "The alert force is boarding the combat ship at Sandvik Base. ETA fifteen minutes."

Whatever is left of the alert force, Idina thought. The QRF usually had just a single platoon on emergency standby, only four squads of troopers, and one of those squads had been in the hotel when it blew up.

"The police and emergency responders from our side are on the way also," Dahl said next to Idina. The Gretian officer holstered her weapon and raised the visor of her helmet. After a moment of consideration, Idina returned her own gun to its holster as well. If there was another trap waiting for them, the pistol would make no difference in the end. The QRF squad had been armed to the teeth and trained to expect trouble, and now they were buried in the rubble of a four-story building.

The site of the detonation wasn't hard to spot even from almost two blocks away. A billowing cloud of smoke rose into the night sky where the hotel had stood just minutes ago. One of the JSP patrol gyrofoils rushed by above their heads and made a wide circle around the block, climbing as it went. The downwash from the engine's rotors made the rising smoke swirl. The smell of the explosives residue triggered unwelcome olfactory flashbacks in Idina's brain, memories of blood and fear and bone-deep exhaustion. This was the scent of a battlefield, not that of a civilian neighborhood.

"Good gods," Dahl said when they rounded the corner of the next intersection.

"The gods had nothing to do with this," Idina replied grimly.

The site of the hotel was half a block ahead and to their left. Whoever had set the ambush had either vastly overestimated the amount of explosive needed, or they had meant to demonstrate their willingness to commit destruction to excess. The capsule hotel was just a pile of concrete rubble and twisted steel girders. Every building in the intersection had taken severe damage from the shockwave and the flying debris. It looked like the aftermath of an artillery strike.

"What do you see, Noor?" Idina asked on the platoon channel.

"Nobody's moving down there but our people," Corporal Noor replied. "Thermals are all over the place. Half the block is gone, Colors. And most of what's left is on fire."

"Everyone stay clear of the damaged buildings," Idina said. "Keep the perimeter secure for when the backup gets here."

"What about the QRF unit?"

She looked at the burning ruin that had been the hotel. The fire that had engulfed the remains of the building radiated intense heat that was uncomfortable on her unshielded face even from half a block away.

"They are being welcomed by their ancestors right now, Corporal," she said. "And I hope they get piss-drunk with them in the Hall of Heroes tonight."

CHAPTER 15

ADEN

"Some smuggling crew we are," Maya said.

On the navigation plot, the icon representing RNS *Minotaur* was almost at the edge of their awareness bubble, a hundred thousand kilometers astern of *Zephyr*. They were burning at two g, nice and easy, but Aden could tell that Maya would go full throttle if she had her way, just to leave the Rhodian Navy behind as fast as possible.

"I feel like I just got a stern lecture from my old teacher," Tess said. "That's a damn funny way to show gratitude to someone who drops a stolen nuke back into their lap. I wasn't expecting a reward. But a 'thank you' would have been nice."

"That was a nuclear warhead," Decker said from above. "Navy people really get their overalls in a wad about those. To be honest, I'm surprised he let us go."

"And you took it to them anyway?" Tess looked a little scandalized.

Henry cleared his throat.

"Nukes are poison," he said. "We did the only thing we could have done that carried the chance for leniency. If that same ship had busted us on that run, we would be on our way to Rhodia right now. To begin our complimentary decade and a half of leisure time in a high-security detention arcology."

"We could have dumped it," Maya said.

"Out in space? Like a bunch of galley trash?" Tess shook her head.

"There's a lot of empty space between the regular transfer lanes. That thing would be floating out there for ten thousand years before someone came across it. Maybe forever."

"I am not dumping a half-megaton warhead for some scrapper to stumble across." Decker's tone made it clear that she wasn't even slightly entertaining that argument.

On the plot, the icon for *Minotaur* disappeared off the edge. Aden let out a little puff of breath. He had come very close to being in the brig on that ship right now even as *Zephyr* went on her way with the rest of the crew, and he was still amazed at the completely unexpected act of mercy from the Rhodian commander.

"And of course we had to get the biggest hard-ass in the Rhody fleet," Decker continued. "I was hoping to run into some patrol corvette. Some green lieutenant on his first tugboat command out of space warfare school. Instead, it's a seasoned frigate crew, with a craggy veteran in charge. I had to really lay on the contrition."

"That jug-eared asshole," Maya grumbled.

"I don't know, I thought he was kind of handsome," Tess said. "Nice blue eyes."

"Captain made the right call. So did the Rhody," Henry said with finality.

Tess got up from her acceleration couch and walked over to the ladderwell.

"I'm going to check my stuff in the workshop again. I hate that those people had their hands all over the ship. It feels like getting felt up without permission while you're asleep. I want to scrub all the bulkheads with antiseptics now."

She climbed down the ladder and disappeared from view.

"If we don't have any more zero-g adventures planned in the next hour or two, I want to throw together some dinner," Tristan said.

"Go ahead," Maya replied. "We're going to stay at acceleration until we get to the turnaround point for Acheron."

Tristan nodded and peeled himself out of his harness, then went over to the ladderwell and followed Tess down.

Aden stifled a yawn and got up to stretch his limbs. After the encounter with the Rhodian ship and the tension of being found out as a Gretian by the Rhody commander, he felt drained. The navigation plot was empty now, but he almost expected to see the icon for *Minotaur* pop up again on the fringes of their sensor range any moment, burning in pursuit at ten g because the commander had changed his mind. Whatever tint of romance and excitement the notion of the smuggling job had held was now thoroughly extinguished in his brain. Maybe he really wasn't cut out for this new career, and this was the fates telling him to go home again. However hard it would be to build something new out of the bits and pieces of his old life, at least he wouldn't have to look over his shoulder like a thief in the night every time a Rhodian warship popped up on the navigation screen.

He glanced up at the command platform to see Decker watching him.

"You look like you could sleep for a week," she told him. "You all right?"

"I'm okay," he said. It didn't seem to convince Decker.

"Go get some bunk time before dinner. Half an hour of sleep. You'll feel better. And maybe you won't plant your face in the meal tray."

Aden nodded and went to the ladderwell to climb down to Crew Deck B, where his berthing compartment was located, next to Tess and across the ladderwell from Henry.

His berth was as clean and neat as any room he'd had in the military. Other than a few sets of clothes and a comtab, he had brought nothing with which to clutter up the space. Even his locker was mostly empty. He had gotten glimpses of Tess's berth whenever they got out or went to their bunks at the same time, and he knew that her space was personalized just like the workshop deck, drawings and sketches all over the bulkheads. As long as he felt like a temporary addition to the crew, it didn't seem right to him to claim his space in that fashion. If they got rid of him again, he didn't want to leave behind anything, least of all intimate glimpses into his personality. Unless he could be sure that day wasn't likely to come, he wanted to be able to pack everything he owned into one bag and walk out with it. And as long as he kept his secret from the rest of the crew, he knew he could never have that certainty.

He took off his boots and crawled into his bunk. His tiredness was fighting it out with the residual adrenaline from their encounter, which seemed to refresh itself a little every time he thought about it. Aden closed his eyes to let the background hum of the ship calm his mind.

Enjoy your new life, the forger Henk had said when Aden had walked out with his new name and ID pass. But he hadn't bought a new life, just a piece of polymer and a few database entries. A life was made of the thousands of little strings that tied people to each other and anchored them in their worlds. Those strings needed time and care to form. No ledger was big enough to buy any number of them, or hurry their connections along, not even all his father's money. Seventeen years of Aden Robertson hadn't managed to erase Aden Ragnar. Three months as Aden Jansen would not get rid of Aden Robertson.

———

"Come on up if you want to try the special," Tristan's voice sounded from the comms panel. Aden opened his eyes and tried to focus on the time readout above his head. It felt like he had barely closed his eyes, but forty-five minutes had passed since he had put his head down on the pillow.

When he climbed up onto the galley deck, everyone was already sitting at the table and talking over food. For a moment, Aden felt a pang of longing, as if he were looking at the scene from the outside. Then Tess saw him on the ladder and gestured to the empty chairs between her and Tristan.

"Grab a seat. Tristan has actually managed to turn the number eleven into something edible."

"Really?" Aden sat down and looked at the ingredients of the foil pan in the middle of the table. The unaltered number eleven was practically a veggie cake, but this looked more like a tagine, a mess of veggies and meat jumbled and coated in a red-tinted sauce.

"I took four number elevens and mixed them with two number threes and two number eighteens," Tristan said. "Took a little experimenting. And a bit of vinegar, citrus juice, and Liquid Sunshine."

"Citrus juice," Aden repeated.

"Yeah, to cut down the salt. You want to add an acid or a sweetener. I added both. The beef from the number three is in a sweet sauce. The tomato sauce from the eighteen adds some more acid."

"How many meal trays did you burn through before you figured out the right ratio?"

"Just what's in the pan. I've been cooking for thirty years, you know."

Aden put some of the pan contents on a plate and tried a bite. The salt was still unmistakably present, but it was no longer the overwhelming flavor.

"It's good," he said and took another bite to prove the sincerity of his assessment.

"Now that we're all here, we need to talk about the delivery job we just flushed down the drain," Captain Decker said. "I've had some time to look at the numbers."

Henry made a face as if the bite he had just taken was mostly citrus juice.

"How badly did we get skinned?"

Decker sat back and flicked a comtab projection over the table, where it expanded above the foil pan with Tristan's dish.

"We sent the deposit to the Rhodies with the rest of the data, so this run has us all in the red. We burned over five thousand in reactor fuel to get to the pickup point and then for working up ballistic speed. Add to that whatever we're going to use up getting back to the shortest-time transfer route to Acheron, and it'll be six and a half before it's done. Plus our time, and whatever we're out by not doing paid work for most of a week."

She looked around the table with a frown.

"Can't really put a number on the missed pay. But just to get the operating budget back to the way it was before I hit 'accept' on that fucking contract offer, we're looking at twenty-five hundred ags per head. Sorry."

They all digested the unwelcome news for a few moments in silence.

"I should cover it," Aden said. "I got you all to listen to me."

"Stop talking nonsense," Maya replied. "Do you believe that these people said what you think they said?"

He nodded. "But if they were just joking around, I rang the alarm for nothing. Maybe I overreacted."

"Best-case scenario, we would have gone through with the job and gotten paid. And there would be a half-megaton nuclear warhead sitting in someone's private arsenal. Not a great best case," Henry said.

"Worst-case scenario, they were waiting for us with guns drawn," Tess added. "Nobody gets paid, and we all die."

"You did your job," Decker said. "That's exactly the sort of thing I want you to do. Keeping your ears open and letting me know when something isn't quite right. That's why I hired a linguist, not a comms operator. I can train any kid fresh out of merchant school to run that gear."

"All right," Aden said, feeling sheepish. "I'll stop talking nonsense."

"It wasn't all on you anyway," Henry said. "We put it to a vote. Everyone agreed to pop the lid on that cargo. And then everyone agreed to take it to the Rhodians."

"So now we all get to pay the bad-judgment tax," Tess said.

Decker waved her hand in front of the screen to shut it off.

"If Aden was right, it's a small tax. And we'll never find out if he wasn't because we didn't want to roll those dice. Fuck the odds. Stakes were too high."

She shrugged and picked up her fork again.

"Besides, it's not all bad news. I got in touch with the people at Tanaka and told them we're free for the three-year overhaul a little earlier than we had planned. They said they can get us in a week ahead of time if we can make the slot. Someone else had to reschedule."

"We'll be done early," Tristan said. "Way early. Are we going to spend an extra week? Because I wouldn't mind that at all."

"As soon as we have the ship back from the Tanaka crew, I'm looking for a new contract on the board," Decker replied. "Something nice and safe and moderately profitable. You may be able to squeeze in a few extra days. But I wouldn't count on it."

"How long are we staying above the table with contracts?" Maya asked.

"That'll be up to vote. But I think we ought to play it square on the board for a while. Until we can be sure that the Rhodies aren't going to impound our ship the next time we dock at Rhodia One."

"Oh, I am fine with *square* right now," Tess said. She had finished her dinner, and now she was taking sips from a half-liter bottle of Rhodian ale while she listened to the conversation. "When I opened the lid and that fucker was thirty centimeters from my face, I swear it took a year off my life."

———

The transit to Acheron was uneventful. At three and a half g, they passed most of the traffic on the transfer route, ore haulers and general-goods freighters chugging along at an easy and energy-saving one g, their crews bantering with *Zephyr* or giving them shit about wasting reactor fuel. When they finally left Rhodian space, Aden felt like the ship had finally passed through a minefield they had been navigating for days. He knew he wasn't the only one who was relieved because the tension on board dissipated over the next day like air from a broken tank valve. By the time they got to Palladian space, they had resumed their communal dinners, Tristan had given him a few lessons on how to sharpen knives with a water stone—the only proper way, according to him—and even Maya had stuck around after meals to socialize a little with Aden and Tess down in the workshop. They had all transferred the money they owed for the operating costs, and nobody had approached Aden to take him up on his offer of paying their share. The 2,500 ags that was his share had been his biggest expense by far since he joined the crew, and he was in no danger of running out of money, so he resolved to pay the communal bar tabs on Acheron until someone pried the comtab from his hands by force.

"You've been here before, right?" Tristan asked him when they were on final approach for docking at Acheron's enormous spin station. The planet was spread out behind the station and taking up most of the forward array's field of view, ochre swirls and intermingling streams that never stopped moving.

"A few times," Aden said. "Long before the war. I was in my early twenties. Gods, was that really twenty years ago?"

"Not much has changed down there. The war just kind of passed this place by. Their fleet yards actually had more business. The Rhodies and the fuzzheads were going through new ships like they were made for one-time use. Lots of replacement orders."

"I wouldn't really say the war passed us by," Maya said from above. "Ten thousand navy spacers killed. For casualty rates, we had higher losses than anyone else. Hefty price to pay for more ship orders."

"But you didn't get occupied for four years," Tristan said. "With the fuzzheads hauling off half of your output every year."

Maya just chuckled.

"That would have been a fun sight," she said. "Watching Gretian drop ships trying to land troops on CoCity. Hard enough to land there when you have permission."

Aden watched the scenery while *Zephyr* was going through its AI-controlled docking ballet with the station, matching rotational speed and lining up with the assigned docking berth, then letting the station controller reel the ship in like a fish on a line.

"All right," Decker said when they had latched onto the station and Tess had throttled down the reactor to standby mode. "Once we're off the ship, the overhaul crew has her for a week. Make sure you pack everything you want to take down to the surface with you. We get one free ride down and back as part of the service contract, or it'll cost you a thousand ags just to get back up to the station to fetch it."

―――

They went through the security locks at Acheron Station and met up with the liaison from Tanaka Spaceworks, a bubbly young woman who was reasonably fluent in Oceanian. She ushered them through the commercial part of the station and to a small private charter shuttle terminal, where the Tanaka people had prepared refreshments for the *Zephyr* crew while the shuttle was prepped and cleared for their ride down to Coriolis City.

"This was all part of the purchase price," Captain Decker said as they were sipping drinks and watching the launch preparations from the terminal's VIP lounge. "Full three-year overhaul package included.

But if you think all these smiling people are going to give us so much as a napkin for free when we show up for the five-year overhaul, I would love to talk to you about some oceanfront property I have for sale on Hades, right near the equator."

"Two weeks of idle time," Tess said. "I'll not touch a single wrench."

"What are you going to do with all that time?" Aden asked.

"There's a racetrack in CoCity," she said. "It's like a regulation track, but scaled down for karts. Whenever they don't have any league events, you can rent twenty-kilowatt karts and flog them around the track. Ten kilometers from start to finish. They charge eighty ags per lap."

"How much did you spend there again last time we were here?" Tristan asked.

"Look, you have your vices, I have mine. I like things that go."

"I'll have to try that," Aden said. "Not that I have anything else planned."

"Let me know when you want to check it out, and I'll take you," Tess said. "Two weeks on CoCity, and you have nothing planned at all? You don't know anyone here?"

Aden thought of Torie, the girl he'd met on *Cloud Dancer* three months ago. He wondered if she had ever started that job with Hanzo she'd accepted, or whether the near-death experience in the life pod had realigned her priorities. But wherever she was now, she probably wouldn't appreciate the physical reminder of that day if he showed up at her residence unit to say hello.

"Not really," he said. "Nobody I can just drop in on."

"You have a big fat ledger full of ags and no attachments," Tristan said. "Coriolis City is made for people like that. Walk around for an afternoon. Check the service directories. Just go out at night and hop into whatever place looks interesting. If you've forgotten how to spend your leisure time, this is the place to learn that skill again."

"Spoken like a subject-matter expert," Decker said. "All right, they're sending over the chipper one to come fetch us. Let's get down there and turn our brains off for a while. After this week, I'm ready for some mindless debauchery."

———

The flight down to Coriolis City was so smooth that it felt like they were in a gentle simulator ride, and the lack of portholes and viewscreens in the shuttle's luxurious cabin only contributed to the effect. When Aden asked about the absence of visuals, Maya told him that it was standard procedure to leave the external views deactivated because too many off-worlders found the daytime descent into the planetary atmosphere terrifying instead of interesting.

Aden had seen the main atrium at the Coriolis City spaceport before, but the effect was still every bit as stunning as it had been the first time he had walked up the ramp from the arrivals area, many years and two lifetimes ago. He thought of the kid he had been back then, still thoroughly wet behind the ears, convinced by upbringing and privilege that everything was laid out for him to seize as he wanted. He had almost nothing in common with the version of him that had looked at the bustling city on the other side of the massive panoramic viewport twenty years ago.

"All right," Decker said when they were all standing in the middle of the atrium. "Drinks tomorrow evening at the usual place. Someone flick Aden the location, please. You know the drill until then."

"There's a drill?" Aden asked.

"When we have a week or more somewhere, we spend the first twenty-four hours by ourselves," Tess explained. "Can be more if you want it to be. Can't be less. No hanging out, no Mnemosyne messages, no vidcoms. We are stacked in close quarters on the ship for weeks and months. The twenty-four–zero rule is so we get some scheduled time off from each other."

"And to have a window where you can do all the weird shit you don't want everyone else to know about," Tristan added with a craggy smile. "All right, I am off for my scheduled weird shit. See you all tomorrow evening."

He winked at Aden and walked off without further ceremony.

Maya nodded at them and followed suit, pointedly walking in a different direction than Tristan had. Then Decker and Henry went off in their own trajectories as well and disappeared in the crowd.

"I sent you the location of the bar for tomorrow night," Tess said. "Try to find your own fun in the meantime. Just don't get killed. And if you get detained, make sure it's a low-bond offense, or we won't be able to get you out. See you tomorrow."

Then Aden was alone in the middle of the vast expanse of the space-port atrium, entirely on his own for the first time since he had stepped into the shuttle off Adrasteia with Decker and Henry three months ago to start his job on *Zephyr*.

After weeks of shipboard life, he didn't feel ready to throw himself into the bustle of the city beyond without some acclimatization first, so he walked over into the atrium mercantile, where dozens of shops offered travel supplies and tourist mementos. He browsed the goods with no intention of buying, just to get used to having strangers around him again. Then he bought a snack and a drink from a food stand and sat down to eat and give his brain a little bit more time to adjust.

The last time I was here, I was Solveig's age, he thought. *Maybe even younger.* He had to think about her precise age—she was born in 900, so she had turned twenty-three in May.

The thought of his sister brought a smile to his face. They had only exchanged brief messages since their Mnemosyne meeting, to keep the electronic intercept opportunities for Ragnar's corporate security division at a minimum. It had been almost a month since their last quick exchange.

I have two weeks off, he thought. *Two weeks in the same location, and the place is littered with Mnemosyne nodes.*

Aden got out his comtab and looked at the translucent slab in his hand for a moment without calling up a screen. Then he decided that the opportunity merited the risk. With that much advance notice, maybe his sister could find the time to meet in the Mnemosyne again.

He brought up a message screen.

> Hey, shorty. Having stationary downtime for the next two weeks. Can we meet in the Syne?

He sent the note off into the Mnemosyne, where quantum entanglement would ensure that his query would reach his sister's clandestine comtab before he'd have the time to put the device back into his pocket, the ninety million kilometers between their devices bridged in an instant because the data bits had no mass.

When he got up and walked back into the middle of the atrium, the sky had taken on a vivid orange hue that was streaked with red, yellow, and white. The slight change in backdrop made the cityscape outside look even more dramatic, as if the orange had increased the contrast of the geometric lines against the chaos of the swirling clouds. There was something undeniably energetic and triumphant about the place, a constant memorial to the resilience and ingenuity of humans, who could find a way to thrive even when it meant spending lifetimes suspended between the heavens and the ground.

If you've forgotten how to spend your leisure time, this is the place to learn that skill again, Tristan had told him.

Aden shouldered his travel bag and walked toward the exit. He had forgotten how to have fun, but now he had time to kill and a bank ledger full of gratuitous spending money, and he suspected that those were the only ingredients he needed to put the truth of Tristan's statement to the test.

CHAPTER 16

DUNSTAN

Minotaur was on the prowl.

They were deep in Rhodian space, on a ballistic trajectory well beyond any of the current transfer lanes after a brisk acceleration burn. Dunstan didn't know who would be waiting for the delivery of the nuclear warhead at the rendezvous coordinates, but he suspected they would find themselves unpleasantly surprised at the nature of the courier vehicle.

"Eleven minutes to turnaround burn," Bosworth said from his station.

"Anything at all on passive, Mayler?"

"Negative," the tactical officer said. "If they're out there, they've got their lights off and their reactor on standby."

"If they're smart," Dunstan said. "Once we turn around and light the drive, they'll see us coming from a long way out. Let's do our best to look like a fast courier and not like a warship. We won't be able to see through our drive plume, but neither will they."

"And then we flip around and light up the neighborhood with the active array, and oops."

"Let's hope the surprise will just be on their side, Mayler. I've had my fill of *oops* moments for a while."

Dunstan looked at the plot, which was empty except for the icon representing *Minotaur*. The frigate was pretending to be a smuggling ship. Sending out recon drones or scanning the space ahead with active sensors would give them away and send their quarry running. Once they turned the ship and fired up their drive to slow down, they'd be blind to anything ahead until the deceleration burn was complete. The element of surprise would work both ways, but he was hedging a bet that *Minotaur* would be able to handle whatever popped up on their active sensors in front of them once they pointed their bow at the target coordinates again. No smuggling crew in their right minds would engage in a fight with a warship of their size, and Dunstan had stacked the cards to make sure running away wouldn't be an option for their quarry either. But if there was one unchanging constant in this business, it was that no engagement ever went as planned.

"Give me a system status on the weapons."

"Green across the board, sir," Lieutenant Mayler replied. "All four rail-gun mounts are warmed up and ready to be energized. Magazines are at one hundred percent. Point defense is on standby."

We're as ready as we're going to be, Dunstan decided. He glanced at the plot again and took a slow breath.

"XO, sound action stations," he said.

"Sound action stations, aye," Lieutenant Bosworth replied. He tapped the comms panel, and the all-ship announcement system blared the alert klaxon.

"Action stations, action stations. All hands to action stations. Set damage control condition Zulu throughout the ship."

Every crew member on *Minotaur* spent the next few minutes securing vacsuits, connecting life support umbilicals, and assuming their assigned battle stations. All over the ship, airtight compartment doors sealed bulkheads to prepare for possible damage. Dunstan had heard the action stations klaxon so many times in his life that the sound would never fail to make the hairs on the back of his neck stand up. He went through his own preparations automatically, his hands performing tasks they had done a thousand times before, tightening restraints and twisting connectors onto receptacles in his gravity couch. There was an odd comfort in the routine, even though it meant they were about to take the ship into danger. It gave his hands something to do and his mind the feeling that he was in control.

"All stations report ready for action, sir," Bosworth said.

"Very well. Midshipman Boyer, commence turnaround and deceleration burn."

"Turn for deceleration burn, aye," Boyer confirmed. This was her first deployment cruise, but after three months of patrol that had included two combat encounters, she had lost all her initial timidity and nervousness. *Minotaur* and her current crew had seen more action than any other fleet unit since the end of the war.

Except for Danae, Dunstan reminded himself. Whoever had waylaid and destroyed the unlucky light cruiser could very well be waiting for *Minotaur* at the end of this deceleration burn. But this ship was ready for a fight.

Still, as Dunstan looked around the battle-ready AIC, he couldn't shake the unwelcome memory of the bodies drifting among the wreckage of *Danae*, a ship that had been ten years newer than his frigate and twice as powerful.

———

"We are down to maneuvering speed," Boyer announced at the end of their deceleration burn. "Cutting the main drive in thirty seconds."

"Steady as she goes," Dunstan said. "Tactical, go active on the forward array as soon as we come out of the turn. Let's take a good close look at the neighborhood."

Minotaur had run her plasma drive at full throttle to slow down from her ballistic coasting velocity as quickly as possible. The physics of a drive plume at maximum thrust meant that they had been flying blind for the last hour and a half because the sensors could not see through the noise and thermal bloom. In thirty seconds, they'd be able to open their eyes again and see what was ahead. As much as Dunstan wanted to get his hands on the people who were trying to take delivery of a weapon of mass destruction, part of him was hoping they'd find nothing but empty space in front of them.

"Standing by for active sensor sweep," Mayler said.

Minotaur's main drive throttled back to its idle setting. Dunstan felt only a slight moment of discomfort as the gravmag generator at the bow of the ship spun down at the same time to keep the gravity on the ship at one standard g.

"Commencing turnaround," Boyer said.

Dunstan watched the tactical display rotate as Boyer used *Minotaur's* thrusters to spin the ship around its lateral axis.

"Turnaround complete. Coasting at one point five kilometers per second."

"Energizing main sensor array," Mayler said. The tactical display changed color to indicate the active radiation they were emitting to scan the space ahead. They had just done the space warfare equivalent of walking backward into a dark basement, turning around, and switching on a very bright flashlight. If any shooting was going to start, it would happen in the next few moments.

Five seconds passed, then ten. The tactical display remained unchanged, with only *Minotaur* sitting in the center of the three-dimensional holographic orb. Then a lone gray icon appeared on the display, accompanied by a notification alert sound.

"Contact," Mayler called out. "Bearing 299 by 11, distance eight hundred kilometers, designate *Sultan-1*. Moving at twenty meters per second."

"Just hanging out and waiting for their delivery," Dunstan said. "And right within ten thousand klicks of the coordinates the courier crew gave us."

"No transponder signal, and their drive is cold, sir."

"They're running dirty. Because *of course* they are. Open comms and give me a link." Dunstan picked up his comms set.

"You're on, sir," Mayler said.

"Attention, unidentified vessel," Dunstan said. "This is RNS *Minotaur*. You are in Rhodian space without a valid transponder ID broadcast or transfer-lane exemption. Identify yourself and state your destination and intent at once."

The comms remained silent. On the plot, the icon for the unknown ship plodded along on its trajectory, still without a transponder identifier. Space-traffic transponders sent their ID automatically every few seconds. They had backups for redundancy, and unless the ship had suffered a complete loss of all power sources, there was only one reason why a civilian ship would turn off their transponder.

"They're not even trying the 'broken comms gear' ruse," Lieutenant Bosworth said. "As if we'll leave them alone if they pretend they can't hear us."

"Well, there isn't much they could be saying, Bosworth. We're a long way from any of the transfer lanes. 'We just happened to be drifting around in the neighborhood' won't cut it, and they know that."

He considered the plot for a moment.

"Helm, lay in an intercept course. Weapons, keep a lock on them with the fire-control system. Just so they don't have any misconceptions about our willingness to play games."

"Aye, sir," Mayler replied.

"Sir, the bogey just changed heading. They've turned away from us and gone to three and a half g."

"Guess they noticed the target lock." Dunstan watched the green icon on the display make a ninety-degree course change and increase speed.

"Match their acceleration and put in half a g on top," he ordered. "Let's have them in intercept range in twenty. No need to rush things."

"The AI is still working on an ID, sir. It's a commercial medium-output plasma drive signature. We aren't close enough for a good hull profile scan yet, and their drive plume is muddling things up now."

"No worries, Mayler. We'll catch up with them soon enough. If three and a half is the best they can do, it'll be a short chase."

"Why would they even try to run? They're too far inside our intercept envelope. It wouldn't make a difference if they burned twice as hard."

"People do dumb things when they panic, Lieutenant. They know they can't fight us. So they went for flight."

Dunstan shook his head at the sight on the plot. *Minotaur* was now burning at almost four g, and the gray icon was no longer increasing the distance. The skipper on the bogey was either supremely optimistic or terrible at math, because there was no way he'd be able to outrun the Rhodian warship bearing down on him.

"If he turns, we turn right along with him," Dunstan said. "Nice and easy. He's got nowhere to run."

The other ship continued its futile flight as *Minotaur* closed the gap slowly but steadily. With every passing minute, the sensor AI got a better picture of the ship they were chasing.

"We got ID on the bogey," Mayler said after a few minutes. "She's an Oceanian merchant. OMV *Winds of Asterion*."

"What does the database have on them?"

"It's a supply ship. Part of the civilian merchant component for their spacelift command. She's supposed to be laid up in the reserve fleet yard."

"I guess someone took her out for a joyride. Any armament on that type?"

"Negative, sir," Mayler replied. "Not from the factory anyway. But it's really hard to bolt something to a merchie hull that'll hurt a warship."

"They're trying to take delivery of a nuke, Lieutenant. I'm not trusting any blueprints. Not after *Daphne*. Assume they're armed to the teeth and getting ready to blow us out of space."

The chirp of a notification alert drew Dunstan's eyes over to the tactical display. Another green icon had appeared, this one in the general path of *Winds of Asterion*'s heading and well in front of them.

"New contact," Mayler called out. "Bearing 23 by negative 39, distance eighty-five thousand kilometers. Designate *Sultan-2*."

He turned to look at Dunstan.

"Sir, contact *Sultan-2* is accelerating. At ten and a half g."

Dunstan stared at the new icon on the plot. The numbers next to it that showed bearing, acceleration, and velocity increased so quickly that the unknown ship could only have a military-grade drive and a gravmag generator.

Guess they brought backup, he thought. He'd been expecting an unpleasant surprise ever since they came out of their burn, but it still sent a chill down his spine to see that his paranoia had been justified.

"Get me a course projection and target ID for *Sultan-2* now. And put out all the drones and set them to active recon mode."

"They're headed for a shortest-time intercept with us," Mayler said. "At our closing rate, time to engagement-range limit is nine minutes. The AI is working on an ID right now."

Dunstan took a deep breath to steady himself. The most agonizing part of being the commander of a warship was the weight resting on his decisions, and right now he had very little time and data to make his next call. The commander of the unknown ship either had strong suicidal ideations, or he was confident he could take on a battle-ready

Rhodian frigate. Or it could be a ruse, and the new contact was a small ship with a powerful drive, intending to throw *Minotaur* off their pursuit and then outrun them. But if he waited for the AI to come up with a definitive ID, it would be too late to make that call. The odds were low, but if he rolled the dice wrong, he'd be forced into an engagement on someone else's terms, with no way to control the situation.

Sometimes it's not the odds that make a bet unwise, he decided. *Sometimes it's the stakes.*

"Helm, bring the drive to emergency power. Have the AI plot us a trajectory that will keep the distance between us and *Sultan-2* as wide as possible for as long as we can."

"Aye, sir." Boyer looked pale, but she jumped into action without hesitation, her hands flying over the data fields on her control panel. When the drive fired up to maximum output, Dunstan could feel the tug-of-war between the plasma rocket that was subjecting them to ten g of acceleration and the gravmag array that countered the g-forces to keep the crew alive.

On the tactical screen, *Winds of Asterion* continued her slow flight, her icon moving from ahead of *Minotaur* to her port side as the frigate made a wide turn. A few moments later, the icon for *Sultan-2* changed its direction as well, nudging the predicted trajectory to converge with *Minotaur's* new course.

"They are coming back on track for a shortest-time intercept," Bosworth reported. "They have almost a full g of acceleration advantage. We won't be able to keep them at bay for very long."

A message screen popped up in front of Mayler's station, and Dunstan could see the tactical officer's face blanch even in the semi-darkness of the AIC's red combat illumination.

"The AI has positive ID on *Sultan-2*," he said. "Sir, it's GNS *Sleipnir*. The Gretian gun cruiser from the internment yard."

There was a moment of absolute silence in the AIC.

"Show me that ID assessment," Bosworth said sharply. Mayler opened another instance of his screen and flicked it over to Bosworth's station, then repeated the process to put another copy in front of Dunstan.

"Eighty-eight percent certainty on the hull," Bosworth read. "The drive profile is a ninety percent match. That can't be right. Where did they get a crew trained for that thing in three months?"

Every set of eyes in the AIC turned toward Dunstan. He knew that the eerie calm he suddenly felt was out of place for this situation. If the AI was right, and the contact bearing down on them was really GNS *Sleipnir*, they were about to head into a fight that would be all but impossible to win. The Gretian heavy-gun cruiser was almost twice the mass of *Minotaur* and far more heavily armed. And it had been designed to hunt and kill frigates and light cruisers. The Gretians had preferred to operate their ships autonomously as commerce raiders, so they had been equipped to outgun everything they could catch and outrun everything that had more firepower.

"Lieutenants, I hope you still remember the simulated scenarios you ran against that ship a few months ago," he said to Bosworth and Mayler. "Because we're about to need that knowledge."

He turned his head toward the helm station.

"Boyer, get ready to hand the conn to the AI for evasive action. Fully autonomous mode."

"Aye, sir. Preparing for AI conn, full auto," Boyer replied. "We can't outrun them forever, sir. Not with their acceleration advantage."

"We don't have to outrun them forever. We just have to keep them at range so we can let our point-defense AI chew up their ordnance. Mayler, how many gun mounts does that thing have again?"

"Six double mounts, sir. Four-and-a-half-second cycle time. One hundred and sixty rounds per minute for the full broadside."

"*Damn,*" Dunstan said. *Minotaur* only had four single mounts, each with eight-second firing cycles, which added up to only thirty rounds per minute.

"And theirs are two hundred millimeters to our one fifties, sir. They have more broadside weight than any two of our cruisers put together."

"They'll want to get in close so they can tear us up with those quick-firing two hundreds," Dunstan said. "With that rate of fire, even the AI can't avoid everything. Not if they get inside a hundred kilometers."

On the plot, the symbol for contact *Sultan-2* had changed to the bright green, denoting a hostile Gretian warship, something he hadn't seen on the hologram in almost five years. *Minotaur* was burning her drive at full power, but the Gretian cruiser was closing the gap a little with every passing moment.

Five years ago, we could have outrun them, he thought. On the spec sheet, they were faster than the Gretian cruiser. *Minotaur's* maximum design acceleration had been almost twelve g when she was brand-new, but that was thirty years and many tens of thousands of reactor hours ago. Now she couldn't break ten g even if they ignored all the safety margins and pushed everything to the limit.

"Four minutes until they are in engagement range, sir," Bosworth said.

Dunstan looked around the AIC. Every face he saw showed the same anxiety and fear. These were the pre-battle jitters, the brain trying to process the reality of impending mortal danger. He knew the junior crew were looking to him to give them reassurance. He was only forty-six, but so many of these officers were not even half his age. To them he was the Old Man, the only member of the crew who had lived through the entire war. He was supposed to know what to do, what to say to make them feel a little less afraid. A lie wouldn't do, but he could put an optimistic coat of paint on the grim reality.

"Bosworth, all-ship announcement," he ordered.

"You're on, sir," his XO said.

"All hands, this is the commander," Dunstan announced.

He paused for a moment to gather his thoughts.

"We are about to do something nobody has done in half a decade. We are about to engage a Gretian warship. The *last* Gretian warship. The only remaining ship of the fleet that killed our brothers and sisters, our friends and comrades. The fleet that we defeated, that's now radioactive debris between Rhodia and Tethys. And once we are done with this ship, there'll be nothing left of their fucking navy."

He was satisfied to see a grim smile on the face of Lieutenant Mayler.

"I don't know who stole that cruiser," Dunstan continued. "I don't know who's crewing it right now. But I do know that we are better at this business than they are. We've been doing this for a while. And we know our ship inside and out. They haven't even had time to get used to theirs. Everyone stand to your posts. Let's give these people an object lesson on why the Rhodian Navy won the war. Commander out."

He nodded at Bosworth and leaned back in his gravity couch.

"The nearest fleet unit is far away. We're on our own. And we can't go up against a heavy cruiser by ourselves and expect to come out in one piece," Bosworth said in a low voice.

Dunstan shook his head with a sigh.

"No, we can't. I think this old girl is about to fight her last battle, Lieutenant. However this plays out."

"Let's make sure it's the last one for that fuzzhead cruiser, too," Bosworth said.

———

For the next four minutes, *Minotaur*'s AI played a cat-and-mouse game with the helm controller of the Gretian ship. The frigate changed course at random to throw off the intercept angles and force the enemy cruiser to respond with a new course change. But with the acceleration advantage the other ship had over *Minotaur*, it was clear that they'd run out of angles for course changes very soon. On the display, the bubble showing the projected range of the Gretian cruiser's armament crept ever closer to the range of *Minotaur*'s own weapons. Physically, there was no limit to the range of a missile or a rail-gun projectile in a vacuum, but in practice, hit probability increased as distance decreased. The point-defense AI could fry warheads and dodge shells with near-absolute accuracy if the flight time of the incoming weapon was long enough.

"Twenty seconds until engagement threshold," Mayler said.

"Open hatches on missile tubes one through twelve. Set tubes four and six to intercept pattern Theta Two Niner and launch as soon as they get in range." Dunstan watched as the two range-marker bubbles approached each other's thresholds.

"If we're lucky, they haven't had a software update for their point-defense AI since that ship was commissioned," he said.

"Their PDS is a slug system," Mayler said. "If the database is right, they never got directed energy mounts."

"That's good. If their point defense is all guns, it means they can run out of bullets."

"Ten seconds. Standing by for launch on tubes four and six. Intercept pattern Theta Two Niner is laid in," Mayler said. He was all business now, surrounded by half a dozen tactical subdisplays, a focused expression on his face.

"Let's stick to the protocol. Give them a warning before we start flinging war shots," Dunstan said. "But don't let on that we know what they are."

Bosworth nodded and opened the comms panel.

"Unidentified vessel on intercept course, this is the warship RNS *Minotaur*," he sent. "Power down your drive and cease your approach immediately, or we will assume hostile intent and open fire."

The reply came just a moment later. It was spoken in Rhodian, not run through a translator AI, and Dunstan could only make out a faint accent that could have been Oceanian or Gretian.

"*RNS* Minotaur, *this is* Valravn. *Here is our counterproposal. Shut down your weapons grid and your active transmissions and set your reactor to standby. Comply in the next thirty seconds, and we will spare your crew. Fail to comply, and we will close in and destroy your ship, and every escape pod you launch.* Valravn *out.*"

"*Valravn?*" Mayler looked at Bosworth and Dunstan.

"The Raven of the Slain," Dunstan supplied. "From Norse mythology. If my memory serves me right. It's been a while since I took that class."

"Well, the Raven of the Slain just crossed into engagement range, sir," Bosworth said. "One hundred twenty kilometers. What's our response?"

"We will send it their way. Lieutenant Mayler, fire tubes four and six. Midshipman Boyer, hand helm control to the AI."

Mayler flipped the safeties off the hardware buttons for the missile-launch tubes.

"Firing four. Firing six."

The igniting drives of the heavy antiship missiles sent a low vibration through the hull. On the tactical display, two more icons appeared next to *Minotaur* and rushed toward the incoming contact.

"Missiles away at fifty g. Both seeker heads are tracking *Sultan-2*. Time to target, twenty-two seconds," Mayler said. "Range is down to one ten. *Sultan-2* is coming about to two hundred degrees relative."

In response to the incoming missiles, the Gretian cruiser had altered its course to show its broadside to the warheads and bring the maximum number of point-defense guns to bear. From now on, it would be a duel between computers, both ships' AI systems trying to outwit and outmaneuver each other, analyzing data and making decisions far faster than any human could.

"Fifteen seconds to impact. *Sultan-2* has reduced their burn to under five g."

"Diverting energy for their point defense," Dunstan said. "I thought you said they didn't have a directed energy PDS."

"No, sir. And no way they could have gotten one fitted. Not in three months."

On the plot, several new contacts popped up between *Sultan-2* and the incoming missiles from *Minotaur*.

"*Sultan-2* is firing at our ASMs," Mayler said. "With their rail-gun mounts."

"At that range? That's a waste of slugs," Bosworth said.

On the plot, the missiles changed course to avoid the incoming rail-gun fire. They weaved through the volley of tungsten slugs and reacquired their target with ease. Rail-gun shot moved at five kilometers per second, which was slow motion to a seeker-head AI at over fifty kilometers, when the computer had ten seconds to calculate an evasive maneuver.

"Welcome to postwar tech," Bosworth commented. "Too bad about those five years of missed software updates."

"Ten seconds to impact," Mayler narrated the plot display. "*Sultan-2* has increased burn to eight g again. Seven seconds. Five seconds."

Maybe this won't be a hard fight after all, Dunstan thought.

On the optical feed, the flank of the distant Gretian cruiser seemed to erupt into flame as hundreds of thermal bloom signatures lit up the hull. One of the missile icons disappeared from the tactical display in a blink. The other changed course, but a second later, there was a brief flash on the infrared spectrum, and the second ASM was gone from the plot as well.

"Both birds are down," Mayler said. "Successful intercept by the enemy at two point five kilometers range. Doesn't look like the ballistic debris scored a hit either."

"Good gods, look at that point-defense fire," Bosworth said. "That's a lot of explosive shells. We'll have a bitch of a time getting anything through that flak field. Modern seeker heads or not."

"We have incoming," Mayler warned. On the plot, a dozen contact symbols appeared next to the Gretian cruiser and rushed toward *Minotaur*. "They're returning fire with their gun battery."

Minotaur's AI analyzed the incoming rail-gun rounds and maneuvered the ship to avoid them. It seemed like a waste of ammunition on the part of their enemy to throw slugs at this range. But five seconds after the first salvo, another followed, then another. By the time the first dozen rounds had covered three-quarters of the distance between the Gretian cruiser and *Minotaur*, twenty-four more were following behind in two intervals.

"Point defense is in autonomous mode and tracking," Mayler said. The ship turned and twisted its way between the trajectories from the first salvo, and the slugs passed harmlessly above and below the hull. But the next broadside was just five seconds behind, and from the way the shots were dispersed, Dunstan knew that the AI on the Gretian ship was trying to anticipate their evasive maneuver, adjusting the follow-up shots to put them where *Minotaur* was likely to be next. The ship avoided the second spread, dropping from an eight-g burn to three g and then back to seven in the span of a few seconds. When the third salvo arrived, the Point Defense System went into action for the first time, blotting two of the rail-gun slugs out of space with a few megawatts of focused energy. And the Gretian cruiser continued to pump out broadsides, twelve slugs every four and a half seconds, saturating the space between them with salvo after salvo.

"We can't stand up to this rate of fire," Bosworth said. "Not even at this range."

Dunstan didn't know how many slugs the Gretian cruiser had in its gun battery magazines, but he doubted that *Minotaur* could keep up this dance until the enemy had shot those guns dry. The reactor was already running at maximum, splitting its output between the main drive and the Point Defense System. And despite their efforts to keep the distance open, the other ship had gained several kilometers on them since they had started their barrage.

Dunstan considered responding in kind and letting Mayler open fire with *Minotaur's* own rail guns, but he dismissed the impulse right away. They only had four barrels, and the energy needed to fire them would divert megawatts of power away from the propulsion and Point Defense Systems. The rate of fire on their guns wasn't nearly enough to duplicate the Gretian cruiser's tactics anyway, he decided.

"Open all remaining missile tubes," he ordered. "We have to give their AI something to do other than aim those fucking gun mounts at us. Maybe it's enough to saturate their point defenses."

"Aye, sir. Opening tubes one through sixteen." Mayler flicked the safety caps off all the launch buttons on his console in quick succession.

"Randomize the intercept patterns and fire. Flush out everything we have left."

"Firing one through three. Firing five. Firing seven through sixteen." Mayler punched the remaining launch buttons. "All birds are away and tracking at fifty g. Time to target nineteen seconds."

The space between the two ships became a chaotic display of overlapping sensor echoes. The Gretian cruiser kept up its broadside fusillades, twelve rounds every five seconds, and *Minotaur* weaved her way through the stream of tungsten slugs. Out of every salvo they dodged, one or two rounds got close enough to the ship to trigger the point-defense emitters. *Minotaur's* missiles rushed past the incoming storm of rail-gun slugs and toward the Gretian cruiser, which turned fully broadside to them again to bring the maximum number of point-defense guns to bear.

A shudder went through *Minotaur's* hull. Over at Lieutenant Bosworth's station, a data screen materialized in front of him and began flashing red text and blinking diagrams.

"We took a hit to the aft port section," Bosworth reported. "Hull penetration between frames forty-four and forty-five. Went through and exited the dorsal section right behind the aft missile tubes. We've lost the capacitor bank for the starboard emitters on the stern."

Dunstan suppressed a curse. With one hit, they had lost 25 percent of their point-defense capability. The slugs from rail guns traveled at five thousand meters per second, and they punched straight through warship hulls wherever they hit. There were not too many angles where a tungsten slug could travel through the hull without hitting anything important. They'd lose essential components with every hit, and the resulting cascade failures would make it easier for the Gretian cruiser to score follow-up hits.

"Time to target on the birds is ten seconds," Mayler said. The fourteen icons representing *Minotaur*'s guided missiles had passed another incoming rail-gun volley and were now starting to converge on the enemy cruiser, the AI seeking to overwhelm the other ship's Point Defense System with warheads coming in from as many angles as possible.

Another hit shook the ship, then a third. This time, Dunstan could tell that something major had taken a blow. The lights in the AIC dimmed, then returned to normal before going out altogether. For a terrifying second, the AIC was in complete darkness. Then the illumination returned, and the tactical hologram and display projections popped back into existence.

"Direct hit on the main power trunk and secondary data core," Bosworth shouted. "We are running on the backup trunk. The number-one water tank is venting into space."

Dunstan returned his attention to the tactical display in time to see the sensor echoes from the Gretian cruiser clutter the space in front of the missiles from *Minotaur*, which were now just a few seconds away from their target.

"Enemy point defense is engaging our birds," Mayler said.

"Come *on*," Dunstan pleaded. The flak field from the Gretian cruiser's point-defense gun mounts was stupendous. On the optical feed, it looked like the side of the enemy ship was on fire from bow to stern. Fourteen missiles turned to eight, then six, then four in just a few seconds. Then the point-defense fire and the explosions of the disintegrating antiship missiles were too much for the sensors to sort out at this range, and the area of space around the Gretian cruiser washed out into a blob of thermal bloom.

It took a few moments for the sensors to burn through the noise again. When they did, Mayler let out a triumphant little shout.

"Target hit," he said. "Some of our birds got through. They're trailing air. Their acceleration dropped to four g."

On the tactical screen, the regular salvos from the Gretian rail guns had ceased. *Minotaur* dodged one more broadside that had been on the way already before the cruiser had switched its fire control to point defense. Dunstan held his breath in expectation of another hit, this one maybe through the reactor core or the AIC, ending the fight on the spot by killing them all in a blink. But the AI weaved the ship through the salvo, and Dunstan released his breath when the last of the tungsten slugs had passed fifty meters to stern. He could practically hear a collective sigh of relief in the AIC.

"We can't take another exchange like this," Lieutenant Bosworth said.

"Our missile tubes are empty anyway. And we'll never survive a gun battle with that thing. Turn us away and get some distance before they get their batteries going again. And give me a damage assessment. For us and them."

———

Minotaur was badly hurt. The second hit had caused damage to the power transfer network and reduced the reactor's output by half for reasons the damage-control AI had yet to figure out. They were accelerating away from the enemy cruiser at an angle to keep from presenting their opponent with an easy stern shot. But whatever hit they had scored seemed to have hurt the Gretian ship at least as much. The cruiser was trailing air and debris, and it made no effort to come about and close the distance again.

"Looks like we got a solid missile hit on their stern section," Mayler reported once the AI had done its damage assessment. "Their drive signature is flickering like a campfire. They're down to three and a half g. The other hit we scored was likely ballistic debris from a close intercept."

"If we nicked their reactor core, they may not have enough juice to run those rail guns," Bosworth said. "We have a half g of acceleration on them right now. We could close in and give them a dose of their own medicine."

Dunstan shook his head.

"That's not a gamble I'm willing to make. If they get their fusion plant patched up while we're chasing them, they'll tear us to pieces in three broadsides. We need to use that acceleration advantage to get out of here while we still can. We're lucky we still have air in the hull. Mostly."

Dunstan watched the Gretian cruiser opening the distance between them on the plot with a mixture of relief and frustration. They were out of the effective range of those murderous rail-gun batteries now, but they had no weapons of their own left to throw at the enemy ship. Space combat between modern warships was short and brutal, and nobody ever went home without holes in the hull and dead crew members in body bags. The screen above Bosworth's station was still scrolling through damage reports and diagrams as the AI's survey and repair units discovered more broken hardware in *Minotaur*'s hull. The third rail-gun hit had almost broken their back. That single 200 mm tungsten slug had torn through bulkheads and hull plating, severed power conduits and data trunks, disabled the ammunition feed for one of the rail-gun mounts, and damaged enough support frames on its short and violent passage through the hull that it would take a month in a fleet yard to put *Minotaur* back into fighting shape. Dunstan knew that his frigate was at the bottom of the priority list for yard work anyway, and there was a good chance the battle damage she had just suffered would see her decommissioned and consigned to the scrapyard.

"Where's that damn merchant? *Winds of Asterion*?"

Mayler expanded the tactical display until the icon for the Oceanian ship showed up.

"Still running away in a straight line, still at three and a half g. Distance is now eight thousand two hundred kilometers."

"And we can't chase them because they've got that gun cruiser between us and them." Dunstan frowned at the green icon representing the Gretian warship.

"We've already alerted the fleet. RNS *Circe* and *Agamemnon* are on the way," Bosworth said. "And half a dozen Home Fleet units. They'll find them and chase them down."

Dunstan knew that *Minotaur* had performed as well as anyone could have hoped for against a vastly superior opponent, and that the missile strike they had scored on the Gretian cruiser would put that ship out of action for a while even if they escaped the Rhodian Home Fleet units that were coming to hunt them. But it still felt like a defeat to have to let the Gretian warship accelerate away without further challenge.

"Got some more good news," Bosworth added. "Casualty report says eleven wounded, no KIA."

Dunstan closed his eyes briefly and let out a relieved sigh. To have lost no crew members after that encounter was almost unbelievable luck.

"I hate calling this a draw," he said. "But that's what it's going to have to be for today."

"Just this round," Mayler said.

Dunstan shook his head.

"If we're counting this in rounds, they won this one by points, Mayler. And I don't think we'll be out of our corner again. Not with this old girl."

As if to underscore her commander's point, *Minotaur*'s AIC lights flickered again, and another row of warning messages scrolled across Lieutenant Bosworth's damage-control screen.

"Set a least-time course for Rhodia One at maximum safe burn," Dunstan ordered. "Bow toward the good guys, stern toward the bad guys. And let's hope nothing essential falls off the ship before we get there."

CHAPTER 17

IDINA

The mood in the Gretian police headquarters was visibly dark. Idina noticed few people standing around in the offices and conversing. Almost every Gretian officer that crossed her and Dahl's path through the building either expressed sympathy to her in some way or simply gave her a grim, knowing nod. No Gretian cops had died in the bombing, but all eight members of the JSP's quick-reaction squad had perished, along with eleven Gretian civilians that had been guests at the capsule hotel. Idina expressed her own anger and grief by wearing her full don't-fuck-with-me combat armor, accessorized with a sidearm, multiple spare ammunition cassettes, and a subcompact machine pistol hanging on a sling in front of her chest armor plate. It would do nothing to save her from an explosion of that order, but it made her feel better, and it sent a clear message regarding her willingness to engage in confrontation.

"The chemical analysis is not complete yet," Dahl said next to her as they walked along the central corridor of the building, causing Gretian officers to swerve out of their way or duck into nearby offices to avoid them. "But all indicators point toward a binary explosive, possibly artillery propellant from Gretian military stocks."

"Surprise," Idina said. "That's how they got my squad out in the field three months ago. A rail gun to draw our attention, make us bunch up and get us all in the same spot. And then boom. I bet you my kukri that these were the same people."

"I would not take that bet," Dahl said. "The odds would be heavily in your favor. And even if they were not, I would never try to claim the win."

"It's a brigade expression," Idina said. "You use it when you are absolutely sure of something. No brigade trooper would ever give up their kukri willingly."

"The residue and explosive strength indicated the presence of at least two hundred liters of binary artillery propellant in the basement prior to the detonation. This is not something you carry into a building in a backpack on short notice. They set that trap for us well in advance."

"Which means Fuldas was part of it. The question remains whether he was in on the whole thing. Or if they decided to shut him up for certain before he could get off the planet."

"It just so happens that we have someone in custody who may know," Dahl said.

"Let's go ask him. And I hope for his sake that he isn't into playing games today. Because I am all out of patience for those."

———

Haimo was seated at a steel table in the middle of one of the small interrogation rooms. He was wearing restraints around his wrist, which had been tethered to an eye hook on the floor, leaving very little slack for movement. He looked up when they walked into the room, and his expression wasn't unsure or fearful anymore. Instead, he looked calm and composed. He gave Idina a pleased little smirk that told her he knew about the bombing. For all their reputation as a hard-nosed law-and-order society, the Gretians were surprisingly lenient with their detainees once they were in state custody. She had been surprised to learn that they were even allowed limited Mnemosyne usage because the state considered access to information a human right.

Some police state, she thought as she returned Haimo's gaze without expression. *On Pallas, you would be in a windowless cell right now, with a hole in the ground for a toilet you'd be shitting blood into after each interrogation.*

Dahl did not offer a greeting. She walked over to the table and put a translator earbud down in front of Haimo.

"The sergeant and I have a few questions for you," Dahl said. "If you would."

Haimo looked at the earbud as if he had never seen one before in his life. Then he raised his hands to the tabletop, which was the maximum range of movement the tether allowed. He picked up the earbud and threw it across the room, where it bounced off the wall and clattered on the floor.

"I will talk to *you*, maybe," he said to Dahl. "I do not want to hear anything out of *that* one."

He nodded his head at Idina with distaste.

Idina looked at him, and he held her gaze, the smug little smile still in the corners of his mouth. It was like looking at a different person. This wasn't the kid they had scared shitless just a few days ago, the one who had been upset about losing his job. Idina was in full battle gear and armed to the teeth, and he was demonstratively unconcerned about it.

I wonder if the scared kid was an act, or if this cocky one is, she thought. Pallas and Gretia had no history of conflict, no major cultural friction points before the last war. She had no idea why this kid and the people like him hated her so much. Maybe it was the fact that of all the other planets, Pallas's population looked the most obviously non-Gretian. Or maybe this kid knew that Palladians had killed more Gretian soldiers on the ground than all other Alliance planets combined. They had given the Gretian veterans a legacy of generational nightmares about sharp blades in dark places. She hoped he hated her for the Palladian battle skills and not for her color, because that sort of rage seemed tiresome and stupid to expend on someone due to the melanin content of their skin.

So much rage, she thought. *It will get you killed before you have a chance to get old enough for knowledge. You'll never even know that you've wasted your life, or why.*

And that would be fine with her right now, except that he wouldn't be the only one who ended up dead. There were eight body bags in the morgue at Joint Base Sandvik right now, and most of them didn't contain anything except a few scraps of tissue. All those young men and women were dead, their histories and ambitions wiped out in a few nanoseconds, every one of them leaving long-lived ripples of grief in their circles of friends and families with the heavy impact of their senseless deaths. And this little shit was happy about it.

"Captain Dahl," she said without taking her eyes off Haimo's face.

"Sergeant."

"I've never asked you for any favors since we started patrolling together. I am asking you now. Go step outside for a minute and get a cup of coffee, please."

Dahl didn't reply right away. When Idina looked at her, the older woman's emotional conflict was obvious on her face. She knew how Dahl felt right now, knew the magnitude of what she was asking of her. Three months of cautious friendship were not enough to put on the scale and be weighed fairly against thirty years of principled service.

"I'll be on the flight back to Pallas at the end of the week. But many of these kids will die. Yours and mine. Our side and theirs. Let me do this one thing before I leave. We can try to put a stop to it."

"You know how I feel about the Pallas way," Dahl said.

"I am asking you to trust me."

Dahl looked from her to Haimo and back. Idina was happy to see the first tiny flicker of doubt crossing Haimo's expression when the Gretian police captain looked at him with something like pity, as if he was already dead.

"I do believe I need some coffee this morning," Dahl finally said. "I did not get enough sleep last night. Too much time spent digging through debris for dead colleagues, you see."

She turned and left the room. The door closed behind her with a soft click that seemed very loud in the silence that followed in her wake.

Haimo looked at Idina again, and the contempt returned to his face. He pursed his cheeks and spat onto the floor next to his chair. Then he sat back as far as his tether allowed and smirked.

Idina had lost any sort of sympathy she had once felt for him due to his age. He'd been shown the road map to the sort of ruin that was waiting for him at the end of the path he had chosen to tread, and he had not taken the chance to step off. Instead, he had quickened his pace. Dumb kid or not, twenty people had died last night, and his deception had been instrumental to their deaths. If he wanted annihilation and ruin, she would give him a taste of it.

She pulled her kukri from its sheath. The blade made a faint ringing sound as she drew it free and stepped in front of the interrogation table. She raised her arm and brought the kukri down on the table with all the force her anger would let her muster. The monomolecular edge bit through the steel surface with an almost melodic pitch as her blow cut the tabletop apart before Haimo could finish blinking in surprise. He recoiled with a yell. She kicked the halves of the tabletop aside. They were still attached to the floor with bolts, so she had to give each half a few kicks to bend them out of her way, but it felt good to stomp something with her boots until it broke. Haimo tried to retreat backward, toppling his chair over in the process, but the tether would only let him get a step or two before it pulled taut and yanked him down on his ass.

Idina swung her kukri in a short arc in front of Haimo. This time, he let out a frightened scream. The blade came down between his legs and chopped through the steel tether and the eye hook that anchored it to the floor. The tether snapped, and the sudden release of tension sent Haimo sprawling on his back. She stepped in front of him. He raised his shackled hands in front of him in an instinctive gesture of defense. She knew that if she aimed her swing well, she could sever both of his arms in one stroke without much effort. All she felt right now was pure, cold, silvery rage.

She pointed the kukri at the earbud Haimo had thrown against the wall.

"Pick it up *now*."

He didn't seem to have any trouble comprehending the meaning of the Palladian words even without the assist of a translator AI. He scrambled to a sitting position, then scooted back until he was up against the wall. When he had made it as far away from Idina as he could, he got to his feet, his face rigid with fear.

She nodded in the direction of the earbud, her kukri still pointed toward it. Haimo made his way around her, as far along the wall as he could, and walked over to the earbud. Then he picked it up and moved to put it into his ear. Once it was seated, Idina nodded with grim satisfaction.

"If that leaves your ear without permission, I will pound it back into your skull so hard that it will remain a permanent part of your head forever," she said. "Now pick up the chair and sit down on it. Don't open your mouth unless you are answering a direct question, or your tongue will be the next thing on that floor. Understand?"

He nodded without looking at her, still all but paralyzed with fear. It took him a few moments to pick up the chair with his shackled hands and put it upright to sit down on it. Once he was seated, she took a step forward to close the distance and crouched down in front of him to bring their eyes to the same level. He flinched when she held up her kukri between them.

"This is what will happen now," she said with certainty. "The Gretian police captain will come back into this room in a few moments. When she does, you will tell her everything you know about the people who did this. You will answer every question without lying or evading. If I think that you are not telling the truth—or gods forbid, if you start talking tough again—I will claim Alliance jurisdiction over you. Then I will haul you off to the brig on Sandvik Base, where I will leave you alone in a locked room with the comrades of the troopers that died last night. The ones whose pieces they had to pick out of the rubble."

She turned the kukri between them. The overhead light in the room glinted off the edge as she moved the blade slowly.

"And every one of the people in the room with you will have one of *these*."

His gaze went from the blade to her. She could almost smell the fear that was radiating from him in waves.

"Do you understand that?" she asked.

It took him a few moments to work up the spit to speak.

"I am not afraid of dying," he finally said, in a strained voice that contradicted the statement.

She smiled without humor.

"But you *should* be," she said. "You should be *terrified*. Because they wouldn't just hack you into tiny bits. They would peel your layers from you first. From head to toe. See how long they can keep you alive while they carve every scrap of skin from your body for what you helped do to their friends. And if you think I am just trying to scare you, look into my eyes and tell me what you see there. Tell me that I am lying."

He didn't take her up on the challenge. Instead, he swallowed hard and stared past her.

"If you dare to test my patience again, you will find that I have none remaining," she continued. "The only reason you're not already in bloody chunks on the floor is because I wouldn't want to deny my comrades the pleasure of dealing with you. They have no outlet for their grief right now. I am hoping you are dumb enough to volunteer yourself for that purpose. It would give me the only true and pure joy I've ever had on this planet."

She sheathed her kukri slowly and deliberately, not so much for psychological effect but out of necessary respect for the weapon. The sheath kept the blade sharpened and in harmless stasis by suspending the cutting edge in a magnetic field, and careless sheathing wasn't wise when that edge could shear through laminated battle armor. When the kukri had locked into the sheath properly, she raised herself out of her crouching stance and walked back across the floor to the spot near the door where she had been standing before, kicking a bent table leg out of her way, demonstratively unconcerned about having her back turned to the now untethered Haimo. He couldn't release her weapons even if he overpowered her, and she knew she'd stomp him into the floor if he tried. But he was cowed now, doubtlessly asking himself if his willingness to die for the cause included getting skinned bit by bit by a platoon of pissed-off Palladians with extremely sharp knives beforehand.

The door opened a silent minute later, and Dahl walked back into the room. The Gretian policewoman looked at the remnants of the interrogation table in front of Haimo. She turned her gaze toward Idina and raised an eyebrow.

"It fell over," Idina explained.

"It fell over," Dahl repeated wryly. "Of that I have no doubt. But I am sure something interesting happened before it did."

"Just working to remove some linguistic barriers, that's all."

"I see." Dahl looked over at Haimo, who still looked like he was a food animal trying to avoid the attention of a nearby predator, intently studying the same spot on the wall without moving any part of his body.

"Well," Dahl said. "Where were we before I felt a sudden need for coffee?"

"We were about to ask Haimo here a few questions," Idina replied. "I do believe we have resolved our earlier technical difficulties in your absence."

"I am very glad to hear it. So, what is it that you think we may want to talk about, Haimo?" Dahl asked in an agreeable voice.

"You want to know about the bombing last night," Haimo replied after a brief, nervous glance at Idina, who returned it stone-faced.

"That is correct. I will not waste my time and yours by playing a game of pretend where you say that you do not know anything about it. We want to know who was behind it. And we will stay in this room until we find out. I may have to go for coffee every now and then."

He looked up at them, the fear and inner conflict evident in his face. After a few seconds, he lowered his eyes, and the tension dropped from his shoulders.

"They are called Odin's Wolves," he said, saying the name of the group in a tone of voice that made him sound like a schoolboy telling his classmates something he feared they would ridicule.

"Odin's Wolves," Dahl repeated. "That is the first time I have heard of them. Who are they?"

Haimo shrugged.

"They are the resistance," he said. "They will rid us of the occupiers. Save us from serfdom to the rest of the system."

"I see. Are you a part of Odin's Wolves, Haimo?"

He shook his head.

"I wish. But they do not take people like me. I was not in the military. I do not know all that much about guns and fighting. But they said there is always a way in if I prove myself."

"And they told you to lead us to Vigi Fuldas," Dahl said.

Haimo nodded.

"They told me that if I got arrested, I should tell the police where I bought the gun if things turned too hot for me."

"Fuldas was with them?"

He nodded again.

"He was not in the military either. But he was good with guns. Fixing them, I mean. Removing biometric locks, that sort of thing. They can always use someone like him."

"Who is *they*?" Dahl asked. "Who set you up with Fuldas and told you to name him if you got busted with that gun? Not the group. I know that name now. Tell me about the people."

The pained look of inner conflict returned to Haimo's face as he considered the question.

"If I tell you and you arrest her, they will know."

"You know what's waiting for you if you don't tell us," Idina reminded him.

He squirmed for a few more seconds, then shook his head and sighed.

"She is someone my father knew in the army," he said. "Someone from his unit. We talked about guns one day, and she told me where I could find one to buy. Her name is Elin."

"Does Elin have a last name?" Dahl probed.

"Elin Sorenson. Corporal Elin Sorenson. But we have not talked in weeks. I do not even know where she lives. I just ran into her one day on the Artery ride home from the spaceport. We met a few times after that, but always out in the city, after work."

"You know what happened the last time you gave us a name and we went looking," Idina said. "You can't be dumb enough to believe we'll fall for the same trick again."

"I did not know," Haimo said. "You said to be honest. I am being honest, I swear it. You know I support what they do. I am not sorry those invaders are dead. But I had no idea what the Wolves were planning."

I don't doubt that, Idina thought. *If these people are military veterans, they know better than to let some expendable kid in on their operational plans.*

She exchanged a glance with Dahl, which told her that the other woman had roughly the same assessment of that answer.

"So Corporal Elin Sorenson said she knew your father. And she told you about Odin's Wolves," Dahl continued. "Go on."

"We got to talking after that thing on Principal Square a few months back," Haimo said. "The bombing. Everyone at work said it was the Alliance because most of the dead were loyalists. She did not tell me anything about the Wolves at first. I was telling her that I wished I knew how to fight back while we still can. Before we become just a Rhodian labor colony with Palladian guards."

He glanced at Idina again.

"She set me up with Vigi. She gave me a loan, too. For the gun. A thousand ags. I told her I would pay her back over time. She said I could make payments whenever I had anything to spare, no hurry."

"Did you sleep with her?" Dahl asked.

From the way his face reddened and his eyes darted around the room before settling on a spot half a meter in front of his feet, Idina knew the answer.

"She is young. Much younger than my father," he said in a slightly defensive tone.

"So you are together. But you have not seen her in a few weeks."

Haimo shrugged.

"She is taking a trip south to Skalanes. To stay with family for a bit. And we are not together. We are just bed friends sometimes. You know how it works. I do not have time to be with anyone."

"I am sure that is exactly what she told *you*," Dahl said. She looked at Idina and sighed. "Young people can be *such* simpletons. Soak a juvenile brain in hormones, and it turns into modeling putty."

"It would have been better if you had told us the full story two days ago," Idina said to Haimo. "You must realize by now that they used you to get us to go after Fuldas."

Haimo shrugged again.

"If that is true, then I have done my share for the Wolves. Once they win, they will open the detention facilities. And people like me will get to leave first. The political prisoners."

Idina suppressed a snort.

"*Political* prisoners," she said.

"That is what I am."

"What you are," she said, "is a single-use tool. And they just used and discarded you."

She could tell he wanted to contradict her, maybe mouth off with something clever, but her warning from earlier still seemed to be fresh in his mind because he bit off his response.

"Fuldas was far more useful to them than you are," she continued. "And they killed him without a second thought when they sprung that trap. Just to tie up a loose end before it could get off the planet and out of their reach. What do you think they would do with you if you weren't in here?"

She shook her head. The rage from earlier had dissipated, leaving only disgust behind in its wake.

"Think about that sometime. In between your fantasies about Elin giving you a hero's welcome."

———

"Do you believe him?" Dahl asked when they left the interrogation room half an hour later, satisfied they'd squeezed every drop of useful information out of Haimo's brain.

"I believe that *he* believed everything he told us," Idina replied. "Whoever recruited him knew exactly what they had in him, and how to use him best. And we fell for it."

"They must have known he would give us the rest," Dahl said. "That is why he only knew one contact other than Fuldas. That way you know exactly who talked when the police come calling. And one person cannot compromise more than one other person in the group."

"So Elin probably knows by now she's been burned."

Dahl nodded.

"If there even is an Elin. They have groomed him for this. They know how to operate in covert cell structures. I very much doubt they would make a mistake and give up one of their own by accident like that. I think that when we go looking for that name, we will find that she died in the war. Or that she never existed."

"There was somebody," Idina said. "Whatever her name is, she recruited this kid. Slept with him, groomed him. Put thoughts of glorious nonsense in his head. Spent time with him in the city. They rode the Artery together. You dig deep enough, you'll discover a face to go with the name. Just look at wherever he popped up in the last three months, and sooner or later you'll find her, too."

Dahl smiled and shook her head lightly.

"Listen to you, giving me investigative pointers. Maybe you have come to like this line of work more than you admit."

"No, thank you. Not enough interrogation tables in the building for that. I'd be bad for the operating budget."

"It was a fair trade, I think. An old table for the truth. What little truth he knew."

"Do you think they made up Odin's Wolves for him, too?" Idina asked. "It sounds exactly like the kind of romantic martial tale you'd spin to rope in young idealists like him."

"There is someone out there behind all of this," Dahl said. "We know they are very organized. They operate in cells. They have money, and access to military equipment. They know how to set sophisticated bombs and execute infantry ambushes. Whether they call themselves 'Odin's Wolves' or not, we have to call them something."

They walked in silence for a few moments.

"Whatever you do once I'm gone, you need to take your steps with care," Idina said. "This is no longer police business, if it ever was. This is well beyond the JSP. It's a full-blown military insurgency. These people know how we operate. And right now they are a step and a half ahead of us everywhere we turn."

"Five years after the war," Dahl said. "Why now? And to what end? They cannot hope to defeat the Alliance on the ground. Not if you gave all the Gretian combat veterans a gun and sent them off to fight in the streets."

"I don't think it's about winning a war. I think it's about starting one. Whoever is behind this wants to turn the clock back about nine years. For whatever insane reason."

They stepped out into the atrium and walked toward the reflecting pool. Outside, the summer was giving one last valiant effort, offering up blue skies and sunshine on a twenty-five-degree day. The third of Gretia's planetary seasons was about to take over and bring with it cool nights and the first frosts.

This place is teetering on the edge of a kukri right now, Idina thought. *If it topples the wrong way, the whole system is going to catch fire again, from Hades all the way out to Pallas. And I have to leave at the worst possible time.*

"*Odin's Wolves,*" Dahl said next to her in a tired voice. "Gods and predators. At what point in all our histories has anything good happened whenever some fool put those on a single banner to march under?"

CHAPTER 18

SOLVEIG

Halfway through the first morning meeting with Hanzo, Solveig decided that her four years of Acheroni language and culture instruction had been mostly a waste of her time.

The Hanzo building made Ragnar Tower look like a drab spaceport warehouse. Hanzo owned an entire block of Coriolis City's most expensive commercial ward, and almost all of that block was taken up by the corporate headquarters, a beautiful structure made of glass and composite latticework that stood a mere three stories tall. It was as delicate as a bird nest and as light and airy as a clearing in a forest. It was also a display of wealth and status, a ludicrously underutilized space in a city where every square meter was precious. All over Coriolis City, Solveig had noticed the predominance of supertall, slender towers that reached into the sky underneath the dome like needles, obviously designed to minimize their footprint on the ground. Hanzo's headquarters showed everyone that the company did not have to concern itself with that sort of sensible efficiency. From what Solveig had learned about Acheron, using space in a wasteful manner was considered uncouth and offensive, but it seemed that she hadn't even begun to understand the dynamics of this culture despite her extended schooling on the subject.

"We do not share the view that the contract between our companies extends to pricing privileges beyond the annual Alon quantities we originally agreed to supply," she said to her counterpart across the table in Gretian.

The Hanzo executive listened to the translation on his earbud and nodded thoughtfully, as if he had heard the statement for the first time just now even though she had told him the same thing in five different ways over the last half hour. Acheroni seemed to have a deep aversion to definitive statements. Solveig had started the negotiations in Acheroni, without the use of translator buds. But she had quickly realized that her limited mastery of the language was a welcome loophole for the Hanzo people to willfully misinterpret her statements in small but important ways, so she had switched to Gretian, irritated that her hosts would try to turn her attempt at courtesy into a negotiation advantage.

"It seems unwise to agree to something that would see us penalized for purchasing more of your production," the Hanzo executive said.

After the initial greeting and introduction by the company president, Hanzo had cycled four different executives through the seat at the head of the table. This one—his predecessor had introduced him as Arata—was a handsome man who looked to be in his sixties, and whose full head of graying hair reminded Solveig of her father's.

"I wouldn't consider it a penalty," Solveig replied. Next to her, Gisbert pretended to listen intently, but he had given up trying to add anything to the conversation a while ago. "Your rate for the out-of-contract quantities you're requesting is better than what we charge anyone else. You still get a favored discount. A *very* favored discount."

"Just not as favored as before," Arata said with a little smile.

"*Exactly* as favored as before," she said. "For the same order volume. Which we agreed upon when our production capacity was much lower."

"And your willing buyers were much fewer in number," Arata said, still with that little smile on his face. "Hanzo has been a loyal business

226

partner since before the late . . . *unpleasantness*. Unlike most of the companies that are now bidding for your increased capacity."

Solveig inclined her head in acknowledgment with an inward sigh.

"We are grateful for your continued partnership. And for the loyalty you have shown Ragnar over the years. Especially through the *unpleasantness*. You are and always have been our biggest and best customer."

Arata nodded.

"But," Solveig continued. "Four years ago, when we resumed operations, you were also our *only* customer. And you got to set the market rate for Alon. Because you *were* the market for us. Now that you are no longer our only buyer, the market rate has gone up. And you have been able to buy at the favored rate while everyone else has driven up the value of the commodity."

Arata turned his palms up. "We abided by the terms of the contract, no more and no less. And we would love to continue our mutually beneficial relationship on similar good terms in the future."

Solveig looked at the compad on the table in front of her, where the main data points of the old agreement were listed in neat bullet format.

"That is also Ragnar Corporation's wish. To maintain the excellent relationship between our companies."

She looked up at Arata again, whose expression had changed subtly. She could tell he knew she was about to make her main pitch, but that he didn't know what to expect, how to translate her polite deflections into a prediction.

"But we cannot afford to continue to sell a considerable percentage of our most valuable product's annual yield at what are now far-below-market prices. Not if we want to remain in business. *Especially* not considering the rate we have to pay for Hanzo graphene composites."

"Ah." Arata folded his hands on the table in front of him. His little smile had returned to his face. "Now we come to the heart of the matter. In the typically direct Gretian fashion."

If we go about this in the Acheroni fashion, I'll be here for three more weeks, Solveig thought. She wouldn't mind the extended time away from home, but the thought of sitting here for days on end and bouncing inoffensive and evasive statements off each other with the Hanzo people had no appeal to her.

A message popped up silently on the comtab in front of her. It was color coded with the data link from her secondary personal comtab, the one whose node number she replaced every few weeks. Only a few people had the address for that node.

Hey, shorty, it read. Having stationary downtime for the next two weeks. Can we meet in the Syne?

Aden.

Solveig suppressed a smile. She looked at the words for a moment and quickly flicked them off the screen before Gisbert could see the message. A glance to the right told her that she was too cautious in this case. He looked like he was about five seconds away from drifting off into a midday nap.

"Forgive the interruption, but I must retire briefly to attend to myself," she said in Acheroni, using the standard phrase she had learned for excusing a visit to the sanitary facilities.

"Of course," her counterpart answered in the same language. He had seen her glance at her comtab, and she knew that he suspected she needed a break to confer with her seniors.

If he wants to think that, so much the better, she thought. *Let him think they just yanked on my leash.*

Arata waved a hand and nodded toward the door, and Kee appeared in the room.

"If you would follow me," Kee said to Solveig with a polite nod. "I will show you the way."

Solveig got up and returned the nod. Kee walked off, and she followed, leaving her corporate compad with the contract details on the table. Another assistant walked in and commenced serving beverages.

"He does not know what to make of you," Kee said to her as they were walking down the skyway in front of the conference room.

"Who, Arata?"

Kee nodded. "He is not used to negotiating with someone as young as you. It throws him off. He does not want to be disrespectful, and yet he does not want to concede or defer too much. You are messing with his . . . what is the word? *Calibration.*"

"His social calibration," Solveig said with a smile. "I get it."

She glanced at Kee, who was wearing a little smile of his own.

"Are you sure you want to be telling me that I make your bosses confused? You should be trying to get information out of *me*. Not feed it my way."

"It amuses me a bit," Kee said. "Even if my parents were directors here, I would not be sitting at a negotiating table yet. One must pay their dues in the lower ranks first. Nobody your age has power here. Not the kind of power to say yes or no to someone like Director Arata. They will hear what you say because of your family name. But they will not believe that the decision was yours."

"As long as they sign whatever we agree on," Solveig said.

If there's anything I know how to handle, it's people who assume I have no agency of my own, she thought.

———

The sanitary suite was more spacious than her living quarters at the university had been, and far more expensively appointed. Solveig did a quick scan of the room with the security sensors of her corporate comtab, which was equipped with the most advanced spy detection algorithms available on the market. When she was satisfied that there were no obvious data sniffers in the room, she took out her personal comtab and opened the message from Aden to reply. Even though the corporate anti-snooping hardware hadn't detected anything overt, she did not allow herself the delusion of thinking her comms to be fully private. They were in Hanzo's corporate headquarters, after all, and she was sure that just like Ragnar, they kept tabs on every data stream in their building. She'd have to change the hardware and the node address of her anonymous device again, and Hanzo would still be able to get through the encryption in a few hours or days. But she wasn't concerned with Hanzo's ability to read her private mail eventually. Personal comms were of little interest to their business, her burner tab would be long gone by then, and she knew that Hanzo would never tip their hand to Ragnar's corporate security anyway.

She read Aden's message again.

> Hey, shorty. Having stationary downtime for the next two weeks. Can we meet in the Syne?

Maybe, but it's hard to get away right now. I'm on Acheron for the company. Corporate escort everywhere, she replied.

She sent the response into the Mnemosyne and walked over to the window of the sanitary suite. It was a piece of Alon that had been coated with a one-way optical layer. Outside, the street was bustling with surface traffic, pedestrians and transit pods streaming by in dense flows. She watched the scene while she turned the comtab in her hands slowly. Aden's reply came a few moments later.

> You're on ACHERON? I'm in Coriolis City right now. We're spending two whole weeks here. Our ride is getting overhauled in the shipyard. Can we meet? In person this time?

Solveig did a double take, and the shock of the surprise felt like someone had electrified her brain stem. They were on the same planet, at the same time. Her habitual paranoia about her father's control and surveillance schemes made her want to erase the comtab and throw it out on the spot. This was too fortunate a coincidence. Six months ago, she would have killed the Mnemosyne conversation, wiped the node address, and flushed the comtab down the sanitary commode. But Aden had used the right one-time code she had given him after their last meeting in the Mnemosyne a month ago. Her sudden excitement at the unexpected possibility of a face-to-face meeting won out over her suspicions.

Who knows when we'll be on the same planet again? she thought. *I told him I don't want to wait another seventeen years.*

Negotiating a new contract, she wrote back. I'll be here for a little while. But they packed my schedule. And I have one of Papa's little birds following me around. Let me see what I can do.

That would be fantastic, Aden replied. But don't take any chances. There's always the Syne later.

Solveig flicked the message string off her comtab screen and tucked the device back into her pocket. Outside of an Acheroni intelligence agency office, this was probably the least private place on the planet for her. Hashing out the details of a meeting with Aden here in this building would be a dumb thing to do. Right now she still had plausible deniability on her side.

On the way back to the conference room, Solveig found that the rush of her short clandestine conversation with her brother gave her step a bit of bounce it hadn't had earlier. Now she was eager to get on with the negotiations and move on with the day. Just like that, the morning had turned from irritating to exciting. It was a chore to work around her father's control mechanisms all the time, but it gave her a dopamine rush whenever she got away with something without his knowledge, and it had taken her a long time to admit to herself that she actually enjoyed the cat-and-mouse game more often than not. And the higher the stakes, the more satisfaction she got out of playing. This wasn't just stealing a liter of ice cream from the service-kitchen freezer right underneath the watchful eyes of the security network sensors and eating it under the bedcovers at night. In the eyes of her father, her secret contact with Aden would be a major betrayal. Falk Ragnar would suspect an insurrection, accuse them of plotting to take over everything behind his back, when all she wanted was to get to know her brother a little better after seventeen years of his absence from her life.

When she walked back into the conference room, all eyes were on her, and she realized that the proceedings had completely ground to a halt while they'd waited for her to return. She was the keystone of the meeting for both the Ragnar and Hanzo people in the room. The Ragnar people would not dare to speak for her because they knew what would happen if she complained to her father about any of them. And to the Hanzo people, she *was* Ragnar, and everyone else in the delegation was a water bearer at best.

If someone else had gone in my stead, they would have continued with Gisbert talking for the company, she thought. *I'm the only one in the delegation who doesn't have an acceptable substitute. Because of the name.*

For the first time in her tenure at Ragnar Industries, Solveig considered that maybe her family name meant that her father's power over her was limited as well.

What is he going to do if he finds out I've been talking to Aden? Is he going to disown me? Exile me?

She sat down and nodded to thank the people at the table for excusing the interruption. Then she looked at her corporate comtab again to focus on the matter at hand, the negotiation of the new contracts between Hanzo and Ragnar. But the thought had nestled in the back of her brain, and now it refused to dissipate.

I'm the only Ragnar left who can be here in his stead. Maybe he needs me more than I need any of this.

They broke for lunch and then returned to the negotiating table in the afternoon, but Solveig was pleased to see that the schedule had a five-hour gap between the conclusion of the day's business and the planned formal dinner with their hosts tonight. In the early afternoon, the Ragnar delegation packed up their compads and their meeting notes to head back to their hotel. It was corporate policy for Ragnar to stay off-site and not in accommodations offered by the hosting company, in order to avoid the appearance of impropriety and safeguard the employees against electronic eavesdropping as much as possible.

The hotel was right in the middle of the busy entertainment district, a thirty-floor slice of a commercial tower that adjoined a shopping and recreational complex. Even from the soundproof windows of her suite on the twenty-fifth floor, Solveig found the bustle of the city almost overwhelming to the senses. It was the opposite of her running track through the tranquility of the Ragnar estate, a constant stream of movement among the regular geometric shapes of artificial structures. In a class on cognition back at the university, she had learned that the human brain wasn't wired to look at right angles and straight lines all day, that doing so put the mind into a constant state of unrest and alert. Something about human evolution made people relax when among the non-Euclidean shapes and green color palette of nature, and stress them out when they went without that soothing factor for too long. This city, with the same number of residents as Sandvik back home but crammed into closer proximity in a much smaller space, brought the lecture back to Solveig's mind, and she fully believed the conclusion now. She was already looking forward to her morning runs again. But this much concentrated life had its own sort of exciting energy as well.

A great place to visit for a week, she thought as she looked out onto the streets. *But I don't think I could live here for good. I'd miss being able to sit under a tree and listen to nothing but the wind rustling the leaves.*

Being in the most densely populated city in the system had its advantages. When she checked her hotel compad for service directories, there was an unending amount of choice. Everything she could ever need to buy or rent could be found within a few blocks from the hotel, even the sort of services that weren't plentiful or easy to find in Sandvik. It seemed logical that a place where physical privacy was a luxury would offer so many ways to have virtual privacy, fuss-free ways to indulge in a desire anonymously.

There were hundreds of pleasure-companion services in Coriolis City. She went through the talent lists of a few of the most highly rated ones, filtered them by the ability to understand Gretian without a translator, and picked a face she liked out of the dozens of choices. For what she had in mind, she would need someone who wouldn't need to rely on the AI of his translator software to understand her intent. She checked her schedule and booked the visit in the middle of her free time slot before dinner, with several hours comfortably buffering the time between the appointment and her evening obligation. When she was finished, she flicked up a screen from her comtab and called Cuthbert to her suite. He rang her door chime a minute later.

"Yes, Miss Ragnar?"

"I have made some plans for the afternoon, Cuthbert. I need a little relaxation after all the sitting and talking this morning. There will be someone here for me in thirty minutes. I will need you to do a security screening."

"We usually use vetted services that have been approved by the security division beforehand, Miss Ragnar."

"Cuthbert, I am not the High Chancellor of Gretia. Nobody is out to assassinate me. And this isn't the kind of service we usually have vetted by corporate. It's someone from a companion agency."

Cuthbert showed only the mildest hint of surprise on his face, but he didn't even blink at her revelation.

"Apologies, ma'am, but you're wrong about that. It's the most common category on the list for Acheron expenses. Right after food and drink providers."

What happens off-world stays off-world, she heard her father's voice. *Thanks for the tip, Papa.*

"Sorry I jumped the gun, then," she said.

"May I see the service listing?"

She brought it up on the hotel compad and flicked it over to his device. He consulted it only briefly.

"Oh, they're on the approved vendor list," he said. "That won't be a problem."

"Good. Just don't tell Marten I made the booking before checking with you. I'll remember next time."

"No trouble at all, Miss Ragnar. Just call me when you get the notice from the front desk, and I'll be right over."

He smiled curtly and left the suite again. Solveig waited until the door had closed behind him. Then she picked up her comtab and looked for a suitable place for her plan. The best spots were in a private business, out of view of the public surveillance systems. It had to be a location that was neither too crowded nor too empty, so she could keep an eye on everything but not stick out too much. And it had to be a place where foreign faces were common and didn't draw special attention.

There was a capsule diner just three blocks away. It sat right on one of the major thoroughfares to the nearby recreational complex, and the guest data showed that it was usually half-full at this time of day. Even the food was well reviewed. Solveig noted the address and sent it on to Aden with a message.

> There's a diner not too far from my hotel. Meet me there in an hour if you can. I may be a few minutes early or late. But I'll be there.

As soon as her message had disappeared off her comtab and into the Mnemosyne, Solveig felt a wave of anxiety well up and twist her stomach. If all went as planned, she'd see her brother in the flesh again in just sixty minutes. The jitters she suddenly experienced were worse than any she had ever felt. Playing cat-and-mouse games with corporate security didn't even register on the scale in comparison. But there was a wild sort of joy to this tension that was never present when she pulled one over on Marten and his crew, or even when she managed to sneak something past her father. Solveig sat down on the lounge chair by the window and forced herself to take slow breaths and get control of her emotions. If she let her nervousness show too much, even Cuthbert would sense that something was off. And if she blew this golden chance to meet Aden, she knew she'd be angry with herself for months.

———

When the companion showed up half an hour later and precisely on time, she sent Cuthbert downstairs to the lobby to escort him up to her floor. She knew he would have been able to do his check in the lobby, where it would have made more sense from a security standpoint anyway, but she also knew that his job was mostly to serve as a status indicator, and doing the check in front of her door was part of the appearance. She watched on the door's observation screen as Cuthbert scanned the companion with the sensors in his comtab and then did a manual pat-down. Finally, he was satisfied that his performance had delivered the expected optics, and he tapped the door chime.

"Your guest is here, Miss Solveig."

She noticed that he had switched to her first name, which he usually didn't do, and realized that it was part of the discretion protocol. She had always wondered why Acheron had always seemed such a desirable assignment for business trips among the executives. Now she suspected she had at least part of the answer.

The companion introduced himself as Yejun. He was almost unreasonably fit and handsome, a slender face with a sharply chiseled jawline and stunning green eyes. Under other circumstances, she would have at least considered employing him for the purpose Cuthbert would think she had in mind.

"Thank you, Cuthbert. Be back to pick up my visitor in an hour, please, and delay all my incoming comms requests with my apologies. Absolutely no disturbances, please. Unless the hotel is burning down around us."

"Of course, Miss Solveig," Cuthbert said and withdrew after one last glance at the companion. She could tell that he wasn't bothered by the fact that she had hired an attractive distraction, just surprised that she had done it.

You weren't expecting that, were you? she thought. He'd be reporting the encounter to her father by way of Marten, of course, and she knew that Papa would look at it as a rite of passage. Part of her suspected that he actually expected and maybe even preferred that she service her urges with high-quality hired work rather than entangle herself in regular relationships. It was certainly a more efficient way to get the sex when you didn't have the time or will to deal with the emotions.

She walked Yejun back to the living room of the suite and gestured at the lounge chairs in front of the panoramic window.

"Sit, please," she said in Acheroni, which he rewarded with a smile.

"Gladly," he replied in fluent Gretian that didn't have a trace of an accent. "Would you tell me what kind of enjoyment you had in mind this afternoon?"

He sat down and looked at her expectantly. She had picked him from his holo image on the agency listing, but even the image hadn't done him justice. On her personal list of encounters, he was easily among the top three most attractive people she had ever met.

The sacrifices I make for family, she thought.

"I would like to purchase your discretion for an hour, Yejun."

"You already secured that when you requested me."

"That's not quite what I mean. I would like for you to sit here and have a drink or three while you look at the scenery for an hour. Or do whatever else comes to mind. As long as it doesn't involve answering the door or leaving this suite."

He smiled and gave her a puzzled look.

"I need my security officer to think that I am busy in here with you while I step out behind his back. I will make sure that you get twice the asked fee if I get back here in an hour unnoticed."

Yejun smiled again and shook his head lightly.

"There is no need for that. I will do as you request if that's what would please you most this afternoon."

"It would," she said. *But only by a hair,* she thought with another glance at the obvious topography of abdominal muscles under Yejun's tightly fitted silk shirt.

"If anyone finds out I am gone, you can tell them I stepped out for a bit. There is no danger to you. This is just some corporate subterfuge. Mixed in with regrettable family issues."

"Believe me, I've had to entertain far more complicated requests," the companion said.

———

Cuthbert had retreated to his own room down the skyway and just around the next corner. Solveig closed the screen she had been using to monitor the space on the other side of her suite's door. Then she put her company compad and her personal device on the little table by the side of the circular bed in the suite's sleeping section.

Might as well play the charade all the way, she thought. *Maybe I should get a proper background sound, just for fun. Punch up some sexy entertainment on the Mnemosyne and play it on low volume. In case he's smart enough to know how to tap into my company device.*

Now she only carried her burner comtab, the one she would have to discard and replace after meeting with Aden today. Through a long string of authorizations and data scrubbings that were the digital equivalent of wiping the floor behind herself after every step she took, she had enabled it to allow her access back into the hotel and onto the floor for the next sixty minutes. What little evidence of her absence remained would be wiped clean when she deactivated the node and destroyed the hardware.

Back at the old game, she thought as she opened her door and looked around in the breezeway outside. *Stealing ice cream from the service kitchen in the middle of the night. Piece of cake once you get busted a time or two and learn enough from your screwups.*

The floor had four skylift banks and half a dozen emergency stairwells. She walked to the side of the building that was away from the rooms of the Ragnar delegation. Then she took one of the skylift platforms down to the atrium and strode across to the exits, careful to move with purpose but not so rushed as to draw attention. The atrium was a busy place, and nobody paid her any mind as she headed for one of the side exits.

Once she was outside, it felt like she had just escaped from a detention facility. She'd never be able to shed her access to the Ragnar wealth, but once she stepped out of the cocoon of Ragnar security, the world became a little risky again. It was enjoyable to have that feeling of unpredictability in the back of one's mind, at least for a while.

Solveig turned and walked down the street, flowing with the crowds that were out and about for leisure this afternoon. The weather here was consistently pleasant, every day a sunny twenty-two degrees, neither too warm nor too cold. But now that Kee had pointed out the circumstance to her, it really was strange not to feel a breeze, not even in the deep canyons between the buildings. Whenever she did feel a slight movement of air on her face, it invariably came from below, where ventilation grids were set into the streets in regular intervals. After a while, it felt like walking around in a gigantic building, which was of course what the Acheroni cities really were—floors, walls, and roofs, just on a much grander scale.

The excitement of executing the sleight-of-hand deception with Cuthbert and Yejun had suppressed her anxiety temporarily, but now that she was out of the building and walking toward the diner, the feeling returned with a vengeance, and it got stronger the closer she drew to the place where she would meet her brother in person again for the first time since she was in primary school.

She checked the time. Nine minutes until the full hour, and only fifty-one minutes until she had to be back in the suite to avoid getting found out by Cuthbert.

Not even an hour, she thought. *That's all I get right now after seventeen years. And I have to sneak it like a thief. At least I will get to find out why he doesn't want his old life anymore.*

CHAPTER 19

ADEN

It seemed like the peak of vanity to buy expensive new clothes, but it was what felt right to Aden under the circumstances.

He had spent the last three months in a rumpled flight suit just like the rest of the *Zephyr* crew, and it really was the most comfortable mode of dress for shipboard life. But the last time he had seen Solveig, at their Mnemosyne meeting three months ago, she had been dressed expensively and impeccably, and he didn't want to feel like a careless slob next to her. Thankfully, Coriolis City was riddled with opportunities for visitors and travelers to turn their disposable ags into custom-fitted threads, and an hour and a half after he had received Solveig's message opening the possibility of a face-to-face meeting between them, Aden had purchased a set of bespoke computer-measured clothes that he dearly hoped made him look fashionable and not like a middle-aged man trying to look like a secondary school student again. They were well-made clothes that looked fine to him in the mirror, but he had lost his sense for fashion styles after living in uniforms for the last seventeen years, and he fidgeted with everything for fifteen minutes before he realized that he was just nervous.

When he left the store, his comtab trilled a notification, and he opened a screen in front of his face without breaking his stride, just like he had seen countless Acheroni do.

> There's a diner not too far from my hotel. Meet me there in an hour if you can. I may be a few minutes early or late. But I'll be there.

The abruptness of the message was a little startling. Solveig's last message had said that she would look into a possibility to get away, and he had expected at least a few back-and-forths concerning timing and logistics. But talking around the hot porridge had never been a Ragnar family trait, he supposed.

At least she said "if you can," he thought with a smile, trying to ignore the nervousness that was now reasserting itself after he had mostly managed to wrestle it under control in the clothing shop.

The message had a directory listing for the diner appended to it, and he checked the location on a map of the area. The diner was a good way from where he was right now, but there was no shortage of available transportation in the city, and the map offered a variety of transit options along with their rates and estimated times of arrival. Aden noted with amusement that he could even elect to hire a private gyrofoil that would pick him up on one of several landing pads within three minutes of where he was standing. It would whisk him off to his location in only three additional minutes, if he had the desire to get there very quickly and didn't mind parting with five hundred ags for the convenience. But his map informed him that at his average walking pace, he could make the location on foot in just forty minutes. He didn't need to save the money for a transit pod, but he had spent most of the last three months in the tight quarters of a small ship, so he opted for the walk, grateful for the opportunity to exercise his legs and move in straight lines that were longer than just six meters.

He was half a block from the diner when he got another message on his comtab.

I'm here. Capsule 47.

Aden flicked the message away. He stopped and turned toward the windows of the storefront to his right and checked his appearance, then chided himself for the gesture.

You're meeting your sister, not going on a date, he thought. *She won't care if you have a wrinkle in your tunic or a hair out of place.*

The diner was an oasis of shade and quiet in the bustle of the district. It was fully automated, with a host console at the entrance and softly lit pathways on the floor to provide directions. He tapped the location for capsule forty-seven, and an orange arrow appeared on the floor in front of the console, pointing into the diner and waiting for him to follow.

It was strange to be in a restaurant with no conversational din in the background. A few people on their way out passed him as he followed the orange arrow, and they passed each other by without acknowledgment. The dining capsules had doors that could be closed, and most guests had chosen to do so, ensconcing themselves in silence for the duration of their meals and shutting out the world completely. It made sense to him that in a city as densely populated as this one, where the hotel rooms were not much bigger than his living compartment on *Zephyr*, quiet privacy was a precious commodity, a premium item on the services menu.

When he reached capsule forty-seven, the door was only slightly ajar. Aden took a deep breath and knocked on the capsule right next to the opening.

"Come in," Solveig's voice answered from the inside. He knew what her adult self sounded like because they had met in holographic form in the Mnemosyne three months ago. But those had been digital avatars, cleaned up and adjusted by the AI to remove commonly perceived flaws and imperfections, ideal versions of themselves smoothed out by a million social and cultural algorithms. This was reality, and there was no easy disconnect option if things got uncomfortable.

Aden looked over his shoulder, almost convinced he'd find a detachment of Ragnar corporate security people walking toward him and blocking his way out, but there was nobody else in the place except for the two Acheroni guests on their way out who just now passed the host station without looking back. Everything about this place was right out of the intelligence textbook in the chapter "Meeting Places to Avoid." It was out of public sight, had no obvious secondary exits, and could have been prepared for the meeting days in advance. But he knew that Solveig had picked the place in a hurry out of necessity, and that her biggest concern was to stay out of their father's field of view, not to avoid enemy spy services. In any case, she was taking a far greater risk with this than he was.

He opened the door all the way before he could give his doubts any more time to muddle things.

Solveig sat at the table inside, hands folded in her lap, and she looked up at him as he entered the capsule. They stared at each other for a moment that seemed to stretch in his perception.

"Hey, shorty," he finally said, and she got out of her chair and rushed over to where he stood. Then she hugged him with a firmness that bordered on ferocity, and kissed him on the cheek. Aden was momentarily taken aback by the sudden display of unanticipated affection, but then he returned the hug with equal firmness.

"Ow," she said. "The beard scratches." Then she pulled away and looked at him in appraisal. "But it suits your face. I kind of like it."

"You think so?" he said with a smile.

"Yeah. You look like a proper spacer. You smell like one, too."

Aden chuckled. "I'm not sure how to take that. How do spacers smell?"

"They all smell the same. Like the inside of a spaceship. It's faint, but it's there. Maybe it's something about the filters or the recycled air. Or maybe you all use the same soap."

Solveig relaxed her embrace, and he held her at arm's length to look at her. She was wearing a dark-blue jumpsuit that appeared all business. Her long red hair was gathered up into a loose tail that reached all the way down to the spot between her shoulder blades. He had inherited their father's height, but she had gotten most of his looks—the shape and color of her eyes, the defined jawline, the minuscule earlobes, just filtered and softened by the genetic card shuffle with their mother's DNA. Everything was like the image she had presented in the Mnemosyne hologram three months ago, and yet this was completely different. It was like the mass of her body standing right next to his own had a gravitational pull on his heart that the hologram had lacked.

"Gods, I can't believe that worked out," she said. "What are the odds?"

She gestured toward the other seat at the table.

"Come, sit. We don't have a lot of time to talk. I have to be back in my suite in fifty minutes, or even Cuthbert will figure it out."

He followed her to the table and sat down. The seats were wide, low-slung benches with cushion pads tied to them, and he had to fold himself a bit to fit into the arrangement.

"Who's Cuthbert?"

"One of Marten's army of weasels. His new understudy."

"Marten's still around, then," Aden said darkly.

"Oh, yes. Papa's loyal company muscle. I think he'll be there forever. He's too grumpy to die."

They smiled at each other across the table. He was studying her face, trying to reconcile it with its younger version just like he had done before in their Mnemosyne meeting, and he knew by the way she looked at him that she was doing the same.

"How did you slip your leash?"

"Slipping the leash," Solveig said. "Funny, that's what I always call it, too. Maybe I got it from you when I was young. When you showed me how to do the sensor hack so we could get into the kitchen at night."

"I had almost forgotten about that," he said with a smile.

"I made good use of that knowledge for years after you left," she said. "But Cuthbert is easier to fool than Marten. Let's just say he's expecting me to be doing something entirely different right now and leave it at that. You don't want to know the details."

"Fair enough," Aden said. "What kind of business is Papa having you do on Acheron?"

"Our contracts with Hanzo are running short. He sent me to get better terms for graphene composites. And use our Alon contract as leverage."

"And how is that working out?"

"They don't want to concede that we're not coming to them as beggars anymore. But they'll come around. It's a seller's market right now. And they can't afford for us to take their Alon quota and sell it to their competitors. Which we will if they make us, even if it costs us our top graphene supplier."

She shook her head. Then she tapped the compad that was built into the table in front of her.

"But I don't want to use our time to bore you with corporate theater. Trust me, I've had a hard enough time staying awake through it this morning. Do you want to order some food while we're here? It'll look a little strange if we don't."

"Sure," he said, and looked at his own order compad, then selected one of the lunch packages. "You sound like you like that stuff just about as much as I did."

"The thing is that I sort of do," she said. "It's like a strategy board game. Once you get used to it, it's really easy to make people commit to the moves you want them to do. The key is to let them think they had the idea first." She laughed and covered her face with her hands for a moment. "Oh, gods. That's exactly the obnoxious sort of thing Papa would say, isn't it?"

He's had you to himself for so long, Aden thought. It would be a wonder if his ways hadn't influenced yours at all.

"Have you heard from Mama lately?" he asked, partly out of curiosity and partly to steer the conversation into a new direction. "I tried to follow the family news when I was in the Blackguards, but she just dropped off the Mnemosyne a few years after I left. I only read the PR release about the divorce after everything was done."

"I was already at boarding school," she said. "Came home one summer, and Papa said Mama had left and gone back to Oceana. I asked her about that, later. She was a little drunk and pissed off at Papa for some reason. More pissed off than usual, I mean. She said he told her to leave and never speak to any of us again if she wanted to keep being financially secure. I never told him about that. On the chance she was telling the truth."

"And she moved to Hades."

Solveig nodded.

"She said she wants to spend her retirement account where the gravity is always low and the drinks are always cheap."

They both laughed.

"She took her old name back. *Jansen,*" she continued. "I can give you her node address if you want to get in touch. She still thinks you're probably dead. Everyone did."

"I'm a Jansen now, too." Aden took out his ID pass and showed it to her. She looked at the card and turned it around between her fingers.

"Oceanian," she said. "Just like Mama's."

"It's a fake," he admitted. "A good fake. But a fake. I couldn't come back and be on the same planet with Papa again."

She put the card down on the table between them.

"I think I have earned the right to know why, Aden," she said. "The reason why you left. The real reason. And Papa sure as hells won't tell me. Not even after a bottle of his Rhodian whisky. Every other year or so, I'll try, and he'll shut me out for a month."

Their food arrived through the serving port next to the table. The automated kitchen conveyor slid two trays in front of them, both with precise arrangements of food on little plates and bowls. Aden considered her request while they each picked up their eating utensils and prepared to begin their meal.

"Why do you think that is, Solveig?"

His sister shrugged.

"Knowing Papa? Because he fears it'll make me think less of him."

"And what if I told you that it will? Would you still want to know?"

"The truth is the truth," she said without hesitation. "It doesn't matter how I feel about it. Or how I might feel about it. Of course I would want to know."

Aden sat back and looked at his sister in silence for a few moments. She returned his gaze evenly. If he had been in her place for so long, he would have asked the same questions and given the same answers. She was an adult now, and her relationship with their father was her business. He decided that if she wanted the truth, he had no reason to keep it from her.

"I met a girl," he said. "I know he told you that much."

"He said he didn't approve of her, and you got mad and left."

"That's what he's been telling you for all these years," Aden said, his anger stirring in his chest.

"More or less."

"How very *Papa*," he said. "He never tells you the whole truth of a thing. Just the part he thinks you need to know. Told from the angle that makes him look the best."

He looked at his plate and shook his head.

"Her name was Astrid. I can't even show you an image of her because I lost all my access to Aden Ragnar's stuff when I became Aden

Robertson. But I'm sure you know how to dig around if you really want to know."

He picked up his utensils and began to eat his lunch, just so he could give his hands something to do other than tear his napkin into progressively smaller bits under the table. She followed suit, and they ate in silence for a few moments. He had already forgotten what he'd ordered. It was a chicken dish with a sweet glaze, mercifully mild for Acheroni food.

"We met in Arendal, when I was just out of the university. I was twenty-four; she was twenty-one. It took us all of a week together to know that we were meant for each other. I still figured we shouldn't rush things. So we waited six months."

"And you brought her home and told Papa," Solveig said. "I think I know how that one went over with him."

"Actually, we got married before we left for home," he said, and he saw her do a little sympathetic wince.

"I know. I *know*. I shouldn't have gone over his head and put him in front of accomplished circumstances like that. But I figured it was better to ask forgiveness than permission."

"Oh, no," Solveig said.

Aden nodded.

"He was polite to her. But it was that icy kind of polite he does with people he loathes. You know what I mean. So we went to the guest quarters to stay for the weekend, and he had me called to the house a little while later, by myself. I figured that would be the part where he'd yell at me a little. Maybe a lot. But then he'd get over it and accept it, eventually. And he would see how good she was for me."

He shook his head at the memory of his own youthful naivete.

"He told me there was no way she could have the family name. Said that she would be entitled to half of my share of Ragnar. Then he claimed that's what she had in mind for me all along. I stood my ground. Told him she was his daughter-in-law now, whether he liked it or not. And he said, 'We'll just have to see about that.'"

"He told you to annul the marriage," Solveig said. "And . . . *wait*. You told him to go to all the hells, and then he went to her and offered her a stack of money to annul it from her end."

"You do know him better than anyone else," Aden said. "She told him to keep his money. He doubled the offer. Then he tripled it. Astrid said she'd not take his money even if he sat there all night and increased his multipliers exponentially. So we left."

"And then what happened?"

He hadn't allowed the memory close to the surface of his consciousness in a long time, and when he did, it hurt as much as ever, undulled by the passage of time. He could tell from the sudden concern on Solveig's face that he wasn't able to keep the grief out of his own expression.

"What happened? She *died*, that's what happened."

She looked at him, crestfallen.

"We went to Sandvik and got a hotel room for the night," he continued in a soft voice. "I didn't want to make Papa extend hospitality against his will. The next day, I sent her back to Arendal on the vactrain. Figured I should make one more gesture of goodwill and go home to see Papa by myself before I left. And her transit pod from the vactrain station in Arendal crashed into a maintenance divider on the city interchange. At a hundred kilometers per hour."

"Gods," Solveig said.

"The police said it blew both the collision avoidance sensor and the safety interlock at the same time somehow. The pod never even hit the brakes. From what I know, it usually stops a pod on the spot when either of those things are disabled. Astrid had some improbably bad luck that day."

"And you think Papa did it," Solveig said slowly. "That he had your new wife killed because he didn't want you to stay married to her."

"It could have been just really bad luck. People die in accidents all the time, Solveig. I know that. But ask yourself the same question I did after it happened."

"Could he do it," Solveig said, her voice almost a whisper.

"With all that you know about Papa, can you say you're absolutely certain that he would never be able to do such a thing?"

She didn't reply. Instead, she just looked at him, her internal turmoil evident on her face.

"I can't tell you how I know, but I do," he continued. "Maybe it was the way he said, 'We'll just have to see about that' when I left that night. Maybe it was the timing. Or the improbability of those safety features failing at the same time, in just the right rental pod. Maybe it's all of those factors when you combine them."

He sighed and let his shoulders drop.

"But I knew that once I had answered that question for myself, I would never be able to stand in the same room with him again without thinking about what he may have done to Astrid. And I would always be only two drinks away from a life sentence. For him or me."

Aden took a slow, deliberate breath and sighed.

"I'm sorry," he said. "This is the first time we've been in the same room in seventeen years. I wanted this to be a pleasant thing. Not to kill all the joy in the room forever."

Solveig shook her head.

"Don't be sorry. I asked you, after all. I insisted."

She reached out and put her hand over his.

"I'm glad I finally know the whole story. Because now I can understand why you would leave. I always felt that you had left me behind. That you walked away from me for no good reason. And now I don't have to be angry with you for that anymore. And that does make me happy. Because I never want to feel anger when I think of you."

He felt a relief he hadn't known he'd needed, and it was so sudden and profound that it brought tears to his eyes. He used his napkin to wipe them away, and when he looked at Solveig, he saw that she was dabbing away at her own eyes. They looked at each other and laughed, in that cathartic way people laugh when some shared grief or misery was eased a little.

"Would you come back home?" she asked. "If Papa was not part of the equation, I mean."

"I don't know," Aden said. "I've been away for so long, I don't even really know it anymore. But I do miss you. And sausage rolls. And good wheat ale. But mostly you."

"Marten's weasels are still on the lookout for you. Papa says they almost caught up with you in Adrasteia."

Aden nodded.

"It was when I got this job. They were doing facial recognition to find me in the crowd, at the choke point to the space station. I had to make a run for it."

"He's not going to stop looking. Now that he knows you're still alive."

"I have no idea why," he said. "I can't take over the business. Not anymore. What else does he want with me?"

Solveig shook her head.

"I would say he wants to make good on the mistakes he knows he has made. But I'm not sure he has the ability to self-reflect to that degree. But I can tell that something is eating at him. I see it whenever he gets drunk. But he's always careful to button up his feelings again in front of me. Even when he's so loaded that he can't get off the bar stool without stumbling."

She checked the time and flinched.

"Hells. I have to be back in twelve minutes, and the walk takes five. Gods, I wish we had more time."

They left their half-eaten meals on the table and got out of their seats. Then they shared a long hug, and for the second time today, Aden wished he could slow the clock with the force of his will.

"I'll be on the planet for another two weeks," he said. "Maybe you can sneak out again."

"Why don't you come with me?" she replied, seemingly on impulse.

"What?"

"Come with me. Tell everyone who you are. Catch a ride with us back to Gretia when we are done. We can spend all the time we want together. And we could dare Papa to do something about it. No more need to sneak."

He laughed at the mental image of the two of them sitting on a couch together and answering Falk's next vidcom jointly, as if nothing had happened in the last seventeen years.

"Tempting," he said. "Just the look on his face would almost make it worth it. But I don't think I'm ready yet. I can't skip out on my new job. And I know I'm not ready for the fight that would follow. I'm not sure that he is either."

"If you change your mind, you have my node address," she said. "And if there are any strings I can pull for you from afar, tell me."

"I need to do this without the might of Ragnar behind me," he said. "Just to know that I can. And that I'm not like him."

"You've never been like him," Solveig said. "I'm the one who has to keep that DNA on a chain. You have no idea how often I look into the mirror and see a shorter version of him. And then I find myself sitting in a conference room at Hanzo, realizing I want to buy the damn building just so I can raze it to the ground, because one of their people just belittled me by accident. And I know that the resemblance isn't just in the mirror."

She kissed him on the cheek again and opened the door to leave before he could think of a soothing denial she would find plausible.

"Bye, Aden," she said as she slipped out of the capsule. "I love you."

"I love you, too," he said to the void she left in the doorframe as she rushed toward the exit.

CHAPTER 20

DUNSTAN

If there was a positive about being a severely crippled ship twenty minutes away from what was likely going to be the last docking maneuver of its long career, it was that *Minotaur* did not have to concern itself with its emissions control anymore. With most of the comms array assigned to the crew's Mnemosyne links and personal communications, Dunstan's vidcom connection to Rhodia's surface was as clear and sharp as never before.

"How long do you think the handover will take this time?" Mairi asked. Dunstan's wife was in the kitchen of their living unit in the Caledonia-4 arcology, down on the northern half of the continent, and now well within line of sight of *Minotaur*'s comms array.

"That's hard to say. I haven't come home with a damaged ship since the war. But she's not getting passed on to another crew. We'll be off the ship in an hour. And then it depends on how long they want to keep us for debriefing and after-action reports."

"You've already done a double patrol," Mairi said. "The navy's had you for six months now. I swear the girls have grown five centimeters since you left."

"You're the one who keeps feeding them," Dunstan said, and his wife rolled her eyes at the well-worn joke. She was trying to go along with his fiction that the engagement had been minor and that *Minotaur* had never been in real danger, but he could tell she wasn't buying what he was selling. They had been married for fifteen years, and the five in the middle had been wartime years, when he had been away for most of the time and only seen his family on leave once a year for two weeks. He knew that she still remembered what it had been like when the battered hulls of shot-up frigates and cruisers had returned to Rhodia One on a near-daily basis, half their crews dead or wounded, a seemingly endless stream of broken ships and broken bodies.

Once, a few years after the war, she had told him that she hadn't slept through a single night while he was deployed, and that the first thing she had done every morning after getting up was to check the unofficial observer reports for the names of the ships that had arrived at the station while she was asleep, always looking for the name of Dunstan's command, and being both relieved and dismayed when it didn't show up on the list. They had gotten used to a peacetime navy again, the predictable routine of three-month patrols followed by three months onshore, with the occasional double patrol thrown in whenever the ship and personnel rosters got too thin. This felt disconcertingly like wartime again, and he knew that she felt the same because of the way the conversation had been dancing around the uncomfortable sharp edges of the subject.

"Where are the girls, anyway? Isn't it nine o'clock in the morning down there?" Dunstan asked.

"Kendra is at socaball practice. Amelia is still in bed. I'm being merciful because tomorrow isn't a school day, and because she volunteered to help me this afternoon with the food for the spouse association meeting."

"That's still a thing?"

"It's never not a thing," Mairi said. "I must have baked a thousand cakes and hand pies for the association over the years."

After the last six months, the screen in front of Dunstan was like a window into another world, a normal one where people didn't have to wear vacsuits, didn't have to memorize the exact location of the nearest escape pod hatch. He was disappointed that he wouldn't be able to see his daughter's faces, but he was glad they were busy with a regular life, unaware of the new hazards that had appeared out here between the planets.

"Two weeks' leave, and then three months of shore duty," he said. "And I have no idea what I'm getting after that. All I know is that it won't be this old girl. She'll be in the breakdown yard by then."

"It would be nice if they doubled up on your shore duty time after socking you with a surprise double deployment," his wife said. She was cutting up strawberries while she talked on the vidcom, her hands trimming the little green leaves and stems with a paring knife seemingly on autopilot.

"It would be nice. But you know it won't happen in this lifetime."

"I know. Because the navy treats its people almost as well as it does its ships." Mairi flicked another strawberry stem into the garbage without having to aim.

"Only because they can sell the ships for scrap when they're done with them," Dunstan said with a smile.

He checked the time on the bulkhead display in his cabin. The countdown to docking was close to the point where he needed to be present in the AIC again.

"I have to go and make sure we dock without putting any more dents into the hull," he said. "Not that it matters much at this point. I'll let you know what's going on once we're on Rhodia One and get our orders for surface transport."

"Okay. I'm glad that you're at least overhead already. And not that I'm happy your ship got damaged. But it's good to know they won't be able to refuel it and send you right back out like they did last time. Love you."

"Love you, too. See you very soon." He blew a kiss at the screen and swiped his hand to make the projection disappear.

Dunstan got up from the edge of his bunk and straightened out his uniform overalls. His shipboard bag was strapped down on top of the mattress, packed and ready to go. Once they docked, he'd retrieve his bag and leave through the main collar, and then he'd never see these bulkheads again. He'd served on many ships, but this goodbye felt more poignant somehow. *Minotaur* had carried all of them into battle and back home faithfully despite her age and the neglect the fleet had shown her, and now the navy would reward her by having her torn apart with plasma cutters.

He opened the door of his cabin and stepped out into the passageway, then took a left turn to walk to the AIC. On the way, crew members made way as he passed through, and he spread around a few words of upbeat encouragement. They'd been in a genuine battle now, not just a brief trading of shots with a pirate corvette. They had fought a far more powerful warship and gotten in a blow or two without taking casualties. Even if the Gretian cruiser had a green crew and no missiles in her magazines, it was a statistically unlikely outcome. It made everyone on his crew stand a bit taller.

The AIC staff looked as busy and alert as ever, but Dunstan knew that this was the part of a cruise when errors were most likely to creep in. With their home planet spread out underneath and the space station just in front, everyone was halfway home in their heads already. He sat down on his command couch and observed the choreography of the procedures ballet for a little while, all the parts of the command machine working together to get the ship to her docking ring as precisely and safely as possible. Rhodia One was as busy as ever, but Dunstan saw mostly merchant traffic, and precious few warships. The navy had started the war with two hundred ships and ended it with

1,300. Now they were back down to two hundred, and almost half of that number were not ready for deployment for various reasons. The rest had to carry the workload of patrolling all Rhodian space and safeguarding the transit lanes as they moved through the navy's sphere of control. It had been enough until recently, when the pirates had started to become more numerous and far more violent seemingly overnight. Now the fleet was stretched to the breaking point and maybe already beyond. The Gretian cruiser was still out there, and its simple presence in Rhodian space had already cost the fleet a destroyed cruiser and a damaged frigate that was beyond repair. And now Home Fleet was short four more ships, tied up on a search-and-destroy mission.

"Sir, we are getting a request from Rhodia control," Lieutenant Mayler said. "They say one of the station's shuttles just had a near miss with an unidentified ship in low orbit. They claim it didn't show on the sensors until the last moment. Control is asking all units in the area to link into AEGIS and do a sensor sweep facing planetside."

Dunstan did a double take.

"That is super odd. Confirm the request, Lieutenant. Link us up with AEGIS and bring up the sensor suite. Helm, bring the bow around to zero by negative one niner, steady on your heading and velocity."

"Bringing the bow around to zero by negative one niner, steady on heading and velocity, aye," Boyer confirmed.

"We have a data link to AEGIS," Mayler said. "Firing up active sensors."

The other ships in the pattern followed the request as well. Within a minute, a dozen nearby navy units added their own sensor data to the big picture, turning themselves into extended arrays for AEGIS, the planetary strategic defense network. Dunstan checked the class tags on the other ships and saw that *Minotaur* was the biggest unit in the line. The rest of the navy presence in the immediate area consisted of tugboats, supply ships, tankers, and a few escort corvettes.

And we're not exactly in prime fighting shape right now, Dunstan thought, trying to suppress a kindling sense of unease. *Let's hope it's a joyriding civvie in a speed yacht, buzzing shuttles for the fun of it.*

They watched the tactical display as the sensors of the combined ad hoc drone fleet swept the space between upper and lower orbit. Three shuttles popped up at various altitudes, all headed for Rhodia One and flashing proper beacons and ID.

"Nothing on active, sir. From us or anyone else," Mayler said. "Just tagged and scheduled traffic. And a lot of background noise from the surface."

"I wonder what the shuttle jockey was drinking, then," Dunstan said. "I don't need any last-minute scares like that."

"Ground-to-orbit transport isn't the most exciting job in the fleet," Bosworth replied. "If I had to do the same hop twice a day for a year, I'd start looking for stuff to dogfight too."

On the tactical plot, two new contacts appeared between the sensor picket and the inner atmosphere boundary. They seemed to stand still in the air for a moment. Then they streaked off in different directions, accelerating so quickly they could only be one thing. The AI classified them as hostile instantly, and the shock of surprise that jolted through Dunstan made him react automatically.

"Action stations," he bellowed.

"Bandit, bandit. Missile launch at 25 degrees by 4, distance 512 kilometers. Accelerating at fifty g." Mayler had jumped to his station and was reading off the values next to the icon as the action stations alert blared all over the ship. His face showed the same profound disbelief Dunstan felt.

"That's way inside the ballistic defense belt," Dunstan said. "Bring the reactor up and set the point defenses to active. Tell the cargo cans on either side of us to keep their distance. And get a trajectory on that ordnance now."

"One is heading our way, the other . . . sir, they fired the second one at the surface. Time to impact on the second bird is two minutes."

"Active search the launch point and scan ahead. *Find* that launch platform."

Dunstan looked at the diverging missile trajectories, and cold fear shouldered aside his disbelief. Whoever just launched missiles had fired from inside the planet's antimissile defense belt, a network of sensors, rail guns, and interceptor missile batteries that orbited Rhodia and extended into the space around the planet for thousands of kilometers. It was meant to protect against ballistic attacks from Gretia like the one that had crippled the energy relays at Hades three years into the war. But these missiles had been carried in and fired at point-blank range, on the wrong side of the defensive ring. What they were witnessing was supposed to be so unlikely as to be statistically irrelevant, but the evidence was in front of them and streaking through the atmosphere at fifty-g acceleration.

"Unannounced planetary defense drill," Bosworth said. "They're checking to see if we're still on our feet ten minutes away from the barn."

"Afraid not, Lieutenant. Unless the AI has gone completely insane," Dunstan replied.

"The first bird is changing aspect. *Sir* . . . it's not aimed at us." Mayler looked up from the plot. "It's aimed at Rhodia One."

A few dozen kilometers to their portside, Rhodia One was taking up millions of cubic meters of orbital space. It was a big and valuable target that had been positioned on the inside of the ballistic defense belt for a good reason. The incoming ordnance streaked in from the wrong side, the one direction the defensive planners never expected to have to consider as a vector for incoming fire. Whatever was heading their way, it was unlikely to destroy the station—*Minotaur* herself wouldn't have been able to do that trick even with her entire load of antiship missiles—but it could still cause catastrophic damage.

"Active searching the launch area. New contact, designate *Zulu-1*, bearing 355 degrees by 10. Small ship, high heat signature. They just lit their drive, sir. Distance six hundred ninety kilometers."

Dunstan opened his mouth to order Mayler to activate the rail guns and get a target bearing but dismissed the idea right away. The missiles and the bogey all had the planetary surface as a backstop. Any slugs that missed would travel through the atmosphere at ten kilometers per second and hit the ground, or whatever got in the way, with enough energy to punch through an arcology's top fifty levels. And the slugs would never catch the second missile, which was now outracing anything they could have thrown after it.

"Lock up *Zulu-1* with the fire control. We have no missiles left, but they don't know that. Maybe they'll do something dumb."

"Target locked," Mayler said. "They are really hauling ass, sir. Bogey is burning at fifteen g, up and away. And it's a weak sensor return even at this range. First missile is headed straight for Rhodia One. It'll cross into our point-defense bubble, but for just a few seconds."

"The starboard capacitor bank is still down," Bosworth reminded them. "We won't be able to engage anything coming up on that side. Helm, turn our bow forty degrees to starboard."

"Forty degrees starboard on the bow, helm aye."

The AIC was barely controlled chaos. Nobody had expected to hear another action stations alert on this ship, not at home and ten minutes from docking. It was like waking up to see a burglar in the room and having to go from a sleep state into a full-on fight in the span of a second or two.

"That bogey is going to outrun us. We can barely do four g. There's nothing in the neighborhood that can catch him," Mayler said.

"Forget him. Nothing we could do about him even with a healthy drive. He's on AEGIS—let the fleet track him. Focus on those missiles, please."

"Missile one will cross our bow and dip into our engagement range in twenty-three seconds. Missile two is headed for the southern continent. Kelpie Peninsula. Time to impact, one minute, ten seconds."

This is going to be bad, Dunstan thought in dismay. *A missile strike on the home world, right underneath the noses of Home Fleet.*

"They're small missiles, sir. AI says they're 550-millimeter antiship ordnance. But there's no signature coming from those seeker heads. They fired them dumb, sir. Ballistic."

"Explains why they felt the need to get so damn close. Point-defense status, report."

"Portside emitters energized; AI is tracking missile one. Crossing the edge of our engagement envelope in ten seconds," Mayler replied. "We'll have less than two seconds for our shot."

"Then don't miss," Dunstan said. "That's an order."

The missile streaked across their bow and toward their port side, a hundred kilometers away, continuing its mindless run at Rhodia One. Without active guidance, it wouldn't be able to dodge point-defense fire, but it also made the warhead impervious to the AI's electronic warfare attempts.

"The reactor is only at sixty percent," Bosworth warned.

"Allocate everything to the portside PD emitters."

"Aye, sir."

"Three . . . two . . . one. *Firing,*" Mayler said.

The lights and consoles in the AIC went out without so much as a residual flicker, turning off every screen projection in the room and leaving them all in complete darkness. A moment later, the emergency lighting came on, and the screens came back to life. The sudden lightness Dunstan felt could only mean that the ship's gravmag unit had stopped.

"Reactor failsafe kicked in," Bosworth read off his screen. "Power is gone. Sensors are down. Gravmag array is down. No propulsion. Point defense is out."

"Hells, just read off what's still working."

"Not much, sir. Comms and data links are coming back on right now on reserve power. That's not going to last long. We have thirty minutes of life support and no gravity. Sending out emergency broadcast right now."

"Just tell me we got that missile," Dunstan said.

Mayler looked at the screen that had just now rematerialized in front of his station. In the red glow of the emergency lighting, Dunstan could see the sweat glistening on the lieutenant's forehead.

"We splashed the first missile, sir. The second one is thirty-five seconds to impact."

"And not a damn thing we can do about that one," Dunstan said. "Put out a distress call. And if you're the praying kind, ask the gods to make sure that bird is going to hit nothing but volcanic rock down there."

"They're tracking it with nine different stations. It'll hit somewhere between the Norfolk-9 and Cumbria-1 arcologies. Twenty-five seconds to impact."

Standard medium-caliber ship killer, Dunstan thought. *Deadly to a frigate, a fart in the wind against a planetary target. Even if it scores a direct hit on an arcology. They should have just fired it at the station as well.*

They watched impotently as the missile followed its projected trajectory on the plot. In the last ten seconds, the AI changed the arc a little to adjust for the friction of the warhead as it sliced through the lower layer of the atmosphere. Dunstan didn't have a visual on the bird, but he knew that the superheated plasma around the shielded warhead would make it look like it was trailing fire.

"Five seconds. Four. Three. Two. One. *Impact,*" Mayler narrated. "Enemy warhead strike on the planetary surface, two point six kilometers east-southeast of Norfolk-9."

At least it wasn't the northern half of the continent, Dunstan thought, and instantly felt shame for his selfishness, thinking about the safety of his own wife and children first.

Twenty seconds of tense silence followed as Mayler tried to get a visual feed from the target area. Then another screen popped up in front of Bosworth's station, and the comms chatter in the background seemed to increase tenfold. Even in the dim red light of the AIC, Dunstan could tell that his XO had just gone ashen faced.

"*Nuclear* warhead strike on the planetary surface," he amended Mayler's report with a cracking voice. "They confirmed the thermal bloom and radiation spike from orbit. Two point six klicks from Norfolk-9. Estimated at twenty kilotons yield."

There were cries of anger and shouts of disbelief in the AIC. Dunstan felt a sudden weakness that would have made his legs tremble if he hadn't been strapped down on a gravity couch.

Not even the Gretians had used nukes against civilian targets in the war. All the combatants had followed an unspoken agreement to limit the use of nuclear warheads to space and against valid military objectives, and even then they had been employed very sparingly over the years. Everyone, including the Gretians, had been afraid of the atomic demon slipping its leash, of things going out of control in ways that ended in wholesale nuclear exchanges between planets. He didn't think much of the Gretians, but Dunstan had always thought that even the most dedicated and fanatical Blackguard wouldn't launch an atomic warhead at a civilian target. Once nukes started flying, there was a terrible temptation on both sides to follow up with more, to seek easy answers to difficult strategic problems in kilotons and then megatons.

Just twenty kilotons. A small tactical warhead, not a city buster. But that close to an arcology. Gods.

"Flash traffic from fleet command," Bosworth shouted into the din. "Planetary Defense Condition 1. I repeat, all military units in the Rhodia AO are ordered to Planetary Defense Condition 1."

The voices died down, and a moment of shocked silence followed. Then Dunstan heard a few sobs. PLADEC-1 was the highest readiness level for the military. It meant that command expected war to be imminent and all but unavoidable. Whatever else it would mean for him and his crew, PLADEC-1 also meant they just had their enlistments extended indefinitely, to serve according to the needs of the navy until the crisis was over. The last time the Rhodian military had gone to PLADEC-1, war had broken out two days later, and Dunstan hadn't come home again on leave for a year and a half.

"XO, all-ship announcement," he ordered, then looked up at his rattled executive officer when the open-channel signal didn't come right away as expected.

"Lieutenant Bosworth."

Bosworth was so shaken that it took him an uncharacteristically long five-second span before his hands could manage to punch the right data fields.

"You're on, sir."

Dunstan took a deep breath and let it out slowly.

What have I done to piss off the gods that I'd have to live through times like these twice? he thought before he touched the TRANSMIT field.

"All hands, this is the commander. There has been a surprise attack on our home world. The fleet is now at Planetary Defense Condition 1."

He paused, momentarily unsure of how much information to give his crew, who were all ready to go home, none prepared to unpack their shipboard bag again and face an unlimited deployment. He still remembered how he had felt when the declaration of war had come across to the fleet nine years ago. The tensions had ramped up gradually back then. Everyone had been able to see it coming. This was brutal in its suddenness. *Minotaur* had a little over 250 crew members, and statistically speaking, it was likely that at least a few of them would be from arcology Norfolk-9. Telling them about the nuclear strike would only add the agony of that uncertainty to the shock of the PLADEC-1 announcement.

"I will share more information as it comes in. For now, we are safe, but we're adrift with no power, propulsion, or gravity. We sent out an emergency request for assistance, and we're just a few hundred klicks from Rhodia One, so we will get assistance to get us the rest of the way. We will rise to this challenge just like we have done before, and we will come out just like we always do."

He closed his eyes and gathered his thoughts for a moment before continuing. When he opened his eyes again, he saw that every member of the AIC was looking at him.

"I won't try to claim we're the best and most powerful ship in the fleet, or that we're blessed by the war gods, or some other horseshit another commander would serve up to motivate his crew," he continued. "We all know that the old girl was a hard-ridden hand-me-down already when we got her. And don't any of you tell me that wasn't your very first thought when you reported to your new command, and you stepped on that shitty worn-out deck liner at the main airlock for the first time.

"But she took care of us, and we took care of her. And I will claim that we have the best crew in the fleet, and I'll fight to the death anyone who tries to shed doubt on that. Nothing that happens after we dock at Rhodia One will take that away from any of us. We may not be the shining heroes in the spotless flagship. But we all know how to do our jobs, and we do them well with what we are given, because we are very good at what we do.

"Whether we serve together or apart, don't ever forget where you were when all of this started. Don't forget the faces of those who stood the watch with you. When we cleaned pirate gunships out of our shipping lanes. When we went toe to toe with a heavy gun cruiser twice our size and four times our firepower and fought them to a draw.

"All of this will be a footnote in a history book someday. But those of us who were there will know what happened, and who made it happen. And now I am wasting emergency power, so I'll cut this short. But know that I am proud to have served with you all. And know that I would be happy to let any of you buy me a drink in any bar in the system. Commander out."

Dunstan closed the channel and leaned back in his couch with a sigh.

"I have a news feed that has a current visual from Kelpie Peninsula, sir," Lieutenant Mayler said.

"Can you bring it up on a bulkhead screen, please?"

"Aye, sir."

Mayler opened another screen and flicked it against the forward AIC bulkhead, where it expanded to fill the available space. The footage was shot from a very high altitude, but the visual was unambiguous. Norfolk-9 was a thousand-meter pyramid of titanium, composites, and steel, a hundred million tons of mass anchored twenty floors into the ground, and not even a tactical nuke going off in close proximity was enough to bring an arcology down. But there were thousands of fires large and small burning on the shattered eastern and southern facades, and it was clear that many thousands were dead down there, maybe even tens of thousands. The angry-looking dark smoke from the fires was already billowing thousands of meters into the sky. To Dunstan, it looked like a funeral pyre of world-shaking proportions.

"All leaves have been canceled. They're calling up the ready reserve," Bosworth said. The stream of news on the screen of his XO station kept refreshing itself, piling alerts on top of alerts, a rushing cascade of words. "Command has ordered a total flight stop for all traffic in and out of Rhodian space except for military units, effective immediately."

"What does it all mean?" Midshipman Boyer asked from the helm station. Dunstan turned his head to look at her.

"What it means, Boyer, is that someone out there is wishing for a war. And it looks like fleet command is about to grant them their wish."

CHAPTER 21

IDINA

Idina had packed her gear the previous night like any good trooper did before a transfer, but that left her nothing to do in the morning. She didn't want to scrub down her quarters for the fifth time, and there was no point in making herself more miserable by drawing out the goodbyes with Fifth Platoon and the rest of the company, so she went for a walk around the perimeter of the base one last time, committing all the details to memory.

She was standing at the fence between the main part of the base and the air and space field, watching the flow of shuttles and gyrofoils taking off and landing, when her comtab sounded an incoming vidcom alert. She opened a screen in front of her with her thumb and forefinger. The caller was a Rhodian lieutenant she didn't know, but from his surroundings, she could tell that he was in the security office at the main gate.

"This is the officer of the watch. You have a visitor at the liaison building, Colors Chaudhary. Can you confirm that you know this person?"

He sent an image of her visitor as required by the gate guard security protocol. Idina looked at the face on the hologram and smiled.

"Yes, sir, I do. On my way. Please tell her I'll be there in ten minutes."

———

"I almost didn't recognize you," Idina said to Dahl when she walked into the JSP's liaison building. "I don't think I've ever seen you in civilian clothes before."

The Gretian police captain stood at the front of the room next to the briefing lectern, just like she always did at the beginning of their joint patrols. She was wearing her hair in the usual tight braid, but the civilian trousers, shirt, and thermal vest she was wearing looked so wrong that it almost caused cognitive dissonance in Idina's brain.

"I am sure you are surprised to find out that I even own any," Dahl said.

Idina walked up to the lectern, and the two women regarded each other for a few moments.

"You shouldn't have come all the way out here on your day off," Idina said. "I'm sure you have better things to do than to see me off."

"Oh, please," Dahl said. "Like what? I would just have breakfast, clean the living space twice, and then go to the office anyway by lunchtime, out of boredom. And we have been patrolling together for three months. It would seem wrong not to say goodbye properly."

"Well, I'm glad to see you one last time," Idina said. "I'm sorry I have to leave you to deal with this mess by yourself."

"I am sure Sergeant Noor will be an able replacement. But I would rather see you in the other seat of the gyrofoil tomorrow night—that is true."

"I'll try to get another deployment," Idina said. "And when I do, I'll volunteer for a JSP assignment from the start. They usually give preference to troops who have done the job before. Cuts the need for familiarization."

"I am sure I will still be on patrol when you do," Dahl said.

"I hope so. Things are getting hot out there. You've done your share. Let someone else stick out their neck for the JSP for a while."

"I am afraid I have done this job for so long that I am just no good for anything else at this point."

"That's supposed to be my personal lament," Idina said.

"Maybe we both are exactly where we need to be."

"Maybe," Idina agreed. "Gods, I hope that's the case. We've got fifty years in uniform between us. It's a little late for second thoughts now."

"You are still young. I am the one who is three years from mandatory retirement. Maybe I can come visit you once they push me out of the door with a pension. If they allow Gretians on your planet again by then."

"I'll make sure they allow you in," Idina said. "You've paid for the privilege, I think."

"I am glad you think so. And I hope you think a little better of this place now. Not all of us agreed with the war. Or the invasion of Pallas."

"I've lost too much here to ever forget," Idina replied. "And I sure as hells can't bring myself to forgive. But you don't need my forgiveness. You had nothing to do with any of it. And if I gave you the impression in the beginning that I thought all Gretians were the same, I'm sorry."

Dahl nodded.

"It would be nice to see you again one day. Here or on Pallas. Or anywhere in between."

Dahl had a bag slung over her shoulder, which she now swung around to the front of her body. Then she opened it and took something out.

"I do not know if this is a Pallas custom, so do not be offended if it seems inappropriate to you. I understand you may not care for a keepsake from your time on Gretia. But I wanted to give you this as a token of my gratitude for our time together."

She handed the item to Idina. It was a folded piece of clothing. When Idina touched it, the unmistakable organic feel of real animal hide greeted her fingers. She unfolded it slowly in her hands. It was a jacket made from heavy cowskin that had been tanned black.

"They issued these until about ten years ago," Dahl said. "They are sort of a marker for the old breed of officers, the veterans. Everything about the new clothing is better. The new jackets are synthetic. Lighter, faster to dry, easier to clean. But when it came time to turn in the old gear, most of the old-timers kept their old jackets and reported them lost or beyond repair."

"That's yours," Idina said. "I can't take that with me." The jacket in her hands probably weighed two kilos or more, and if that was indeed real leather from live Gretian steers instead of vat-grown leather or synthetic replicate, it was worth thousands of ags in material alone.

"I still have my own," Dahl said. "I found a colleague who is close to your build, and whose midsection has expanded considerably in the last ten years. So I talked him out of it. Do not worry. I would not give up my own even under threat of death. But I figured that you should have one of your own. If you care to keep it, that is. You, too, have paid for the privilege."

Idina folded the jacket again and held it to her chest with one arm.

"Thank you," she said. Then she held out her hand, and when Dahl moved to take it, she seized the other woman's forearm in a firm one-handed grip, the Pallas Brigade greeting and farewell.

"When we aren't in uniform anymore, we'll meet up," Idina said. "Here or on Pallas, or anywhere in between. And we'll wear our steer-hide jackets and have drinks and bore the shit out of the other patrons with our stories."

"If the gods have any goodwill left for us at all," Dahl said. "And if they do not, we will tell them to stuff themselves. And then go do it anyway."

———

The orbital shuttle in front of the transit lounge was a Gretian design, part of the military inventory the Alliance had taken over with the rest of the base. It was shaped like a slender arrowhead and painted in what Idina guessed had been a brilliant titanium white with orange accents once upon a time. Now it was flecked in various shades of gray and brown and black, and the paint had scrapes and scuffs everywhere. The Alliance had elected to keep utilizing the Gretian equipment because it was there and because it interfaced with the spin station overhead without a fuss. From what she heard, they had expected the Gretian shuttle fleet to last maybe two more years after the occupation had started, but now they had been here for half a decade, and the birds were still lifting off and landing reliably every day despite their obvious surface wear.

If they engineer their duty clothing as well as they do their spaceships, this thing will outlast me without popping a thread even if I decide to go to sleep in it for the next fifty years, Idina thought as she tucked the leather jacket Dahl had given her into her gear bag before putting it into the cargo conveyor's loading chute. Then she walked through the boarding door and plodded across the metal gangway that connected the transit lounge with the main airlock of the shuttle. Now that she had said her goodbyes, she wasn't much for lingering and taking in some final impressions. She had all the memories she'd ever need of the place, and if it wasn't for the kinship she felt with Dahl, she would have been skipping merrily all the way to the shuttle airlock while humming a happy tune.

Her fellow passengers were mostly Rhodians and Palladians, with a few Acheroni and Oceanian marines sprinkled here and there. The Pallas Brigade troops she passed on the way to her assigned gravity couch nodded at her respectfully. A lot of those faces seemed impossibly young to her. Most of the troops who had received their kukris with her were now either dead or retired, and the former group was considerably larger than the latter. Maybe it was the knowledge that she was being sent home early like a worn-out piece of machinery, but as she strapped into her couch, she felt a deep and profound fatigue that seemed to go all the way to her bones.

Maybe a year or two as the brigade museum curator is all I have left in me, she thought.

She went through the launch prep and listened to the automated briefings with her brain on autopilot, knowing full well that none of the safety features would change the fact that her fate would be out of her hands for the ninety minutes it took to get to the orbital spin station. Then the hull of the shuttle vibrated as the service lines and gangway retracted for takeoff and the engines came alive.

"We are cleared for departure. Launch sequence initiated. Prepare for main engine ignition in thirty seconds," the flight deck announced to the passengers. Idina closed her eyes and leaned back in her gravity couch in anticipation of the g forces she'd feel momentarily. The Gretian shuttles didn't have gravmag units fitted, so the couches would do all the work to compensate for the thrust from the engines. This was the part of the trip she usually disliked the most.

The thrumming from below died down gradually. A few moments later, the hull was silent again. They spent the next minute in silence. In the cabin around her, some troopers started chuckling and talking in low voices.

Great, Idina thought. *I got the defective shuttle. But I guess it's better for the stupid thing to break now than halfway up to the station.*

"All passengers, our launch clearance has been canceled. Please maintain position and remain in your harnesses until the flight deck signals the all clear."

It took a few more minutes for the all clear to come from the flight deck. Idina unbuckled her harness and raised her couch into the egress position to climb out of it. Outside, there was clattering and clanging as the gangway returned to the side of the shuttle and the service lines locked back into their receptacles.

"Now what the hells is going on, Colors?" the young private in the seat next to hers asked.

Idina shrugged.

"I haven't the slightest idea, Private. I guess we'll find out in a minute. But I'm guessing we won't be docking at the spin station in ninety minutes."

———

Annoyed, Idina walked back across the gangway with short steps that made the metal clang. Nothing on the outside of the shuttle gave any indication why they had aborted the launch. There were no emergency pods pulling up on the outside, and nobody had directed them to hurry with the disembarkation, so she guessed it wasn't a critical technical defect.

She didn't even register how quiet it was inside the transit lounge until she was already half a dozen steps into it. Everyone in the room was paying attention to the information screens on the wall, which all showed the same visuals, high-altitude shots of a structure on fire. All around her, people were opening smaller screens on their comtabs to check their own information sources. Idina looked at the feed on the lounge screens, and a sinking feeling materialized in her stomach.

"What's happening, Corporal?" she asked a nearby brigade trooper.

"There's been a nuclear strike on Rhodia, Colors," the young corporal said. "Just a few minutes ago."

"You have *got* to be joking."

The corporal just shook his head. He turned his attention back to the nearest screen, and Idina followed suit. The images on the screen were underscored by a scrolling band of text updates.

. . . WARHEAD IN THE TWENTY-KILOTON RANGE. PRELIMINARY REPORTS SUGGEST TWENTY THOUSAND CASUALTIES, BUT THE INITIAL ESTIMATE IS ALMOST CERTAIN TO CLIMB. RHODIAN FLEET COMMAND HAS ISSUED A PLANETARY DEFENSE CONDITION ONE ALERT FOR THE FIRST TIME SINCE THE GRETIAN WAR. EMERGENCY PERSONNEL ON THE PLANET ARE IN FULL MOBILIZATION . . .

Who the hells got a nuke through those defenses? Idina thought. *This has got to be a mistake.*

But then one of the screens showed an inset from a sensor feed on the ground. From the perspective, Idina could tell that it was maybe fifty kilometers away from the event. The mushroom cloud from the thermonuclear detonation was unmistakable. The sight of it made Idina's heart sink with dread. Fusion plants didn't explode when they malfunctioned. Only a high-order fission event would produce such a cloud, and the only use anyone had for that dirty and dangerous old technology was in atomic warheads, precisely because the tech was dirty and dangerous.

"What did they hit?" she asked the corporal.

"One of the arcologies. They say it's on fire. The Rhodies went to PLADEC-1."

"Well, I fucking *bet* they did."

Every single duty comtab in the room went off with the attention-seeking chirp of a military priority message. All around her, there was a flurry of movement as everyone took their devices out of their pockets or made screens in the air in front of them to check the incoming comm.

This isn't likely to be good, Idina thought as she pulled out her own device and activated it.

FROM: Supreme Headquarters, Alliance
Military Command

TO: All Alliance Units and Personnel
RED ALERT, RED ALERT—Effective immediately, all active alliance units are ordered to full combat alert STATUS LEVEL RED. All leaves and movement orders are hereby canceled. All personnel report to your units without delay. Hostilities expected or imminent. This is not a drill. REPEAT, THIS IS NOT A DRILL.

She took a few slow breaths to keep her heart rate low, then pocketed her device again.

"You read the message," she said loudly into the room. "Everyone get your asses moving and report to your units. For those of you who are unsure, that's the place you came from before you got on that shuttle. Even if you have movement orders."

"What about our kit, Colors?" the young corporal next to her said. "All our gear is still on the shuttle."

"Report to your unit. You are still wearing your uniform, aren't you? If there's something that needs shooting soon, they'll give you your weapons and your armor. Your toiletries can wait."

"Yes, Colors." He rushed off, seemingly happy to get some authoritative direction.

"Anyone with the JSP company, form on me," she called out. "Come on, people. The enemy aren't going to wait around."

Whoever the fuck the enemy is, she thought as the JSP troopers in the room made their way toward her.

"Attention all personnel," an overhead announcement sounded. *"Alliance High Command has ordered an indefinite flight stop for all inbound and outbound Gretia space traffic, effective 1220 hours Universal Time. All scheduled transports are canceled until further notice. All personnel, report to your units immediately."*

Idina looked at the anxious faces of the scattered JSP personnel that were now gathering around her. She was willing to bet good money that this was their first full-scale Level Red combat alert that had ended with the words "This is not a drill." Her last live one had been half a decade ago, when they had started the occupation of Gretia. None of these kids was higher than corporal in rank, and none looked to be older than twenty-one.

"All right," she said when they had all assembled in a loose cluster. "Let's find some transportation. And if we can't source any in this mess, it's an easy two-klick run back to the company building."

As they moved toward the exit as a group, with Idina in the center, she thought about Dahl, and wondered whether the captain had been off the base already when the Level Red alert had sounded. Right now, the base was getting sealed off from the outside world, and no traffic would pass through the main gate in either direction for a good while.

I can probably find you a bunk and a meal somewhere, Captain Dahl, she thought. *Let's just hope we're not about to look at mushroom clouds of our own down here before nightfall.*

———

Outside, the base was in a state of controlled chaos. The group pod that had brought Idina to the transfer terminal was gone, likely commandeered by some other group looking to get back to their own unit. Trying to flag someone down seemed like a waste of time in this mess. All around them, troops were rushing somewhere else in a hurry.

"All right," Idina said to her JSP gaggle. They were a dozen strong, eight of them Pallas Brigade troops from First and Fourth platoons, and the other four from the Rhodian and Oceanian companies, with a single Oceanian marine in the mix. They all looked like they were expecting nukes to fall out of the sky any moment, looking around as if they were a herd of goats about to bolt from the scent of a predator. A brisk run would help channel their barely suppressed panic and give it a release valve.

"Form up in three-abreast running formation," she ordered. "Corporal, you take point. We are moving out in this direction." She indicated it with her hand.

"Yes, ma'am." The corporal stepped onto the roadway outside of the transfer center. Overhead, two combat gyrofoils roared into the sky and away from the airfield. Her JSP stragglers looked up at the war machines as they got into formation as if they were expecting the gun turrets to start thundering any moment.

"*Today*, people," Idina prodded them along. "Corporal, move 'em out, double-time."

She caught up with the formation as they started their run, then kept the pace alongside them. If she had intended to turn off the minds of the young troops and get them focused on something other than their anxious thoughts, it worked on her just the same. It was good to do something physical, to move with a goal and a purpose.

"Corporal, how about a cadence?" she shouted.

The Palladian corporal took up the challenge and began to belt out a popular and highly bawdy brigade running cadence. The Palladians in the formation picked it up after a moment, and Idina could hear their boots hitting the road surface with a little more authority. The Rhodians and the solitary Oceanian in the group didn't sing along because they weren't familiar with the language, but tuning into the rhythm required no understanding of the words. Within a few moments, the whole formation was running along in perfect time, the Palladians sounding off loud enough for a platoon instead of a squad.

Maybe we are both exactly where we need to be, Idina heard Dahl's voice in her head. Ten minutes ago, she wasn't at all sure about that sentiment. But right now, she knew with certainty that she was at least where these young troopers needed her to be.

Another pair of gyrofoils roared overhead, then another right behind it. The craft took up a staggered formation and roared toward the distant skyline of Sandvik. On the road in front of them, a company of personnel carriers appeared, wedge-shaped chunks of armor with autocannon mounts on top, rolling on heavily studded honeycomb wheels. They turned onto the road in the direction of the main gate and dashed off at high speed. The vibrations from their nearby passage made the surface under Idina's boot soles shake. If war had a smell to Idina, it was the scent of fuel in the air that heavy combat machines left in their wake. She was glad that the red alert hadn't come five minutes later while she was already on the way to orbit, that she had been on the right side when the portcullis came rattling down. Whatever happened next, she'd be facing it with a gun in her hands and a platoon under her guidance, not witnessing it from afar while condemned to observer status.

As they ran along the road that would take them back to the JSP complex, Idina realized that the bone-deep fatigue she had felt earlier had lifted from her completely.

I guess the brigade museum will have to wait for now, she thought. *There's a war coming up. And gods help me, I am glad not to miss it.*

CHAPTER 22

SOLVEIG

The dinner with the Hanzo directors was a boring affair that didn't even really loosen up when the formal part ended and the Acheroni plum brandy bottles came out. Solveig made a mental note that a dull corporate drone continued to be a dull corporate drone even after seven shots of high-strength liquor, and that the alcohol just removed the self-restraint from the dullness and gave it an aggressive quality. She had nursed one small glass of the stuff all evening, never letting it drop to below half-full because she was aware of the Acheroni custom to always refill an empty glass for a guest. Gisbert hadn't been aware of that custom, and he had toasted himself into a near-catatonic state by the end of the dinner, studiously avoided by even the most hospitality-minded Hanzo people. Solveig had observed a long time ago that alcohol didn't bestow new personalities on its consumers but merely amplified the existing ones—or in Gisbert's case, the lack of one.

They returned to the hotel just before local midnight. Gisbert had his assistant on one side of him and his security agent, Lanzo, on the other as they maneuvered him the short distance from the skylift platform to the door of his suite. Solveig hoped he'd be sick enough in the morning to bow out of the first round of negotiations so she wouldn't have him hovering just behind her right shoulder for hours, alternating between looking at her compad screen and dozing off.

"If there is nothing else, I will see you in the morning, Miss Ragnar," Cuthbert said when they had reached the door to her suite.

"Good night, Cuthbert. I wasn't planning on any nighttime excursions, but I will let you know if I change my mind and decide to go to a nightclub or something."

"Of course, Miss Ragnar. Good night to you."

The smile he gave her had a slightly pained quality to it, as if the thought of having to escort his protectee out into the nightlife of Coriolis City caused him physical discomfort. For a young guy, he wasn't very adventurous.

Solveig closed the door behind her and stepped out of her shoes. Then she walked over to the seating arrangement in the middle of the living space. The ambient floor and ceiling lights came on with a soft blue-white glow.

"Room, open blinds," she said.

The multi-segmented blinds in front of the panoramic window moved aside soundlessly. Beyond, the city was a sea of lights. It seemed brighter out than it had been at midday in full sunshine. She tried to imagine what Coriolis City looked like right now from the outside, floating among the dark clouds with all the buildings and streets illuminated, a bubble of moving light in the swirling darkness of Acheron's night side.

There was an ample supply of security-screened refreshments in her suite, water and snacks and a variety and quantity of alcohol that would have been enough to fuel a decent dormitory party back at the university. Solveig made herself a little plate with salted almonds and grapes and poured herself a glass of Gretian red wine. Then she took her drink and snacks over to the seating arrangement and sat down. The wine was a good dry grape and vintage, captured sunshine squeezed into a vat and left to ferment for a little while.

She was halfway through the glass and the bowl of almonds when her private comtab hummed with an incoming request for a vidcom. She checked the ID code of the caller.

Here we go, she thought. *Time for me to report on what I've learned in school today.*

Solveig put the wineglass on the table in front of her and brought up a screen at eye height above the table surface. Then she leaned back on the recliner seat and accepted the incoming vidcom.

"Hello, Papa."

"Hello, daughter of mine," Falk said. He was sitting in his usual spot at the bar in the main house. Behind him, Solveig saw the flickering from his multiple news screens, silently blasting content into the room.

"I see that it's wine hour where you are," he said and nodded at her half-full glass. He raised his hand, which had his own glass in it, this one with two fingers of Rhodian whisky over ice cubes. That was one area where she knew she was not like him at all—she didn't mind whisky, but she'd never pour an expensive one over ice. And expensive ones were the only kind he drank.

"We just got back from the Hanzo dinner," she said. "Gisbert got so loaded that his poor little assistant had to help carry him home. She's half his size. If that doesn't merit bonus pay, I don't know what does."

"Gisbert's a bumbling idiot," her father said. "But he has one redeeming quality. He does what he's told."

"Are you even supposed to call me like this?" Solveig asked.

"It's a loophole," Falk said. "Neither of us are on Ragnar property, and you are off the clock. And we're not talking business. I'm just a father checking in on his daughter, who's on her first trip to a new planet. How was your day?"

"Perfectly all right. If I could tell you about the business, I'd probably complain about the Hanzo people taking three hours to ask a direct question. I could be on the way home already if I could find just a single subdirector among them who can say and understand the words yes and no."

Falk laughed. His teeth looked very white in the semidarkness of her suite's living room.

"Welcome to the Acheroni business world. Where intent and semantics are everything. Gods, I miss mixing it up with those little bastards."

He looked at her intently and took a slow sip of his whisky. She could tell that he had something on his mind, and he did her the favor of getting to the point right away, unlike the Hanzo negotiators.

"I know who you've been meeting," he said. The smile that followed was his usual toothy dominance display, without a trace of good cheer or humor in it. He took another sip from his glass as he waited for her reaction.

Solveig felt the shock of alarm trickling down her spine. She sat up and reached for her glass to give herself the second she needed to smooth out her composure.

If he knows, then he knows. And then at least I don't have to pretend anymore.

"You do," she said. "And how do you know that?"

"Some little birds told me, Solveig."

Birds, she thought. *More like weasels.*

Now that his surprise was out of the bag and failed to make her crumble with the shock of it, his expression switched from predatory cheer to restrained anger.

"I expected better from you. I never would have thought that you'd have such abysmal judgment."

"I did what I thought I had to do," she said evenly and took a sip of her wine, giving him another second or two to start showing his hand without folding hers.

"You thought you had to sleep with the police detective who's investigating our company? Oh, Solveig. Maybe I have overrated your critical thinking skills."

He's talking about Berg, she realized, feeling a wild wave of relief coursing through her that she was equally careful to keep out of her expression.

"He closed the investigation. He said it was a dead end. They handed it all off to the military investigators. It's not our concern anymore. He's no longer involved in any cases that touch Ragnar."

"So he figured he'd do some touching of his own, I guess. What if that's all part of the investigation? What if it's still in progress? Have you thought of *that*? What if he wants to see if you're holding anything back? You've given him backdoor access to the company's pulse, Solveig. You don't sleep with the *enemy*."

"He's not the enemy. I haven't even slept with him. We've gone out a few times for dinner. That's it. Not that it's any of your business, Papa."

He took a quick little sip from his glass and put it down on the counter with a sharp click of glass on wood.

"I beg to differ. When it comes to anything Ragnar, it's very much my business. Regardless of what those Alliance people put into writing. And you are the future of Ragnar. Only you, Solveig."

Then nothing I do will ever fail to be your business, she thought, and the sudden anger she felt warmed her middle better and far more quickly than the wine had. This wasn't even about Aden, and he was treating it like a personal betrayal, just because she had dared to make a judgment call that disagreed with his.

"I like him. I think he likes me. He seems like a good man. I may sleep with him in the future, or I may not. But that's my choice to make, not yours."

"We will talk about that when you're back home," Falk said.

She closed her eyes briefly and took a slow, deliberate breath. This was a fork in the road, and her next statement would put her on one of two paths. If she stepped the way she had always done, she could feign acquiescence and recognize his sovereignty over every aspect of her life, resign herself to getting her way only whenever she could tiptoe past him. She'd have to be content with sneaking the ice cream from the freezer at night occasionally.

Or she could step the other way, on a new path she'd never taken before. She could be more like him, but in the way he would least appreciate. That path had far more thorns and brambles on it. But whatever she would find at the end would be hers to claim entirely, whether it was good or bad.

She made her decision, and as soon as she opened her mouth, the contentment she felt made it clear that it had been the right one.

"I love you, Papa. You know that. And I respect your opinions and your counsel. But my love life is absolutely none of your business, either now or after I get back home. And I will not discuss this any further. Good night."

She gave him a stern glare and wiped the screen away to terminate the vidcom.

Her father was not used to people ending talks with him. *He* was the one who terminated the connection, and only when he felt that you knew he was done with you. Solveig knew that there was probably a whisky glass exploding against one of the walls in the bar right now. His fury would be red-hot when she got back from Acheron. But she knew that if she had yielded to him on this, it would have been a universal adapter for him to attach himself to every part of her life and never let go again.

Solveig put down her wineglass and shut off her private comtab before her father could send another vidcom request. She got up and walked over to the panoramic windows to look out over the city and let her emotions ebb a little. The anger at her father's intrusion was battling it out with the relief she felt that his network of snoops had followed the wrong track, leading her father to Detective Berg instead of Aden. The tiredness she had felt when she had walked into her suite was gone now, and she knew that she'd need either a good, brisk run or another glass of wine to wind down enough for bed again. After a few moments of consideration, Solveig decided to choose the easier option. Going for a run in a strange city in the middle of the night wouldn't make her security detail happy.

She had just topped off her wineglass at the bar when the door chime sounded. She looked over at the screen that materialized in front of the door to show her who was outside. It was Cuthbert. He was holding his comtab and wearing a concerned expression.

"What is it, Cuthbert?" she asked. "If that's my father trying to talk to me, tell him I'm not taking any more comms tonight."

Cuthbert looked up from his comtab and shook his head. She couldn't recall the last time she had seen him flustered or upset, but he was clearly in crisis mode.

"It's not your father, Miss Ragnar. May I come in? Something awful has happened."

Solveig gestured at the door to allow him access, and it retracted silently. Cuthbert walked into her suite and past the bar nook into the living area, where he activated the information system and opened a screen that filled the wall on one side of the room completely. He dismissed the hotel's courtesy service feed and brought up several news feeds, then flicked them to arrange the screen into quarters. All showed variations of the same visuals: a large, roiling cloud rising into the sky, and a huge building on fire. The scenery was unfamiliar to Solveig, but the planetary background looked like Rhodia—fields of volcanic rock and gravel, and low, barren, snow-capped mountains in the distance. Text updates were scrolling past at the bottom of each screen quarter, too fast for Solveig to try to make sense of the Acheroni script.

"What is going on, Cuthbert?"

"Someone dropped a nuclear weapon on Rhodia, Miss Ragnar. It's all over the Mnemosyne. It hit one of their arcologies."

"*Gods,*" Solveig said. She put down her wineglass and walked over into the living space. Cuthbert was furiously working the text-entry field on his comtab in between glances at the news feeds.

"I've summoned the others to your suite, Miss Ragnar. I hope that is all right. You have the biggest space."

"That's perfectly fine, Cuthbert. Now what in the worlds is going on? Who would drop a *nuke* on the Rhodians? The war's been over for five years."

"I don't know who would do such a thing. I just know that it happened. And that it's very, very bad news."

That sounds like the understatement of the decade, Solveig thought as she looked at the news feeds with growing horror. As she watched, Cuthbert changed the feeds and their captions to Gretian. TENS OF THOUSANDS DEAD OR MISSING, Solveig read. STATE OF EMERGENCY DECLARED FOR ALL OF RHODIA.

Cuthbert looked like he was expecting an impending assault on the city any second. He closed the blinds of the panoramic windows, then paced in front of them like a restless predator, still reading messages on his comtab and firing off his own into the Mnemosyne.

"I don't think we're in danger here," she said. "Rhodia is a hundred million kilometers away. And Papa said the cities on Acheron are safe from ballistic missiles because they're never in a fixed place."

"And the Rhodians have the best ballistic missile defense system in all of Gaia," Cuthbert said. "This city is ten kilometers across, Miss Ragnar. If someone wants to hit it, there's a way."

And how will you protect me from a nuclear strike? Solveig thought. *The Acheroni didn't even let your security detail bring sidearms into the city.* But she recognized that falling back on his basic job functions made Cuthbert feel like he had a little bit of control over the situation, so she kept the thought to herself.

They watched the news feeds as the other members of the Ragnar delegation trickled into the suite: Solveig's assistant, Anja; Gisbert's bodyguard, Fulco; and his assistant, Inga. Gisbert himself was still passed out in his suite, and Solveig had no desire to send Cuthbert to try and get him to his feet because she knew he'd be worse than useless in his current state.

He's going to wake up with a beast of a hangover and find that the world has shifted under his feet while he was out, she thought.

Even with instant transmission of information across millions of kilometers, the networks could only report what they got from the scene, and after a little while, the images on the screen started to become repetitive to the point where Solveig could begin to predict the angle changes of the limited variety of high-altitude shots.

The information text scrolled across the bottom of the screen: Rhodian fleet on full alert status, Ministry of Defense expected to invoke Alliance to declare system-wide military emergency.

"Are we going to war with Rhodia again?" Anja asked. She looked shaken and afraid, completely unlike her usual put-away professional persona.

"We aren't," Cuthbert said. "Not as far as I know. We don't even have a fleet anymore. But it looks like *someone* is at war with them."

He nodded at the screens, which were showing the footage of the dark, roiling mushroom cloud rising into the sky above Rhodia again from several different angles.

An incoming message chirped on his comtab. He scrolled through it, then softly muttered a curse.

"What is it, Cuthbert?" Solveig asked.

He looked at her, and in the moment he appeared even younger than he usually looked, all wide-eyed anxiety.

"The Alliance has just announced a full blockade of Gretia, effective immediately," he said. "They've halted all incoming or outgoing traffic until further notice. All inbound ships are ordered to hold station or make for alternate destinations."

"They can't do that," Fulco said. "That will bring the economy to a halt. Ours and theirs."

"Ours more than theirs," Solveig said. "They can still trade with the rest of the system. We can't trade with anyone off-planet."

"Well, they just *did* that." Cuthbert pointed at the display, where the summary of the Gretian blockade announcement had begun to scroll across the screen, framing the foreboding footage of the nuclear detonation and the burning arcology.

"So does that mean we can't go home?" Anja asked.

"Not unless they lift the blockade by the time we're done with the Hanzo talks. Looks like we may be here a little longer than intended," Cuthbert replied.

Good, Solveig thought. *That will give Papa's anger some time to cool.*

Solveig immediately chided herself for her selfishness. Somewhere on Rhodia, tens of thousands of people were dead, wounded, or missing, and her first reaction after the initial shock was relief at the prospect of not having to return home soon to face her irate father.

As if our family fight is more important than the fate of two planets. Gods help me if I am starting to think like Papa after all.

She walked over to the bar and picked up her wineglass again, but the visuals unfolding in front of her had made her lose all taste for the indulgence. She poured the contents of the glass into the bio-recycler. Getting drunk wouldn't help her go to sleep any better. She'd just feel as bad as Gisbert in the morning.

"What do we do now, Miss Ragnar?" Anja asked. Solveig looked up to see that everyone in the room was looking at her.

Now you act like I'm in charge, she thought.

She looked past them all and at the window, where Cuthbert had left a small crack in the alignment of the blinds. The scene outside was unchanged, brightly lit city streets busy with late-night crowds. If there were nukes headed for Acheron and Coriolis City, the blinds wouldn't shield them, and nothing would matter anymore. And if there weren't any nukes, then it didn't matter either, not in the moment.

"Let's act as though all the worlds will still be turning tomorrow," she said. "We have talks to resume in the morning. If the blockade isn't lifted when it's time to go home, we figure it out then. But for now, we should probably all go to sleep and go ahead as if nothing has changed."

She could tell that they weren't entirely convinced of the wisdom of her suggestion, but nobody else had any alternatives, and she was glad to see that things were at the point where not even Cuthbert wanted to contradict her openly.

They all filed out of her suite again one by one. The last to leave was Cuthbert, and from the anxious look on his face, she was almost convinced he'd take up station just outside her door and sleep in the hallway. After she closed the door behind him, she walked into the living space and extinguished all the screens with a wave of her hand, already tired of the repetitive coverage of the very limited information everyone had so far. Tomorrow they would have more data, enough for her to make better decisions. Staying up and trying to keep on top of the incoming news would be a waste of time right now, time that was better used to let her brain reset for whatever was to come.

She did her nighttime ablutions and slipped into bed. Outside, Coriolis City was still humming with people and activity, unaffected by the drama that was unfolding a hundred million kilometers away on Rhodia. Solveig felt a strange sense of calmness as she listened to the faint sounds of the busy city outside her suite's windows. It was oddly freeing to finally have some bigger worries than her father's disapproval.

Chapter 23

Aden

The bar was called Halo 212. The directions Tess had sent him led Aden to one of the superslender Coriolis City towers that jutted into the sky underneath the dome like needles. Aden's stomach lurched a little when he stepped onto the skylift platform in the atrium of the building and realized that the number in the bar's name stood for the floor where it was located.

When he walked into the lobby of the 212th floor only a minute later, he understood the complete logic behind the name. Halo 212 was a circular platform that wrapped around the building and jutted out high over Coriolis City. The effect was unsettling and breathtaking at the same time because the bar was constructed almost entirely out of transparent material.

After a moment of hesitation, Aden stepped out onto the floor, which afforded a clear view of the cityscape below. The ring that made up the bar was cantilevered on a thin frame of what looked like titanium and graphite composites, but the wide spaces between the thin spokes of the load-bearing structure were filled in with long slabs of Alon that looked to be at least thirty centimeters thick. Aden knew the properties of the material, but even the knowledge that a slab of that thickness would stop an antiship missile didn't entirely mollify the primitive part of his brain that objected to walking out into seemingly thin air. He hadn't kept up with the current price of Alon, but he had a good idea that the cost of this bar's materials constituted a fair percentage of the building's total construction bill. They had aligned the thermal welds of the Alon slabs with the spokes of the frame to make the floor look as seamlessly clear as possible, and the end result was frighteningly effective. He knew they could have simulated the same view at a much lower cost and effort with viewscreens in the floors, so the whole thing was an ostentatious display of extreme wealth and engineering prowess.

Drinks in this place are going to start at fifty ags, he thought as he walked out into the middle of the transparent floor.

The walls and ceiling were almost entirely transparent as well, with only the most minimal concessions to the need for a visible support structure. The floor jutted out from the building for thirty meters, and the farther Aden got out into the ring, the more complete the illusion of floating in midair became—the streets below, the dark night sky above, all in a grand panoramic vista that was only occasionally broken by a razor-thin composite spar between the massive slabs of Alon.

It took a little while to spot the other members of the *Zephyr* crew, which gave Aden a bit of time to adjust to the feeling of being suspended high above the city streets.

"This is an interesting spot for a bar," he said when he walked up to his crewmates, who were sitting in a group of skeletonized chairs by one of the windows on the outer edge of the bar. There were two empty chairs in the group, and he sat down on one very carefully, dubious that the thin latticework of the furniture could hold his weight. But it did so with ease, and it was far more comfortable than it looked.

"Isn't it?" Tristan said. "I love this place. Even if it is an overpriced tourist trap. But you can't beat the view."

"No, you sure can't," Aden said. He looked down at the space between his feet, which gave a clear view of the plaza in front of the building. "How high up is the 212th floor?"

"Eight hundred fifty meters, give or take a few," Maya said. "That's a thirteen-second free fall in one g, in case you're curious."

"I'm sure he could have done without that information," Tess said.

"It's fine," Aden assured her.

"Have a drink or two, and you'll enjoy it much more," Tristan said. He was leaning back in his chair, one leg crossed over the other. His white linen shirt was unbuttoned to a point just under his sternum, and there was the light-gray stubble of a three-day beard on his face. He looked supremely relaxed, sipping an amber liquid from a bulb-shaped glass.

"How does one go about doing that in this place?" Aden asked.

"There's a bartender station every ten meters on the inner wall," Tristan pointed. "Or you can summon the live waiter, but that'll cost you fifteen percent extra."

"I'll do the station," Aden said. "At least until I know how much they charge for a drink here."

He walked over to the nearest bartender station and selected the cocktail menu on the service screen. It wasn't quite as bad as he had feared, but the place didn't give anything away either. They had been allowed alcohol in the prison arcology, but only beer, wine, and cider. He still wasn't used to drinking anything stronger, so he selected a local brew. The service station produced an ice-cold aluminum bottle a moment later, and the screen told him that the ten ags for the beer had been subtracted from his ledger.

"You got yourself some new clothes," Tess said to him when he returned to the group and reclaimed his chair.

"I did," he said. "It felt like I'd been wearing nothing but that flight suit for three months."

"It's a good look. Not that you look terrible in a flight suit."

"Thanks," he said and took a swig of his beer to give himself a second to deal with the unexpected compliment.

The light in the bar was dimmed to enhance the effect of the entire space appearing to float in the night sky, so when someone a few seating groups away opened a screen on their comtab, it was noticeable. Aden looked over in annoyance only to see several more screens opening all over the room. The low din of the conversations in the room picked up, and even though Aden couldn't understand the Acheroni coming from the seating groups on either side, he could tell that their tone had changed. A tense mood seemed to roll gradually across the bar.

"Something is going on," Maya said.

She flagged down a passing server and engaged in a quick-fire conversation in Acheroni, then turned back to them with a disturbed expression as the server rushed off.

"Check the networks," she said and pulled out her own comtab.

"Which one?" Tess asked as she did likewise.

"I don't think it matters," Maya said. "It'll be on every one of them. She said there's news that someone dropped a nuke on Rhodia."

That revelation stunned them all into shocked silence. Aden took out his own comtab. Almost everyone in the room had a comtab out and a viewscreen open now, bar etiquette temporarily put aside.

"Shit," Tess said softly when she read her own screen.

The news reports were frantic and repetitive, but they all conveyed the scale of the incident. Aden's stomach twisted at the sight of the footage of what was unmistakably the mushroom cloud of a nuclear detonation in the clear blue sky of another planet. He knew the scenery well after looking at it for five years, even if he was unfamiliar with the shape of the arcology that was ablaze with hundreds of fires.

"That is *insane*," Henry said. Aden had never seen a hint of fear on the Palladian's face since he joined the crew, but he looked afraid now.

For the next few minutes, they all watched the news feeds and exchanged low-voiced commentary among each other, all variations of the same Oceanian rote invectives reserved for shock and disbelief.

"That puts us in a bad spot," Decker finally said when the reality of the event had settled in. "A really bad spot."

"We gave the Rhodies what we had," Tess said. "That wasn't anything *we* did."

"Someone just nuked an arcology on Rhodia," Henry replied. "Not even a week after we hand-delivered a black-market nuclear warhead to the Rhodian navy. There aren't that many nukes floating around out there."

"It doesn't even matter if our nuke is connected to that one somehow," Decker said. "The Rhodies sure as hell are going to assume they were. The minute we cross back into Rhodian space, they'll reel us in. If only to make sure they have every bit of information they can squeeze from our brains about that bad client."

I used up all my good luck with that Rhodian commander a few days ago, Aden thought. *If we cross paths with the Rhodies again, there won't be any acts of mercy or forgiveness. Not for a former Blackguard.*

"Odds are we weren't their only supply line." Tristan picked up his drink and slugged the contents of the glass. Then he grimaced and scratched his head with his free hand. "Nice load of shit we took on with that quarter-ton container."

"It happened. We all agreed to take it on. And then we all voted to take it to the Rhodies. Now we have to live with the fallout," Decker said.

"So what do we do now?" Tristan asked. "Once we have the ship out of overhaul. Do we just avoid Rhodian space for the next few years? Half our contracts come from the Rhodia-to-Pallas route."

"I don't see how we can go back there," Aden said. "Not until the Rhodies figure out who dropped that nuke. Because I am pretty sure they won't just take our word for it that it wasn't us."

Maya got to her feet and snatched her empty bottle off the glass table in front of the chairs.

"Before we vote ourselves into another disaster, let me get another drink. Maybe something stronger this time."

"No rush," Decker told her as she walked off. "We're not going to decide anything tonight. Ship's docked for another two weeks anyway."

———

When Maya returned, someone else was with her. Aden looked up from his comtab to see a handsome, lean man with short black hair by her side. His first thought was that she had met a local friend or maybe picked up someone on her way to the bartender station, but when he saw her stiff expression, he knew that something wasn't right. Across the table, Henry's body language shifted into an alert posture, and seeing the Palladian's hand creep close to the hilt of his kukri set off all kinds of alarm bells in Aden's head.

"And who might you be?" Henry asked.

The man had wrapped one arm around Maya's shoulders. It would have looked like a casual embrace except for his other hand, which he had pressed against her side. He nudged her downward into one of the empty chairs and sat down in the one beside her, all in one smooth and fluid motion. Aden could see something white and pointy in that hand.

"If your hand goes any further toward your knife, I'll stick mine straight through her heart," he said to Henry in a pleasant tone. His voice was honey poured over polished steel. "Your blade may be sharper, but my blade is faster. Do you understand me?"

After a tense moment, Henry nodded slowly and pointedly moved his hand away from his beltline.

"Who are you, and what do you want?" Decker asked.

"My name isn't important," the man said. "It wouldn't mean anything to you anyway. But if you have to have a name to go with the face, you may call me Milo." He spoke Oceanian, but with the sort of neutral inflection that indicated very expensive and thorough language training.

Aden looked at Maya's face, which was equal parts fear and anger, and he tried to judge if he could make it to her from his side of the table. From Tristan's body language, he could tell that the ship's cook was having the same thoughts. The intent must have been too obvious in their faces, because the unwelcome guest looked at them and shook his head with a slight smile.

"If I see anyone's asses getting out of any chairs even a little bit, your young friend here dies, and I'll take my chances with the rest of you. I've got two of these. Don't want to use them tonight, but don't think that I'll hesitate."

Tristan held up his hands in appeasement, anger etched on his face. Aden kept his own hands where they were, on the armrests of his chair.

Maybe he's bluffing, Aden thought. *But if he's not, I won't give him an excuse.*

Milo prodded Maya lightly with the point of his blade, and the way she sharply sucked in her breath dispelled all notions of a bluff from Aden's head. This man would do exactly what he said, and there was nothing anyone at the table could do about it. Aden knew he could leap out of his chair and cover the meter and a half to Maya and Milo in just a second, but he also knew that he'd be half a second too late.

"All right. Like I said, my name isn't important. I'm here on someone else's behalf. You owe a debt to my employer, and I have come to collect payment."

"You work for the people who hired us to smuggle the nuke for them," Decker said.

The black-haired man nodded.

"The cargo you surrendered to the Rhodian navy was very expensive. Hard to obtain. Almost impossible to replace."

"My heart is broken," Decker replied. "If you're coming to collect your advance, we had to turn it over to the Rhodies. And I hope you aren't asking us to buy you a new black-market *nuke*."

Milo shook his head.

"I'm afraid that would be impractical. It took my employer long enough to source the one you lost."

"So what did you come to collect?" Henry asked.

"Twenty million ags," Milo said. "That is what my employer has lost due to your breach of contract. And they were generous and didn't add the ancillary damage they incurred after you surrendered their cargo."

"Twenty million," Tess said with a snort. She looked like she wanted to laugh out loud but didn't quite dare.

"Who walks around with twenty million on their comtab?" Aden asked, taken aback by the casual way Milo had thrown out a number that would have been hard to raise on the spot even if Aden still had access to the family fortune. People with twenty million ags on their ledgers didn't spend their time chasing courier contracts between the planets.

"We don't have a tenth of that between all of us," Tristan said. "You've come a long way to stick your hand into an empty jar, I'm afraid."

"I know you don't have the money in your ledger. But you have something of roughly similar value. A Tanaka Spaceworks model two thirty-nine."

Decker shook her head and chuckled.

"We couldn't give you our ship. Even if we wanted to, which we most certainly do not. *Zephyr* doesn't belong to us. She is owned by a consortium."

"I know who owns the title to that ship, Captain Decker," Milo said.

Aden noticed that Milo still had his arm around Maya's shoulder. To any casual observer, it would look like someone being tender with a partner. But the hand that held the knife hadn't wavered since he had taken his seat.

"I also know she's docked at Tanaka right now for her three-year overhaul. You can be glad for that because it gave me a reason to come here and make a business proposal instead of just disposing of you all one by one. You're not half as wily or clever as you think you are. I got to the spaceport two hours ago, and I had you all tracked down forty-five minutes after I got here. The ride on the travel pod to this place took longer than that."

"She already told you the ship's not ours to give," Aden said. "She doesn't hold the legal title for it."

"And without the title, she's useless for what she was built," Tess added. She looked profoundly offended, as if Milo had proposed they all surrender their eventual firstborn children to him. "You can fly her, but you can't dock her anywhere without getting flagged for a stolen ship. That's not some rack-grade freighter whose registry plate you can just renumber in the command deck. They only made four two thirty-nines."

Milo smiled and shook his head.

"If you are quite done with your interplanetary legal advice, I'll give you my proposal. Or we can decide to start stabbing each other. Just know that I kill people for a living. Your Palladian friend there may give me some hassle, but he's across the table. I will have three of you bleeding out on the floor before he can get to me, and I'd put even money on being able to add at least a fourth."

From the way Henry's hands were flexing almost imperceptibly, Aden could tell that the first officer was evaluating that claim and considering putting it to the test. Just like it would be impossible to stop Milo from slipping the knife into Maya's heart, Aden knew that it was equally impossible to keep Henry from launching himself across the table if he chose to try his luck.

Don't do it, Aden thought. *You'll kill him. But not before he kills her first.*

"Let's hear your proposal," Decker said. "And why don't we stop talking about blood and stabbing."

She reached over to Henry and lightly put a hand on his knee without taking her eyes off Milo.

"You'll take possession of your ship after the overhaul is complete," Milo said. "Then you will fly her out to coordinates I will supply, where you will simulate an emergency that requires you to abandon ship in a life pod. Then one of our subsidiaries will come in and take over. You will be returned to Acheron, and we can all go our own ways, with clean ledgers."

"Simple as that," Decker said. "And you won't just blast the life pod into pieces."

"You want to claim a salvage title," Tess said. "That's pretty devious."

"It'll work better if you are alive to corroborate the story, of course. So no, they won't blow the life pod away. And your ship will have just had its overhaul, so a mishap wouldn't be out of the ordinary. Dockhands screw up all the time. Things don't get plugged back in, or they get plugged in the wrong way. You know how it goes. You have a good engineer. She should have no trouble faking a convincing emergency."

Aden glanced at Tess. He knew her well enough by now to realize that the proposal was morally unpalatable to her, and that Milo might as well have asked her to strangle a crew member and use the corpse for emergency rations.

"If you think that's going to happen, you are out of your mind," Tess said dryly.

"The proposal I just gave you is Option A," Milo replied. "If you choose to do anything else, you will have picked Option B. You can fly off and try to go about your business. Maybe report the whole thing to the Rhodies again. But rest assured that no matter where you dock, we'll catch up with you sooner or later. And there will be no Option C at that point. We will get that ship one way or another. The only difference is going to be whether we'll have to mop blood off the deck once we have her."

The air between them was thick with the possibility of impending violence, a highly combustible mix that would take just a quick gesture or a slipping temper to ignite and consume them all. Aden had no great martial abilities, but he knew he'd join in if anyone else tried to lunge across the table and pry Maya away from the hard-eyed, smooth-talking black-haired man who still held her in an almost friendly embrace. But he also knew that he'd probably end up bleeding on the floor with the rest of them. He hadn't been in a violent line of work, but as an intelligence officer, he had dealt with people who were. This man reminded him of those professionals—his utter calmness in the face of a close-quarters fight with six people, one of them a Pallas Brigade veteran armed with a monomolecular blade.

Whatever Aden had seen in their unwelcome visitor, Henry seemed to have come to the same assessment. His hands relaxed, and he let out a deep, slow breath. The Palladian martial ethos was their way of life, and Aden had a good idea what kind of self-control the first officer had to exert to keep himself from drawing his kukri and taking up the challenge. But even if Milo wasn't quite as good as he thought, Maya would die. Aden wouldn't have made that trade, and he was glad to see that Henry wasn't willing to make it either.

"Can we have some time to think about it?" Decker asked.

Milo shrugged.

"Personally, I don't know why you would. It's a simple A or B choice. Like I said, there is no C. But you have two weeks anyway. Until you go back up to the spin station to get your ship back from Tanaka."

He stood up carefully, pulling Maya up with him as he straightened out.

"I will send you the coordinates I mentioned before you leave the dock. If you get the bright idea to pass them on to the Rhodians, rest assured we will know. If you do anything else other than make best speed to that spot and abandon ship once you get there, I will come to collect the payment on Option B."

He flicked his wrist a little to let them see the knife he was holding against Maya's side. It had the dull white shimmer of ceramic composites.

"I will walk toward the atrium in just a few seconds. Please don't get the idea to rush me and start a fight. I have two of these, and I'm very good with them. Don't put too much stock in that flashy parade knife on your first officer's belt. I don't care how many mudlegs he killed with it during the war. But if you want to roll the dice, go right ahead."

In a smooth movement that looked almost gentle, Milo pushed Maya back into her chair. Then he turned around and walked off without another word. Aden held his breath, but Henry remained in his own chair, his face tense with controlled rage.

When the trim black-haired man with the ceramic knives had disappeared in the atrium beyond the bar's entryway, it felt to Aden like someone had pounded the relief valve off a pressure tank with a hammer.

Decker and Tristan leaped out of their chairs and rushed over to Maya.

"Holy shit," Tess said. "What the fuck just happened?"

"Are you all right?" Decker asked.

"I'm fine," Maya replied. She unzipped her flight suit and lifted one side to look at her rib cage. The white compression shirt she wore underneath had a fist-sized bloodstain on it.

"Fucker only poked me with the tip. Half a centimeter maybe. Just to let me know he meant it. Sorry, everyone. He came out of nowhere. I walked up to the order station, and he was right behind me."

"Don't worry about it," Tristan said. "Let's get that shit bandaged up."

"Thank you," Aden said to Henry.

"For what?"

"For not trying to take his head off. I don't think he was talking big. He absolutely meant it."

"Oh, I know he was," Henry replied. He got out of his chair and looked at the atrium entrance for a moment. Then he flexed his hands and balled them into fists.

"How'd you know?" Aden asked.

"He walked up to six people and started talking about killing them and taking their ship," Henry said. "Anyone who does that is either insane or really sure of their skill. And that man wasn't insane."

"Ceramic blades," Tristan said. "Only two kinds of people really use those. Cooks who are too lazy to sharpen their steel every day. And professionals."

Aden didn't have to ask what sort of profession Tristan meant.

"Well, he didn't look like a fucking cook to me," Maya growled.

———

"We should split up," Aden said a little while later, after Tristan had patched up Maya in the sanitary suite and gotten everyone a round of expensive Rhodian whisky. "Junk our comtabs and get new ones. Rent different rooms every night. Make it hard for them to track us."

Captain Decker shook her head.

"We're better off staying in a group. Watch each other's backs. Switching comtabs won't do us any good without different ID passes to link to them."

She tilted her glass and watched as the liquid's surface changed its angle as well, beholden to the gravity of the planet.

"We don't have many options here. Rhodia is going to grab us as soon as we dock there. Gretia is blockaded—not that I want to go to that shithole anyway. We can't go to Hades because we don't have the shielding for the approach. We'd just toast the ship and give ourselves a radiation overdose. That leaves us with Pallas and Oceana."

"We'll have a hard time making our operating budget with Oceana-to-Acheron runs," Tristan said.

"Or we stay on Acheron for now," Tess suggested.

Henry shook his head. "With the docking fees and everything else, we'll be burning up our operating budget inside of a month."

They mulled the situation while sipping the whisky Tristan had provided. On the floor underneath Maya's chair, Aden noticed a few drops of blood that had dripped from Maya's side onto the Alon, where they had formed an irregular little pool of crimson.

I can still go my own way, he thought. *Ditch the comtab, disappear in the crowd, get passage to Oceana or Hades. I have enough in my ledger to stay somewhere for a year, maybe two if I live cheaply.*

But then what? And how many nights would I spend awake, looking at the ceiling and wondering what's happening with the rest of them?

"The way I see it, we have two good options," Decker said. "Because turning over the ship to these people isn't one. We either head home to Oceana and lay low for a while. Or we go to the Rhodies, turn over the ship to them, and try our luck with their legal process."

"That sounds like one good option and one sure way to spend the next ten years in a Rhodian prison," Tristan grumbled. He looked at Maya.

"You could ditch us," he said. "Take a long leave of absence. This is your home planet, after all. You'd be safer here. We'll make for Oceana and hole up somewhere for a while."

"Not likely," Maya said. "I can't leave. None of you can fly the ship for shit."

That got the first chuckle out of them since Milo had appeared next to Maya at their table.

"We have two weeks to figure it out," Decker said. "But Maya isn't bailing on us, and none of you are asking to cash out right now and get the hell away from this mess. So whatever we do next, it looks like we will do it together."

———

The sun was coming up by the time they left the bar and walked out into the plaza below. The sky on the other side of the dome was a roiling sea of orange and red currents, constantly intermixing and flowing apart again, an endless kaleidoscope of atmospheric fury. The streets were as busy as they had been any other time of day. The encounter in the bar felt almost surreal to Aden in the daylight, like a bad dream after one too many glasses of liquor, but the bloodstain on the side of Maya's flight suit served to anchor the event back in reality when he glanced at her.

"Well, crap," Tristan said. "We're on two shit lists now. The Rhodies and whatever fucking gunrunner cartel sent that prick with the knives. This will be an interesting month."

"Your idea of 'interesting' doesn't really overlap with mine," Henry said.

Aden could tell by the swaying and the unsteady gaits that all of them were still more than just a little drunk, even Maya, who usually nursed a single beer all evening.

"It was a pretty good evening, though," Tess said. "I mean, except for the part with the knives and the blood and the death threats." She was walking next to Aden and using him for balance control by holding on to his arm, and he found that he didn't mind at all. He knew that if they had ended up in a fight, he would have jumped in front of her, or Maya, or any other member of the crew without hesitation.

And I've only been with them for three months, he thought. *Until this moment, I never would have thought about taking a knife for anyone except Solveig.*

He thought of his sister, who was just a few kilometers away, probably asleep in her hotel suite. The fates had deposited them both here in the same city at the same time. If she couldn't go back to Gretia at the end of her negotiations, maybe it meant they'd be able to get together in person again. The knowledge that she was in walking distance from him, and away from the turmoil that was sure to erupt on Gretia, made Aden feel a sense of profound relief.

Whatever we do next, we'll do it together, Decker had said. Maybe it was the drink clouding his judgment, but right now Aden found that he was fine with that idea, even if the crew voted to go to Rhodia and he ended up in a prison with them for the next decade.

There are worse things in life than having to tend a garden and share communal meals with people you like, he thought.

They walked down the steps of the plaza and out into the street to hail a transit pod. Tess stumbled a little and held on to him for balance, and her weight made him lose his step as well. For a moment, they teetered on the edge of tumbling down the stairs together, but then he caught himself and kept her from falling as well.

"You all right there, Aden?" Decker said.

"Yeah," he said. "I'm good."

And for the first time in what felt like an eternity, he found that he meant it.

ACKNOWLEDGMENTS

The list of people who had a hand in finishing this book is always a long one, because writing is a bit of a team sport. Even if I was the one to get the ball across the finish line, plenty of others were instrumental in the process: clearing obstacles, setting up passes, or handing me metaphorical energy drinks in those neon-colored little squeeze bottles.

(You can probably tell I am not all that great at sportsball lingo, but let me just run with that one.)

First thanks are always due to my wife, Robin, who keeps the daily intrusions of life off my back and without whom this book—and all my previous books—would not exist except as vague ideas in the back of my head.

On the professional side, I want to thank the production team at 47North, especially Adrienne and Jason, who have a lot of patience when it comes to tolerating my fluid definition of the word "deadline," and Andrea Hurst, who makes sure the final product is always much better than the first draft.

On the personal side, I have to thank my close friends and beta readers, who keep providing me with encouragement and motivation: my Doge friends Paul, Tracie, Monica, Tam, Laurie, and Stacy, and my VP pal and collaboration partner, Kris Herndon.

Thanks to George R.R. Martin, who said some extremely nice things about this book's predecessor, *Aftershocks*, and who was kind and generous enough to send those extremely nice things to my editor in written form to be used for blurbs.

And as always, thank you to all the readers who have bought my books and recommended them to others, and who have followed me to this new world and cast of characters. I appreciate you very much, and I hope you stick around for what comes next.

ABOUT THE AUTHOR

Marko Kloos is the author of two series of military science fiction, the Palladium Wars and the Frontlines, and is a member of George R. R. Martin's Wild Cards consortium. Born in Germany and raised in and around the city of Münster, Marko was previously a soldier, bookseller, freight dockworker, and corporate IT administrator before deciding that he wasn't cut out for anything except making stuff up for fun and profit. Marko writes primarily science fiction and fantasy—his first genre love ever since his youth, when he spent his allowance on German SF pulp serials. He likes bookstores, kind people, October in New England, fountain pens, and wristwatches. Marko resides at "Castle Frostbite" in New Hampshire with his wife, two children, and roving pack of voracious dachshunds. For more information, visit www.markokloos.com.